The Courtship of Princess and Pirate

The Courtship of Princess and Pirate

KASTLE FORTUNES
BOOK ONE

TINA KNIGHT

Day and Knight
Romance
Publications

Day and Knight Romance Publications, LLC

DayAndKnightRomance.com

Cover illustration by Lisa Bell Roden, Shadow House Media.

ISBNs: 9781953306104 (paperback), 9781953306111 (eBook)

For my children, for being my greatest adventure

Prologue

In the waters near China. 1860...

Christopher Kastle had heard that a man's entire life passed before his eyes just as he was about to die. That wasn't what he saw now, though. Forced to kneel on the cold, wet wood of his ship's deck, his left eye swollen shut, his blood dripping down the back of his throat from a thoroughly broken nose, Christopher couldn't see his life passing before his eyes. All he could see were the faces of his sisters.

He could see all seven of them, just as they had been on that day, three long years ago: standing in a row, watching him ride away from their family estate on his way to join the Royal Navy. He saw Daniela, with her brow cocked and lips pressed together while she waved a disapproving goodbye; Juliette, with giant, brimming tears in her bright blue eyes; the twins, Ruby and Pearl, pulling on each other's pigtails even as they tried to behave; Constance, clutching her favorite doll with her soft gaze cast down; and Octavia, a sleeping babe in Cora's arms.

Cora. Christopher's Cora. She wasn't the closest sister to him in age, but she was the closest in spirit. She'd spent her life at his heels, challenging him and fighting him and making him laugh until his eyes watered. Cora's face was the one he could see most clearly right now, even with the sun baring down on him and the remainder of his ship's crew, blinding each of them to anything but the brutal pain that had been inflicted on them today.

The sight of Cora would forever be burned into Christopher's brain, just as she'd looked when his twenty-year-old self had abandoned his family for adventure on the high seas. Cora hadn't just been angry then; she hadn't just been sad; she hadn't just been in pain. She'd been all those things and so much more. He took something from her that day — he took something from all of them — and he'd done so under the guise of duty and honor.

One of the few men still alive and kneeling on the deck with him groaned in agony, making Christopher suck in a shallow breath against his cracked ribs. Sweat dripped down into his eyes, the sting of the salt barely noticeable against the other traumas to his body. Still, the agony of the gashes and bruises he'd gained today felt justified, while he took what he assumed were his last breaths on this earth. He knew it was good and fair that he should feel this pain, since he could finally acknowledge to himself that joining the Royal Navy wasn't done out of duty or honor.

Christopher had simply *run* that day.

He'd run like hell away from the responsibilities of a family who depended on him with their very lives. He'd run from their ancestral home, the home that had lost a beloved mother and harbored a barely functional father. He'd run from the burden of seven younger sisters and an estate full of servants who'd all looked to him, the young and foolish heir of Nightingale, for guidance and leadership. He'd run...straight into this.

A pistol fired a few feet away from him, followed by the thud of another body slumping lifelessly onto their ship's deck. He turned his head to see his captain's form lying at the feet of a viciously large man with stringy black hair and a wicked grin. The man kicked at the captain's chest before he moved down the line of kneeling bodies to the next member of Christopher's crew, a boy named Max who was barely a year older than Cora — Maxwell Taylor — an orphaned lad who'd emulated Christopher from the moment he stepped foot on this ship.

The dark-haired pirate dropped his smoking pistol to the deck in order to pull a sword from the scabbard at his waist. He poked the tip of the blade against Max's chest and cackled. Max winced but he did not cower.

"Stop," Christopher growled through clenched teeth. "Stop this now."

"No, brother. Don't," the man kneeling beside him hissed.

Christopher turned his head to see Nicholas Marlow, his childhood friend and fellow shipmate, at his side. Nick's nose bled into his mouth, his teeth red as he grimaced and shook his head.

"I have to try, Nick. I have to..."

Christopher didn't get a chance to finish his sentence. Not before the large, imposing pirate removed the tip of his sword from Max's chest, took several steps down the line of kneeling men, and brought his blade swiftly to rest on the back of Christopher's neck. "What did you say?" the pirate spit out, pressing the sharpened silver into Christopher's skin.

"I told you to stop this," Christopher answered, forcing his words past the metallic taste in his throat. "You will not kill any more of my crew."

"*Your* crew?" the man clarified, his brutal gaze roaming across Christopher's stained shirt and breeches before returning to his face. "And who made *you* captain of this ship?"

Blood dripped down his spine as the pirate's blade dug a sharp, shallow trench into his neck. "You did. Just now. When you shot that man."

The pirate glanced back to the fresh body lying on the deck, amongst all the other bodies he and his band of men felled this day. Except it wasn't *his* band of men. Christopher knew this voracious executioner before him wasn't in charge here. He also knew his only hope for saving the few shipmates he had left was to appeal to the ranking officer of this pirate crew: a man he assumed to be shrewd and intelligent, based on the organization of the attack he'd witnessed today.

"Well, then," the stringy-haired pirate continued, "aren't you the brave lad, taking responsibility for what's left of this ship. And you get to be captain, too — at least, until I remove your head. Which, unfortunately for you, is at present. So, I hope you enjoy your elevated status for the next two seconds."

Christopher forced himself to keep his one good eye open while the pirate pulled his sword back, hoisting it into the air in preparation for a swift downward stroke. He could only see Cora's pained face in the silver reflection of the blade, the harrowing image forcing him to scream in a vain attempt at salvation. "Don't be a daft ass, pirate! You're throwing away your own treasure!"

"Sid!" a voice shouted from behind the pirate. "Sheath your sword!"

The command came barely in time, and the dark, looming man Christopher now knew as Sid bore a look of absolute disgust when he obeyed. Sid lowered his weapon and shifted to the side, standing before Nick while turning to face the man who stepped toward them across the deck. "Captain," Sid acknowledged with a bow of his head.

"What seems to be the problem here, Sid?"

"This boy says he's captain of this ship now. I was going to teach him a lesson by taking off his head."

"I see," the pirate captain answered, his tone even and calm. "You're a worthy teacher, Sid. Although lessons often do better if the person remains alive to learn from them."

Sid's eyes narrowed, but he still averted his gaze to the ground when his leader came to stand beside him.

Christopher stared up at the captain. He wasn't nearly the size of Sid, and yet this man wielded more power in his voice than Sid did in his entire massive body. Christopher's stomach sank to his knees when the captain's discerning gaze landed on his face. "What is your name, boy?" he asked, his English words tilted with an accent to match his obvious Chinese heritage.

"I am called Christopher."

"Very well, then. Do tell me why you think I'm throwing away my treasure, Captain Christopher."

"It...it's just that..."

"Speak quicker. Or I'll allow Sid to behead you, as he desperately wishes."

Christopher swallowed against the lump in his throat when the meaty pirate's fist tightened around the grip of his blade. "*We* are the treasure," he replied as quickly as he could.

"You?"

"Yes, us. Men are rich property. We could be your property."

The captain's brow rose. "Why would I want you to be my property?"

"Because I have a strong back, and a strong mind, and I know these waters through and through. I cannot speak for the remainder of my crew, since each man here must choose for himself. But as for me, if you allow me safe passage on your ship, I will pledge you my servitude for as long as you desire it."

A smirk tugged at the captain's sun-weathered lips. "*Safe* passage? Do you believe the existence of a pirate is a safe one, Captain Christopher?"

"No, it's...no, Sir. I do not." Christopher glanced at the bodies piled on the deck around them, his ears filled with the grating caw of carrion birds circling above. "But this existence is not safe, either," he realized, refocusing his good eye on the man standing above him. "All I am asking for is a chance."

A chance to make it off of this ship alive. A chance to find my way back home one day. A chance to take care of my sisters as I should have done three years ago, to make up for my selfish choices and lack of courage. A chance to see Cora again — to see her and hold her and tell her I'm still here for her.

"A chance for what?" the captain questioned.

Christopher shifted his knees against the bloodied wood of his ship's deck. "For life, Sir."

The pirate captain did not respond. He simply stood and stared at Christopher, measuring him for what felt like hours. Eventually, Sid's grating voice clawed through the quiet. "Captain, you cannot honestly be...."

"Silence, Sid."

"But he's...he's one of *them*!"

A flash of metal appeared, the taut edge of the captain's cutlass pressed instantly to the leathery skin beneath Sid's chin. Christopher absorbed the even, unmoving gaze of the captain as well as the slight but distinct glimmer of fear in his subject's eyes. Sid gulped, causing a drop of his own blood to slither down the captain's blade.

"Do you and I have a problem, Mr. Bishop?" the captain asked.

Another drop of Sid Bishop's blood slithered down the blade. "No...no..."

"What was that?"

"No, Captain."

The elder pirate removed his cutlass from Sid's throat, the metal re-sheathed against his body before Christopher could even register the rapid action. He stared up into the eyes of his new captain. Eyes that held fathomless determination. And undeniable pain. And unquestionable fatigue.

Christopher could not be certain if he would live to see the light of another morning. But if he did, if this gamble he'd taken granted him a chance at life, then he would owe his allegiance to this man. And he would serve him well, at least until the moment he could break free forever.

The captain held deathly still, the lines in his weathered skin a makeshift map of all he'd seen and done. For a moment, Christopher doubted the possibility of earning mercy from such a man. He braced himself for the swing of the captain's swift blade, but didn't shrink from his fate. Instead, he held the head pirate's steel gaze, maintaining his ground on the rocking deck.

The pirate finally nodded his head. "My name is Fan Cheng. I am your master now, Christopher. And you will address me as Captain."

"Yes, Captain," Christopher replied, although the pirate had already turned away. He focused his limited eyesight on the long black hair hanging down Fan Cheng's retreating back.

"Bring him!" the captain shouted over his shoulder at Sid Bishop. "And anyone else who still breathes!"

A smile spread Christopher's lips, even as Sid stepped in front of him.

"I don't know why you're smiling," Sid grunted. "That man isn't going to live forever, and the instant I become captain, you will kneel before me again."

"Well, until then, I guess we'll have to learn to get along, Mr. Bishop."

Sid huffed out a laugh. "I don't think so."

Christopher still smiled in reply, even when Sid balled his fist and struck Christopher's jaw, knocking him down hard onto the bloodied wood.

CHAPTER 1

Home

Nightingale, England. 1865...

Christopher made the final journey to his home on a horse.

After three years in service to the Royal Navy, and another five years lost at sea, he'd stepped off the dock at Nightingale Port in the middle of the night, to no fanfare at all. Nick Marlow, Christopher's childhood best friend and fellow sailor these eight years, stepped off the dock with him. The two men embraced briefly before parting ways.

Within minutes of landing on English soil, Christopher purchased a horse from an innkeeper using one of the few gold coins in his pocket. It was severe overpayment for the bony creature, but he couldn't waste time haggling. Not when his home and family were finally within his reach.

Moonlight illuminated the path of the horse's hooves while he galloped them toward the Kastle estate. He appreciated the cover of night and trees, not wanting any of the locals to recognize him yet. He didn't want rumors of the return of Lord Christopher Kastle, heir to the Earl of Nightingale, to spoil that surprise for his sisters. He hoped his return would be a good surprise. He hoped Cora would be waiting for him. He hoped all of his sisters would be waiting, of course...but especially Cora.

God, how many of them would already be married? Daniela, Cora, Juliette, Ruby, and Pearl would all be of marrying age by now. Each of them could already have estates and families of their own, which would leave only Constance and Octavia to greet him upon his return. Sadly, Octavia would not even know him, since she'd been a mere babe when he left. But Constance might recall him. Some of the older servants might, as well. And their father – Quinton Kastle – should know his only son. That is, if Quinton still lived.

When the horse rounded the edge of the extensive wooded path and found the opening of the lengthy entryway leading to the Kastle lands, Christopher focused on the manor in the distance. His ancestral home looked even bigger somehow, as he drank in the sight of the place he'd dreamt of every night for the past eight years.

Please let someone within those walls remember me. Please.

The horse's hooves beat a steady tattoo on the dirt path lined with overgrown shrubs. Christopher frowned at the sight of the unkempt entryway, his grimace settling deeper while evidence of deterioration grew more pronounced. Vines now overtook the front face of the manor and crumbled brick and mortar lay in piles beside the once proud parapets surrounding the entrance. Even the adjacent fields, which harbored thriving crops in his youth, appeared barren and still.

He slowed his horse's movements, easing the willowy steed to a trot as the trepidation in his chest rose. He'd left this place and these people to fend for themselves these eight years. Seeing the current state of their home, Christopher now knew they had not fared well in his absence.

That realization made his scars ache. Not the elusive scars within his mind, but the actual scars littering his body. During periods of great stress, he could feel each one. They had all healed over time to varying degrees, but he still knew the location and circumstance of every stab, slash, and burn he'd amassed through the years. At this moment, they all dug at his heart.

"Don't hate me," he whispered to the people he could not yet see, his gaze fixed on the dilapidated face of his home while he brought the horse to a halt before the front door. "Please don't hate me."

Christopher dismounted as the door opened. He blinked his eyes, trying to make out the dark figure illuminated from behind by the warm glow of the manor's innards. The person in the doorway was a woman – he could tell by her small form and curved silhouette – but he didn't know which woman she was.

"It's me," he offered in a hushed tone, stepping forward in caution, hoping to not scare the tiny creature. "It's Christopher."

"Christopher? *Christopher*? Is it really you?"

"Cora? Is that you?"

She launched herself at him. He caught his fiercest sister against his chest, his arms folding twice over her back as he lifted her from the ground.

"Oh God, oh God, you're here," Cora breathed, her trembling arms circling his neck. "How is this possible? I thought you were dead. We all thought you were dead."

"I'm not dead," he insisted, even though he knew it was a lie. The brother Cora remembered had died years ago, and the one who came home to her tonight was another man entirely. But he had come home, at least. "I'm here, Cora. I'm here."

"Thank the dear heavens," she sang, her words catching in her throat while tears fell down her face to dampen his skin. "I've missed you so much, Christopher. I love you."

He held her tighter, clinging hard, allowing eight years' worth of tears to seep from his eyes. "I'm home now. I'm home."

~

Pennyshire, England. Ten months later...

VIOLET BELL WALKED among the primly kept gardens of the Bell estate, soaking in the beauty of their family manor in the distance. The home Noah Bell had purchased for his wife Liza, as well as Violet and her sister Gwendolyn, was vast and ornate and quite simply gorgeous. Violet remembered thinking the estate was a castle when her parents brought her and her sister here ten years ago. She'd been twelve years old then, and Gwen only nine, when this became their life.

Even now, Violet couldn't believe this was indeed her life, filled to brimming with household servants, rich foods, and silk clothes. She appreciated all her father had managed to provide their family, even if the polished dresses she'd donned these past ten years came accompanied by rather irksome undergarments. They were undergarments she refused to wear, if for no other reason than their intent to confine. To be perfectly honest, the fact that her refusal to wear knickers vexed her mother was a tiny amusement in an otherwise dull new world.

But a lady of status should always wear knickers, Violet. That is who you are now: a lady of status. Or, at least, a lady in the making.

She frowned at the sound of her mother's voice in her head. Violet supposed she would never grow accustomed to the idea of being a lady, instead of the London street urchin she'd been ten years ago – running amok in filthy alleyways, contentedly covered in dirt. Besides, she was not truly Lady Violet. Not yet. Not until the day she would be married into title.

"*Forcibly* married into title," she corrected herself with a shiver.

Flopping down in the lush grass beneath a sun-shading elm, Violet cleared her thoughts of her ominous future in order to concentrate on the beauty of the present. Pulling her spectacles from the pocket of her overcoat, she perched them on the tip of her nose. She unfolded the London newspaper she'd pilfered from her father's study last night, a jolt of thrill flitting down her spine with the memory of her sneaky accomplishment. Grasping the page in both hands, her eyes moved purposefully over each story, her brain soaking in the information and cataloguing it in an instant.

She lovingly read every word, from the notifications of Parliament down to the paper's advertisements: sellers announcing various miracles ranging from insomnia cures to hair-restorative tonics to nerve-soothing tonics, those namely being gin, brandy, and rum. Violet laughed while she read, envisioning a gaggle of distinguished gentlemen dozing off in their Parliament chairs while sporting overgrown hair and rum-soused grins. Shaking her head at the farcical image, her eyes travelled to the most exciting story on the page, the one she'd reserved for last:

The pirate Blackheart struck disaster upon another Chinese village this week, looting and destroying at will...Efforts to capture Blackheart have been futile yet again and he remains at large...Rewards continue to grow for anyone aiding in the capture of this menace and his crew...

A chill flitted up Violet's spine at the thought of a beast such as Blackheart wreaking havoc upon the world. She wanted to say her chill originated from fear, since that is the reason a lady of status should shiver with such a thought. But she knew her heart better, and allowed herself a moment to indulge in the fantasy of Captain Violet Bell of the Royal Navy, avenging the world with the pirate Blackheart beneath her blade. She would bring the beast to his knees before her. Then she would collect the bounty on his head, after which she would have her own riches and the means to support herself. And never be forced to marry any man she did not love.

Violet grinned with that daydream, her smile remaining even after she stood from the ground, refolded the newspaper, and slipped both the page and her spectacles back into the pocket of her peach overcoat. The fine matching gown beneath flowed softly across her knicker-free thighs as she walked toward the backside of the Bell estate. She headed purposefully for the kitchen door, despite it being solely a servants' entrance. Holding her breath, she strained to hear voices emanating from inside.

The chattering of two women – Beatrix and Harriet, the family maids – tickled Violet's ear and made her smile broaden. Liza Bell often complained about the inability to find more cultured maids to work in their household, despite Pennyshire being only a half-day's carriage ride away from either London or Nightingale. However, Violet did not share her mother's sentiments on the topic. She loved the fact that their family's "new" money would not attract more refined servants, because no matter how many of her father's newspapers Violet pilfered, there would never be a better wealth of information in the world than the mouths of maids.

"Good morning," she addressed the women while she entered the kitchen.

Beatrix and Harriet spun around to face her. "Miss," they said in unison, both giving her a curtsy. Each of the maids were a few years older than her, and each were quite beautiful, with long, dark hair and tall, shapely bodies outlined by pinstriped gray uniforms.

Violet shifted a loose blond curl behind her ear while glancing down to the basket of fruit resting on the counter. "It is a beautiful day, is it not?"

"So beautiful, Miss," Harriet agreed. "Would you like a piece of fruit?"

"Yes, thank you," Violet agreed, grabbing an orange amongst the apples and grapes, grateful that such offerings were a staple in their household.

"Hope you'll have a lovely day, Miss," Beatrix added.

"You as well." Violet nodded to both of them, making eye contact and exchanging smiles, before stepping through the kitchen out into the hall.

Violet's foot landed firmly on the squeaky floorboard to the right of the kitchen door. She bounced against it a few times, with lesser and lesser intensity, making it sound as if she were walking away. After completing her task, she stepped off to the side of the board and leaned against the wall beside the kitchen, stilling her concealed body while opening her ears.

"Did you see that, Beatrix?" Harriet's voice drifted into the hall. "She picked a fruit!"

Beatrix cackled. "Indeed! The Picky Princess of Pennyshire actually managed to pick something!"

Violet winced at her assigned title as she eavesdropped from her favorite spot outside the kitchen door. *The Picky Princess of Pennyshire.* Would she never live that down?

The maids giggled together until Beatrix scoffed. "Can't really blame her though, can you? For not picking the heir to the Earl of Centreville?"

"Why can't I blame her?" Harriet bit back. "Lord Wellington Chaney is a true gentleman. Not to mention rich, and of a pleasing countenance. The

Picky Princess would have had everything a woman could want if she'd accepted him for a husband."

"Listen to you, Harriet. Of a pleasing countenance? You're starting to sound like one of these stuffy country fools. And I can most definitely see why Violet refused him."

"All right, then. Go on and tell me how she could possibly be justified in refusing Lord Chaney's courtship."

"Because he's entirely too young and pure of heart. He never would have ravished her. Not once. And even worse, there's his name."

"What's wrong with his name?"

"Wellington? Do you really have to ask what's wrong with Wellington? Can you imagine screaming that in bed? Oh, Wellington! Give me your manly cock, Wellington!"

Violet's hand flew to her mouth, her eyes watering as she worked to muffle the ghastly, indiscreet noises creeping up her throat.

"Beatrix! You're evil!" Harriet shrieked. "And bloody hysterical!"

"Wellington! Oh, Wellington!" Beatrix persisted. "Don't stop rutting me, Wellington!"

Harriet's laughter resounded through the kitchen as Beatrix grunted and groaned quite animatedly. Violet's fingers nearly drew blood in their efforts to keep her mouth shut and her presence undetected.

"But you know Violet and Gwen call him *Welly*," Harriet defended once the other maid's unearthly noises dimmed. "That isn't so terrible."

"It is terrible," Beatrix snipped. "And even if his name were better, he's still barely a man. I wouldn't want a little boy between my legs."

"But he's an heir! Who else could you possibly want?"

"You mean if I could pick any man in the world?"

"Yes. Any at all."

"Hmm," Beatrix considered. "I suppose I'd pick the pirate Blackheart."

Violet's eyes nearly popped out onto the squeaky floorboard.

"Blackheart?" Harriet echoed. "Why on earth would you spread your legs for that creature? I heard he's old and grizzled, with stringy black hair and dark, cruel eyes. And that he eats the limbs off of children for breakfast."

"That's rubbish! I heard he's young and fine, with long, flowing black hair and a chiseled jaw. And that he beds a dozen wenches a night."

"Young and fine? He's been terrorizing ports for over twenty years! How could he possibly be young and fine?"

"Well, what if he's discovered the Fountain of Youth? Just think of it – to be young and beautiful forever – and a pirate's bride!"

Harriet clucked her tongue. "Young and beautiful are all well and good, but I don't believe pirates take brides. Only mistresses."

Beatrix snorted. "I suppose I'll have to be the head of Blackheart's mistresses, then. But I'll keep his hands so full, he'll only be able to bed *six* other wenches a night!"

The maids burst into ferocious giggles while Violet stood stiff as a board in the hall. She dared not move a muscle, until a lowly whispered, "Tsk! Tsk!" drew her attention. Her gaze flew down the long corridor to where Gwendolyn now waited at the very end.

Violet pinched her lips as she stared at her sister, who frantically motioned her away from the kitchen door. Dropping her shoulders, Violet shimmied sideways across the silent floorboard by the wall until she reached the end of the hallway. Once removed from the maids' range of hearing, she stepped over onto the finely woven rug in the adjoining corridor.

Gripping the orange in her hand, she looked to Gwen with the most innocent expression she could muster. "What is it, dear sister?"

Gwen shook her head. "Why do I always know where to find you?"

"I must gather knowledge any way I can," Violet answered with a grin.

"I highly doubt what our maids say can be considered knowledge. And I think you would know, better than most, not to listen to gossip."

Violet frowned at the withered look on her sister's face. "I hear their gossip, but I don't pay mind to it. I assure you, there's a world of information inside their idle musings – a world I cannot glean from books or newspapers."

"I know you believe that. I also know you want to fill your mind with all the knowledge there is." Gwen ran her hand soothingly down Violet's arm. "Even if there are some things you do not wish to hear about."

"What does that mean? Are you privy to something I'm not?"

"I'm afraid I am."

Violet watched her sister's eyes fill with concern, which made her stomach plummet. "What is it, Gwen? Just tell me. Please."

Gwen exhaled. "Papa wants to see you. And he's wearing his *serious* wig."

"Good heavens, not the wig."

"Yes. The wig."

"Dear God," Violet breathed, knowing Papa's ridiculous wig could only mean one thing: Judgment Day. "I suppose I'd better be off to see him, then. I assume he's in his study?"

Gwen nodded as she fell into step beside her, both of them walking in sync while turning several corners through the manor. "Do you want me to come in with you, Violet?"

"No, thank you. I must do this on my own."

"But you know I'd do anything for you."

Violet stopped a few doors down from Noah Bell's study, pivoting to meet Gwen's eyes. Her sister contrasted her in nearly every way: Gwendolyn was taller and thinner, and had brown hair and eyes in opposition to Violet's blond and blue. But mostly, Gwen was the vision of an angel, as pure and glorious as fresh fallen snow sparkling in the sun.

Bending over to avoid displacing the wide bell cage of Gwen's stylish maroon skirt, Violet pecked her on the cheek. "I know you would, Gwen, just as I would do anything for you. Do not worry about me. Everything will be fine, I'm sure."

Gwen grabbed Violet by the shoulders and gave her a quick hug, unable to hide the tears in her eyes when she released her and turned away. Violet watched her sister glide down the hallway, hearing the soft rustle of her fine dress even after she floated around the corner. The moment she stood alone, she took a deep breath in and inched toward her father's door.

"Are you in here, Papa?" she called when she arrived at his study, cautiously stepping over the threshold. "Gwen said you wished to see me?"

"Yes, Violet. Do come in."

She saw her father then, sitting behind his stately desk with his frumpy white wig of curls pulled down hard over his head. Even with the potential doom stretched out before her, she couldn't help but smile. "No one wears those wigs anymore, Papa," she chided, stepping forward to embrace him as she always did.

Noah Bell held his hand out before him, stopping her advancement. "Violet. Do not. We have serious matters to discuss."

Her footsteps halted in front of his desk. This was not like her father. He never refused her affections. Even in his foulest mood – when he might refuse the company of his wife or his younger daughter – Noah never refused Violet. Not before now.

"I...I do not understand what could possibly be so serious that I cannot hug you," she said, unable to hide the quaver in her voice.

Noah's brow knitted. "You will see soon enough. Sit down, please."

Violet placed the orange in her hand on the edge of his desk before moving to sit in the ornately carved chair facing him.

"Now then, my eldest daughter," he began with unfamiliar formality, "you and I both know there is a matter we have not yet settled in your life. The matter of a husband."

Her heart pounded. "Oh, Papa, we do not need to visit this silly business again, do we? Don't you agree that I'll be of more use to you and Mama here?"

"You cannot stay with us. You must marry into title. You know this."

"But, why can't I…"

"You will marry into title and that is final!"

His barked words made Violet blink rapidly, fending off the moisture springing to her eyes. She schooled herself and nodded. "Yes. I do know what is expected of me."

Noah's body remained stiff, despite the earnest awareness in his gaze. "Violet, the expectation I place on you is of vital importance to the future of our family status. Our money is plentiful, but it is not old or noble. I need you to marry a noble man of noble birth. As such, I have decided to give you a choice between two men of appropriate standing."

A choice? He is giving me a choice this time?

Violet clasped her hands in her lap, gripping onto her fingers while awaiting the verdict.

Noah leaned forward, pinning her eyes. "The first suitor I have selected for you is George Susserby, Duke of Dunworthy."

Acid clawed its way into her throat. "The Duke of Dunworthy! You cannot possibly be serious! He's older than you, Papa! With sons older than me!"

"Yes, but it is proven he can have sons, since he has had them with his three previous wives. And even though your son with the Duke will not be first in line to the Dunworthy estates, he will still be titled."

"But how can you be certain a man that old can even give me a son?"

Noah sighed. "Men can have children quite late in life. It is the woman who must have a young womb to grow her husband's seed."

Violet's eyes narrowed. "Would you like me to *moo* now, Papa?"

"What?"

"Well, if I'm going to be treated as cattle, I thought I could *moo* to complete the picture."

Noah's voice fell to a frighteningly low level. "You will watch your tongue with me, Violet. I know I often indulge your manner of speaking, but your frankness is neither proper nor desired amongst people of society. And despite your ill thoughts, I am *not* the villain in this story. I found you a suitable man – a young, intelligent, pleasant man – and what did you do with my efforts? You refused him! You refused the heir of Centreville, flat out! Honestly, after that decision, you should be grateful I'm giving you *any* choice in the matter."

Violet clenched her teeth, unable to keep herself from glaring across the desk at her father, even though she knew he spoke the truth. She *had* refused Welly, which led her to this very moment. "So," she said, trying to remain motionless when all she wanted was to run for the door, and keep on running, forever. "Would you care to tell me who my other choice of husband is?"

Noah settled back into his chair. "His name is Lord Christopher Kastle. He's the heir to the Earl of Nightingale."

Her jaw fell open. "You mean the Royal Navy sailor who was lost at sea for five years?"

"Yes, that's the one. Apparently, he and a fellow shipmate were castaways for that time period, but they've been back in England for nearly a year now. The Royal Navy gave them each an honorable discharge secondary to the suffering they endured. The heir is at home in Nightingale, attempting to manage his estate."

"What's wrong with his estate?"

"It fell into disrepair in his absence. His father, Quinton Kastle, the Earl of Nightingale, has not been well for some time. Christopher is responsible for the upkeep of their manor, as well as the care of his seven younger sisters, all of whom are unmarried and require dowries."

Violet's breath caught. "You're...you're saying that my *one* dowry can provide for *seven* others?"

Noah sighed. "I am a very wealthy man. You know this."

Her heart sank inside her chest. She'd never felt more like an object for sale than she did at this moment. The realization brought fresh tears to her eyes.

Her father's shoulders dropped at the sight. "Violet, my dear child, please see that I am trying to be reasonable here. I realize I did not give you a choice a few months ago, when I presented Wellington Chaney as your one and only suitor. But I am giving you a choice now."

She shook her head, since this wasn't really a choice. Even if she could choose which man she would marry, she still couldn't choose neither. She could not choose her own direction for the path of her life.

A knock at the door startled her, nearly toppling her from her seat.

"Come in," Noah declared.

Violet turned to see a sharply dressed man step into the study, carrying a large black case. She looked back to her father. "Who is this, Papa?"

"This is Mr. Havensborg. He is a photographer."

"Who is he taking a photo of?"

"You. The photo will be placed into a locket, to be sent to the man you choose to marry."

Blood boiled behind her eyes, instantly drying her tears. "How lovely. I'm glad my husband will have a chance to view his goods before he purchases."

"Daughter!" Noah barked.

"Good Lord!" she bit back. "Fine, Papa. Just...fine."

Violet sat quietly, attempting to calm her nerves, as Mr. Havensborg assembled his equipment and placed a stool in the middle of the room. She moved to the seat when instructed and posed as told. Yet her eyes still drifted to the floor while she considered the options she'd just been given: to be the fourth wife of an old man who did not need her for anything more than a place card; or to be the much-needed but probably unwanted wife of a returned castaway with a home to rescue and seven sisters to provide for.

Sadness descended into Violet's chest with either thought. Marriage was her only option for lands and support, yet her father would never allow her to marry solely for love, which meant her life would never truly be her own. Her decisions would always be made for her by one appointed man or another, so this ruse of a choice was not really a choice at all.

The popping noise of the camera snapped Violet from her sullen thoughts. She glanced up to see Mr. Havensborg had completed his task. "But I wasn't even looking up," she protested, although she knew it didn't truly matter. This photo would simply prove to her future husband that she lacked significant physical malady, and hadn't been born with three eyeballs.

"I'm sure it will be fine," her father dismissed with a wave of his hand, turning his attentions back to the other man. "Please have the photo placed into a fine metal locket, Mr. Havensborg. I would like this chore completed as soon as possible."

"Of course, Mr. Bell. Where would you like me to send the locket?"

"I will messenger you the address by the end of the day."

Violet's brow shot up with those words, her gut churning anew. Rising from her seat, she stepped to the far corner of the room to stare at the bookshelves, seeking comfort in the volumes she loved so much. Yet even the sight of these treasured books could not ease her overwrought mind.

The moment she heard Mr. Havensborg leave the study, Violet spun around to face her father. "The end of the day? You're only giving me until the end of the day to make my choice?"

Noah's stern gaze did not falter. "That is correct."

She sucked in a deep breath, fully prepared to argue over this injustice until she collapsed utterly from the effort. But then one of their maids entered the room, carrying a basket of fruit. "Pardon me, Mr. Bell," Harriet offered. "I was just bringing you some food."

"You can place it on my desk," Noah told the woman, his discerning gaze never leaving his daughter.

Violet glanced to Harriet, watching as she deposited the basket before turning silently toward the wall. Harriet pulled a dusting cloth from her apron and began moving it idly across the frame of a painting. Violet stared at the maid's back, wondering when on earth the woman would leave so this harrowing discussion with her father could resume.

However, as she watched Harriet's sloth-like actions, the wheels in Violet's mind shifted in an entirely new direction. She already knew that further protests over her current situation would do her no good. Nothing she said to her father, whether she gave him a well-spoken argument or an outrageous fit of screams, would alter his mind on this matter. Her only hope was to gather more knowledge, to properly inform the dreaded decision she must make.

Looking back to the man in the wig, Violet straightened her spine, stared him in the eye, and spoke very clearly. "What you are saying, Papa, is that I must make a choice – a choice between the two men you have picked for me to marry. I must either choose to wed Lord Christopher Kastle, heir to the Earl of Nightingale, or to wed Lord George Susserby, Duke of Dunworthy. And you are only giving me until the end of the day to make that choice."

Violet did not have to look at Harriet to notice the hitch of her breath.

Noah's head tilted. "That is exactly what I'm saying. But thank you for repeating it all in summation, since I am now certain you have heard me."

"Oh, I heard you," she replied, her eyes darting to Harriet's back as the maid scurried from the room. "I'll have my answer by the end of the day."

"See that you do," he said, his tone still stern and formal. But then her father exhaled heavily, his eyes softening. "And please try to understand that I do this for your own good. For your future and the future of your children."

Violet nodded, even though she didn't want to hear his gentle words or witness the concern in his eyes. She could not accept that from him right now, not so soon after giving her this wretched ultimatum. Instead, she simply curtsied before diverting her attention to the exit.

She strode to the door with poise, yet the moment Violet stepped out of the study and into the hallway, she began running as fast as her legs would carry her. When she arrived at the end of the corridor leading to the kitchens, she took great care to not step on the squeaky floorboards. She shimmied with her back to the wall, across the quietest part of the flooring, until she was close enough to the kitchen door to hear the maids. Although she didn't really have to be so close, since Harriet was already screeching like a banshee.

"Beatrix! Beatrix! Beatrix!"

Violet heard the door to the back of the house slam, followed by footsteps into the kitchen. She held still against the outer wall and listened.

"Bloody hell, Harriet! You're going to crack my ears!" Beatrix bellowed. "I could hear you all the way outside!"

"But you are not going to believe what I just discovered!"

"Calm yourself! I can't hear my own thoughts over your racket."

Harriet snickered riotously. "Oh, Beatrix! It's *so* good!"

"Very well. Out with it, then."

"It's the Picky Princess! She's been given another pick!"

"Another pick? Do you mean her father found her a new suitor?"

"Not just one! Two! She gets her pick of *two* men now!"

"Oh, God, this *is* good! Tell me! Tell me!"

"Her first choice of suitor is Lord Christopher Kastle, heir to the Earl of Nightingale."

Beatrix gasped. "Lord Christopher Kastle? Are you certain you heard that name correctly?"

"Indeed, I did."

A solemn hush fell over the kitchen. Violet squinted her eyes in the hallway, as if that might help her to hear better.

Beatrix inhaled sharply and spoke with grave certainty. "This is not good. Perhaps Violet should have chosen Wellington Chaney after all."

"You're changing your mind about her refusing Welly? Why?"

"Because, Harriet. As much as Wellington Chaney is a boy, Christopher Kastle is a man. And although I don't rightly care what becomes of the Picky Princess, I still don't think it's proper to expect one so innocent to take on such a formidable degree of a man."

Harriet sighed. "Perhaps Christopher Kastle was a force to be reckoned with, once upon a time. But I don't think that's true anymore, not since he returned from sea. I hear his time as a castaway beat him to the pulp. Now, he's only a broken shell of a man. Nothing left but the skin on his bones."

Violet's heart thudded painfully in her chest.

A broken shell of a man. Nothing left but the skin on his bones.

Beatrix gave a haughty laugh. "Perhaps Lord Kastle does only have the skin on his bones left. But let me tell you, that's some bloody handsome skin."

"Really? Have you had your hands on his skin?"

"Unfortunately not. However, I know many a maiden who sought his company back when he was a young and wild buck, trolling the streets of London with pockets full of gold coins and brandy flasks. I hear he's still as fetching as ever, perhaps even more so now, after all that time spent laboring at sea. His muscles may have actually grown muscles. God, I'd give anything to bed the man in order to find out."

Violet shifted on her feet, doing her best to stare silently at the wall.

"I see," Harriet hemmed. "But is that what a wife should want, though? Just a pretty shell for a husband? I fear no man could return home – after being lost for five long years – with his heart entirely intact."

"Blimey, Harriet! When did you become such a sop?"

"All I'm saying is it makes sense for his heart to be damaged."

Beatrix harrumphed. "Honestly, I don't care about the damage to his heart, as long as his body is still intact. After all, Lord Kastle has a history of being quite the rake, fully capable of rutting any woman in a good and proper way. In fact, my cousin's best friend's sister personally knows a dozen different girls the young heir bedded before he left to join the Royal Navy. They all say he's hung like a bull with the stamina to match."

Violet nearly swallowed her tongue.

"And if that's all true," Beatrix continued, "then I do not think it matters if Lord Kastle is a broken shell or not. A man with that past doesn't forget how to take care of a woman's needs, no matter how broken he's become."

The kitchen quieted, although Violet's heart thumped louder.

A moment later, Harriet exhaled. "I suppose you're right. Even if he is damaged goods, I imagine he's still a better choice of suitor than the other."

"Really? Who is the other option for the Princess?"

Harriet giggled. "Are you ready for it?"

"Yes, yes! Tell me now!"

"It is Lord George Susserby, Duke of Dunworthy."

Beatrix's shriek resounded into the hallway, making Violet jump.

"Good God, Harriet! Tell me you're joking!"

"I'm not! I swear I'm not!"

"But the Duke of Dunworthy is old enough to be her grandfather!"

"I know! Can you imagine choosing that? Although..."

"Although what?"

"I heard he has vast, fine estates, filled with the best of everything London has to offer. The Princess would want for nothing."

"Nothing except passion, lust, and desire," Beatrix scoffed. "If she picks *that*, she'll turn to dust within the year, simply from lack of use."

"Oh, dear, that's probably true. I heard the duke falls asleep in his soup bowl at the dinner table. And that his last three wives all died of boredom."

"I heard he only has one ball hanging beneath his shriveled old cock."

Violet vomited a bit in her mouth.

"Only one bollock? Bloody hell, that's horrid."

"Isn't it, though?"

"God, I cannot imagine having such a choice to make," Harriet mused, her voice falling low and hushed. "For once, I can honestly say I do not wish to trade places with the Picky Princess of Pennyshire. Not at all."

"Neither do I. We may only be working girls, but we can at least choose our own mate based on good-and-lusty desire. Or based on love, if you believe in that sort of thing."

"I do believe in love, Beatrix, and I'm grateful I can love any man I wish. But the Picky Princess cannot. She can only choose to live out her days with a wrinkled old duke who will kill her with boredom, or to throw herself into the arms of a handsome ex-rake who is already dead. And that is not really a choice at all."

With those words, Violet fled down the hallway, not mindful in the least of the noise her feet made while trampling over the squeaking floorboards.

~

CHRISTOPHER STARED at the shrub before him. It was an unruly boxwood, living beside another of its kind in one of the many congested gardens behind the Kastle manor. But it would not be unruly for much longer.

Hoisting his sword above his head, the metal of the blade gleaming brightly in the noonday sun, Christopher poised himself. His eyes sought out the overgrown, skewed branches, his body preparing for the kill. He brought the sword down in a swift, sure stroke, cleaving the unwanted foliage with sharp precision. He repeated the motion again and again, until the plant bowed to his command.

"There you have it," he acknowledged to himself while inspecting the newly squared shrub. "It is perfect now."

"I'd say so," a voice replied from behind, forcing him to spin around and direct his sword at the intruder, all in one rapid, blurred motion.

Cora didn't even blink when the tip of his blade pointed at her chest. "Hello to you, too, Christopher."

He instantly dropped the sword to his side, fisting the grip. "You shouldn't sneak up on me like that, Cora. I could have hurt you."

"But you wouldn't," she stated with a shrug.

Christopher heaved out his held breath. Swiping at his sweat-soaked brow with the long sleeve of his white cotton shirt, he returned his attention to the boxwoods. He raised his sword again, preparing a fatal blow for the next unsuspecting plant.

"I see you trimmed your hair," Cora spoke to the back of his head.

"I did. The length was irritating me."

"It looks darker, since you've cut it so short. No more blond streaks now, just a light brown. I remember when you were a lad and had hair nearly white as snow."

Christopher huffed. *And I remember when you were a babe and didn't track my every move.*

"But you've kept the prickly scruff on your jaw."

"That's correct," he acknowledged, bringing his blade down to slice off another section of unkempt branches, hoping his sister had finished stating the obvious.

Cora sighed. "Why do you do this?"

"Do what?"

"Constantly attack things with your sword? There's no one to battle here. You're home. There's nothing to fight."

Christopher didn't turn around. He also didn't respond, since it felt like there were still many things to fight, regardless of what Cora thought.

"You worry me when you do this," she continued with a hitch in her voice. "It makes me frightened that you plan to leave us again."

"I'm not leaving. I'm home now. I told you that the night I came back."

"Yes, you did. You told me then that you'd come home. But it's been ten months since you rode to our doorstep, and I still don't think you're home." Cora moved to his side, working to gain his attention. "In truth, I have yet to see my brother. I mean, you look like him, but you don't act like him. All you ever do now is hack at things with your sword. And please do not think me ungrateful – we have the finest sword-maintained shrubs in all of Nightingale, I'm sure – but even though you've hardly left our estate since your return, you're still not truly here."

Christopher took a deep breath before looking to her, but the fullness of his lungs didn't stop the constriction of his chest when he witnessed her pain. He dropped his gaze to the ground, trying for the thousandth time to clear his mind of the fathomlessly wretched things he'd done in the years he was away.

Cora stepped closer. "It's as if you left a world out at sea – a whole other world that expects your return – and you pine for it as you lie here in wait."

He shook his head with her presumption, even though his sister was right about the fact that he'd left a whole other world behind him. But it was not a world he wanted to return to. Not ever.

"You don't smile anymore," she persisted in his silence. "Do you know that? You don't laugh, either. I mean, I don't expect an uproarious chortle at every turn, but a little chuckle from time to time seems fair. Although, at this point, I will settle for a simple smile."

Christopher forced the tip of his blade into the soil at his feet. He turned his body fully toward hers. He dragged his lips up at the corners.

Cora shuddered. "Good Lord, I hope that isn't your definition of a smile."

"That was a perfectly fine smile."

"No, it was not. That was terrifying, to be honest. I swear you're just like Father sometimes. Except instead of hacking at things with a sword, Father sits in his antechamber all day, pickling his innards with brandy and waiting for the hours to pass until the Reaper takes him away."

Christopher grimaced when his sister's joust hit him square in his chest. He didn't want to be the man their father had become, wallowing in misery and wishing to die. He wanted to be so much more than that, but with all he'd seen and done, he truly didn't know how.

Cora's brow knit at the look of consternation on his face. His obvious lack of direction made her tenacity understandable. After all, Cora and Daniela had worked to hold this estate together since the moment he'd escaped to the seas nearly nine years ago. They'd grown into fearsome women, able to do the work of any servant and still hold themselves poised in the face of society. Daniela had become their family's unfailing leader, and Cora could wield a sharpened blade – both an actual sword's blade, as well as the cutting blade of her tongue – better than most men. They were exceptional, and he wanted to be the brother they deserved. He wanted to be a man each of his seven sisters could look up to, since Quinton Kastle had failed them all on that front.

"My dear Cora," Christopher entreated with both his voice and his eyes, "please understand that I'm doing the best I can. I perform all the chores Daniela requests of me. I've been tackling these gardens, beating them back into shape slowly but surely. I do everything our servants would do, if we had any remaining. I don't know what other function I can perform to make you accept the fact that I am here to stay."

Cora stilled as she regarded him. "I've not seen you cry since the night you returned home. Despite the pain you must have endured in your time away."

Christopher dragged a hand through his hair. "Is that what you expect of me, then? To burst into random fits of tears?"

"You have to let someone in," she insisted, craning her neck to meet his blue eyes with her green. "It doesn't have to be me. But for your own good, you must let someone in. It is the only way to find your joy again."

"Thank you for your concern. But I am quite well as I am."

She placed her fists on her hips. "Promise me you'll try, Christopher. Promise me you'll try to find a reason to smile."

"Cora..."

"Promise me!"

He stared down at the tiny ball of determination standing before him – with her worn gray work dress, crudely pinned brown hair, and deep, fiery eyes – and he huffed out a laugh. "Aye, Captain. I promise you."

Cora grinned with the title he awarded her. Then she curtsied, which appeared strange coming from such a ferocious creature. "I'm going to head back to the house now," she stated, turning on her heels. Yet her tracks stopped as soon as they started. "Oh, I almost forgot to tell you. Nick has come to visit. He's in the kitchen, speaking with Daniela."

Christopher groaned. "Back again so soon?" he questioned, grasping his sword to fist the hilt. Cora led him to the rear entrance of their manor, clearing the distance from the gardens in just a few minutes. He heard Nick Marlow's voice before he even stepped inside.

"The years have been so kind to you, Daniela," Nick offered the eldest Kastle sister in a deep, soothing tone. "I'm sure you've heard that before."

"I heard it just two days ago," Daniela replied as Christopher and Cora entered the kitchen. "From you, Nick."

The dark-haired Mr. Marlow leaned against the counter in the center of the room, his entire body focused solely on Daniela. He straightened the instant Christopher entered his line of sight. "Well, if it isn't Lord Kastle. Bloody good to see you, mate."

Christopher unclenched his jaw. "Did you come to see *me*, Marlow? Or did you come to see my *sister*?"

Nick's gaze drifted back to Daniela, allowing Christopher to observe the wistful, besotted look on his friend's face. He remembered how his father used to look at his mother like that, like the sun rose and set within her. He also remembered how Quinton Kastle had spiraled into hell the moment Miranda was lost to them, sinking into a world of drinking and gambling, of self-pity and sorrow. It was a fate Christopher would save any man from, if he could.

"Well, I'm here to see you, of course," Nick answered once he managed to drag his eyes from Daniela's.

"Good," Christopher bit back. "Why don't we go for a walk, then? Just you and I, out in the gardens."

"The gardens? Are they even capable of being walked in?"

Christopher gripped his sword harder. "They are getting there."

Nick glanced down to Christopher's clenched hand before offering the two women a lazy smile each. "Lady Daniela. Lady Cora. I do hope to share your sweet company another time."

Daniela gave him a soft nod before turning much stricter attentions to her brother. "Christopher?"

"Yes?"

"The rugs in the main hall need to be taken outside and beaten. I cannot lift them myself, and would appreciate your help."

"I'll get to it later today."

"Very well."

Christopher took one last glance at Cora before he led Nick out of the kitchen and onto the path behind the estate. His friend fell easily into step beside him, as he knew he would. After all, he and Nick had spent most of their lives together, in one form or another: from childhood playmates, to companions in youthful debauchery, to fellow sailors, to the many roles they'd filled in the five years they were lost at sea. Christopher knew he could count on the man for anything, since they were brothers in every way that mattered.

"So," Nick began, breaking the calm silence of their walk. "I suppose you've heard the newest tales of the pirate Blackheart."

Christopher's fingers twitched on the hilt of his sword. "No, I have not."

"Don't you read the newspapers?"

"They say nothing that would concern me."

"They say Blackheart is looting and destroying villages in China."

Christopher halted in his tracks, meeting his friend's intent gaze. "And that is what pirates do, is it not? They loot and destroy."

Nick smiled, but it did not reach his eyes. "I suppose they do."

Christopher looked away, to the vast, uncultivated fields stretching behind the Kastle gardens. "We are back now. Back to civilized society, to the life we always wanted to live. We must let go of the past."

"And how are you doing with that, old friend? Have you been able to let our past go? Because I'm having a bloody hell of a time letting *anything* go."

"Damn it, Marlow, don't say that. We're...we're good here. Things are good for us now."

Nick shook his head. "How often do you have to tell yourself that lie in order to believe it?"

Christopher spiked his sword into the earth. "God, I tell myself that lie constantly. And I still don't believe it."

"I know. I know exactly how you feel."

He allowed his shoulders to fall. "It will get better, won't it, Nick? If we tell ourselves it will get better, then it will. Right?"

Nick didn't reply for the longest time. Eventually, he offered a genuine smile. "I do know one way I can make things better for you, and also for me."

Christopher eyed him cautiously. "I'm listening."

"Well, you must realize that your sisters are all beautiful. They are kind and brave and intelligent, yet they're all still unmarried, since they lack the funds to attract advantageous suitors. I'm sure they could each find suitable husbands if they had proper dowries. And, as you know, my family has money. Lots of money. Therefore, I could..."

"No. Absolutely not. I won't accept charity."

"But it won't be charity, Kastle. It will be repayment. I owe you. In a hundred different ways, I owe you my life. You know that as well as I do."

"You don't owe me anything, since I would do it all again in order to bring us home. I will not accept your money. Only your friendship."

"And you'll always have that," Nick assured. "Always."

He opened his mouth to speak further, but Christopher merely folded his arms across his chest and looked back out to the fields. Nick fell silent beside him, laudably aware to not push him too far, especially since Christopher felt quite done with this particular discussion. He was certain he could never accept charity from his oldest friend. Yet he was equally certain he had no earthly idea how to earn the money his sisters needed to live vibrant futures. He only knew he owed it to all of them to figure out the answer.

CHAPTER 2

Decisions

Violet sat on the edge of her bed, focused on the marble floor. She gripped the velvet duvet lying atop her mattress, the fisting of her fingers a vain attempt to stop their trembling. Night had nearly fallen, and she still had not made her decision. The Picky Princess had yet to pick a husband.

She can only choose to live out her days with a wrinkled old duke who will kill her with boredom, or to throw herself into the arms of a handsome ex-rake who is already dead. And that is not really a choice at all.

"Violet. My dear girl."

Her eyes drew up from the floor to see her mother standing in her doorway. Violet had been too entwined in her maid's haunting words to even hear Mama enter. Now, she could only sigh as she met her empathetic gaze.

Liza Bell didn't rush forward to throw her arms around her daughter's neck, as usual. Instead, she moved to the opposite side of Violet's bedchamber to open the first of her three enormous wardrobes. "I thought we could look over your dresses together. We need to pick something perfect for you to wear for when your betrothed comes to call on you. We'll also want to have several new dresses and corsets made to enhance your assets during courtship."

A tear rolled down Violet's cheek. She brushed it swiftly away.

"Although, if you choose the Duke of Dunworthy, your courtship will have to take place at his home. I'm told he does not care to travel anymore," Liza informed, turning away from the wardrobe to stare at her daughter. "Honestly, I believe the duke may be the right choice here. After all, he has a more prestigious title and a very breathtaking estate. In addition, he'll put few demands on you, since he already has sons from his three previous marriages. He also has an extensive library where you can read to your heart's content. You can live there in peace, and when the duke passes away – which I imagine will be sooner rather than later – you'll be allowed to remain in his home for as long as you desire. Your father has made certain of that."

Violet took a shaky breath in. Her mother never used to be like this, so poised and controlled, with her wild blond hair pulled into a tight bun and her full lips pressed into a line. Mama used to be bright and bubbly and raucous, back when their family was poor. Back when Papa used to laugh.

Liza glanced down before meeting Violet's eyes. "However, there is also the heir of Nightingale to consider. Lord Kastle's title is not as elevated, and his home not as lavish, as the duke's. But he does have many sisters to keep you company, until the dowries you provide allow them to find husbands of their own. They could all be friends of yours, I suppose. You may even find that Lord Kastle himself could be your friend, as he is only seven years older than you. I've also heard he has quite a pleasing countenance, and there is mystery about him, what with him being lost at sea for so long. I do know how you love a good mystery, little one. You might actually learn to grow fond of him."

Violet couldn't reply. She could only sit in silence, replaying every word she'd heard today in her overworked mind.

"Oh, do say something," Liza pleaded, gathering her hands together in front of her wide, copious skirts. "Say anything. Ask me a question. Tell me a story. It is not like you to be so quiet, and this silence is deafening."

"I, um...I do have a question for you, Mama."

"Yes? What is it?"

"How many balls is a man supposed to have?"

Liza's brow rose higher than ever before. "You mean balls for sport? Like croquet balls? Or rugby balls?"

"I just, it's...never mind." Violet shook her head, fighting the sharp pain behind her eyes.

Liza stepped forward, her gaze narrowing. "Do not be ungrateful for this choice, Violet. You are lucky to even be in such a position. You do not remember what the dregs of London were like for us. You were too young in our past life – too young to recall the filthy, unwashed people, the refuse in the streets and rivers, the sickness, the..."

"I do remember, Mama. I remember everything. And I swear I am not ungrateful for what you and Papa have provided us here, for this posh and privileged life you've given to me and to Gwen. But please understand, this decision of a husband is still a difficult one to make."

"I do understand," Liza amended, although the kindness of her words did not soften her stare. "I am truly sorry there are not better choices for you than these two men. But you have a reputation now, and eligible suitors were more difficult to find because of the way society sees you. At least your father is giving you an actual choice this time."

You have a reputation now. God, it all came back to the Picky Princess of Pennyshire. It all came back to her refusal to wed the heir to the Earl of Centreville. Society judged her so harshly for that decision.

No one understood that Violet actually had every intention of marrying Lord Wellington Chaney. From the moment her father had offered him as a suitor, she had set her mind to the goal. She understood that they were all a family – Papa, Mama, Gwen, and her – and being a family meant sacrificing for one another.

Violet had been fully prepared to give up her treasured freedom to marry into title, doing her part to legitimize her father's fortunes. She'd even gotten excited for the possibility of learning to love Welly, and the hope that he could learn to love her in return. She believed they might be able to find happiness together, if given enough time in each other's company.

That is, until the day Welly first came to call on her. The instant he stepped through her doorway, he focused in – singularly and completely – on Gwen. At that moment, Violet may as well have not even been in the room. At that moment, she feared her hopes for finding a husband who would love her, and her alone, were merely a child's dream.

"Are you listening to me, Violet?"

She refocused on her mother's stern voice. "Yes, Mama, I heard every word you said. I am grateful Papa gave me a choice, and I promise I will make my decision by tonight, as instructed."

Liza studied her for a while before nodding. "Then I'll leave you to your deliberations. We'll start working on your wardrobe selections tomorrow."

"Very well."

Liza opened the door to leave just as Gwen came around the corner, bumping into her. "Oh. I'm sorry, Mama," Gwen offered with a curtsy.

"It's no problem, sweet child. Talk to your sister. I believe she needs you."

While Liza fluttered away down the corridor, Gwen stood stiffly in the doorway. "May I come in, Violet? Or would you rather be alone?"

The sparkling sound of her sister's voice instantly eased the pain in Violet's head. "You know you are always welcome."

Gwen crossed the room to slip onto the mattress. As she sat, her wide cage skirt bowed out around her. "May I lay my head in your lap?"

Violet smiled with the familiar request. "Most certainly."

Flopping onto her side, Gwen settled her head on Violet's thighs. "You do know you have the best lap in the world, right?"

"You say that all the time."

"Yes, well, I mean it all the time."

Violet reached to Gwen's hair, brushing it back from her forehead like she used to do when they were little, when Gwen would wake with nightmares from the sound of rats scurrying about their hovel of a home. They were both much older now. Yet she still looked small and innocent at this moment, with her cheek pressed against the folds of Violet's peach silk gown.

Gwen's fingers curled into fists with her next words. "I'm sorry this is all happening to you because of me."

"It's not all because of you."

"But it is. I know it is. If I hadn't fallen in love with Welly, the two of you would already be married. There would be no talk of a Picky Princess, and no need for you to choose between two such terrible men."

The distress in Gwen's voice hurt Violet deep in her heart. She hushed her sister softly as she continued to draw her hand over her hair. "I'm sure they are not terrible men, or else Papa would never have selected them. Besides, we both know Welly never wanted me. Even if you did not return his feelings, it wouldn't have mattered. His heart was lost as soon as he saw your face. That is not your fault. It is no one's fault. Love simply is."

"Thank you, Violet. Thank you for choosing to leave Welly a free man, so we might one day have the chance to be together. Thank you for letting him still come here to visit you so that I may see him. I'm so grateful we are able to spend time together, although it wracks me with guilt to think you've sacrificed your happiness for mine. Truly, no amount of gratitude is enough to give you in repayment."

"You do not need to feel guilty or grateful, dear sister. And you do not need to repay me, for it was never a choice in my mind. You and Welly love each other, and I have always believed love deserves a chance."

Violet's breath caught with her own words. *I have always believed love deserves a chance,* she repeated in her mind, the idea making her heart race.

"My heavens, Gwen. I think I just solved my own dilemma."

Gwen turned to look up to her. "You did?"

"Yes. I do believe so."

"Tell me. Please."

"Well, I've been sitting here all these hours, trying to decide between the lesser of two evils. But now, I see that I've been looking at this entirely the wrong way. I cannot wallow in self-pity, wondering what path my life might take if I were not in this situation. This is my life now: the life of a future lady. I must learn to embrace it, and if I am to have any hope of happiness in this life, I must seize whatever chance I have at love."

"You think you have a chance at love with one of these men?"

"Not with the duke," Violet insisted. "As comforting as it sounds to live out my days in a well-stocked library with a grandfather to guard me, I do not wish to be married to a man who falls asleep in his soup bowl at the dinner table. What I want is someone who can be my partner, and can view me as a partner. What I want is a man who can look to the future with me and see all the possibilities before us. What I want, at the very least, is the opportunity to fall in love with my own husband. Do you think that is too much to ask?"

Gwen shook her head, her dark hair shifting over Violet's skirts. "It's not too much to ask. You deserve to be loved, always. I just hope Lord Christopher Kastle is capable of giving you what you deserve."

Lord Christopher Kastle.

He's a broken shell of a man. Nothing left but the skin on his bones.

Violet cringed with the words that still rattled inside her brain. Perhaps the heir of Nightingale had indeed returned from sea as a broken shell. Perhaps his heart had been beaten to a pulp and could never be revived, even with all the love in the world. But maybe, just maybe, that wasn't true at all. Maybe it was only idle, venomous gossip. After all, Violet knew better than most how destructive gossip could be.

"I do not know if he can," she voiced her uncertainties aloud, although more to herself than to Gwen. "I don't know if Lord Kastle is capable of giving me anything I desire. He was a castaway for five long years, and that experience must harm a man. But if he's not entirely broken – if I can find some part of him that wasn't lost at sea – then perhaps we can discover something wonderful together."

Gwen grinned ear-to-ear. "Wouldn't that be grand? To find love with your own husband?"

Violet laughed for what felt like the first time in forever. "That would be grand, indeed. But I'll need to meet him soon, and be courted by him for a long while, to see if that is even a possibility."

Gwen's smile edged downward. "That may prove difficult, though. I don't know how much time Papa will allow you."

"I fear you are right. He may barely allow me any time at all with my betrothed before the wedding. Even if I beg."

"Oh, if you beg, I'm sure he will acquiesce. Papa loves you with all his heart. If he didn't, he would never have given you this choice in husband. Honestly, he would never have let you refuse Welly in the first place."

"I suppose you're right. Although what I want from him now is more than I have ever asked before."

"And what is that?"

"I want time – several months, at least – to be courted by Lord Kastle. And I want to do it away from here."

Gwen stiffened. "Why do you want it away from here?"

"Because I don't want Mama and Papa hanging over us all day. Their constant attentions would be insufferable, and I would get nowhere in discovering the man beneath the myth of the Nightingale heir. I need to be alone with Lord Kastle, not watched over endlessly."

"Alone with Lord Kastle? Do you even hear yourself, Violet? That is not only a brazen proposal, it is an entirely awful desire. We are ladies now, or at least ladies-to-be, and you must be chaperoned at all times."

"Well, of course, Gwen. Good Lord, I'm not suggesting that I bed the man before our wedding night. I know I must be chaperoned, but just not by two people with such eagle eyes as Mama and Papa. How can I possibly learn anything deep and true about Lord Kastle if they're forever present and fussing over us? I want time alone with him. I *need* time."

Gwen scrunched her nose before bolting upright, her voice rising along with her body. "Oh! I know! What if you are courted at the Wilmington estate? Aunt Tildy can barely see two feet in front of her face! And her manor is close to Nightingale Port, as well!"

A smile overtook Violet's whole body. "God, that's brilliant, Gwen! Brilliant! Aunt Tildy's estate is definitely grand, and filled with all sorts of nooks and crannies. I'm certain Lord Kastle and I could be afforded some privacy there. Now, I just have to figure out a way to get Papa to agree to let me be courted at Wilmington."

"Can't you just ask him?"

"Goodness, no. He's wearing his serious wig today. If I'm to have any chance at success, I'll have to make him think it's *his* idea."

Gwen threw her arms around Violet's neck. "Good luck, dear sister. I have utmost faith in your powers of persuasion."

"Thank you for your confidence," she offered while drawing back.

"Although, you do know Papa will demand that you accompany me to Aunt Tildy's, right?"

"Most certainly. I'll be by your side through everything. I wouldn't have it any other way."

Violet pressed a kiss to her sister's cheek before rising from the bed and stepping to the doorway. Traversing the long hall before her with purpose and determination, Violet headed straight toward Noah Bell. Unfortunately, the shivers inside her belly made her footsteps far more unsteady than she wished.

When she reached the door to his study, she knocked and stepped inside.

Noah looked up from his desk. "Have you come to a decision, Violet?"

She smiled while moving toward him. "You look more handsome with the wig off, Papa."

He tensed, running his fingers through his thinning gray hair before his shoulders finally fell. "Flattery will get you nowhere today, dear girl. You know I expect a decision from you."

"I've made my decision. I will wed Lord Christopher Kastle, heir to the Earl of Nightingale."

Her father obviously hadn't expected such an easy answer. His mouth hung open until he cleared his throat. "Oh. Well. That is wonderful. I will make the arrangements tonight."

"Yes, please do. Although I have one small request."

He exhaled slowly. "What is that?"

"It's not much, I promise. I just...I would like some time to get to know Lord Kastle before we marry."

"How much time do you want?"

"Perhaps five or six months?"

Noah huffed. "Violet, time does not matter in this situation. You will marry the heir of Nightingale when I say so. And if you refuse to marry him, then you *will* wed the Duke of Dunworthy."

"Yes, Papa, I will marry at your discretion. But if you allow me the chance to learn about the man who shall one day father my sons – your grandsons – I shall be most grateful for your generosity and graciousness. Honestly, it will mean the world to me."

Violet plastered a grin to her lips the instant she finished.

After several stoic moments, Noah sighed. "Very well. You may have *two* months with the man. No more. Lord Kastle may court you for that time, and then plans will be made for your wedding."

"Thank you," she said, pleased to have been allotted any time at all. "And may I assume, for courting purposes, that he'll come to our estate to stay?"

Her father's brow pinched. "Well, yes, I suppose. It's too far to travel from Nightingale to Pennyshire each day. We'll have the servants set up quarters for Lord Kastle in the far wing."

"Perfect," Violet said, grinning for one more minute before slowly wiping the smile from her face. "Although...hmm."

"What is it?"

"Oh, it's nothing, really."

"It's obviously something. Tell me."

She wrinkled her forehead. "It's just that I'm a bit concerned. For Lord Kastle, that is."

"Why are you concerned?"

"Well, from what we know of his history as a castaway, he's been forced to be so far from his home for so long. I fear that asking him to come all the way to Pennyshire, and expecting him to remain here for two straight months, could be jolting. I wish there was somewhere we could meet for our courtship near Nightingale Port, where he could be closer to home and therefore feel calmer. Just to ensure a smooth transition to our life as husband and wife."

Noah's eyes flared. "Good God, child! You're not suggesting I send you to the Kastle estate to be courted, are you? I was going to let you go to Dunworthy for the duke, but only because he's old enough to not..." Her father gulped before taking a breath. "I could have sent you to Dunworthy with some assurance. But not to the Kastle estate. Not unattended."

"My goodness, Papa. I agree with you completely."

"You do?"

"Very much so. It would be entirely untoward for me to be courted at Lord Kastle's home. And societal dictations require that I be chaperoned, of course. I simply hoped there could be a way to put him more at ease, and ensure his comfort, by finding a suitable neutral ground for our courtship."

Noah stared solidly at Violet. She held as still as possible. Although she could not control the ferocious pounding of her heart against her ribs.

Eventually, he nodded. "I suppose you're right. Lord Kastle may feel better closer to his home. We could ask your Aunt Mathilda about use of her estate."

"Aunt Tildy?"

"Yes. She lives close to Nightingale Port, and since her husband's passing, her house is quite unused. Except for all her servants, of course. I imagine she'll be gracious enough to host you and your betrothed for courtship."

"What a wonderful idea, Papa."

Noah narrowed his gaze. "But you *will* be chaperoned. At all times."

"Absolutely. I'm sure Aunt Tildy will do a grand job of it."

"I would certainly hope so. However, I will also send your sister to accompany you, just to be sure."

"Splendid. I will go inform Gwen right away. Thank you." Violet curtsied before turning toward the door.

"Daughter?" he called, halting her escape.

She pivoted back to him. "Yes?"

"Why do I get the feeling that going to Aunt Tildy's was precisely what you wanted?"

Violet's cheeks flushed, for her father knew her all too well. "I suppose because it was what I wanted."

Noah watched her for a long while before a tiny smile tugged at his lips. "I hope Lord Kastle is prepared for you, my dear girl. And I hope he finds a way to deserve you."

Violet grinned brilliantly. "I love you, Papa," she assured, just before she turned and ran down the hall to find Gwen.

~

"Lift your arm a bit more, Cora," Christopher corrected his sister as they fought amidst the overgrown flowers and foliage of the Kastle gardens. "And tighten your grip. Your form is sloppy."

"It is not!" Cora insisted, attacking Christopher's sword with hers, the metal clanging in the still morning air surrounding their estate. "You're only saying that because you refuse to admit a woman could best you!"

Christopher circled Cora's blade with his own, nearly pulling her sword from her grasp. Yet she managed to hold on. "You cannot best me in this, little sister. But you are good. I'll give you that."

Cora gave his sword one last pounding, enough to make Christopher's bicep tense in response. Then she dropped her blade to the ground and straightened before him. She stood as tall as possible, even if that meant the top of her head barely came to his shoulders. "I'm glad you can admit I've become an amazing swordfighter in your absence."

He shook his head before allowing his sword to rest at his side. "I didn't say you are amazing. I said you are good. Although I don't understand why you even continued to practice the sword after I'd gone to sea."

"Because someone had to be the man of the house, Christopher."

Her pointed words jabbed beneath his skin, making his eyes drift to the backside of the Kastle manor in the distance. Christopher could easily identify the second-story window belonging to his father's bedchamber. He wondered if Quinton Kastle sat before the glass panes now, slumped in his frayed chair, staring wistfully at the unkempt gardens where his children played and fought.

Wrenching his gaze from his father's window, Christopher searched out the ancient, twisted tree beside his mother's favorite garden. The younger Kastle siblings were all there now: Juliette, sitting at the base of the trunk with her nose pressed into a book; Ruby and Pearl, hanging precariously from the extensive branches; Constance, twirling and humming around the thick ground roots; and little Octavia, giggling with the excitement of watching her older sisters play.

In truth, Christopher treasured moments like these. Daniela didn't allow the girls much recreation. She had rigorous schedules designed for them, between the upkeep of the house and of their teachings. She'd managed to do a fine job acting as a governess to her younger sisters, ensuring each of them could read, write, sew, sing, and play the piano. She'd made certain all of the girls grew into worthy women, or were well on their way.

But times like this, when they each took a few minutes to relax and be themselves, allowed Christopher to remember how glorious their life had been before their mother died. Before their father crumbled in misery. Before Christopher left them all alone to fend for themselves.

That last thought sobered him from the gentle joy of the girls' giggles. Gripping hard to his sword, he turned away from the beauty of his family and began to hack at the shrubs of the garden where he and Cora stood. His actions made his fiercest sister huff almost immediately.

"There you go, retreating into your shell once more," Cora sighed. "Every time you do it, I always think the exact same thing."

He continued to whack at the branches. "What do you think?"

"That you're going back to sea. That you're leaving us all again."

Christopher turned to pin her gaze. "Why do you bring this up over and over? I've told you a hundred times: I'm home now."

Cora took two steps forward, glaring up at him. "Do not speak to me as if I don't know you, Christopher Kastle. I can see the urge to run in your eyes. And I am telling you, you had better not ever leave me again. I forgave you the first time you left. I hated to watch you go, yet I understood that losing Mother was hard and you needed to escape to the sea. But then, when we heard your ship was lost and you were dead – dear God, the *pain* I felt – I cannot describe the pain."

She stopped speaking for aching seconds, catching a harsh breath before she continued. "Therefore, I need you to hear this, and to understand it: I will not forgive you if you leave me again. I *will not*. If you plan to head back out to sea, you sure as hell better take me with you. No questions. No discussions. I come with you, wherever you go. Or you won't have this sister to return home to next time."

Christopher hung his sword at his side, his limbs heavy as he stared into Cora's blazing eyes. "I'm sorry," he offered. "I'm so sorry for all I put you through. But I swear to you, there will not be a next time. I am not leaving again. I am not."

Her lower lip quivered with his words. "I wish I could believe you. I wish you would give me a *reason* to believe you."

"Cora..."

"Christopher!" Daniela called, her stern, distant bellow unnerving him.

He stared into Cora's watery eyes for one more moment before raising his gaze to their eldest sister, who walked toward them both from the back of the manor. "Yes, Daniela?"

She halted several feet away. "Father wishes to speak with you."

Christopher handed his sword to Cora, giving her arm a gentle squeeze before moving toward the house. "What does he want from me?"

Daniela shrugged. "I do not know, exactly. A messenger arrived while you were out here, and shortly afterward, Father called for you."

"Very well," Christopher said, more than a little confused by this turn of events. Quinton Kastle did not receive messages anymore. He didn't do much of anything anymore.

Christopher entered the house alone, moving through the kitchens and down the back hallway to the grand circular foyer. His eyes lifted to the second floor as he ascended the right half of the double stairway unfolding to each side, the thinning wood steps squealing beneath his solid weight. He traversed the lengthy upper hall, passing the anteroom to his own bedchamber, before reaching his father's room.

He knocked on the door as he eased it open. "Father? You wished to see me?"

"Yes, Christopher. Please come in."

Quinton Kastle sat in his frayed old chair before the window with a blanket resting across his frail legs and a decanter of brandy at his side. He looked a bit livelier than usual today, which was to say that his yellowed cheeks displayed a hint of rosiness. Unfortunately, his hunched shoulders remained unaltered, even when Christopher stepped to his side.

"I have good news for us, my son. Well, I believe it is good news." Quinton's fist opened to reveal a gold locket, oval with an intricately carved pattern across the front, resting inside his crinkled palm. "A courier arrived today with a parcel and a message. It is a message I could not be more pleased with."

Christopher shook his head, since the only message he could imagine pleasing his father was one that said Miranda Kastle had returned from the dead. "What is the message?"

Quinton looked up to him with dull, pale eyes. "Christopher," he whispered, clinging to the name. "I know I've gambled away our fortunes. And all I do now is sit up here and drink. I've sinned against this family, against your sisters. I've left them with a crumbling home, no dowries, and no hope for families of their own."

Christopher didn't protest the words. He simply stood and listened.

"But now, for once, I think I can repair at least some of the damage I've done," Quinton continued. "If you'll help me."

"How can I help?"

"By agreeing to the deal I managed to arrange for our family."

Christopher's brow quirked. "You've struck a deal?"

"Yes. I still have some connections, you know. Maybe they aren't as reputable as they once were, back when your mother was alive, but I have them. And I was able to find you a...a wife."

"A *wife*?"

Quinton's fingers squeezed around the locket. "Her name is Violet Bell. Her father is quite wealthy. The Bell money is new, but it is vast. Mr. Bell is willing to offer us an immense reward – enough to save our estate and provide dowries for all your sisters – if you wed his eldest daughter."

Christopher stood stiffly in front of his father, attempting to absorb so much information at once. Although one particular item stood out above all others. "Mr. Bell made his daughter's dowry so large that it will save every one of my seven sisters from financial ruin?"

"Yes."

Bloody hell. What on earth is wrong with this girl?

"Father, I'm a bit confused. Why would a man with that degree of wealth desire his daughter to marry *me*?"

"Because you are Lord Kastle, heir to the Earl of Nightingale."

"Oh. Right." Christopher often forgot the fact that he was a lord. He couldn't remember the last time he'd felt like a nobleman, if he ever had. "So... how is it that you came to strike this deal with Mr. Bell?"

Quinton's skin blanched. "Well, while you were away at sea, I spent a great deal of time in the gambling dens down on Wharf Street. During that period, I made the acquaintance of Mr. Noah Bell, who came from poverty and yet still assumed control of all the gaming houses in Nightingale Port in just a few short years. As you can imagine, one does not accomplish such a feat without bending rules and making enemies. Mr. Bell is a shrewd businessman, to be sure. I imagine he has managed to avoid persecution of the law by paying constables, and even inspectors, to avert their eyes to his misdeeds. But while his amassed wealth is great, it lacks connection to title and nobility. That is what Noah Bell seeks for his daughter: to remove her from the dangers of his activities by attaching her to title. Her marriage to you will provide a noble future for the Bells at the same time it returns the wealth of the Kastles. Honestly, it is an ideal situation for both families, given their current statuses."

"I see," Christopher said, working to wrap his mind around the truth. "And his daughter, Violet? Does she approve of the arrangement?"

"She does. She's agreed to marry you after a period of courtship. Mr. Bell has asked that you travel to his sister-in-law's home, a Lady Mathilda Wilmington, who lives near Nightingale Port. Once there, you will commence with a two-month courtship of Violet Bell, who will remain at her aunt's home with you. Lady Wilmington will act as your chaperone, and after those two months have passed, Mr. Bell will begin the preparations for your wedding."

"I see," Christopher repeated. "Then this arrangement has already been planned out in detail. And it is what you wish of me."

"Yes, my son. This is my request. I want you to wed Violet Bell."

The moment his father said those words, something inside Christopher changed. He settled. Calmed. Eased.

Good God, this sounded perfect. It probably shouldn't sound perfect: marriage to the unseen daughter of a criminal. Yet it was. It was an opportunity he didn't have to go in search of, but rather one that had fallen into his lap. This was a chance to care for his sisters in real and tangible ways. A chance to save his ancestral home from ruin. A chance to prove to Cora that he wouldn't leave her again.

Christopher did understand that he would have to get married in order to take advantage of this opportunity, but he took no issue with that condition. Back in his younger days, when he'd believed his life would flow smoothly out before him like a gently babbling brook, he'd accepted that he would eventually get married. But then, when the babbling brook mutated into an ocean tempest, he'd deemed himself too lacking for marriage.

He hadn't even attempted to return to the formalities of English society since his return to Nightingale, knowing the ceremonial balls and cotillions would only open him to the scheming of matchmakers. He hadn't resumed the role of an eligible bachelor because he honestly didn't know what he had left to offer a wife. And even if he could find a way to act as a proper husband, he remained unwilling to fall prey to the pitfall his father had: the treacherous pitfall of loving a woman with all his heart. He'd seen firsthand what that kind of love did to a man, having watched his father crumble with its loss, and couldn't imagine choosing it.

Christopher didn't want the kind of love that brought a man to his knees. He knew what it felt like to be on his knees, both literally and figuratively, and nothing in this life would ever do that to him again. Not ever.

Consequently, an arranged marriage was actual perfection. Violet Bell's dowry would fix his crumbling home and provide vast opportunities for his sisters. Also, taking his place as a husband would prove to Cora that he was here to stay. And most importantly, Christopher could walk into this arrangement with his eyes open and his heart closed.

Sucking in a breath of the room's kempt air, he nodded to the man sitting before him. "All right, Father. I will marry her."

Quinton's mouth gaped. "Really? That is everything you have to say on the matter? No arguments? No reservations?"

"No. None at all."

"Oh. Well. Very good, then." He shifted in his seat, reaching his hand out to his son.

"What do you hold there?"

"It is a locket with Violet's picture inside. Mr. Bell sent it over for you to see her before you meet. I will send a message back to him, stating you'll make the journey to Lady Wilmington's estate at the end of the month."

Christopher forced himself to edge closer to his father so he could accept the locket. The weight of the gold trinket lay heavy in his palm. "Yes, please do. I will be ready to meet my betrothed at month's end."

Quinton placed his hand over Christopher's while looking up to his eyes. "Thank you, my son. I know by asking you to do this, I am asking you to atone for my sins. I also know I have no right to do so. But even if you do not do this for me, I appreciate that you will do it for your sisters."

Christopher nodded even as he withdrew from his father's touch. "I do this for all of us," he replied, giving a tight smile while turning away.

He made it out of his father's chamber and into the hallway before his nerves took hold of him. He wasn't having second thoughts about his betrothal. On the contrary, this marriage was exactly what the Kastle family needed. But the Kastle family wasn't the only family involved here. There was the Bell family to consider. There was Violet Bell to consider.

"Violet," Christopher said aloud, accustoming himself to her name while standing in the empty hallway. "Violet Bell. Violet *Kastle*."

His fingers tightened around the locket as he brought it up to his chest. He knew this trinket may contain evidence of an entirely wretched woman – a woman so hideous that it cost the dowries of seven others just to pawn her off. "It doesn't matter what she looks like," he told himself. "She will be your wife, regardless."

Christopher listened to his words, and even accepted them, yet his heart remained in his throat while he studied the ornate gold front of the oval. He didn't breathe at all when he pressed the top clasp, flipping the locket open. Then he stared in stupor at the photo inside.

My God, she's lovely.

Violet Bell was absolutely lovely. She did not present the picture of lofty attractiveness one would see with modeled London fashions, nor did she force the painted-on allure he'd witnessed in the brothels of his youth. Violet was, plainly and simply, beautiful.

The photo had no color, of course, but he could tell her complexion was smooth and light, and her loose hair blond. Her lips were full and a natural shade of rose. He couldn't see if her eyes were light or dark, however, since she wasn't looking up in the photo. She looked down, as if focused entirely on the floor. In truth, she looked quite sad.

Christopher's thumb shifted of its own volition, to stroke the gentle slope of her jaw. *Why are you sad, Violet?*

His brow furrowed with the question. What could cause such a lovely young woman to appear so melancholy? Was she always unhappy? Or had her mind only latched to a forlorn thought when this photograph was taken?

As his thumb eased across the delicate curves of her face, Christopher realized he had not yet considered the personality of the woman he was to marry. Probably because he'd had very little time to think of her at all. Yet now, seeing her soft, sad face, he wondered what his Violet would be like when she stood before him.

Would she be controlled and directive, like Daniela? Or fierce and outspoken, like Cora? Would she have Juliette's wistful, romantic heart? Or the mischievous tendencies of Ruby and Pearl? Would she sing and dance like Constance? Or giggle and squeal like Octavia? Would Violet be some combination of all of these women, and more?

Christopher smiled as he memorized the arch of her brow and the outline of her lips. He didn't know what kind of woman resided inside his betrothed, but felt certain she would reveal her true self the instant they met. Even though he knew firsthand that looks could be deceiving, the woman in this photo definitely wasn't hiding anything. She wore her heart on full display, her emotions bared for all to see.

"Violet," he sang, her name on his lips already familiar and oddly right.

A loud knock against the front door downstairs startled him, finally drawing his attention away from her picture. He heard the purposeful walk of footsteps toward the entryway and Daniela's direct tone as she spoke to the caller. He could discern Nick's deep voice even from this distance.

Christopher's spine stiffened at the sound of his friend. He closed the locket and slipped it into the pocket of his trousers while he strode down the hallway. When he began to descend the grand staircase to the first floor, he saw his oldest friend standing in the foyer, speaking with his eldest sister. He took note of how Nick's voice had lowered just for Daniela's ears, of how his body leaned toward hers, and of how her lips curved up with his whispered words.

Witnessing the closeness of the couple, Christopher's mind latched instantly to the image of Violet's face. His fingers twitched in anticipation as he considered the possibility of one day being able to lean into his betrothed the way Nick leaned into Daniela. Christopher wondered what it would be like to feel Violet's cheek beneath his fingertips. He wondered if her skin would be as soft to the touch as it appeared in her photograph. He wondered if her eyes would widen, and her lips part on a gasp, at the feel of their contact.

When he arrived at the bottom of the stairs, Christopher cringed with the simplistic beauty of his thoughts. He tried to assure himself that he only had these visions of Violet because he'd been too long without bedding a woman. But deep inside, he knew his yearning to touch her had little to do with carnal desires.

"Love brings a man to his knees," he muttered beneath his breath as he approached his sister and her would-be suitor. "You are entirely better off without it. You don't want to love a woman the way Father loved Mother. Or the way Nick loves Daniela."

"Nick! You're back again!" Cora announced from the opposite side of the lower halls, entering the foyer at the same time Christopher did.

"Yes, he's back again," Christopher huffed. "To see *me*, of course."

Nick straightened from Daniela in an instant. "Always happy to see you, Lord Kastle."

He gave his friend a smirk.

"What did Father want with you, Christopher?" Daniela questioned.

"Did it have anything to do with the messenger who arrived earlier?" Cora added, coming to a standstill beside their sister.

"It did," Christopher answered, feeling all eyes on him. He inhaled steeply before his announcement. "Father has made arrangements for me to marry."

Cora and Nick's jaws dropped simultaneously.

Daniela scowled. "Marry? Who on earth are you going to marry?"

"Her name is Violet Bell."

A choking sound escaped Cora's throat.

"Are you serious?" Daniela scoffed. "You're actually going to wed the Picky Princess of Pennyshire?"

Christopher cocked his head. "The who?"

"Oh, the Picky Princess of Pennyshire," Nick chimed in. "I've heard of her. I guess she finally stopped being picky and decided on a husband."

"The Picky Princess?" Christopher echoed.

"Strange that she chose another heir to an earldom," Daniela considered, "when she's already refused the heir to the Earl of Centreville."

Nick chuckled. "Well, with the amount of money stuffing her father's pockets, I imagine she can refuse whomever she likes."

"Money?" Cora asked.

"If I've heard correctly, the Bell family has even more wealth than mine," Nick confirmed. "And my family has a shocking amount of wealth."

Cora's face fell as she turned to Christopher. "You're having to marry her for the money, aren't you? So that you can support us?"

He reached for Cora's hand, squeezing her fingers inside his own. "Look at it this way: If I'm getting married, it means I'm not leaving. Isn't that what you wanted? The reassurance that I will stay?"

She held his eyes. "I don't know. It still feels like you're leaving."

"Only to gather my bride, and to bring her home with me."

Cora scrutinized him before finally releasing his hand. "If you say so."

"I do."

Daniela shifted on her feet. "So, how much money is she worth?"

Christopher's jaw clenched with the impolite question. "If you're asking what her dowry is worth, it's enough to provide for all the necessary renovations to our estate. As well as dowries for all of you."

Daniela gasped. "You mean we will *all* have dowries?"

"Yes. All seven of you."

"Bloody hell," Nick breathed. "Her father is coughing up enough money for seven dowries, just to get rid of one daughter? What in the hell is wrong with her?"

Christopher growled at the question, even while inwardly ashamed that he'd wondered the same. "Don't be rude, Nick."

"I'm not being rude, old mate. It's a serious question. Can the girl walk? Can she talk? Does she have extra appendages?"

"Yes, she walks and talks and has the appropriate number of limbs."

"Well, isn't that wonderful," Daniela cut in, stepping closer to her brother. "For your sake, I do hope the only thing wrong with her is her pickiness. But if this woman and her money are to be the saviors of our family, then we have a much more pressing issue than her limbs."

Christopher met Daniela's piercing gaze. "And what is that?"

"She has to *like* you, dear brother."

"What's not to like about me?"

Nick's hand flew to his mouth, concealing a sudden fit of snickering.

Christopher scowled at him.

"*That* is what's not to like," Daniela informed. "That scowl of yours – the permanent insignia of the grumbling, growling Christopher we've all had the pleasure to witness each day since your return from sea."

He turned to his other sister in search of support, but Cora merely shrugged. "She's not wrong, Christopher."

"Well, thank you both so much for that," he admonished. "But I am not always grumbling and growling, despite what you may think. And besides, Violet is betrothed to me now. She'll be my wife regardless."

Daniela shook her head. "That's simply not true. The Picky Princess has already turned down one earldom without recompense, so I don't see any reason why her father won't allow her to refuse another."

That thought made Christopher's chest constrict. Violet's face sprang to his mind again, so quickly and easily. He pictured the curves of her full, rosy lips, wanting to hear his name spoken on those lips in pleasing ways only. He never wanted Violet to refuse him anything.

"Try to remember what you used to be like," Daniela instructed in his silence. "Try to be dashing around her. You do remember what it is to be dashing, do you not?" Her eyes darted to Nick's. "You and Mr. Marlow certainly had your share of dashing moments with the ladies in your youth."

Christopher cringed with his sister's harsh but accurate comment.

Nick looked downright crushed by it.

"I think I'll manage just fine with my bride-to-be," Christopher insisted, not wishing to dwell on the thought of Violet's potential refusal.

Daniela snorted. "I do hope so, for all our sakes. But until such time as you marry the Picky Princess – if she'll have you – there's plenty of work to be done around here. Let's get on with it." She turned, grabbing Cora's arm to pull her down the hallway toward the kitchen.

"I'll be there soon," Christopher told her. "And Daniela?"

She pivoted back to him. "Yes?"

He glared into her eyes. "I want you to stop referring to my betrothed as the Picky Princess. Her name is Violet."

"Very well," Daniela conceded, her brow pinching before she dragged Cora from the room.

Christopher turned to his friend as soon as his sisters disappeared down the hallway. He did not miss the way the Nick's gaze followed Daniela's retreating form to the last possible second. "So? What do you have to say to me, old friend?"

Nick's face hardened when their eyes met. "Are you actually going through with this insanity?"

"You mean getting married? Yes, I am."

"But why? Why would you agree to the ancient custom of arranged marriages in this day and age? Especially since I've already told you I'll give you all the money you need for..."

"No. Absolutely not."

Nick threw his hands in the air. "So, you'll sell your soul to some girl you've never met, rather than accept help from your best friend?"

"I won't take your money, Nick." *And I no longer have a soul to sell.*

"Good God, man! You have no idea what you're getting into! What if she's a simpering half-wit? Or worse, a tyrannical snit? I highly doubt a woman comes to be called 'the Picky Princess' without being a horror."

Christopher pinched his lips shut, since he apparently had to work on being dashing. Growling at his best friend would not be a very dashing thing to do at all, even if it angered him beyond reason to hear anyone speak ill of his wife. "I don't know why people call her that, Nick. But you know as well as I do that a person is not always who they seem from a distance, and not always the same as their name implies. I honestly find it hard to believe that you put so much value in idle gossip."

Nick's shoulders fell. "I'm only trying to look out for your best interests here. You haven't even seen this girl. Just because you know she has all of her limbs doesn't mean she's agreeable to the eyes. What if your bride has a hooked nose? And ears like an elephant?"

Christopher's hand flew to his pocket to retrieve the locket and prove to his brother that Violet was lovelier than imaginable. But he stopped the moment his fingers curled around the oval. He didn't want anyone else to see her yet, not before he had the chance to lay his eyes on her in the flesh – and to figure out why such a heartfelt young woman looked so sad.

"I'm sure it will be fine," he insisted, resting the photograph back into his pocket. "Besides, her appearance is of little consequence. This is a business arrangement. Her family gets a title. My sisters get dowries. That's all this is."

"Hell, I know that much," Nick agreed with a chuckle. "I certainly wasn't suggesting you'd fall in love with her."

Christopher's stomach twisted into knots. "No, of course not. I definitely won't fall in love with her."

CHAPTER 3

First Sight

Gravel grumbled and growled beneath the carriage wheels as Violet watched Aunt Tildy's home come into view in the distance. Violet peered over at Gwendolyn, who sat beside her on the cushioned coach seat with wide eyes and an even wider smile. Gwen had always loved visiting the Wilmington estate when they were children. Violet had also enjoyed the adventure of it, since it felt like a whole other world from their lowly London roots. But while a youthful Gwen saw only the beauty of intensely manicured grounds and the plushness of daily freshened bed sheets, Violet's younger self dreaded witnessing the cool civility between their Aunt Tildy and Uncle Gilroy.

Turning to glance out of the carriage window, Violet listened to the constant clip of horse hooves that brought the manor closer and closer. The spacious manor could house several families in lush comfort, yet this was merely Tildy and Gilroy's summer home. The couple had birthed only one son, who now resided in the main Wilmington estate in London with his own family, leaving this country home to his mother after Gilroy's passing.

As Violet soaked in the vision of the grand entryway doors, along with the broad windows highlighting the expansive gold-inlaid foyer beyond, a memory crept into her mind. It was a remembrance of her 10-year-old self, hiding in an alcove to the back of the foyer, listening to Mama and Aunt Tildy speak in hushed tones.

"You don't have to go back to him, Liza. Stay with us. I've spoken to Gilroy, and he's agreed to take on you and the girls until they are of marrying age."

"Tildy, I've told you a thousand times. I love Noah. I want to be with him."

"But what has he done for you? What has he given you? You live in a hovel. You have no jewels, no fashionable dresses. Your children are lacking in proper education and more often than not are covered in filth."

"They're children. They like to play."

"They'll be women one day, Liza. Before you know it. And then what will become of them? They should be ladies, as you were once a lady. Just because you chose to throw all of that away to marry for love doesn't mean your daughters need succumb to the same fate."

"Oh, Tildy. Love is not a fate, my dear sister. It is a gift."

Violet smiled in contentment with the memory of how happy her mother had been back then. Liza Bell's eyes positively glowed whenever they'd finished visiting Wilmington and went back home to Noah, where they belonged.

"We're here," Gwen said, taking Violet's hand.

She jumped with the unexpected contact.

Gwen's brow rose. "Are you all right?"

"Yes, of course."

"Are you sure? You're quite jittery."

A tremulous laugh escaped Violet's throat. "Well, it isn't every day you meet your husband, is it?"

Gwen petted her arm. "Please try not to be nervous. You know how your mouth opens when you're emotional, and if you end up saying something untoward in the presence of Lord Kastle, it will only make you more anxious. I'm afraid it will become a downward spiral."

"That's good advice. I'll try to take it. Although I don't know if this amount of nerves could ever be controlled."

"But this is what you wanted," Gwen reminded with a squeeze of her fingers. "You'll be here with your betrothed – accompanied by Aunt Tildy's extreme nearsightedness and penchant for idle napping – and you'll have time to learn about each other. I'm certain, once Lord Kastle gets to know you, he'll be absolutely enraptured. For you are wondrous and lovely in every way, and if he cannot see that, then he truly is a broken man."

Violet forced a smile, since she knew Gwen meant well. Unfortunately, her choice of words festered inside Violet's brain. Would Christopher Kastle truly be broken? Would he arrive here as a wilted creature, hunched over on his horse, with a drawn mouth and dead eyes?

A chill crept down her spine when the carriage pulled to a stop in front of the manor, because she honestly had no idea what to expect from Lord Kastle.

She would also never be properly chaperoned here at the Wilmington estate, no matter how lofty her aunt's intentions may be. And while that was precisely Violet's purpose in coming here, the current chill wracking her body still spread and festered in the most alarming way.

You must take control of your mind, she admonished herself. *Gwen is right. This is what you wanted. You have two months to learn all you can about your future husband, so stiffen your spine and get to it.*

Drawing a deep, calming breath, Violet straightened against the seat. "Thank you for your support, Gwen, as always. I do promise you, even though I may be nervous, I am truly ready for this adventure."

Violet gave her sister's hand one last squeeze before the coachman opened her door. Her soft suede boots hit the gravel along with the hem of her crimson riding cape as she stepped down from the carriage. An older man approached them from the manor doorway, a welcome apparition from their past. "Mr. Rodchester? Is that you?"

"It is me, dear girl," the weathered caretaker replied, showing off his few remaining teeth with a gentle grin.

Violet grabbed hold of him, certain his frail frame could only benefit from a thorough hugging. "I'm so grateful you're still here."

"Yes, I still live, thank the heavens," Rodchester assured when she released him. "I'm fortunate enough to care for the sweet Bell sisters once again."

"Mr. Rodchester! How wonderful to see you!" Gwen squealed from the other side of the carriage, running over to hug him.

Violet grinned at the sight of their embrace, turning away only when she heard another coach pull to a stop behind theirs. This second carriage had remained close ever since they left Pennyshire early this morning, bringing their trunks of necessities and finery along. Mama had insisted on as many changes of clothing as possible for Violet, so she may be courted in elegant style. She'd let her mother fuss over packing, but she'd put her foot down about wearing the fashionable crinoline bustles that made her skirts obscenely wide and sitting down ridiculously difficult. Although Mama had still put one cage in, for good measure.

"I'll have your trunks brought in," Rodchester informed when he came to stand by Violet. "Everything will be in place before your betrothed arrives."

"Lord Kastle is not here yet?"

"No, although his trunk of clothing arrived yesterday. I made sure it was carried into his bedchamber. Which is, of course, on the other side of the house from your own bedchamber."

Violet grinned. "Thank you, Mr. Rodchester. You always take such good care of me."

"I'm just happy to have you back. It's been far too long."

"You're right. It has."

"Well, come now, sweet girls. Your aunt wishes to see you before you settle in."

~

AN HOUR LATER, after greeting Aunt Tildy with a hug and seeing Gwen into their adjoining bedrooms, Violet left her sister in order to roam around the house. She didn't bother to change out of her riding outfit, other than to remove the cape, and the simple dress swirled about her ankles as she traversed the stretching second-story hallway. She'd told Gwen she needed a few minutes to reorient herself to the manor, but in truth, Violet simply felt too wound and tight to sit still.

Ambling slowly to the main staircase, she descended into the foyer where they'd first arrived. Dog barks resounded in the distance when she approached one of the tall windows overlooking the outside entryway. She saw Mr. Rodchester in the distance, carefully guiding the hounds back to the horse stables. Uncle Gilroy's dogs still remained here at the manor, remnants of his love of hunting. Tildy's late husband bred the hounds for sport, but Violet could remember when they were just happy, drooling pups. She preferred to think of them that way.

She watched Mr. Rodchester settle the hounds into the far stables before starting back towards the manor entrance. She imagined the kind, elderly care-taker kept a vigil outside, awaiting Lord Kastle's arrival. Violet knew she shouldn't even be here in the foyer right now. She certainly could not meet her betrothed for the first time unattended, without her aunt and sister present. That would be an atrocious crime, to say the least, and Tildy might never recover from it.

"If Lord Kastle arrives, I'll simply hasten upstairs," she assured herself as she continued to observe Rodchester through the window. After all, Violet had no desire to act in any way her aunt might disapprove of. She wanted Tildy to like her betrothed, probably because Tildy had never liked her father.

Noah is a scallywag, Liza. I'll never understand why you married him.

The memory of Tildy's common admonishment to her sister brought a sad smile to Violet's face. She wasn't sad for her mother, who'd married for love. On the contrary, Violet was sad for Tildy, who never knew love. Aunt Tildy and Uncle Gilroy had chosen to spend their days being polite to one another and their nights in separate bedchambers. Meanwhile, back in the dregs of London, Mama and Papa had chosen to spend every moment they could in each other's arms. They held hands. They kissed. They laughed. Those were the things that made Violet happy – not the house and the gardens and the servants – but the love.

She sighed, her eyes glassing over with ancient memories as she watched Rodchester come to a standstill near the front entrance. A huge part of her wished Papa had never fulfilled the promise he gave Mama the night he proposed to her. When Noah Bell made good on his word, and found a way to give his wife back the privileged life she'd given up for him – when he purchased their home in Pennyshire and pulled on his curly white wig and made deals to protect their family – he lost the spark that Violet loved so much. He lost the spark that united them all, and she could only sit and watch as her mother slowly ceased laughing and turned back into Lady Liza.

Violet knew everything her parents did was to benefit their daughters, but she would have much preferred to remain in the filth of London with her happy, loving family. Love was what she wanted in her life above all else. Love was why she wanted to be here with her future husband. She wanted them to learn about each other, to laugh together, play together, and know joy in each other's arms. She wanted to love Christopher Kastle with all her heart and have him love her equally in return.

He's a broken shell of a man. Nothing left but the skin on his bones.

Another shiver wracked her body when those words jumped into her mind yet again. Violet didn't want to believe them, but she also understood how they could be true. Her betrothed had been lost at sea for five long years. She had no idea what he'd endured. She had no idea who the man coming to court her was, deep inside his soul.

A thumping noise rattled inside her brain, right alongside her thoughts. The thumps grew louder and more distinct, until she realized they belonged to a galloping steed, moving ever closer to the front of Tildy's estate. Violet's gaze sharpened when she stared out of the foyer window, watching an impressive white stallion charge forward. The horse carried on its back a statuesque man in a navy-blue riding jacket, white breeches, and black boots. The gentleman commanded the sizeable steed with minimal effort, riding with his long spine straight and his sights fixed pointedly on the entrance to Wilmington manor – the entrance where Violet still stood.

She froze. Well, her body froze. But her mind moved faster than ever.

It's him! Lord Kastle is here! You need to leave this foyer immediately! Don't look at him any further! Just leave!

Unfortunately, it was too late to listen to her sensible inner voice of panic. Rodchester had already moved forward to take the reins from Lord Kastle's hands. Violet continued to stare out of the window, unable to move a muscle, as she watched her betrothed pull his steed to a stop before the front door. Her mouth gaped when he dismounted, her eyes fixated entirely on his body as he drew one of his long legs over the stallion's back before shifting effortlessly to the ground.

Good gracious, the man was tall. And muscled. The top of his short, light brown hair came nearly flush with his horse's head, his broad shoulders pulling at the constraint of his riding jacket while he approached the Wilmington caretaker.

Violet could only gawk at Mr. Rodchester as he spoke with Lord Kastle, her heart tripping over itself when the older man directed the younger to enter the house with a wave of his hand. She actually managed to back several steps away from the window before her legs stopped working altogether. The air thinned around her when she saw Lord Kastle turn toward the front door.

Violet knew what she should do. She should flee to the stairs this instant, lest she meet her betrothed unintentionally unattended. But as she watched him advance up the short path to the master doorway – his sharp eyes intent on his destination and his thick body moving with the grace of a panther – she could barely breathe, let alone lift a foot.

Dear heavens, if this is what the man looks like broken, I fear seeing him in full command.

Christopher Kastle entered the massive door and closed it behind him. He glanced around for a moment before moving lithely inside the house, taking several long strides forward until he stopped entirely. He ceased walking the moment his gaze met hers.

Ten years of training to act the part of a lady abandoned Violet's brain the instant her betrothed's deep blue eyes fastened onto her. She honestly could not remember what to do or say right now, since it was far too late for retreat. She stood stiffly before him, only vaguely recalling something about a curtsy and a "my lord" being the proper order of address. But all she could manage to do as she looked on his ridiculously handsome face was to breathe out the word, "H-hello."

Lord Kastle didn't move at all. He simply watched her, with no change in his stance or expression. Violet wasn't even sure if he'd heard her whispered greeting until he finally replied in kind.

"Hello."

Goodness, his voice was deep. And the slight shift of his chest when he spoke pulled his shirt against the breadth of his muscles perfectly. Just one word uttered, yet everything about him tantalized. Violet could listen to his voice for hours. And she would. She would listen to his voice for the rest of her life, because this man was her husband.

A squeak snuck out of the back of her throat. *This man is my husband,* her brain realized. Then her mouth opened, much to her chagrin.

"So...I guess I'm...I'm your wife. I mean, I'm not your wife *yet.* Obviously. Since I've literally just laid eyes on you. Good gracious! I'm getting ahead of myself, aren't I? I'm getting ahead of both of us, as there's still the courtship and engagement and wedding to be had. But I will be your wife, I suppose. Well, I don't suppose. I mean, I suppose I actually know. Since this has all been arranged. You and me, that is. Although I'm sure you're aware, since that's why you're here. And it's also why I'm here. Because we're to be married."

Violet winced with the words she couldn't stop from flowing. "Unless you'd like to call the whole thing off right now, which I assure you I would completely understand, since I am apparently unable to stop talking. But I will. I will cease to speak. This instant," she announced, pressing her lips shut.

She fully expected Lord Kastle to run screaming in the opposite direction. She waited for him to turn on his heels, burst back out of the front door, wrestle his horse's reins from Rodchester's frail hands, hop back on his mount, and ride violently away until he and his steed both collapsed from sheer exhaustion. Although she imagined it would take a great deal to exhaust him, because he was so big. Big and broad and muscular and – dear God – she might faint this instant, just from looking at him.

He should definitely run. Away from me. Immediately.

He didn't run, however. He only continued to watch her.

Violet stood as stone, with her mouth shut, her eyes wide, and her fingers twisted into the silk of her skirt. She waited an eternity for him to respond.

Eventually, he did. He smiled. Christopher Kastle smiled at her, and it was warm and genuine and lit up his entire body. The sight allowed her hands to finally relax at her sides.

Lord Kastle bowed his head. "It is a pleasure to meet you. *Violet.*"

She managed to curtsy in return, even while her mind spun. She had never heard her name spoken in such a way: like it was a question and an answer, all in one. "It is a pleasure to meet you as well, my lord."

Taking a single step toward her, he shook his head. "Christopher. Please. Call me Christopher."

"Christopher," she agreed, taking a step toward him as well, although not consciously recalling the decision to do so. They remained several feet apart, across the expanse of Aunt Tildy's ornately gilded parlor, yet Violet could see nothing but the fathomless blue of his eyes, the etched line of his stubble-covered jaw, and the flawless beauty of his smile.

He held himself with noble poise, even while slowly and steadily drinking in the curves of her face. In any other situation, with any other man studying her in such a tender way, Violet would have been self-conscious about her appearance. Especially since she hadn't even taken the time to pin up her hair or change into a more suitable dress. But she couldn't muster the energy to doubt herself – not with the way Christopher gazed upon her. He looked positively enraptured, and for a moment she didn't doubt anything in the entire world. At least, not until her sister entered the room.

"Violet? Did I hear horse hooves? Has the heir of Nightingale come to…oh!" Gwen's words faltered as soon as she comprehended the scene playing out before her. She reached Violet's side in an instant, halting her footsteps to focus her attention on their guest. "Pardon me, Lord Kastle. I didn't realize you'd arrived."

Violet looked to her sister with a jolt of panic. She suddenly remembered standing in the parlor of the Bell manor, watching Lord Wellington Chaney as he caught sight of Gwen for the very first time. Violet couldn't even glance over to Christopher at this moment, fearing the pain of witnessing another suitor succumb to her younger sister's perfectly natural charms.

Nibbling against her lip, she swept her hand out to her side. "May I introduce my sister, Gwendolyn Bell."

"Pleased to meet you, my lady," Christopher spoke to her.

Gwen laughed her gorgeous laugh and Violet's stomach twisted.

"No need to call me a lady, my lord. I'm not married, so do call me Gwen."

"All right, Gwen. And I prefer to be called Christopher, if you will."

Gwen curtsied. "Christopher."

Violet could barely fathom the thought of looking back to her betrothed, but she knew she had to get it over with. Pulling her attention away from her stunning sister, Violet drew her gaze slowly up to his face. She expected him to still be entranced by the dark-haired beauty beside her. She expected him to have that same besmirched look in his eyes that Welly had the day he'd stepped foot into the Bell manor.

But Christopher did not stare in dumbfounded appreciation of the woman at Violet's side. He did not look anywhere else. His eyes were for her and her alone.

Christopher stared directly at Violet, with his entire body focused on hers, and she couldn't have looked away even if she wanted to. Which she did not. She stared straight back at him. She was not shy or demure, as she knew a proper lady ought to be. She looked on her future husband boldly, even though she had trouble catching her breath with the realization of the preference and vigilance he already held for her. She may never have moved again, if not for a harsh, harrumphing noise coming from behind her.

"Great heavens! What is all this about? Violet! Why are you here with Lord Kastle? I was not even informed of his presence!"

She flinched with the sound of her aunt's voice, dropping her eyes immediately to the ground. "I'm so sorry, Aunt Tildy, I just..."

The heavy-set woman's booted footsteps clanged against the marble flooring, ringing like a death toll in Violet's ears. "Well, I never..." Tildy began her admonishment, straightening to her full, short height when she reached Gwen's side.

"It is my fault entirely, Lady Wilmington," Christopher cut in before Tildy could continue her diatribe. He took several steps toward the older woman with the firmly planted frown. "Mr. Rodchester asked me to wait here in the foyer until he had time to settle my horse in the stables. I assure you, my arrival caught your niece purely off-guard."

Violet risked glancing back to her aunt's face, watching in sheer amazement as the widow's crinkled nose eased the instant Christopher bowed before her. "I hope you will accept my apologies, most sincerely," he added with a sparkling grin. "It is such a privilege to be invited into your lovely home and I never wish to act in any manner you deem inappropriate."

Aunt Tildy's cheeks flushed with more color than ever before seen, a startling contrast to her black dress and gray hair. Violet bit into her lip to keep from giggling. It seemed even her aged, opinionated aunt was not immune to the allure of Christopher Kastle.

Sweet heavens, this man could charm the knickers off a snake. If a snake wore knickers, that is. And he could certainly charm my knickers off. Although I don't wear knickers, either.

Violet flushed hotter than Tildy. *Goodness, where has my mind gone?*

Mr. Rodchester burst through the front door then, saving Violet from the bizarre travels of her brain. "Oh dear, you're all here already. I beg your pardon, Lady Wilmington. I was only placing Lord Kastle's horse in the stables and..."

"Yes, yes, Rodchester," Tildy barked, returning to her crotchety old self the moment her eyes left Christopher's. "I was informed of your whereabouts. Do introduce our caller officially, as should have been done before."

Rodchester bowed to Tildy before coming to stand at Christopher's side. "May I introduce Lord Christopher Kastle, heir to the Earl of Nightingale."

Violet looked back to Christopher, watching his attention drift smoothly from Rodchester to Tildy to Gwen before settling firmly in on her. A gentle smile pulled at his lips when their eyes met. Then he bowed deeply, his intent gaze never leaving hers.

"And may I introduce my niece," Tildy stated with regal clarity, "Miss Violet Bell, daughter of Mr. Noah and Lady Liza Bell, of Pennyshire."

With the announcement, Violet curtsied as she knew she should. But she didn't exactly know what to say to her betrothed now, since Christopher had already asked her not to call him "my lord" and she didn't know how to address him. She opened her mouth to speak, but nothing came out.

In her floundering silence, he stepped forward, rescuing her once again. "It is a pleasure to meet you. *Violet,*" he repeated his words from earlier. Only this time, he added a slight twitch of his eyelid that she could have interpreted as a wink. If a wink were not perfectly untoward in this circumstance.

Her fingers fisted as she fumbled a response. "And, uh, yes, it is a pleasure to meet you as well, my...my...um..."

"Christopher. Please call me Christopher."

"My...Christopher," Violet breathed, relaxing for only a second before her eyes widened in horror. "Oh, God! I didn't mean to say *my* Christopher. I just meant *Christopher.* Since you're obviously not *my* Christopher. Not yet. Not until we're married. Which we will be, but still, I..."

Gwen grabbed her hand and squeezed, enabling Violet to shut her mouth.

"Good heavens, child!" Tildy snorted as she turned to look on their guest. "I beg you to forgive the impropriety of my niece's words, Lord Kastle."

Christopher's gaze remained glued to Violet's as he slowly shook his head. "Forgiveness is not necessary, Lady Wilmington. Not at all."

Violet lost the air from her lungs with the honesty she saw in his eyes. Did he really not mind her manner of speaking? That would be a miracle.

"Thank you, Lord Kastle," Tildy offered. "And now, I shall have Rodchester show you to your bedchamber so you can settle in. We will meet you back in this foyer to escort you to dinner, promptly at six."

Christopher had yet to turn his eyes from Violet's. "I shall be here, anxiously waiting to see you again," he promised.

Violet may or may not have sighed in a rather loud and obscene sort of way.

"Gwendolyn! Bring your sister to her room! Now!" Tildy barked.

Gwen's fierce grip pulled Violet backwards, following on Tildy's heels. But even as her aunt and sister tried to separate them, Violet kept her gaze fastened to Christopher's for as long as she could. He gave her another smile – and sweet heavens, it was absolutely stunning – so she could only grin giddily in response while resisting the tug of her sister's hand.

"Violet," he offered in farewell, his voice caressing her name in the most pleasurable way.

"Christopher," she breathed in return.

The sound of his name on her lips lit a spark in his eyes.

Violet could barely feel her legs as Gwen finally succeeded in dragging her out of the foyer.

~

"You've been awfully quiet," Gwen noted when she put the last curl of Violet's blond hair up onto her head, fixing it in place with another tiny pearl hairpin. "I don't know if I've ever seen you so quiet."

Violet glanced up at her sister through the looking glass in the vanity where she'd been sitting for her evening preparations. "I'm sorry. I hope you know how grateful I am for your care. You've done a blissful job of making me presentable for dinner."

Gwen rested her hands on Violet's shoulders with a gentle smile. Violet smiled back, happy for this time alone together. Aunt Tildy had offered both of them a handmaid for their stay here, but they had politely declined. They were perfectly capable of helping each other dress and preen. They also preferred to keep their personal discussions private.

"You are not just presentable, Violet. You are gorgeous. Christopher will think himself the king of the world when he sees you this evening. Although, based on what I witnessed in the foyer earlier, he may already think that."

Those words propelled Violet from her seat to pace about the room.

Gwen sighed. "What is it, dearest? Are you not happy with him?"

"*Happy* with him? My goodness! Did you even *see* him?"

"Yes, I saw him."

Violet spun around to face her sister, causing the smooth cobalt blue silk of her skirts to shift softly across her legs. The newly made dress had a low, off-the-shoulder neckline, and hugged her small waist tightly over the laced corset Gwen had cinched around her. The full skirts flowed out from there, and because Violet refused to wear knickers, the sinfully soft material caressed her thighs and calves in wickedly wonderful ways.

She'd never thought much about being caressed when she was younger. But during the last year, since she'd first been informed of her expectation to marry, things had been different. After all, Violet had grown to the ripe old age of two-and-twenty without ever knowing the touch of a man. Her curiosity in that regard was quite large, to say the least. She'd often imagined what a kiss on the lips, or even on the neck, might feel like. Yet now, after actually seeing her betrothed, she wasn't sure if her imagination could have possibly prepared her for anything.

Her hand flew to her chest, attempting to contain her riotously pounding heart. "Wh-what did you think of him, Gwen?"

"I don't think that matters. All that matters is what you think of him."

"Well, I think he's...he's...beautiful."

Gwen gave her a sly grin. "Oh, is he? I didn't notice."

Violet laughed, relieving some of the pressure in her chest. "How could you not notice? How could *anyone* not notice?"

"I know! The man even had Aunt Tildy blushing, and I didn't know that was a possibility! Although please do not tell Welly that I also noticed the beauty of Lord Kastle."

"I would never do that," Violet assured, since the fact that her marriage to Christopher would clear a path for Welly to wed Gwen was one of the happiest things about all of this. "I know how much you love Welly."

Gwen stepped closer, her own new mauve silk dress highlighting her taller frame. "I do love Welly, and I think you could love Christopher."

Violet considered that statement, recalling how her betrothed had defended her earlier, rescuing her from Tildy's recriminations as well as from her own fumbling. "I do, too. I think I could love him so easily."

"Then I do not understand the problem. Isn't this what you hoped for?"

"Yes, but...what if I am not enough for him? I overheard Beatrix say that he was quite the rake in his youth, and now that I've seen him, I can see how it could be true. I'm sure he's been with many women. Stunningly beautiful women, wonderfully worldly women, exceptionally accomplished women..."

"Violet! Were you not in that foyer earlier today?"

She glanced back to Gwen's eyes. "Yes, I was there."

"And did you not see the way that man looked at you?"

"I – I saw it. At least, I believe I did. I've been thinking of it so much these past hours, I don't know what I saw anymore."

"Well, I know what I saw. You enchanted Lord Kastle. Honestly, I may as well have not even been in the room. Truly, none of the rest of us were in that room at all. Not as far as he was concerned. He only saw you."

"Do you really think so?"

Gwen grabbed hold of her unsteady hand and held it tightly. "I know so, dear sister. Now let's go to dinner, so you can see it for yourself."

"God, I've never been so nervous to eat dinner in my life. Not even when we were children and didn't know where our next meal might come from."

"It will all be fine, I promise. Just remember that Christopher is going to be your husband, and you wanted this time to learn who he is. Starting tonight, you'll have the opportunity to do just that."

"You're right. I must gather my thoughts and focus on the man beneath the breathtaking exterior."

Gwen grinned as she linked Violet's arm in hers and tugged her out of the bedroom door. "Breathtaking, indeed."

~

BREATHTAKING MAY BE A GROSS UNDERSTATEMENT, Violet considered when she arrived at the top of the staircase. She decided *heartbreaking* was a far better description of him, since her heart both squeezed and swelled the moment she laid her eyes on Lord Kastle.

Christopher stood in the middle of the foyer, his gaze drawn to the window as he awaited her arrival. He wore a black suit jacket and trousers, with a matching black vest over his crisp white shirt. A cobalt blue cravat wrapped proudly around his neck, the color oddly matching her dress.

His outfit was not the newest London style, and may have been a bit too snug in cut, but it didn't matter in the least. The clothes simply begged to show off the man beneath, and Violet noticed far more than she should. She held tight to Gwen's arm as her sister guided her down the staircase, grateful for the support lest she tumble over her own feet and land in a heap at the bottom of the steps.

When the sisters began their descent into the foyer, the movement attracted Christopher's gaze. Violet tried very hard not to look at him, since she was using all of her concentration to get down the staircase in one piece. But her curiosity still got the better of her, and when his blue eyes landed on hers, she missed the final stair and hopped awkwardly down to the foyer floor. Thankfully, Gwen caught her before she made a complete fool of herself.

Her misstep brought her betrothed instantly forward with his hand outstretched. For the briefest moment, Violet thought he might touch her arm to steady her. The mere possibility of feeling his touch made her heart leap straight into her throat.

Christopher stared at her arm for several intent seconds. Then he straightened himself and dropped his hand back to his side. "Good evening, Violet. Good evening, Gwen," he offered with a formal tip of his head.

Violet curtsied at the same time her sister did, trying to convince herself that she was not upset by his decision to not touch her. After all, it would be entirely inappropriate for him to touch her yet. There would be time for touching once they were married. Plenty of time, hopefully.

"Good evening, Christopher," Gwen supplied in the absence of her sister's voice. "Violet and I have been so looking forward to this dinner."

His eyes drew to Violet's. "Have you?"

"Yes, we have," Violet managed to respond despite the muting power of his intent gaze. "Quite looking forward to it."

He gave her the same genuine smile he'd given her in the foyer earlier. "I have as well," he assured, just as Tildy entered the room.

"I see we are all present and accounted for, right on time," Tildy announced in a clipped tone before marching past. "Follow me to the dining room straightaway."

Christopher stepped aside, sweeping his arm out in invitation for Violet and Gwen to precede him. They all strode quietly behind Tildy, out of the foyer and down the hall to the grand dining area. A large chandelier lit by oil-burning flames brightened the vast room. A uniformed butler stood at the head of the table, pulling out the master chair for Tildy when she arrived. The second butler seated Violet and Gwen to Tildy's right side while Christopher sat to Tildy's left, across from Violet. Their party took up very little room on just one end of the extensive table, making Violet grateful that Tildy allowed them to sit as closely as they were.

"I normally do not eat in the formal dining room anymore," Tildy mentioned while her servants brought bowls of soup to each person at the table. "But I feel as though we should all show Lord Kastle a proper time during his stay here."

"I truly appreciate the effort," he offered while picking up his spoon.

Violet barely moved as she watched him take several sips of his cream porridge. The more Christopher ate, the more relaxed she became. If she'd had any doubts remaining over which suitor she should have picked, his lively consumption reaffirmed her choice of the man who did not fall asleep in his soup bowl at the dinner table.

"Your home is quite lovely, Lady Wilmington. How long have you lived here?" Christopher asked when he'd finished the first course of their meal.

"My husband, Lord Gilroy Wilmington, had this estate built as a summer home when we'd been married but a few years. He designed a good part of the structure himself."

"That is most impressive. Lord Gilroy sounds like a fine man."

"He was, indeed. He loved architecture and hunting and..."

Violet sat quietly beside her sister as their aunt recounted tales of Uncle Gilroy's gaming expeditions to Africa. However, she didn't hear much of anything her aunt said, since she focused almost wholly on the man across the table. Even as the butlers brought course after course of their meal, and Violet stuffed her mouth with many savory and wondrous flavors, she remained intent on her betrothed.

Christopher spent most of their dinner paying rapt attention to Tildy's near-constant speech, which was most polite and proper of him. Even though Violet missed having his attention, she was excited to think he was working his way onto Tildy's good side. To be honest, Violet couldn't imagine anyone not liking him. The man was quite likable. In fact, as he sat here so perfectly attentive and amenable, she became certain that Christopher Kastle was just plain loveable. And she could barely believe her good fortune in being betrothed to such a man.

How is he not already married and father to a dozen children? she wondered, since she could only assume that any wife of his would want to be pregnant constantly. Or, at the very least, constantly performing the act that could make her pregnant.

Violet flushed wildly with her errant thoughts, seeing as she was to become that wife. Even if she could not fathom why he'd waited for her.

He's a broken shell of a man. Nothing left but the skin on his bones.

Tildy cleared her throat then, after finishing an exceptionally detailed story about Gilroy's hunt for a famed white tiger, finally pausing her speech to take a of sip of wine. "Enough about me, Lord Kastle," she announced when she set the goblet back on the table. "I want to know more of you."

Christopher wiped his mouth on a napkin before folding his hands on the tabletop. "What would you like to know, Lady Wilmington?"

"Well, I'm told that after three years served in the Royal Navy, you spent five more years shipwrecked. It must be an interesting tale, to say the least."

The mention of Christopher's time at sea made Violet sit fully upright in her chair, her eyes glued to his face even more raptly than they had been all evening.

The excitement of discovering new and uncharted knowledge of her betrothed raced through her veins. And yet, in the same instant, she noted a change in his manner. It wasn't much – just a slight tilt in the angle of his shoulders and a tiny shift of his jaw – but she understood that he did not wish to discuss this topic. No matter how much the people at the table wanted to hear his story.

"Yes, I was shipwrecked for a time," he answered his host in a slow and steady manner. "My childhood friend and fellow sailor, Mr. Nick Marlow, and I were marooned on an island off the coast of China."

Tildy's brow shot into her hairline. "Marooned? For five years?"

"That's correct."

"Hmm. What on earth did you eat?"

Christopher grimaced with the question, making Violet's chest cave in as her aunt waited expectantly for an answer despite his obvious discomfort. "Was it coconuts?" Violet offered, keeping her voice light and whimsical.

He turned to her for the first time in what felt like hours, meeting her eyes across the table. His lips curved up in a tiny smile. "Yes, that's it. Lots of coconuts."

Violet returned his smile as brightly as she could.

Tildy shook her head in blatant dissatisfaction. "So, you were stranded on an island of coconuts for five years, alone except for one other man?"

His gaze dropped to his plate. "No, Lady Wilmington. There were natives on the island."

"Island natives? Good Lord! Trapped on an island with natives for all that time? It's a wonder you retained your manners."

Christopher looked back to his host while pulling up the corners of his lips once again, but Violet could tell how forced this smile was. "Thank you for confirming that I still have manners, my lady. I imagine my mother would be pleased to hear it."

Tildy snorted. "Yes, I'm sure she would. If she were not dead."

"Aunt Tildy!" Gwen gasped, capturing the older woman's attention.

The widow had the grace to frown at her own words before turning back to their guest. "I apologize, Lord Kastle, if my frankness upset you. My Gilroy has passed on as well, therefore I can assure you I do understand loss."

Christopher squeezed his fingers together on the tabletop. "Apology accepted," he said, drawing his eyes slowly back to Violet.

She stilled the instant she witnessed the pain inside his deep blue. "You lost your mother?" she whispered, intending the question for his ears only, even though everyone else would surely hear.

"Yes," he answered her alone. "She died giving birth to my youngest sister."

"I'm...I'm so sorry."

"Thank you, Violet. It was a difficult time. And I still miss her, every day."

She nodded in sympathy, her gaze holding deftly to his. She wanted nothing more than to reach for him to soothe his pain. Especially since he kept his focus solely on her.

"What are your sisters called, Christopher?" Gwen asked, her cheerful tone lightening the sudden thickness of the air.

His eyes remained fixed to Violet's for another moment before he turned to Gwen. "Daniela is the oldest, then there is Cora, Juliette, the twins Ruby and Pearl, Constance, and Octavia."

"Octavia is the youngest?" Violet clarified.

Her voice instantly recaptured his full attention. "She is," he confirmed, his face falling swiftly. "I...I named her."

"You did?"

"Well, I had no choice, unfortunately. My father did not feel up to it."

His teeth clenched after he replied. Violet knew it hurt him to speak of it, and yet he'd still answered. For her. "Your father probably didn't feel up to much of anything at the time," she realized.

Christopher offered a sad smile in response. "No, he didn't. Honestly, he hasn't felt up to much of anything since."

Violet's heart ached for her betrothed. She paused her queries, wanting to give him a measure of peace while her mind chewed on every morsel she'd learned. She almost felt guilty for how eagerly she craved information about him, given his obvious unease. But when his tense shoulders finally dropped from his ears, she allowed herself one more question. "If you don't mind me asking, did you name your sister Octavia because she was the eighth child?"

His brow rose with her deduction. "Yes, I daresay I did. I was not exactly creative at that point in my life."

A giggle burst from Violet's lips, even though she tried to repress it. She didn't want him to think she found his misfortunes humorous and would feel truly terrible if he did. But Christopher didn't rebuke her amusement. He chose to laugh along with her, instead.

A chuckle escaped from deep in his chest as he watched her from across the table. Everything about him was so glorious in this moment – when he stopped looking lonely and forlorn and allowed himself a bit of joy – that Violet's pulse bounded for being the one to bring him this spark of happiness. "Well, I certainly hope you'll feel more creative when naming *our* children," she said without thought, caught up in the moment between them and not weighing the full implications of her words. At least, not until Gwen kicked her firmly under the table.

Violet jumped in her seat even before Tildy began hollering.

"Miss Violet Bell! You will mind your manners while in this household! You and Lord Kastle are not yet married and you will show restraint in speaking of such delicate matters!"

"I am so sorry, Aunt Tildy," Violet acquiesced, bowing her head to stare at the tablecloth. "You are very gracious to open your home to us and I regret speaking inappropriately. I do beg your forgiveness."

Tildy exhaled in exasperation. "You know I love you, Violet. But sometimes that mouth of yours feels as if it will be the world's undoing."

"I understand," she replied, knowing better than to argue, especially if she desired to remain here for her courtship. Which she did. Very much.

Violet continued to stare at the table linens, mortified in more ways than one. Only when she heard the clamor of dishes, and knew her aunt and sister had resumed eating their dessert, did she dare to risk a peek at her betrothed. With her heart lodged in her throat, she drew her eyes back to his, hoping beyond hope that he would not look on her with recrimination or disgust. As it turned out, she had nothing to fear.

Christopher caught her gaze the moment she raised it. The only thing he did was smile. He gave her an intent smile – a secret smile – meant only for her. Violet knew in this moment that he did not admonish her words. He did not judge her. He actually looked at her as if soaking her in entirely, and she refused to look away.

She sat riveted for an eternity, focused entirely on the depths of his soulful eyes. The only time she glanced away, even for a second, was when he moistened his lips with his tongue. That motion drew her attention for more reasons than she wanted to admit, and by the time Violet managed to meet his penetrating gaze once again, she knew the flush of her cheeks had spread down her neck and across her shoulders. Her betrothed either didn't notice or didn't mind. He simply continued to hold her without a single touch, allowing the expansive room to close in around just the two of them, erasing everyone and everything else.

Until Aunt Tildy cleared her throat loudly and spoke even louder. "Well, then. The two of you obviously want to spend time alone together."

Christopher's brow shot up with Tildy's unexpected summation.

Violet's mouth dropped open. "Aunt...Aunt Tildy," she stammered, "I don't think that..."

"Oh, hush, Violet. You can cut the tension in this room with a knife. And since you've already gone so far as to speak of children at the dinner table, I say we call a spade a spade. I am fully aware that all men and women wish to be alone for courting."

Violet looked to her aunt with a glimmer of hope.

Tildy immediately shook her head. "But you know that is not why your father sent you both here – to run amok on your own. I will ensure the two of you remain chaperoned *at all times*."

Her words came out hard and clear, dimming the light in Violet's chest. "Yes, Aunt Tildy. I rely on your good judgment, as always."

The widow huffed. "That statement is certainly up for debate. However, I am not an entirely unreasonable woman. Since Lord Kastle presents the picture of good manners, and has assured me he does not wish to act in any manner I deem inappropriate, I will allow the two of you one walk a day alone together, out in the gardens. During which time I shall sit on my balcony and observe you, of course."

"Really?" Violet questioned, her incredulity at the offer accompanied by a full-faced grin.

Christopher turned toward Tildy. "That is most gracious of you, Lady Wilmington. I appreciate your understanding and confidence more than I can say, and look forward to taking a walk each day with my bride-to-be."

Bride-to-be.

Bride. To. Be.

Good heavens.

Violet knew she would be Christopher's bride one day, but to hear that confirmation from his lips was more than she was prepared for. Her corset suddenly squeezed far too tightly against her ribcage, making her whimper. The indelicate noise drew the attention of every person at the table.

"Violet? Are you well?" Gwen questioned, taking her hand.

"Oh, y-yes. Quite well."

Tildy scrunched her nose. "Hmm. She probably just needs time to digest her meal. Why don't we retire to the parlor, where there are more comfortable chairs? You can play the piano for us, Gwendolyn. I'm sure that will make your sister feel better."

"I shall be happy to," Gwen agreed.

Christopher stood, waiting politely for all the women to rise from their seats, before he followed them from the dining room. The group headed purposefully down the hall until Tildy entered the parlor with Gwen close behind her. Violet slowed her footsteps when the two women disappeared into the next room, idling behind in order to wait for her betrothed.

"Would you like to choose your seat?" she asked when he joined her by the doorway. She worked to keep her voice even, trying her best to act more civilized around him, knowing she should not sigh and shiver simply because he stood a full head taller than her and that fact made her skin tingle.

He bowed gently. "Thank you, Violet. You are most kind."

She nodded in reply, feeling like they painted a portrait of a perfectly proper English couple embarking on a perfectly proper courtship. But then Christopher stepped one foot inside the parlor and saw the raging fire in the hearth. In an instant, the illusion vanished.

Violet watched in confusion as the light of the flames caught him completely off guard. His breathing turned shallow while his feet shifted unstably on the marble flooring. She almost reached her hand to his arm in an effort to steady him, but she knew she had no right to touch him. Instead, she cleared her throat, drawing his eyes back to hers. "We do not have to sit by the fire," she offered in her softest voice.

Christopher swallowed hard. "That – that would be appreciated."

She gave him a reassuring smile before moving into the parlor. He followed close on her heels. Tildy had already seated herself in her favorite high-backed velvet chair by the hearth and Gwen had assumed her position on the piano bench across the room.

"Bring Lord Kastle over by the fire, Violet," Tildy instructed when they walked inside. "You can both warm yourselves while we listen."

"Actually, Aunt Tildy, I still need to digest my meal and I fear the heat may cause me difficulty. May Christopher and I sit closer to the piano?"

"Oh, I see. Yes, that is fine," the widow replied, remaining snugly in her seat while Violet guided Christopher across the room. She offered him the brown leather chair that stood a few feet from the piano, as it was the farthest from the hearth. Afterwards, she took the matching seat beside him.

He glanced to her eyes once they both settled down, silently mouthing the words, "Thank you."

She nodded softly in response, threading her fingers together in her lap and turning her attention to the piano. When Gwen began to play, Violet worked hard to concentrate on her sister's skillful music and not on the extraordinary man beside her. The man who'd lost his mother and been forced to name his own sister. The man who'd spent five long years lost at sea. The man who'd most likely lost something – or someone – to a fire. The man she would one day marry.

Gwen's initial selection of song was light and lively, and the second even more so, while the third shifted to somber. Violet looked at the piano keys, and at the woven wool rug beneath her feet, and at her own fingers, but she did not look to the chair on her right – no matter how much she wanted to. She did not want to test the limits of Tildy's generosity, and certainly did not want her aunt to rescind the invitation of a walk in the gardens with her betrothed, simply because Violet stared bug-eyed at him in the parlor after supper. Although, after the way she'd acted toward Lord Kastle all day, she could only imagine the choice berating her aunt would eventually bestow upon her.

Thankfully, by the time Gwen's third song progressed into the fourth, Violet realized she did not have to fear her aunt's condemnation at this point in time. Tildy had begun to snore quite soundly, the sawing noise reverberating through the room, even louder than the strike of Gwen's fingers against the ivory keys. A moment later, Christopher chuckled beneath his breath.

The joyous sound of laughter drew Violet's eyes to his. "I'm sorry," she whispered, knowing he could still hear her hushed words, since mere inches separated their chairs. "My aunt's snores are a bit loud."

"It's no problem," he assured, gracing her with one of his heart-stealing smiles. "Your aunt is quite interesting. Is she much like your mother?"

"Um, it's...uh," Violet fumbled, her brain scrambling in response to his dastardly delightful grin. "To be honest, Mama and Tildy are nothing alike. My aunt was twenty years old and already married with a son before my mother was even born. The two of them have very little in common."

"I see. Unlike you and your sister?"

"Oh, Gwen and I do have our differences. But she is my best friend, my confidant, and truly one of my reasons for living."

"Hmm. I understand that. Sisters become a part of you, a part you cannot fathom being without."

"They do. And you have *seven*."

"Yes, seven," Christopher agreed with a gentle laugh. "Each unique and each a part of me."

"I look forward to meeting them all one day."

"They will all love you, I'm certain."

He spoke the words casually and yet Violet felt them to her toes, hoping there would come a time when he could love her as certainly as he believed his sisters would. "Thank you for the reassurance, Christopher."

"You are most welcome," he replied, his eyes drifting over to Gwen. "Your sister plays the piano quite well."

"Yes, she's very accomplished."

"Do you play?"

"No, I'm afraid not. Music is not my forte."

He turned in his seat to face her fully. The movement brought his knee within an inch of her skirts. "Then what is your forte?"

Violet ogled his extremely close leg before matching his intent stare. "Um, I suppose I would say learning."

"Learning?"

"Yes."

"What do you like to learn?"

She squeezed her fingers together, wrapping her mind around the thought that her betrothed actually wanted to get to know her. "Anything. Everything. I love reading newspapers, books, and stories of all kinds."

His lips pulled up into another perfect curve. "How wonderful. Perhaps one day you could read to me."

"You would like that?"

"I would. You have a lovely voice. I wish to hear more of it."

Well, that sounded ridiculous. No one ever wanted to hear *more* of her. No one except Gwen, who was stuck with her. Although, in truth, Christopher was stuck with her now, too.

Except he didn't look stuck. On the contrary, he looked intrigued and entranced and even...happy. Violet could hardly believe he desired to hear more of her voice, yet she could see nothing but truth in his eyes: his big, bright, delightfully blue eyes that held her captive in a most wondrous spell.

The fire on the far side of room crackled then, causing Christopher to jump nearly from his skin and decidedly breaking that spell. He cringed at his overreaction, his gaze dropping to the floor for a long minute before pulling back to hers. He plastered on a smile – a fake one this time – and Violet struggled to smile in return.

He does not like fire at all, she realized, wanting nothing more than to march over to the hearth and stamp out the flames entirely. Except her actions would surely wake her aunt, and she did *not* want that.

Christopher reached up, adjusting his neck scarf with tremulous fingers.

Violet sighed. "I like your cravat," she said, hoping to draw his attention from the fire. "The color even matches my dress."

His fake smile transformed to a genuine one. "Yes. Yes, it does."

"That is quite a coincidence."

His eyes drew to hers, aglow in the dim light. "It is not a coincidence at all, actually. I asked Mr. Rodchester what color you planned to wear tonight."

"Really? Well, that explains why he came to check on us earlier. But may I ask why you would employ such effort?"

"I suppose I thought...I thought it might put you more at ease. Also, my sisters suggested that I may not be dashing enough for you, so I hoped the matching cravat might help to earn your endearment."

Violet's brow flew skyward. "Your sisters don't think you are dashing enough for me?"

"No, they do not."

"Why on earth not?"

Christopher shook his head. "Apparently, I've been a bit grumbly at home since I returned from sea. I was informed thusly by Daniela and Cora, who also said you might not like me very much if I did not improve."

"So, that's what you've been doing today? Acting dashing around me?"

"As best I can," he confessed, looking to her with more than a little uncertainty. "How am I doing at it?"

A delirious laugh escaped her lips. "My goodness, Christopher. You are the most dashing man I have ever met."

"Truly?"

"Most truly."

"Well, that's good to hear. I'm pleased to think I haven't entirely forgotten how to exist in a civilized world," he admitted, his shoulders stiffening as the words left his lips. "Although I certainly do not mean to suggest that I've been insincere with you, because I have not. I've sincerely enjoyed meeting you today. I've sincerely enjoyed every moment I've spent with you. I just wasn't sure if you would enjoy meeting me, so I've tried to be on my best behavior."

Violet watched his eyes soften with his words. She angled her body toward his, bringing them truly face-to-face. "You should know that I have thoroughly enjoyed every moment we've spent together, as well. You should also know that I don't need you to act dashing for me."

"You don't?"

"No. I'd much rather you act as yourself, whoever that may be."

His gaze shifted over her face for lingering seconds. "Thank you, Violet."

She nodded slowly, enchanted by his admiration. He studied her with ardent interest, his eyes drifting down to her lips, hovering on her mouth before dropping lower to ease over her chest and onto her arm. He stared hard at her hand where it rested against her skirts, making her fingers twitch with the urge to touch him. Gwen's sweet piano music and Tildy's steady snores filled the air, but Violet heard little except the sound of her own heartbeat as her gaze fixated on Christopher's hand, willing it to take hold of her own.

He leaned toward her, softly and subtly. So subtly that Tildy would never have noticed, even if she'd been awake. But Violet noticed.

Christopher didn't touch her. She knew it didn't actually happen, and yet she thought it may have. The more his body leaned into hers, the more heat she felt – warm, lovely, embracing heat, emanating from his skin and pulling her closer – a deeper, more comforting heat than any fire could afford.

She looked back to his eyes, only to find them latched onto hers. She wished beyond reason that he would just touch her already. She wished he would take her hand, even for a second, just to feel the texture of his skin. Just to ease the hum and burn of her own skin.

Violet almost did it herself. She almost reached out and placed her palm against his, no matter how indecent the action. But the moment her fingers ventured near his, and his brow rose with the realization of her intention, Aunt Tildy woke herself with a brisk, resonant snore. The piano music ceased at once, bathing the room in stark silence.

Christopher and Violet pulled apart from each other immediately, as Gwen straightened on the piano bench and Tildy straightened in her chair.

"What? Where?" Tildy mumbled with a sluggish blink of her eyelids. "Oh, yes...the parlor." She scooted to the end of her seat. "Lovely songs, Gwen. You play beautifully, as always."

"Beautifully," Violet echoed, trying to conceal the quiver in her voice.

Christopher cleared his throat. "Quite lovely, indeed."

Gwen blushed beneath the praise. "Thank you so much."

"Right. Well, off to bed now," Tildy announced. "For all of us."

Christopher stood from his chair with the command, stepping aside to allow Violet to rise unencumbered. She tried not to look at him – she tried not to look at any of them – afraid her eyes would too easily reveal the impurity of her thoughts.

"Gwen, escort your sister to her bedchamber," Tildy insisted.

"Certainly," Gwen said, stepping over to take Violet's arm.

"Thank you for a lovely evening, Lady Wilmington," Christopher offered along with a bow.

"Certainly, Lord Kastle. You are quite welcome."

Violet didn't miss the tiny grin tugging at the corner of Tildy's mouth in response to their guest, just before the silver-haired woman turned toward the opposite exit door. Gwen held tight to Violet's arm while she led the rest of them from the room. Violet strolled beside her sister, sensing Christopher's presence behind them as they eased their way out of the parlor, down the hall, and back into the foyer.

The winding walk allowed Violet time to think on all her betrothed had revealed tonight. He'd been kind, sweet, and perfectly dashing, while she'd merely been herself. That understanding made her realize she owed him an apology. She probably owed him several, but definitely at least one.

Once they reached the foyer and Gwen began to guide her toward the main staircase, Violet pulled back. "Give me a moment to speak with Christopher, dear sister. Please?"

Gwen's brow scrunched. "All right. A moment only."

Violet smiled in appreciation, pivoting swiftly on her heels to catch her betrothed before he escaped to his bedchamber on the far side of the house. Yet when she turned back to him, he had not moved to leave at all. He still stood at the entrance of the foyer with his eyes pinned on her.

She blushed while closing the scant distance between them. "I – I just wanted to wish you goodnight," Violet explained when she arrived in front of him. "I also wanted to see if you'd like to take a walk in the gardens tomorrow, since my aunt said we could, much to my surprise. You seemed to think it was a good idea, so I hoped we could have that time together."

"I would like that very much," he replied, his firm tone leaving no doubt.

"Then perhaps you'll meet me here at noon? If that time is agreeable."

"Noon it is."

"Perfect," she said, gazing dreamily up into his eyes. Her joy lasted mere seconds before she worried her lower lip in her teeth.

"Is there something else on your mind, Violet?"

"Um, yes, there is. I fear I owe you an apology."

"An apology? For what?"

"For all of my verbal indiscretions today. Especially at the dinner table, when I spoke so untowardly of our children. You see, sometimes I say things I shouldn't, because my mouth is…"

"Quite wonderful, actually," he interjected. "And frankly, I don't know how skilled I'll be at naming our children when the time comes. Therefore, I must insist you have the final say in the matter." Christopher leaned into her, his warm breath ghosting over her face as he lowered his voice. "Lest they all be given numbers."

Violet wanted to laugh, because she could imagine a herd of their wild children responding only to numerical summons, and that was a humorous picture, indeed. But she found it difficult to laugh, or even to breathe, with the depth of his eyes so close to her own. Heavens, she could get lost in those eyes. And she wanted to. Lord, how she wanted to.

"Numbers are good. I like numbers," she said, although she probably shouldn't have.

Christopher chuckled, which lit his entire being. The beauty of it made her grin despite the ache of her awkwardness.

"Come now," Gwen urged from the bottom of the staircase. "We must hasten to our rooms before Tildy hears the two of you talking."

"Oh. Right." Violet exhaled, having difficulty with the concept of leaving him. "I guess...I guess I should go."

He gave her a soft smile. "Goodnight, Violet. Until tomorrow."

"Goodnight, Christopher. Until tomorrow," she agreed, stepping backwards so she could watch his smile for as long as possible, until her sister finally hauled her away.

CHAPTER 4

First Touch

Christopher stood before the looking glass in his guest bedchamber, evaluating his reflection as he prepared to meet Violet for their first walk together in the Wilmington gardens. Being able to spend time alone with his betrothed was more than he could have hoped for, before he'd come here to court her. Everything about Violet was more than he could have hoped for, which made his fingers fumble while he dressed.

As he struggled to button his starched white shirt up to his neck, his mind reached to the moment he'd arrived in this opulent manor the day before. When he saw his betrothed standing in front of him for the first time, bathed in the light from the foyer windows, the soft contours of her face had come as no surprise. After all, he'd viewed her photograph in his locket mere moments after his father handed it to him. But Christopher hadn't only viewed her image that once. He'd looked on her many times each day since. He'd looked on her far more than he should have, growing accustomed to the feel of the portrait inside his pocket and learning to enjoy how her likeness found an easy home on his person.

He'd formed his opinion of Violet before he'd ever met her, deciding she would be warm, kind, and heartfelt. His firm beliefs had only deepened in the weeks that followed, as he awaited the day he would finally see her in person. He'd craved meeting her, craved the ability to perceive dimension in the curves of the face he'd memorized. His veins hummed with energy as he'd ridden his horse up to the Wilmington entrance yesterday, but when he stepped into that foyer and witnessed her standing there – when he saw her eyes widen and her cheeks flush with the sight of him, and heard the rapid, flustered words escaping her perfect pink lips – he found himself enchanted in a way he couldn't have foreseen.

So...I guess I'm...I'm your wife, she'd fumbled, her words landing hard inside his chest. Christopher had already accepted Violet as his wife before he'd ever laid eyes on her in the flesh. But once he saw her, and heard her sweet voice, and listened in awed wonder as she spoke so indiscreetly about their children at the dinner table, he knew without question that he actually wanted Violet as his wife. He would even demand it, if challenged.

The thought of being challenged for her affections made his shoulders bunch beneath his shirt. He reached up to run his hand across the scar on the back of his neck, ensuring his high collar would cover that marred section of skin. Thankfully, his clothing should conceal all of his scars. Not just the physical ones, but the emotional as well.

Christopher studied his likeness in the looking glass, seeing the picture of a fine, upstanding English gentleman staring back at him. He forced a deep breath into his lungs, working to calm his nerves while pulling on the double-breasted vest and finely tailored charcoal gray overcoat that matched his trousers – clothing remaining from his younger years, when his family could afford such finery. The outfit was no longer the height of fashion, given that nine years had elapsed since he'd last worn it, yet he could still pass easily as a nobleman. Although the material did pull across his arms and chest now, where he'd amassed the broad muscle his foolish younger self had only dreamed of possessing.

In all honesty, Christopher hated these clothes. While he had pined for his lost homeland every day he'd been at sea, he had never yearned for the ridiculousness of English society and privilege. Alas, his distaste for the culture did not matter now. He would wear this stifling outfit without complaint. He would hold himself to the standards of a gentleman and act the part of a refined and worthy suitor. He would do all of it...for her.

Violet deserved this much, at the very least. She shouldn't have to see his scars: the etchings wrought from beatings, burnings, and blades. Even though he knew, if they really were to be husband and wife, she would see them all eventually. But not now. Not yet. Not while he could still conceal them with fabric and finery.

Christopher turned away from his reflection with more disgust than he wanted to admit. He viewed the bed on the far wall of his guest chamber, examining the sheets he'd rumpled this morning, making sure it looked as if he'd slept in them. He didn't want the servants to suspect otherwise, lest they spread that rumor through the household. Regrettably, this particular gossip would actually be true. He hadn't managed to sleep in a bed for as long as he could remember. A blanket and the floor had offered him a few hours of rest last night, which was more rest than usual.

Damn it. I'm going to have to learn how to sleep in a bed again.

He gritted his teeth as he studied the tousled bed linens. No one had cared where he'd slept since his return to Nightingale. But his wife would care. Violet would care.

"This arrangement is going to be harder than you expected," he admitted to himself in the quiet of his bedchamber. This arrangement may well prove to be entirely unmanageable, not only because he had to mind his manners and be proper with his actions and relearn to sleep in a bed, but also because he'd truly intended to come into this marriage with his eyes open and his heart closed. Christopher now feared he may only be able to keep half of that promise. For his eyes were indeed open, and he saw her.

He saw Violet's wonder and joy, her kindness and innocence, brought to life before him. He saw her with utter, crystal clarity, which made him fear – after just one day in her presence – that she'd already gotten inside him. He feared she'd threaded her way into a place where he would never be able to remove her entirely.

That thought scared the living hell out of him, as it should. After all, Violet deserved the same kind of love his parents had shared. She deserved a man who could give her the very best in life. She deserved a man who would willingly fall to his knees for her. She deserved a whole man: one who could love her with all his heart and soul.

Christopher knew he could not be that man. He hadn't been whole in years. He had nothing to give her. He would never be all she deserved, and yet Violet was stuck with him now. She was stuck with him, and his entire family needed her, so he would have to maintain this impeccably-dressed illusion of intactness for as long as possible. Even if he felt like a duplicitous thief, out to steal her heart under the most heinous of false pretenses.

With a disparaging shake of his head, Christopher turned to leave his chamber. He slipped through the door, scrutinizing the empty hallway while also listening intently to the sounds of the manor. He'd already accustomed himself to his new surroundings, having explored the house in secret late last night, and now took a right turn from his bedchamber instead of the expected left. This alternate route led him to the far staircase on the other side of the manor, down past the servants' quarters on the ground floor.

He moved quietly through the corridors, his footsteps silent against the flooring, a skill of stealth he'd mastered under great duress during his years away. He did appreciate that covert ability now, however, when the final hallway emptied out at the rear entrance of the foyer where Violet awaited him. She did not realize he'd arrived, and her eyes remained focused on the great window, which afforded him the chance to look on her before she comprehended his presence.

His betrothed wore a dress of deep purple silk today. It hung off her shoulders, showcasing the smooth skin of her neck and the upper curves of her shoulder blades, like her dress last night had done. Her hair was also up again, as it had been at dinner, still glimmering with the tiny pearls holding her blond curls in place. He wondered if she'd slept like that and woken up this morning just as beautiful as she'd been when she'd gone to bed. She probably had. He imagined she would be beautiful in the morning no matter what, provided she woke beside him. And most especially if she'd spent the previous night lying beneath him, bared to his eyes and moaning in pleasure.

Dear God, man! You must keep those desires at bay!

Christopher chastised himself silently but firmly, his instant attraction to her unnerving him on too many levels. He tried not to imagine her naked body pressed fully against his, knowing his heady thoughts would only lead them to places they could not go – yet. But despite his best efforts, the perfectly sinful image still managed to instill a lump in his throat. The unsettling feeling forced him to cough, which drew her attention.

The moment Violet turned to him, she gasped quite indelicately. He paid rapt attention as her chest rose on a sharp inhale, straining the rounded tops of her breasts above the tight, low-cut bodice of her gown. He figured she wore a corset beneath the purple silk, lined in stiff herringbone and cinched around her ribcage, since that was the current fashion. But he was not accustomed to the manner in which it showcased her curves, pushing her flesh into places he shouldn't notice as blatantly as he did. A flush of energy coursed through his veins, the kind that used to prepare him for a fight to the death, and yet the rush of it now was only for her.

Christopher stepped forward, compelled to move closer and closer, until his body stood mere inches from hers. The sunshine filtering through the windows highlighted the transparency of her sky-blue eyes as she raised her chin to meet his gaze. He cleared his throat, praying his voice would not catch when he spoke. "Good day, Violet."

The words came out deeper than he meant and her eyelashes fluttered. "Yes, it is good, is it not? It's so very, very good. Everything is just so...so good."

Her hand flew to her face, touching her reddened cheek before she shook her head and pushed her arm back down. Clasping her trembling fingers tightly together in front of her waist, she released a shaky exhale.

"I suppose we should go for our walk in the gardens now?" she questioned. "That is, if you still want to."

"I do want to. Very much."

"That is wonderful."

He nodded. "Wonderful, indeed."

"Indeed. And before we venture any further, I'd like to say that I appreciate all your efforts today. Because you are so good. I mean, you are dressed so good. So *well*. You are dressed so *well*. God, I can't even speak correctly."

A smile crept across Christopher's lips, a smile he could not have prevented if he wished. "I appreciate your efforts, too. Since you are also dressed very...good."

Violet giggled, brightening her face and making him feel thoroughly pleased with himself. "Should we proceed to the gardens?" he offered, struggling to keep his voice steady.

"Certainly. They are just through the back door," she replied, her hands still clasped together in front of her stomach.

Christopher considered holding his arm out for her, since he very much wanted to feel her fingers wrapped around his coat sleeve. But he wasn't sure if she would be able to manage that contact right now. This situation wasn't the same as it had been last night in the parlor, when he'd thought for a moment that Violet might reach out to touch his hand. That had been a surreal instant – to think a young, innocent woman of her status would initiate such contact – yet he would have relished the opportunity to feel her skin on his, no matter how shocking her actions.

Sadly, they were no longer sitting together in the piano parlor, caught in the odd spell of music and snores, and wrapped up in their own little world. This was the cold light of day, and his betrothed trembled and fumbled here. In truth, Christopher was quite accustomed to all manner of people being disturbed by his presence – for various and sundry reasons – but he didn't want Violet to feel that way. He wanted her to be comfortable with him, to let her guard down, to just be...her. Even if the dastardly part of his male pride relished her obvious attraction.

"Please lead the way," he said, falling into step beside her, careful not to touch.

Violet ventured to the far end of the foyer, leading him through a set of large, stained-glass doors at the back of the manor, bringing them out onto a walkway. They took several steps into the bright, warming sunshine, following the carefully inlaid path of flat stones, until she paused to glance behind them up to a second-story balcony. Christopher tracked her line of sight until his gaze landed on Tildy, seated in a chair overlooking the gardens. He nodded to the elderly woman in greeting, but their chaperone didn't respond. Honestly, he wasn't even sure if she could see them from this distance.

Not wishing his betrothed to feel anxious about her aunt's lack of acknowledgement, he offered assurance. "Lady Wilmington will supervise our walk, just as she promised."

"I'm sure she will," Violet agreed, although her fingers remained balled.

"Her attentiveness is good and proper, of course."

Violet gave him a little smile. "Of course."

He returned her smile, waiting patiently for her to begin their walk amongst the detailed gardens. As they moved along side-by-side, Christopher made the decision to keep quiet, holding his tongue in the hopes that Violet could use the peaceful silence to accustom herself to his companionship. His plan seemed to work, since her shoulders eventually eased and her hands unclasped and fell to her sides.

He looked around them while they stepped slowly in sync, soaking in the beauty of their surroundings. The estate gardens boasted the lavish skill of the Wilmington groundskeepers, rivaling what he recalled of his mother's gardens back in the day. Ornamental urns, sculptures, fountains, and gazing balls took center stage in the individually divided sections of shrubs and foliage. A dozen shades of pinks, purples, and greens filled his eyes as they moved in silence between well-plotted areas of carpet flowers, rose bushes, and strands of ivy climbing carefully placed wooden trellises. The elaborate yet simple beauty reminded him of times long past and felt oddly like home, settling his unsteady heartbeat.

After a long while, Violet finally turned her face up to his.

Christopher instantly met her direct gaze.

"I wish to thank you," she said, with only a slight tremor to her voice.

"Oh? For what, exactly?"

"For agreeing to come here to the Wilmington estate for our courtship."

"That isn't necessary. Honestly, I feel as though I should thank you."

"Why would you thank me?"

"Because I appreciate the ability to remain close to my family's lands in Nightingale. I don't know if you had anything to do with that decision, but I assure you the effort did not go unnoticed."

"Well, perhaps I did suggest to my father that you might be more comfortable close to your home, instead of all the way out in Pennyshire."

"Then I thank you for your thoughtfulness."

A fresh flush lit her cheeks. "You're welcome. Although, I must admit, I had ulterior motives for coming to the Wilmington estate."

"You did? What kind of ulterior motives?"

Laughter bubbled up from her chest, a sound more beautiful than any of the resplendent nature surrounding them. Christopher held his breath as he awaited her reply.

"I – I wanted us to be able to enjoy these gardens, for one," she offered, her feet coming to a stop when they reached a bifurcation in the walkway.

"The gardens are quite lovely," he admitted, looking to the left and right where the trail split apart. "Which path do you think we should take?"

"The left one, most definitely. There's an adorable gazebo at the end of it. I would love to show it to you."

"That sounds grand."

She turned onto the left path and he fell into step alongside her.

"You obviously know just where you're going, Violet. I take it you're quite familiar with these gardens?"

"I am. I came to play here often as a child. It felt like another world."

"Another world? Is your own home not like this one?"

Her eyes darted to his and then back to the walkway. "Well, now it is, since my father amassed his great wealth. But it wasn't always this way for us."

"It wasn't?"

"No. We were quite poor in my youth."

"Oh. I'm sorry."

Violet's gaze drew back to his. "Surely you already knew these things?"

"Actually, my father mentioned only the basic facts when he informed me of this arrangement. I knew very little about your family before I came here."

"Hmm. I must say, that's genuinely surprising. I thought everyone from Pennyshire to London had heard of the Bells." She paused her speech, her fingers fiddling against each other again. "But if you have not heard anything of us, then you should be made aware that I have quite the reputation. I've even been given my own terrible title. And then there is my father, Noah. The stories of how he collected our family fortunes by probable-but-not-provable illegal means are of nearly legendary status. At least, I believed they were, before just now."

Christopher held her nervous stare with as much calmness as possible. "My father may have mentioned a few of those things, but I believe in assessing every situation for myself. Also, I do not hear much gossip. And the gossip I do hear, I do not place much value in."

"Then you've never heard me called the Picky Princess of Pennyshire?"

His jaw clenched. "Well, I...I may have heard that one."

She nibbled her lower lip in her teeth.

"Do you wish to tell me why people call you that?" he asked, wondering if it might be better for her to recount the story herself. "Or would you rather leave the topic alone? Because I can assure you, I do not hold any judgment based on that stupid moniker."

Violet smiled up at him, deep and genuine, causing his heart to squeeze. "Thank you for that assurance, Christopher. I sincerely appreciate it. All I would like to say on the subject is that I am called the Picky Princess because I was betrothed to another man before you, a Lord Wellington Chaney, heir to the Earl of Centreville. But I refused him, even though the marriage would have been most appropriate and appreciated by my family, as well as the rest of society. It all happened many months ago, yet Lord Chaney still comes to visit my home quite frequently. Therefore, everyone now assumes that he pines for me and that I am a cold woman who spurns him for no reason."

Christopher shook his head, his stomach filling with acid at the thought of this other heir insisting on visiting Violet when she'd already refused him. He would have some very choice words for the man, if he ever dared to call on her again. "Truthfully, Violet, the whims of society are beyond my comprehension. Especially in this instance. I mean, aren't there simple form letters for women such as yourself, allowing you to refuse a suitor with ease?"

"Yes, there are. But I suppose I do not qualify for the same allotments as other women, since my father's money is neither old nor noble."

"Well, I find that notion ridiculous. And I hope you'll lend no weight to the ranting of gossipers, since they are obviously all wrong. You are not cold at all. In fact, you may be the warmest creature I have ever met."

Her eyes darted to his. "How can you say that? You don't even know me."

"I may not know all of you yet, but I have a good sense of people. I've come across enough cold ones to know the warm ones on sight."

Her brow furrowed. "I appreciate the compliment, most certainly. Although I do not like to think of you having to know so many cold people."

"Unfortunately, that is the way of the world sometimes." Christopher shrugged, eager to change the topic. "So, I assume you do have your reasons for refusing the other heir?"

"Yes, I do. But I would like them to remain *my* reasons, for the time being. If you don't mind."

"I don't mind," he agreed, knowing he would be the biggest hypocrite on earth to demand that she tell him her darkest truths. "Everyone has their secrets, after all."

Violet nodded. "Thank you for not pressing the matter."

"Certainly. The way I see it, Lord Chaney's loss is simply my gain."

"Oh," she said, gazing into his eyes while sighing in contentment.

The sweet sounds she made drew Christopher's attention to her parted lips. His fingers twitched at his sides with urges he knew he shouldn't fulfill. Yet her mouth was so delightfully pink and perfectly shaped, and he couldn't help imagining how soft her lips would feel beneath his when he kissed her for the first time.

Bloody hell, how had his mind returned to these thoughts so quickly? He hadn't even touched her hand yet, and it was definitely far too soon to consider kissing her. Nevertheless, he could not stop himself from staring.

Violet stumbled beneath his heated gaze, righting herself as swiftly as she could. "We're, um...we're here, Christopher."

"Where?" he asked, not at all interested in looking away from her.

"Here, at the gazebo."

"Hmm. That we are," he realized when he finally lifted his eyes to the lofty octagonal structure. He wasn't quite sure how they'd arrived here without his knowledge, since he prided himself on being deftly attuned to his surroundings. This building had simply materialized out of nowhere.

"Would you like to come inside with me? There's a bench to sit on."

His brow rose with her invitation before he looked over his shoulder to where her aunt sat on the balcony. From this distance, Lady Wilmington appeared little more than the size of a beetle. "Are you certain we may go inside the gazebo together? Your aunt will not be able to see us anymore."

"Oh, I think it will be all right. If she greatly disapproves, she can always send the hounds after us," Violet offered, giggling at her own suggestion. Christopher worked to laugh along with her, since she obviously did not know what it felt like to be attacked by animals.

He followed on her heels as she ascended the three steps into the white-painted wood structure. The inside was empty except for a wrought iron bench in the center of the floor. Glass panels framed the gazebo on seven of the eight sides, but so much ivy had grown on the outside of the glass that it was impossible to see clearly from them. The climbing foliage blocked out the rest of the world, with sunlight coming only from the entrance and the glass ceiling, which meant he and Violet were entirely concealed and perfectly alone.

Christopher watched as she moved to the ornate bench and settled herself down on one side. He glanced at the space she'd left open for him to sit on, but decided to step over toward one of the glass panels instead. He rested his shoulder against the ivy-coated window, attempting to look poised yet nonthreatening, while turning his gaze to hers. Violet did not look back at him. She busily adjusted her skirts around her legs, much more than necessary, her fingers twisting in the dark fabric. That behavior continued for a solid minute before she finally glanced up to him.

When their eyes met, she whimpered. Next, a tiny laugh escaped her throat. "I – I suppose you can tell that I'm a bit nervous around you."

Christopher sighed. "I think it's understandable for us to be nervous. We've only just met and yet our future as husband and wife is already decided. It's an awkward situation, at best."

"It is, isn't it?" she agreed, squaring her shoulders as she leaned toward him. "But I would like for us to speak openly about all of this, if that's agreeable. It will help calm my nerves if I believe we each know where we stand."

"And where is it that we stand, exactly?"

"Well, we're both aware we had to come together under obligation. You need funds to save your ancestral estate from ruin and provide dowries for your sisters, and I must collect a title for my family so my father's money can have a proper lineage attached to it. Therefore, ours is not the most romantic arrangement."

Christopher shifted on his feet. "You do speak openly, don't you, Violet?"

"I'm sorry."

"Don't be. I very much appreciate your open manner. Although I would like to voice my objection to one of those things you mentioned."

"Which one?"

"The one about the lack of romance in our arrangement. Since I believe we can still have romance, if we so choose." He said the words before he truly thought about them, and he honestly wasn't sure why they'd left his mouth. Violet was right, after all. This was supposed to be a business arrangement. Yet with the places his mind had already traveled today, he couldn't imagine keeping this marriage in name only.

"You wish for our relationship to be a romantic one?" she questioned, perching herself forward to the edge of the bench.

"God, yes," Christopher answered despite himself.

Her fingers finally eased inside her lap. "I would like that, too. I think romance between a husband and wife sounds quite...lovely."

She smiled then. It was a brilliant smile, like pure light radiating from her soul, warming him from the inside out. Violet Bell simply took his breath away, making him wonder how he'd come to be this fortunate.

"Why me?" he whispered, watching her smile fade with the question but unable to keep himself from pressing on. He had to know why she'd refused one earldom, only to turn around months later and accept another. Especially since she'd now accepted an earldom that lacked funds, and proper gardens, and harbored a lord like him, who had to work like hell just to function in normal society. "Why did you choose me, Violet?"

She glanced to the floor as her mouth opened. "To be perfectly truthful, after that unfortunate business with Lord Chaney, my father was quite angry with me. He insisted I marry another man with title and gave me a choice between two suitors. It was either you or the Duke of Dunworthy, and he only has one ball."

Christopher's jaw unhinged with that last word.

Violet's eyes darted back to him, wide as saucers. "Oh, my God! I should not have said that!"

He stood straight and still for a moment, stunned into silence. But then he saw her fingers grip ferociously to the edge of the bench, her lips quiver, and her eyes water. Christopher forced himself to respond as calmly as possible. "May I ask how you came to know of the duke's...situation?"

"O-only because the maids said so. My maids, I mean. The ones at my home in Pennyshire."

"Your maids speak to you of such things?"

"Well, no, they don't speak *to* me, exactly. They were talking to each other in the kitchen and I – I overheard."

A grin overtook his lips. "So, you were spying? On your maids?"

"Spying? No, I wasn't *spying*. I was merely listening advantageously, trying to discover something of my future. Then I learned that unfortunate tale about the duke and his man parts – or part, as it were – which was frightening, to say the least, considering his other three wives supposedly died of boredom and I don't know if that had anything to do with his one ball or not. Honestly, I'm not even sure of the proper number of balls. I believe it's two, but..."

"It's two," Christopher confirmed, trying his damnedest to not burst into laughter. "And I promise you I have both of mine."

"Oh. Well. Good. I mean, thank you for the reassurance."

"Of course."

"Not that I would look at you differently if you only had one. Although what are the odds of both you and the duke having only one ball each?"

A chuckle escaped Christopher's throat. "I honestly have no idea."

With his laughter, Violet's hands flew to her face, her small fingertips pressing hard against her eyelids. "Oh, great heavens. I don't know why I'm saying these things to you, my lord. You must think me a fool. A childish fool, and a thoroughly ridiculous creature."

He finally moved, stepping swiftly across the floor to sit next to her on the bench. He didn't dare touch her, as that would be far too untoward. But he did lower his voice, relaxing his body beside hers in an attempt to settle her fears. "Violet, please listen to me. I do not think any such things. I find you bright, sincere, and lovely. Truth be told, you have captivated me entirely."

She dropped her fingers from her eyes to meet his frank stare. "Really?"

"Really. And as I've told you before, I do not want you calling me 'my lord'. It's Christopher. Just Christopher."

He could tell the exact moment his reassurances caught up with her rapidly moving mind, as Violet rewarded him with another wondrous smile right then. She sat so close to him now – with only scant inches separating them on this bench – and the urge to touch her nearly overpowered him. His breath hitched while he gazed on her, his hands shaking with the effort of keeping them to himself.

He had to shift his body back a bit, clearing his throat in order to speak. "Will you call me Christopher from now on?"

"I will," she agreed, grinning at him again before her face fell completely.

"I can see there is something else on your mind," he observed as her fingers twisted together. "Care to tell me what it is?"

"How is it that you already know me so well, Christopher?"

"I am simply in tune to your movements," he explained, watching her cheeks flush in response, their fresh pink color quickening his pulse. "Please tell me what you're thinking."

Violet stiffened her spine intentionally, even if her eyes now focused on her skirts. "I just want you to know, in case our previous conversation didn't make it blatantly obvious, that I am...I am a virgin."

Christopher thought she'd been blushing already. Yet he had no idea of the color that could light her skin until she said the word *virgin*. The crimson flushed even higher over her cheekbones and down her neck, spreading to her chest and dipping below the bodice of her dress. He wondered how far the blush went. He wondered if he'd be able to see it ease over the peaks of her breasts and down further still, across her stomach and onto her thighs, if she stood bare before him.

He wondered how she would react on the day he took her virginity from her. He wondered if she would be shy afterwards, ducking her head into a pillow on the bed beside him. Or perhaps, she would feel so comfortable with him by then that she would be bold and impetuous – as she often was in her speech – and let the daring side of herself run free.

Perhaps she would take joy in their lovemaking. Perhaps she would want it, or even demand it. Perhaps she would cling to him and beg him to love her again and again.

Christopher wondered many things about his Violet in this moment, including exactly when he'd started thinking of her as *his* Violet. However, he did not wonder if she spoke the truth. She was definitely innocent to man, since no woman with carnal knowledge would ever look this anxious while attempting to speak so directly.

"I thank you for the clarification," he said when he managed to form words. "But I'm uncertain why you thought the reassurance necessary."

"It's because I'm aware most women my age are already married," she spoke to her skirts. "And since I'm not, I don't want you to worry that something might be wrong with me. I assure you I am still innocent. I am not tainted goods, and I don't want you thinking I am used up, or deficient, in that way."

Tainted goods? Used up? Deficient?

Her words struck him in the worst way, making his chest constrict to the point of pain. Violet's eyes flickered back to his, their light blue rife with anguish. Christopher wanted nothing more than to reach out to her right now. He wanted to take her in his arms and just hold onto her. But he knew that would be the wrong thing to do, given their present conversation.

He shook his head. "You...you speak of yourself as property."

"Is that not what I am?" she countered, her voice rising. "Is that not what all women are? Are we not just property to be dealt, traded, and sold, under the guise of family honor?" Her eyes flared with conviction when the words left her mouth. Yet the moment she'd finished speaking, she looked down again. "Forgive me, my lord. I did not mean to be so bold with my words. I did not mean to..."

"Violet," he breathed, keeping his voice as soft as possible while his heart thudded hard with his own memory: the memory of being forced to his knees on the bloodied deck of his ship, and offering himself up as property to a pirate. "Look at me, please."

She took another moment to fortify herself. When her gaze drew back to his, she met his intense stare without faltering. "Yes, my lord?"

"Do not ever apologize to me for speaking your mind. I want to know your mind. I want to know *all* of you." He hadn't meant to emphasize the word *all* as much as he had, but when he witnessed the flutter of her eyelashes, he couldn't bring himself to regret what he'd implied. "I want you to tell me what you think. I want you to be bold when you're with me. And for the love of the heavens, please, *please* stop calling me 'my lord'. I am Christopher to you. I will *always* be Christopher to you."

Violet didn't say anything for stretched seconds. He held his breath in anticipation of her response. Then she smiled. So beautifully. Her entire body settled down with the upturn of her lips, and he could breathe again.

"Thank you, Christopher. I don't believe anyone in the world has ever granted me such an open invitation to speak my mind. Not ever."

"Well, consider this invitation permanently open."

"My goodness. You are very, very kind to me."

"I'm glad you think so. I certainly want to be," he assured, sliding toward her to keep her focus directly on him. "Also, please know I desperately want to tell you that the world does not see you as property. I wish I could say it this instant, but sadly, I cannot. What I can tell you is that I do not see you as property. I see you as a person with your own thoughts and wishes. And even though you've come to me now under familial obligation, I hope one day you'll grow to care for me. I hope you'll actually choose me as your husband, of your own free will."

By the time he finished speaking, Violet's lower lip quivered and her eyes glinted with moisture. "I...I don't understand," she whispered.

"What don't you understand?"

"I don't understand how I got so lucky, to be here with you. I don't understand why you are not already married and father to a dozen children. I don't understand how you can say you don't think of me as property, when I stood in the foyer yesterday and called you *my* Christopher. In front of everyone."

He couldn't help chuckling. "You did call me that, didn't you?"

"I did. I hope you'll forgive me for it."

"There's nothing to forgive. I didn't mind it then, and I still don't mind it now. Belonging to you doesn't sound like a punishment. Nor does it sound like something I would not enjoy."

Violet grinned even as she brushed back her tears. "Are you saying it's something you would enjoy?"

"Yes, I do believe I would."

"Well, good. I mean, not good as in I want to own you, but good as in I'm glad you like being with me."

"I do like being with you. And since we're being so honest with one another, I should confess that I have already started to think of you as *my*

Violet. Not with the thought that I want to own you, but with the understanding that I want you beside me. For you are kind and beautiful and wondrous in every way, and I simply want you here."

Her shoulders fell. "God, you're just...you're perfect. Aren't you?"

The question caught him entirely off guard. Christopher reared back, putting a bit of necessary space between them. "No. No, I'm not," he stated, struggling to get the words past the constriction of his throat. "I'm not perfect at all. And I don't want you to ever think I am."

"But I don't understand," she responded with a crinkled brow. "Why do you not want me to hold you in high regard?"

"Because I don't deserve it."

"Why on earth not?"

He had to take a moment then. Christopher had to take time to calm down and breathe, for no matter how much he wanted to maintain an illusion of intactness, she needed to understand this fact without question. "I do not deserve your regard, Violet, because things – things happened while I was away all those years. Bad things happened, and they affected me in the deepest of ways, so now I can assure you I do not deserve your generous sentiments."

She immediately scooted toward him on the bench, closing the tiny distance he'd placed between them. Her thigh pressed firmly against his, their hands nearly touching as she looked to his eyes. "I know you were lost at sea, Christopher. I am not innocent enough to think you didn't suffer. I wish you hadn't. I wish you'd never met anyone cold and you'd never experienced bad things. But you are home now and I am here. I want you to know I'm here for you, if you ever wish to unburden yourself of your past. And no matter what you tell me, I promise I will still hold you in the highest regard."

He stared at her for the longest time. Not only because she'd pressed herself against him and now took up all his personal space, but because she looked so desperate to help and he honestly didn't know what to do about it. Violet had assured him that she was not tainted goods, but he could never give her the same assurance. She had no concept of how dark the past few years of his life had been, and he couldn't imagine telling her. He couldn't risk her being inked with that blackness, especially since he realized now that all he wanted was to have a fresh start. Here. With her.

"I'm...I'm sorry," Christopher apologized. "I do not wish to speak of it, although I do appreciate your compassion. Most sincerely."

She gave him a tender smile. "Very well, then. I promise I will not push you to tell me anything about that time. But if you ever change your mind, please know I'm here. I'm here to listen to anything you desire to say."

He searched her eyes, finding only truth. "Thank you, Violet."

"You're quite welcome," she answered, still smiling as her eyes drifted down. Her breathing turned stuttered the instant she focused on the sight of her skirts pressed against his trousers. When she realized just how close she'd gotten to him, she instantly began to back away.

Christopher couldn't fathom letting her go. He reached out, taking her hand inside his own.

Violet gasped and he nearly released her. Yet a mere second later, her fingers gripped onto his. She held tight to him, looking to his face with eyes brighter than ever before.

"Is this touch acceptable?" he questioned.

"Yes, it's...it's quite fine."

"And may I...may I..."

"May you what?"

"May I kiss your hand?"

She swallowed hard, shifting the long column of her throat. He didn't know which one of them was more nervous. Then Violet nodded. A lot.

"Yes, Christopher. Please do."

With her ascension, he grinned as giddily as a lad. Actually, giddier than he ever remembered being as a lad. He took his time bringing her hand up to his chest, giving her the opportunity to change her mind. But even though her eyes widened, she made no protest at all.

He lowered his lips to her skin, her entire body trembling when he pressed his mouth to the back of her hand. Christopher felt that vibration in her fingers and also down her leg, since her thigh remained pushed against his. He kissed her as gently as possible – just a mere touch of his lips to her soft flesh – listening intently while Violet sighed with the contact. Her sigh spoke of both excitement and serenity, and he knew exactly how she felt, so he allowed himself to close his eyes and simply breathe her in.

She smelled delightful, like a finely milled French soap of sweet cream and honeysuckle. She smelled like happiness, like home, and he lingered against her skin. It was all he could do to pull away, even after realizing he'd spent far too much time with his mouth pressed against her flesh.

Once he managed to straighten his spine, Christopher forced himself to rest her hand back on her skirts. But he did not let go of her. He kept her fingers wrapped inside his own, and she made no move to release him.

The moment he could refocus, he fastened his gaze on her face. He couldn't have been more pleased with what he saw. Violet's pupils were wide and black as pitch, her cheeks flushed in roses and pinks, her lips moist from the darting of her tongue.

A shaky laugh escaped his throat. "Was that all right?"

She grinned wildly. "It was wonderful. A bit scratchy, but wonderful."

He reached his free hand to his cheek, to feel the short scruff on his jaw. "Do you want me to use a straight razor? I could make my skin smoother for you, although it will never be as soft as yours, I fear."

"Oh, no, you do not have to shave on my account. I like your short beard. Actually, I found the rough feeling quite stimulating. I mean, dear heavens, that sounded very untoward. I didn't mean to suggest that the feel of your beard stimulated me. I only meant to say that I found the sensation interesting. Although, to be perfectly honest, it was indeed stimulating. In every sense. Unless...perhaps you don't want me to be that honest?"

Her fingers gripped almost painfully to his hand at this point, since she'd squeezed harder and harder onto him the more she spoke. Christopher smoothed his thumb across her knuckles. "As I've said, I like your honesty very much. And since you enjoy my scruff, I'll keep it groomed as you prefer."

Violet sighed loudly, her entire body softening as she watched him. "How wonderful. I look forward to feeling more of your beard on my skin."

When she finished speaking this time, he expected her to tense from the many possible insinuations of her statement. But she didn't stiffen, or correct her speech, or shift her body away from his. She was far too occupied with staring, her gaze roaming softly but surely over his mouth and jaw, as if trying to connect the sensation she'd felt on her skin with what she saw before her. Then she took a deep gulp of air into her lungs, continuing to hold tight to his fingers while bringing her other hand slowly up to his face.

Christopher didn't dare move. He knew his betrothed meant to touch him and he didn't want her to stop. He waited in painful anticipation, closing his eyes when her fingers had almost reached his cheek. His heart pounded in his chest, his entire being desperate for the feel of her.

The jolting barks of dogs thundered in the distance, shattering the perfect silence and startling them both into jumping apart. Violet's hands flew to her chest. Christopher succumbed to nervous laughter.

When the bellowing ceased, he looked back to see the blush on her cheeks renewed with fervor. He soaked in the vision of that color, wishing he could reach out to touch her face the way she'd almost touched his. *There will be plenty of time for that later*, he assured himself, although it still caused him grievous pain to not act on his impulse here and now.

"I suppose that is a sign for us to head back to the manor," he announced as he knew he should. "Lest the hounds come to find us."

"I suppose you're right," Violet sighed, not hiding her dejection at all.

Christopher tried not to take too much pride in her obvious desire to remain on this bench with him. He stood instead, not wanting to give his body any further opportunity to stay beside her, since the longer he stayed, the harder it would be to leave. However, he did allow himself one further indulgence.

"Would you care to take my arm for our walk back?" he asked, angling his elbow out when Violet rose from the bench.

"I'd love to," she agreed, not wavering for an instant before wrapping her hand around his forearm.

Christopher pulled his arm into his side the moment she grasped it, pressing her hand against his body. He felt her fingers curl into his sleeve, gripping onto him as he guided her out of the gazebo. He tensed when they walked down the three steps to the stone pathway, fearing seeing the hounds on their way to attack them. But all that attacked them were the warm rays of sunshine and the fragrance of roses, so he let down his guard and simply enjoyed walking through the gardens with his Violet by his side.

She fell silent while they strolled, just as she had been when they'd first left the manor, yet this quiet was different. His betrothed no longer felt like a ball of nerves beside him. She felt closer to him now, in every way, and that made him happier than he could fathom.

"Thank you for the walk," he said, even though the simple sentiment couldn't possibly express his gratitude for all she'd offered him today.

Violet met his gaze. "Thank you, Christopher. I've truly enjoyed it."

"I have, too. Especially since these gardens remind me of home."

"Really? Does the Kastle estate have gardens such as these?"

"Well, no, not anymore. But they did when I was younger, before my mother passed. These days, all I'm able to do is control their overgrowth."

"Hmm. Perhaps I can help. If you'd like."

His brow rose. "You wish to help me tame the gardens?"

"Certainly. I mean, assuming we'll live in your manor after we're married. Assuming you want me there."

"I do want you there," he assured without a second thought, tucking her hand closer to his side. "I look forward to bringing you home with me."

She smiled ear-to-ear with his declaration. Christopher could have kissed her here and now, propriety be damned. Unfortunately, they were too far out in the open, within view of Lady Wilmington's balcony once again. As they approached the manor, he forced his attentions away from his future wife and looked toward her aunt instead.

He straightened his spine purposefully, trying not to appear too close to the woman at his side, lest their chaperone have cause for clucking her tongue. But when he looked up to where Tildy sat in her balcony chair, he realized he need not be concerned about disappointing her. After all, the silver-haired woman slept quite soundly. Yet again.

A chuckle rumbled deep in his chest while he listened to their chaperone's distant snores. "I'm very sorry to tell you this, Violet, but I think your aunt may have stopped watching over us at some point."

"Oh, yes, I know. But even if she wasn't sleeping, she still wouldn't be watching over us. She's terribly nearsighted and barely sees two feet in front of her face, let alone across the gardens." Violet's entire body tensed the moment the words left her mouth. "And I suppose I shouldn't have said that."

Christopher met her uncertain stare with a nearly permanent smile etched on his lips. "Is that because you don't want me to know that our walks alone in the gardens each day will truly be walks alone?"

Her eyes drew to his mouth. He knew he should regret his husky tenor, since the rise and fall of her breaths came more rapidly now, causing her breasts to press tighter against her bodice with each labored inhale. Yet he couldn't bring himself to regret anything, even if the realization of how swiftly her body drew to his made his desire for her all the more palpable.

"Please don't be concerned," he forced himself to add in the thickened silence. "I promise I will remain a gentleman with you at all times."

He didn't miss the look of utter disappointment on Violet's face before she plastered on a smile. "Well, that's good to hear. Thank you."

"You're welcome," he offered, thoroughly amused by her obvious displeasure with his vow to *not* take advantage of her. "Although, I must admit I am curious about something."

"About what?"

"Actually, perhaps I shouldn't speak of it. I fear my question would be a bit untoward."

"Goodness, Christopher. After all the untoward things I've said to you in the past day, I believe you have the right to ask me any question at all."

"Well, if you truly don't mind, then I shall. I find myself quite curious, since you mentioned earlier that you had ulterior motives for asking your father to have our courtship here, if it was your plan for us to be chaperoned by a woman who has dreadfully poor vision and is prone to fits of slumber?"

Violet sucked in a sharp breath with his deduction, her fingers digging into his arm. He bit back a laugh, not wishing her to feel anxious. After all, he wasn't laughing *at* her, he was laughing *because* of her – because of her delightful mind, sweet charms, and innocent desires – and he couldn't recall the last time he'd felt such joy.

Christopher succeeded in containing himself rather well. He even managed to offer her a calm, reassuring smile. After several edged seconds, Violet relaxed again beside him.

"It...it may have been my plan," she admitted.

"I see," he confirmed, guiding her beneath the balcony where Tildy slept. He led them both to the back entrance of the foyer, stopping only when they reached the stained-glass doors. He dropped his arm down, freeing Violet's hand to return to her side, before glancing around to ensure no one else could see them.

Christopher looked back to her face. "I want you to know, as much as I appreciate your forethought in securing a means for us to spend time alone together during our courtship, I do still promise to remain a gentleman," he reiterated, taking a determined step toward her, forcing her to lift her chin in order to meet his steadfast gaze. "However, I would like permission to kiss your hand again, because I've had a lovely walk with you today and I would like to end it in a lovely way."

Violet's eyes lingered on his as she leaned closer. "You don't ever have to ask for my permission again, Christopher."

"I don't?"

"No. You have free rein."

"Free rein," he echoed, his entire body pulling toward hers of its own volition. "Please preface that by saying I only have free rein to kiss your hand, Violet. Otherwise, I might think it means something else entirely."

"Wh-what might you think it means?"

He stepped forward, not stopping until he could feel the warmth of her flesh seep through his clothes. "Well, since you were so honest with me about enjoying the stimulation of my beard, I'm going to be honest with you, as well. I'm going to tell you that giving me free rein will cause me to struggle most egregiously. For I may take it to mean that I can feel more of your skin than just your fingers. I may choose to believe that I can kiss more of your body than just your hand. And I shouldn't rightly have those thoughts of you. Not now. Not yet. Therefore, it will be best for you to say that you give me free rein in hand kissing only."

Violet swayed on her feet when he finished his indecent speech. Christopher's heart thudded heavily in his chest, fearing he'd gone way too far with her, way too soon. He wouldn't blame her at all if she turned and ran. Hell, she'd confessed mere moments ago that she was innocent to man, and now he felt like the Big Bad Wolf, come to steal her virtue under the guise of a trusted companion.

He knew he should apologize for his impropriety. He almost did just that. Until Violet lifted her arm toward him.

"Well, then. I suppose we should stick to hand kissing only. For now."

Christopher sighed in relief with her generous answer, bowing his head in both respect and appreciation. He took her hand in his own and pressed his lips to the back. He didn't miss the little shiver that coursed through her fingers when his mouth touched her skin. Nor did he miss the gleam in her eye once he straightened. "Thank you, my lady."

Violet shook her head as he released his hold. "I'm...I'm not a lady."

"Yes, you are. The title won't be official until we're married, but that is only a formality. You are a lady, Violet."

She smiled, soft and sweet. He felt it dead center in his chest.

"Thank you, Christopher."

He nodded before glancing to the door of the foyer, dreading the thought of her leaving. His shoulders fell when he recaptured her eyes. "I know you must hasten inside. But I will get to see you for dinner, won't I?"

"Oh, yes. Most certainly."

"Wonderful," he sighed before stepping back.

Violet didn't move. She just continued gazing up at him.

After a long, silent minute, he huffed out a laugh. "If you don't return to your room soon, I imagine someone will come looking for you. Maybe not your aunt, but someone."

Violet shrugged. "Perhaps. Perhaps not," she said, her eyelids falling to half-mast. "I shall see you tonight."

"Tonight," he agreed, watching intently as she turned and glided past him into the foyer. He stood in silence, absorbing her every movement, unable to hide the ridiculous smile on his face even after she disappeared from sight.

Christopher wondered what Cora would think of her grumbly brother, if only she could see him now.

CHAPTER 5

Daydreams and Nightmares

After returning to her room from her walk in the gardens with Christopher, Violet spent the rest of the day in near constant fits of squealing. Yet her sister never complained. Gwen simply sat on the edge of the bed, watching and listening as Violet gushed about her betrothed being the perfect gentleman, paying attention to every word she said, assuring her he also desired a marriage of romance, and kissing her hand.

"Not once, Gwen, but twice! Twice!"

Violet used the word *perfect* a hundred times in her descriptions of him, even though Christopher didn't consider himself perfect. He actually considered himself quite damaged, despite being nothing like the damaged men she'd seen in the streets of London during her youth. She'd witnessed those ex-soldiers returned from battle only to lie around on the docks, drowning themselves in gin and urine as they waited for work on some passing merchant ship.

Christopher was entirely different from those unfortunate men. He was trying to do right by his family. He was trying to do right by her. And even if he wasn't perfect – because she understood no one truly was – he was still as close as she could imagine any man being.

He encouraged her to be bold and to speak her mind. He assured her he didn't consider her his property and thought of her as a person with her own thoughts and wishes. He even hoped she would grow to care for him, and choose him as her husband, of her own free will.

Lord Christopher Kastle was honestly too good to be true, yet Violet didn't want to disparage this situation just because everything he said and did was exceptional. Besides, she'd understood before she even accepted this courtship that her betrothed had demons from his time at sea. She didn't know what happened during his years away to make him think of himself as broken, but what she did know was that this Christopher Kastle – the one who'd come to court her now – was kind and tender and giving. If this was the man his time at sea had turned him into, then she wasn't going to lament the years he'd been lost. She would only lament the pain he'd endured and the sadness still held in his heart.

"But perhaps I can alleviate that sadness, Gwen," Violet concluded after hours of unrelenting speech. "Perhaps I can be the one who finally brings Christopher happiness by soothing the scars on his soul. I want to become his beacon of light. I want to prove to him that love can indeed heal all."

Violet finally stilled herself and stared at her sister, awaiting some reply.

Gwen observed her for lengthy moments before standing and grasping her hand. She held tight to Violet's fingers while staring her down. "That is a heavy burden to embrace, dear sister. Your need to help your betrothed is noble, to be sure, yet it may be based almost entirely on wishful thinking. Are you truly certain you desire to take Lord Kastle's scars upon yourself?"

Violet's face fell with her sister's concerns, but she refused to let sensibility deter her. "Yes, I'm quite certain. Christopher is my husband. I mean, he will be soon. I want that. I want it more than I ever thought I could. Therefore, I shall be present for him in any way I'm able."

Gwen didn't smile, but she did nod her head. "Then let us get you ready for dinner with your husband."

~

THAT EVENING, Violet and Gwen walked together down the lengthy upstairs hallway. Violet wore an exquisite off-the-shoulder emerald dress for tonight's dinner gathering. Gwen had tied her into both her undergarments and her outer ones before fretting over her pearl hairpins, making certain she looked the picture of a lady. For once, Violet didn't mind all the fuss.

When the sisters reached the upper step of the staircase leading to the foyer, Violet glanced down to see Christopher waiting for her. He wasn't looking out of the window, or toward the door. He looked straight up the stairs, his eyes fastening onto hers the moment she emerged from the hall. Her breath caught when she saw him, yet it was not due to nervousness. Tonight, her lack of air originated solely from the handsomely statuesque vision he struck in his fitted black suit.

In just two days, her betrothed had quelled her fears over this marriage, transforming their courtship into the romantic journey she'd scarcely allowed herself to hope for. She couldn't prevent the smile spreading her lips while she glided down the steps beside her sister, watching him stalk forward in anticipation. His intent gaze never left hers as she descended, but she neither tripped nor stumbled when she arrived to stand before him.

Christopher reached for her fingers the moment he could, bringing them to his chest while bowing his head. "Violet," he breathed, just before pressing his lips to the back of her hand.

Gwen whimpered but Violet only held tighter to him, relishing the delicious scrape of his course scruff on her skin. When he raised his head, Christopher smiled into her eyes. "Gwen," he addressed without ever looking away from his betrothed, "would you mind if I escorted your sister to the dinner table tonight?"

"Oh. No, not at all. That is, if she doesn't mind."

"I don't mind in the least," Violet assured, which made him smile deeper.

Christopher straightened but did not release her. He gathered her fingers and pulled them around his forearm, pressing them into his coat sleeve. His hand settled over hers as they walked across the foyer and down the hall.

Violet's entire body honed in on the feel of his large, warm palm engulfing her fingers. She almost didn't notice when they arrived in the dining room, until she saw Aunt Tildy already seated at the head of the table. Violet put an inch of space between her and Christopher when her aunt's gaze honed in on their hands wound together around his arm. To her service, Tildy didn't say anything in condemnation of the affectionate display. She merely waited in silence while he walked Violet to her seat and pulled her chair out for her, much to the chagrin of the eagerly waiting butler. Christopher then assisted Gwen into her chair before striding around the table to take his place beside their host.

"Such a gentleman, Lord Kastle," Tildy remarked once they were all seated. She even smiled, just a little.

"You are very gracious to have me here, Lady Wilmington. Behaving as a gentleman is the least I can do."

Christopher's eyes darted to Violet's when he said the word *gentleman*. Her cheeks flushed with the memory of his promise to her earlier today: the promise to remain a gentleman, even though he desired to kiss more of her body than just her hand. She'd managed to tell him that they should stick to hand kissing only, which was definitely the proper thing for a lady to say, despite her regrets over such a damning restriction.

No, Violet. Restrictions are good. He's not your husband yet, she reminded herself once the soup bowls were placed before them. She stared across the table, watching Christopher grasp his spoon in his long, sculpted fingers, caressing the silver in a way that appeared unlawful. She bit her tongue to keep from whimpering, since she could only imagine how warm and strong those fingers would feel when gliding over her body.

"Violet!"

The bark of her name startled her from her wicked musings. She forced a deep inhale before looking to the head of the table. "Yes, Aunt Tildy?"

"I called upon you three times just now! Where is your head?"

"Oh, it's...I'm...I'm sorry. What did you need?"

Tildy's nose scrunched. "I need to know if you are still prone to pilfering newspapers from your father's study at home."

Violet couldn't help grinning. "Yes, I am still prone to that."

"And have you pilfered my paper today, by any chance?"

"No, unfortunately, I've not had the time," she replied, hearing Christopher chuckle warmly from across the table.

"Well, I actually wish you had pilfered today's paper," Tildy confessed. "I'll even give it to you outright, for I found the stories quite interesting and I desire to speak of them."

"What stories are those?"

"In specific, there is another egregious tale from across the seas, regarding the dastardly pirate Blackheart."

Violet barely opened her mouth to respond when Christopher coughed, harsh and rough, choking on his soup. The sound of his distress instilled a panic in her chest unlike anything she'd ever known. Violet jumped up from her seat, thrusting her body across the table to plant her hands on the linens as close to him as possible. "Christopher! Good gracious! Are you well?"

He nodded, grasping his glass of wine and drinking deeply. "Yes, yes, quite well," he insisted once he replaced the glass.

Violet stared him down from her perch overtop his soup bowl, seeking the truth of his assurance in his eyes.

"That's certainly good to hear," Tildy offered. "We're all happy to know our guest isn't going to choke to death at the dinner table. And now that we are sure he is well, you can *sit down, Violet.*"

The hard inflection of her name forced her attentions back to her aunt. Seeing how far Tildy's brow had risen into her silver hairline, Violet winced. "Oh, well, I...yes, of course," she stumbled as she crawled backwards to resettle in her chair. Dropping her gaze into her lap, she tried to not feel mortified by the fact that she'd wholeheartedly lunged at her betrothed in front of every-one, simply because he'd had a cough.

Tildy huffed the moment her niece was reseated. "As I was saying, the pirate Blackheart has reportedly given up his normal pillaging in China and is now moving toward the African coast with his fearsome band of men. Isn't that the most dreadful thing you've ever heard?"

"Yes, it is quite awful," Gwen agreed, overcoming the gap left by her sister's awkward silence.

"You're right, Gwen," Tildy confirmed. "Especially since the Royal Navy has done such a fine job of clearing the seas of pirates over the years. And yet, for some reason, they cannot apprehend this most vile Blackheart. It makes me grateful that my Gilroy isn't still alive and traveling to his hunts in Africa, for I could not imagine the level of worry I would feel over his ship being attacked by pirates."

Christopher cleared his throat, still recovering from his cough. Violet's eyes flew to his, but he didn't look back at her. He didn't look at anyone. He only studied his soup bowl, which he no longer sipped from. "I hope your husband never had to endure such an experience at the hand of pirates, Lady Wilmington."

"That is very kind of you, Lord Kastle. And no, Gilroy was never attacked, thank goodness."

Christopher's shoulders sank with a heavy exhale.

Tildy turned her short, thick body toward him. "I'm quite curious, though. Did you ever hear any tales of pirates in your time at sea?"

Violet watched a tiny grimace pull at the corners of his lips.

"I suppose every sailor hears tales, although many rumors turn out to be false, or grossly exaggerated," he answered, lifting his gaze to meet his host's. "I wouldn't place much value in those so-called reports."

Tildy hummed in consideration while the butlers served the next course of their meal. "Well, that's good to hear. I hate to think Blackheart will get tired of raiding Africa, as he's gotten tired of China, and make his way around the coast toward England."

Gwen reached out to clasp Tildy's hand. "I'm sure there's nothing to worry about, Auntie. You shouldn't get yourself worked up over such things. It isn't good for your health."

Christopher nodded. "Gwen's right. The sail around the tip of Africa and up the coast to England would take four or five months at least. I doubt Black-heart would go through the trouble of it, especially not with the Royal Navy out for justice. You should rest easy, Lady Wilmington."

"Very well. I thank you for the assurance, Lord Kastle."

"Anytime," he replied, his body finally resettling in his seat.

Violet held stone-still, cataloguing everything in her mind. When her betrothed eventually looked to her, she offered him a smile of gratitude for placating her aunt's concerns. He smiled back, perusing her with his deep blue eyes, before refocusing on his food.

The rest of their meal passed in amenable silence, with only bits and baubles of discussion over the weather, and no more talk of pirates. Violet was grateful for the change in topic, as it obviously did not sit well with Christopher. Yet she couldn't help but wonder how deep his knowledge of pirates ran, and she lamented her promise to not inquire further about his time at sea.

"Gwen," Tildy announced once the servants removed the plates from the table, "why don't you play the piano again? We can all retire to the parlor."

Without even looking across the table, Violet could sense Christopher's tension at the prospect of spending another evening beside a roaring fire. She shook her head as she turned to her aunt. "Actually, I think we should allow Gwen a rest, Aunt Tildy. She would never complain, but I'm sure her fingers are sore after playing so long last night."

Violet gave her sister a tiny kick beneath the table. Gwen jumped in her seat before agreeing. "Oh, yes, you're right. My fingers are very sore today."

The widow's brow furrowed. "Well, if we cannot hear your sweet music, then what shall we do?"

"I thought we could play cards in the game room," Violet offered, glancing to Christopher to measure his approval of the change in venue.

He bowed his head to her. "That sounds like grand fun, Violet. Thank you for the suggestion."

Tildy chortled. "I would not be so quick to thank her, Lord Kastle. You have not seen her play cards yet. It may not be the best idea to witness it."

"Oh? Why is that, Lady Wilmington?"

"Because she plays like a shark, that's why. She's uncanny at it, and as I've always said, it's unnatural for any woman to play that well."

Violet wet her lips. "I...I won't play as I normally do," she promised.

Christopher's gaze drifted to her mouth before he met her eyes. "On the contrary, I insist you play as best you're able. I'm quite certain I need to see this shark for myself."

She smiled wildly despite the presence of onlookers. "Are you sure?"

"Positive," he answered with a glowing grin.

"Then it's settled," Violet announced. "We'll head to the game room."

Tildy grunted. "Don't say I didn't warn you, Lord Kastle."

"I assure you I am forewarned, Lady Wilmington."

They all rose from the table, with Tildy and Gwen leading the way from the dining room into the hall. Violet moved instantly to Christopher's side, grasping onto his outstretched arm, although it was a short distance to the game room and most certainly did not require guidance. Yet she still clutched his coat sleeve without hesitancy, allowing him to pull her body even closer to his. As they navigated the hallway, she reached into the pocket of her skirt to extract her spectacles.

Christopher glanced down to her hand. "You wear spectacles?"

"Only for minute sight, like reading or playing cards."

"Hmm," he considered. "Perhaps I should ask you not to wear them, if your aunt's warnings are accurate. Maybe then I'll actually have a shot at winning against the infamous card shark."

Violet laughed. "I am very sorry to tell you this, Christopher, but you don't stand a chance against me."

He slowed their steps, allowing Tildy and Gwen to disappear into the game room beyond. Once he and Violet stood alone in the hallway, he gave her a devilish smile before lowering his lips to her ear. "I do believe I've already learned that," Christopher whispered, his warm breath and warmer words sending a sinful shiver up her spine.

VIOLET COULDN'T SLEEP. Too much had happened today – between the walk in the gardens, the squealing with Gwen, the conversation at the dinner table, and the events in the game room – and it churned her mind to an uproar. Despite the late hour, Violet rose from her bed, pulled her robe over her thin ivory nightgown, and tiptoed out of her room, hoping a short stroll through the darkened house might assist her into slumber.

The manor sounded deafly quiet once she stood in the hallway. The dim light of an oil lamp in the foyer crept up the stairs, adding an air of mystery to her current venture and imbuing her with all manner of unsuitable thoughts. She didn't know exactly where to go, although the wickedly wanton part of her craved sneaking to the opposite side of the house in search of Christopher's bedroom. But she would never do that, since such an action would be terribly indecent for a lady to commit. And because she feared walking into a servant's room by accident and having to explain why she was out of bed and entering other rooms in the middle of the night. And also because she didn't know what she would do if she actually found his room...other than to stare at his large, muscular, prone body, and imagine how it would feel to be pressed fully beneath him on his mattress.

Blushing with that sinful image, Violet padded across the floor with great care, desperate to remain silent as she wandered. When she came upon the entrance to the main second-story balcony, she recalled how her aunt had supervised her garden stroll with Christopher from here earlier today – or how Tildy had made a show of supervising them, at least. Repressing a giggle, Violet eased opened the double doors and stepped out into the moonlight.

Moving seamlessly across the balcony floor to the edge overlooking the gardens, she came to a standstill in front of the black iron railing. Violet gazed up at the overwatching moon, staring into the bright white globe for several minutes. The moon's vivid glow muted the stars a bit, but she could still soak in their beauty as she listened to the stillness of the night. She basked in that gorgeous quiet, breathing the cool air deep into her lungs, until her ears filled with a strange, unexpected sound. The sound of...grunting.

Grunting?

Her eyes drifted down to discover the source of the noise. She absorbed the sight of the dimly lit gardens. Then she saw the man standing there.

Christopher.

Her breath hitched the instant her gaze landed on his broad form. It took only a second to realize he didn't grunt due to the briskness of a rapid walk along the garden path. Christopher held a long sword in his hand, practicing the art of war with it, jabbing and slicing the fearsome blade through the night air. Violet could not hear every noise he exerted, but she could definitely see him in the glow of the moonlight – the looseness of his white shirt, the tightness of his dark breeches, and the shimmer of his black boots – as he stabbed at unseen things.

She knew she should leave. Her betrothed performed his solitary swordplay with an intensity she could not fathom, and this was clearly a private matter. She should retreat this instant to allow him time to himself.

Yet she couldn't. Violet couldn't tear her eyes away from the magnificence of his measured movements. Despite the immediacy of her guilt, she allowed herself to watch him from her high perch, knowing full well that her secret imposition would eat at her tomorrow.

The width of Christopher's body was not awkward or fumbling as he fought. If anything, his large form granted an imposing strength she'd never before seen. He moved with grace, power, and purpose, bringing her to the realization that her future husband was no ordinary person. His time at sea had turned him into a fierce warrior. And a very lethal man.

That thought should rightly scare her. It didn't. Even while witnessing his current fearsome state, Violet knew he would never be lethal with her. She'd been in his presence for only two days, and yet she understood without question that he would never harm a hair on her head.

Her Christopher was a tender, loving, family-centered soul. If anything, he would fight to protect her – and whatever children they might one day be blessed with – from every evil in the world. Therefore, his excellent swordsmanship did not frighten her at all. His skill actually reassured her. It even soothed her.

She remained on the balcony for some time, just watching him fight. She watched him slice his blade through the air, again and again. She watched her betrothed until her eyelids drooped beyond recovery.

Violet bid him a silent goodnight before leaving the balcony. She sealed the doors behind her as quietly as she could. Then she found her way back to her chamber, collapsed onto her bed, and sank into a deep, peaceful sleep.

VIOLET WOKE LATE the next morning. She barely had time for a bedside breakfast before her sister came to preen her. Gwen chatted about the excellent weather, servants, and food here at Wilmington as she braided Violet's hair, twisting the braid around itself before pinning it into a tight bun at the nape of her neck. Violet listened but didn't converse much, her mind wrapped fully in the events of the previous night.

She normally wouldn't hesitate to share any of her thoughts with her younger sister, but she didn't wish to discuss what she'd seen while standing on the balcony in those dark hours. After all, Christopher's skill with the sword was his secret to tell, not hers. Violet couldn't bear to divulge what she'd witnessed to anyone else, not with the amount of guilt she still felt after watching her betrothed's private moments without his knowledge.

I'm going to have to tell him what I saw last night, she decided when she stood to grip onto her bedframe for leverage. Her knuckles turned white against the mahogany wood post while her sister yanked hard on the back laces of the most fitted corset in her courting arsenal. Violet sucked in a steep breath as the ties tightened almost unbearably around her ribs and waist, forcing the tops of her breasts up to her collarbones.

She ignored her current level of discomfort as she dwelled further on thoughts of Christopher's swordplay. She knew she must confess her stolen knowledge, since she didn't want to keep any secrets from him. Well, except for the one about Welly and Gwen and the truth behind the Picky Princess title – but only because that was also not her secret to tell.

"There you are. All set to dazzle," Gwen announced when she finished fitting Violet into a brand new, and daringly bold, bright red dress.

Violet glanced down to the gold embroidery decorating her exceedingly low-cut bodice. "Is it...too much?" she wondered aloud, fearing a single deep breath might cause her elevated breasts to pop right up out of the top.

Gwen's nose crinkled. "Is anything too much during courtship?"

The sentiment made Violet laugh. "I suppose you have a point."

"Off you go, then. Your prince awaits."

Violet pecked her sister on the cheek before making her way out of her bedchamber and into the hall. She concentrated on breathing evenly as she walked, since a breast-popping-out event was a possibility she was not currently prepared for. She also needed to calm her nerves over admitting to what she'd seen last night. Would Christopher chastise her for watching him without his permission? Would he condemn her for her unladylike actions?

He already waited for her in the foyer, turning toward her when she reached the top of the staircase. His mouth dropped open the instant he saw her state of dress, his gaze traveling scandalously down her body while she traveled carefully down the steps. His eyes did not return to her face until she reached the floor, his pupils now wide and dark.

Christopher took her hand in his, pulling it up to his chest. "You look stunning, Violet. As always."

"Thank you," she whispered, her words faltering with the pressure of his warm, strong lips on the back of her hand.

When he stepped to her side, he guided her fingers to wrap around his arm. "Should we head to the gardens?"

She nodded, holding tight to his coat sleeve as he steered them toward the back of the foyer. Once they stepped out through the stained-glass doors and onto the stone pathway, he kept them both moving forward, not bothering to verify if Tildy watched over them from the balcony. They walked together in amiable silence, although Violet did notice Christopher's gaze drifting to her bodice on several occasions. He actually spent a good deal of time absorbing the sight, all while his heated palm shifted across her fingers.

His attentions unsettled her, leaving Violet's breaths stuttered and skin humming as they moved in time. "Is it too much?" she finally questioned.

"Is what too much?"

"My dress? I know I'm very...tightly pinched in here."

Christopher chuckled, the soothing rumble buttering her insides. "I hope you are not uncomfortable in such tight garments."

"Well, corsets are uncomfortable by nature, I think. Although they do enhance certain things."

"Yes, they do," he admitted, glancing to her neckline again before focusing on her eyes. "I hope you'll forgive me for noticing as much as I have. My only excuse is that you are very beautiful, and I'm merely a man of flesh and blood."

Violet grinned. "I shall take that to mean you like my new dress."

"Oh, I do. Quite."

"That's good. It makes all of my mother's fussing seem worth it."

"Do you not like her fussing over you?"

"Not really. Especially not about clothes. It seems rather dreadful for one single person to have so many new dresses, but Mama insisted that I wear all of my finery for our courtship."

"I take it you do not agree."

Violet shrugged. "I simply do not share her love of clothing."

"No? What do you share with your mother?"

"Um...blond hair and blue eyes?"

He laughed. "You must be your father's daughter, then."

Her hand tensed around his forearm. "I am. Although I shouldn't admit to it, should I? Noah Bell is supposedly the criminal mastermind who took control of every gambling house in Nightingale Port in just a few years."

Christopher didn't miss a step as they continued traveling the stone pathway. "Actually, that would offer a perfect explanation as to how you walloped me so thoroughly at cards last night."

Violet smiled despite herself. "I hope I did not hurt your pride."

"Not at all. Although you do play better than any man I know."

"Thank you for the acknowledgement. My father taught me the games when I was young, and they simply made sense to me. Once something makes sense to me, it becomes very easy to master."

Christopher searched her eyes. "Your mind is exceptional. Isn't it?"

She stared into him as they walked, drinking in his unbound admiration, and for once in her life she didn't feel ashamed of this truth. "Yes, I do believe my mind is exceptional, even if it is untoward for a woman to speak of such things. Had I been born with man parts, I would have pursued a noble profession. Perhaps in law or government."

"You would have made an excellent barrister, I'm sure. I truly wish you'd had the opportunity to pursue whatever profession you desired, since I'm certain the world could only benefit from your intelligence. However, I must shamelessly admit that I'm very pleased you were born with lady parts. Especially in this dress."

He winked at her and Violet burst out laughing, straining her breasts egregiously against her bodice. The sight of it made Christopher clear his throat, averting his gaze to the gardens even as his arm pulled her closer. She continued to grin when they reached the bifurcation in the trail.

He brought them both to a stop. "Shall we go back to the gazebo today?"

"That sounds delightful, if you'd enjoy it."

"I would," he assured, turning them onto the left path.

They took several more steps in comfortable silence, and as much as Violet enjoyed the peace she felt beside him, she also knew this was the perfect time to divulge her guilty conscience. Clutching onto his arm, she raised her eyes to his. "Christopher, I have a confession to make."

He met her gaze immediately. "A confession?"

"Yes."

"Very well, Violet. I'm listening."

"I – I saw you last night. In the garden. I saw you practicing your sword."

She didn't know exactly what kind of reaction she'd expected. But if he'd been angry, or hurt, or even stunned, she wouldn't have been surprised. Yet Christopher was none of those things. He simply smiled at her.

"Were you spying on me?" he asked with a twinkle in his eye. "As you do with your maids back in Pennyshire?"

Violet's jaw dropped. "Spying? I wasn't *spying*. I just had trouble sleeping, so I took a little walk. I found my way to the balcony, and stepped out to see the moon, and there you were. I swear I didn't have any idea you would be there, but once I saw what you were doing – swinging your sword around so forcefully – I just couldn't look away. Therefore, I stayed and I watched and..." Her voice trailed off as her eyes widened. "Oh, good heavens! I *was* spying on you, wasn't I?"

Christopher laughed, which brightened his entire face. "I must say, you are the loveliest spy I've ever come across in all my travels. And I do apologize if my actions last night appeared unseemly, but I often practice my sword in the gardens at home and I've grown quite used to it. I've even been known to trim the shrubbery with a swift blade stroke."

Her brow rose. "You garden by sword?"

"Sometimes. I know it's not a traditional gardening technique, but it is effective and quite good exercise. It's also more than a little cathartic, I suppose." His blue eyes caught hers once again. "Although I would never dare to disturb any of your aunt's shrubbery, so I would appreciate it if we kept my late-night venture as our little secret. For I do not wish to get on Lady Wilmington's bad side. At all."

"Oh, no, you do not want that. Trust me," Violet confirmed.

Christopher gazed down at her with an affectionate grin, warming her whole body with the realization of how smoothly this dreaded discussion had transpired. The ease with which they could converse made her even more attracted to him – a feat she didn't know was possible – and caused an interesting thought to pop into her head. It was a delightful thought. A daring thought. A thought which made her giddy even as her pulse sputtered.

The gazebo appeared before them and Violet felt the pull of his arm guiding her forward. She knew they would be truly alone together the moment they stepped inside, so she reached her free hand out to grab at a jutting branch on a nearby tree. She managed to break off a long twig, holding onto her little treasure with clamped fingers while he drew her up the three steps and into the wood-and-glass enclosure. Christopher led them both to sit on the bench inside, but she pulled her arm from his instead.

Taking several steps away, Violet stood before an ivy-coated window and jabbed the twig out in her best imitation of swordplay. She felt his eyes on her as she whipped the branch back and forth, wondering if she had the nerve to actually act on her daring, delightful idea. After all, this was only their third day together – and they'd agreed to stick to hand kissing only – yet she could not prevent herself from wanting more. Would his desire to touch her overcome his vow to act as a gentleman? Did she possess the ability to coax him further if she requested his instruction in sword fighting?

If he does oblige me, it won't be altogether untoward, she assured herself. *If he just stands a little closer, and touches a bit more of my arm, that will still be perfectly acceptable behavior. Unless he sees through my flimsy ruse, at which point he should rightly refuse my request. And that would be mortifying, to say the least.*

Violet blanched with the thought. She considered not going through with her diabolical plan, but decided that nothing would be gained from fear and many things could be gained from bravery. Gripping onto her branch, she asked, "Have you ever taught anyone the sword, Christopher?"

He cleared his throat behind her. She felt the sound beneath her skin, even with the distance now separating them. "I have. I taught my sister."

Violet turned toward him, drawing his eyes to hers. "Which sister?"

"Cora."

"Is she a good swordfighter?"

"Yes, she is. Honestly, she's excellent. Although please do not tell her I said so, for she loves to deride me in a younger-sibling manner and would never let me live the words down."

Violet giggled despite her nervousness. "I cannot wait to meet Cora. I look forward to the day we can travel to your estate so I can meet all your sisters."

"I look forward to that day, as well," he agreed, his voice shifting deeper. "Honest to God, I cannot wait to take you home with me."

The darkly alluring look in his eyes stole all her air. Violet's fingers curled tighter and tighter around the stem of the twig, until the wood popped and made her jump nearly from her skin. She looked down to the branch, trying to focus her thoughts under the spell of the unearthly man before her.

"Well, then. Since you garden by sword," she said, lifting her gaze back to his, "I think it's important I be trained to use the sword, also. I mean, we did decide that I'm going to help tame the gardens when we get to your home, didn't we?"

With those words, Christopher stepped toward her. His large, lithe body moved with feral grace across the gazebo floor, honing in on her without a moment's hesitation. "Yes, we did decide that," he confirmed when he arrived before her, his proximity pulling her eyes higher.

Violet gulped despite the fact that his closeness had been her goal in this twig endeavor. She simply wasn't prepared for the extent of her body's instant and aggressive response to his.

"Although I want to make one thing perfectly clear," Christopher added, his warm breath shifting across her cheeks.

"Wh-what is that?"

"The moment you step foot in the Kastle manor, it will be *our* home."

"Oh...I...wonderful...please," she breathed, not entirely sure of what she'd said, but hoping he understood the intention.

He pressed closer, his chest nearly brushing against hers. "So, do you want to begin your training now?"

In that moment, staring up into his fathomless eyes, Violet honestly had no idea what he was talking about. "What training?"

A deep chuckle emanated from his throat as his hand drifted to her arm, his fingers closing over hers around the stem of the little tree branch. "Your sword training, of course. Isn't that why you brought this twig in here? To be used as a makeshift sword?"

The warmth of his palm settled into her skin and she whimpered. "Yes, that is what I want. I definitely want training. Because you are obviously very, very capable of teaching me."

Christopher shifted his hand to run his fingertips across her knuckles. He inhaled deeply, the movement causing his shirt to brush against the low neckline of her bodice. "And you would know of my capabilities, wouldn't you, Violet? Since you stood on that balcony last night, alone in the dark, just watching the way my body moved."

Her mouth fell open, because she was appalled. Not by his words. She had no right to be appalled by his words, when everything he said was the absolute truth. No, Violet was appalled by her body's response to his words, and by the atrocious ache settling low in her belly as she envisioned the solid wall of his chest pushed even harder against her.

"I did watch you," she admitted, her voice surprisingly even. "I stood there all by myself and watched you for a very long time. I like looking at you. I like seeing the way you move." His pupils dilated dangerously with her words. "Do I...do I need to apologize for my actions, Christopher?"

"God, no," he sighed, his fingers tightening on hers. "I feel exactly the same way about you. I want to watch your movements every day for the rest of my life."

His words slid deliciously over her skin. "Well, if we plan to spend our lives in such mutual admiration, I imagine there are many things I must learn."

"Like what?"

"Like how to spar with each other. With...with swords, I mean."

"You wish to learn to spar with me, Violet?"

"Yes, I do. Very much."

His heated gaze lingered on her face. "All right. If you honestly want to learn to spar, the first thing we'll have to work on is your stance. But before we get started, I need you to realize this instruction will involve me touching you quite a bit. In order to teach you properly, I'll need to stand behind you and wrap my arms around your body. To fully demonstrate the best positioning techniques."

"Oh," she gasped, his words suggesting a great deal more contact between them than she'd even hoped for. Her blatant desire for that contact made her mouth run dry in anticipation, forcing her to lick her lips.

Christopher fixated on the movement of her tongue without any pretense of restraint. A long while later, his eyes dragged back up to hers. "The instruction method I envision will involve us being pressed quite closely together," he told her. "And as we've agreed to only allow hand kissing at this point in time, I want to make sure it's suitable for me to hold onto you in such a way. Since I imagine this sort of contact will feel much more intimate."

More intimate. More intimate? Dear God.

"Well, that's, um...yes, I think it will be quite suitable. I mean, since this is for learning purposes and everyone knows how important it is to learn. Therefore, it should be fine for you to hold me. In this instance. For learning."

A dark, tempting smile eased over his lips with her pitiful justification. "I couldn't agree more. Now, I must ask you to turn around so we can begin."

"Mm-hmm," she murmured, unable to find the words to accompany her current state and thinking it best not to try.

He dropped his hand from hers, taking a step back to give her more room. Violet turned on her heels as he'd instructed. She presented her back to him, fixed her eyes on the window, and held her breath.

Christopher stepped into her at once, pressing his broad, solid chest against the length of her spine. He bent his head until his prickly cheek rested beside her smooth one, making her eyes roll back in her head. Violet struggled to keep her wits about her, wanting to catalogue every sensation in her mind so she could revisit this moment at any time in the future.

The first thing she focused on was his strength. She absorbed the hardened sculpture of his chest muscles, loving how the smooth fabric of his shirt rested flush with her upper back. She'd never been so pleased to have her hair pinned, baring her neck and shoulders to his sight and his touch.

The next thing she concentrated on was his scent. He currently enchanted all of her senses, but especially her sense of smell. She'd never been pressed this close to him before, with his face directly beside hers, and she relished the subtle aroma of fresh soap with hints of leather.

Her mind labored to record every tiny, titillating observance, until Christopher lowered his mouth to her ear. "The initial step you must take, as a swordfighter, is to assess your surroundings," he informed. "Be aware of your situation. Ensure there are no dangers you have not foreseen."

All rationally formed thoughts in her brain dissolved then, obliterated by the throatiness of his words. "I see no dangers here," she assured.

He brought his hands to her arms, cupping her elbows with heated palms before smoothing his fingertips down to her wrists. "Are you certain?"

"Y-yes. Quite certain."

Christopher threaded his fingers into hers. She barely kept hold of her twig. "Very well, Violet. If you're certain there are no dangers here, the next thing you must do is part your legs."

"*What?*"

Deep, genuine laughter rumbled through his chest, infusing through her dress and into her spine. "You must widen your stance for stability. And press the soles of your feet to the floor for balance. You must keep yourself grounded, or you might feel as if the world is spinning around you."

"Oh. Right. I could see how a person might feel that way."

His fingers tightened in hers. Violet did as he said, despite how she craved this deliciously unbalanced sensation. She moved her feet to shoulder-width apart and pressed her soles to the floor. But she also settled further against him – pressing into his body with the backs of her legs, spine, and neck – simply because she wanted to. She didn't know exactly where her wicked courage came from, but felt rather victorious when he groaned in response.

Christopher slid the side of his face onto hers. "The experience of engaging your opponent in a heated battle can be earth shaking if you are not prepared," he continued, shifting just enough to cause the stubble of his jaw to scrape brazenly against her cheek.

Sweet heavens, did he do that on purpose?

Violet thought the scrape of his scruff against her hand was stimulating enough. Yet as his scratchy jaw continued moving slowly down her skin, every surface of her flesh sprang to life at once. He rested his chin on her shoulder, pausing for a moment only, before easing his beard up the side of her neck. The coarse, prickly path he drew left a trail of heat in its wake. Violet shivered, which pulled his lips into a smile she could feel against her cheek.

God, yes. He's definitely doing all of this on purpose.

She swayed on her feet, barely keeping herself upright, until Christopher released his hold on one of her hands to bring his arm to her waist. He flattened his palm over the bright red fabric covering her stomach, securing her solidly onto his body. Then he tightened the fingers of his other hand around hers, clasping the little branch they held onto together.

"Do you mind if I support you like this while you learn, Violet?"

"No. I don't mind at all," she asserted, quite proud of her bravery.

"Very good," he praised, his jaw shifting over her cheek again. "Now, you'll always want to keep your sword drawn in front of your opponent." He lifted her hand so the wooden twig stood centered before her. "And you'll want to keep your shoulders back and your chest forward when you swing the blade. To keep from losing your balance."

Violet obeyed him. She pressed her shoulders back and thrust her chest forward, straining her breasts against her bodice more scandalously than ever. She knew by the pressure of his chin on her shoulder that he now stared directly at her near-to-bursting cleavage. Her barely concealed nipples tightened in anticipation of his reaction.

She'd never heard a man growl before. Not like her betrothed did now: deep and guttural and pained. The delectable sound sent a thousand bolts of lightning skittering across her skin. Violet moaned in response – a lurid, unruly, thoroughly indecent moan – rivaling the intensity of his growl.

As the wanton noises they both made echoed off the walls, his jaw clenched hard beside her cheek. "Damn it," Christopher cursed beneath his breath. "We should...we should stop this lesson now."

"No. Not yet. Please. I need to know what happens next."

His fingers dug into the lines of stiff herringbone running the length of her corset. He pulled her tighter against him, bringing her bottom flush with his hips. She bit egregiously into her lip, fully aware she should retreat this instant, yet unable to convince herself to do so.

"All you need to know from here on out," he spoke against her ear, "is that you must maintain control. You must learn to relax in the face of danger, to keep your mind sharp and never panic, or else the situation will take control of you before you realize it."

"I must relax?" she echoed. "In order to maintain control?"

"Yes. It is very important that we maintain control. Before anything happens that should not."

Christopher's hot breath skimmed over the tops of her breasts. Violet whimpered as she discarded the twig to the floor. Curling her fingers into his, she wrapped both of his arms fully around her waist. Their hands clasped together while she closed her eyes and slumped backwards, giving herself over entirely to the shelter of his body.

"How is this, Christopher? Have I relaxed enough?"

He shifted his nose to her hair and breathed in deep, pressing his lips to the shell of her ear. It wasn't a kiss. Not exactly. But it was warm, gentle, and perfect. "You have done beautifully, Violet. And God, you're beautiful. In every way."

A soft smile curved her lips. "Then perhaps we can stay here, just like this, for a bit longer."

"I think that's a fine idea," he agreed in a soft whisper, banding his arms around her to encase her completely.

She sighed as she tucked her face into his neck. "Thank you for my lesson."

"Hmm. I believe I'm the one who should be thanking you."

Violet savored his sincere words, rejoicing in the realization that he wanted this just as much as she did. Christopher began to sway them then, moving her side-to-side in a purposeful yet tender dance. She merely continued to smile, allowing herself to follow his lead.

∾

THAT AFTERNOON, Violet drifted back to her bedchamber on a cloud. She didn't know what to think about the time she'd spent with her betrothed today, since her mind could not fully grasp what had happened during her sparring lesson. She could still feel Christopher's arms wrapped around her, the prickles of his beard against her cheek, and the warmth of his breath on her skin. He'd held onto her forever, and when he'd finally released her from the enveloping comfort of his embrace – guiding her from the gazebo with his fingers wrapped in hers and kissing her hand by the foyer door – Violet knew she would be content to float on this cloud for the rest of her days.

Sadly, her cloud burst the moment she walked through her bedroom door and found Gwendolyn standing by the window, trembling and sniffling while holding tight to a sheet of paper in her hands.

Violet dashed to her sister's side. "Gwen? Are you all right?"

Gwen met her gaze with moisture-glinted eyes. "No. I'm not."

"Please tell me what's wrong, dearest."

With a swift shake of her head, Gwen's tears ran down her cheeks. "I received a letter from Welly today."

"Oh, my. Is it bad news?"

"No, it's...it's good news," she countered, crying even harder.

"Come here, dear love," Violet encouraged, taking her sister by the hand and guiding her to sit on the bed. "Come lay your head in my lap."

Gwen complied immediately, dropping her wet cheek onto Violet's skirts the moment they were seated. "You have the best lap in the world."

Violet smiled as she petted Gwen's hair. "That is what you always say. Now please tell me about Welly's letter."

"Oh, Violet, he misses me. Desperately. He says his days without me have no purpose or meaning and he needs me with him always. He says if he cannot see me soon, he has no idea what he shall do."

"Goodness, that is quite the letter. However, I should think those words would make you smile, not cry."

"I don't want to cry. I just...I just..."

"You miss him, too. The same way he misses you."

Gwen turned her brimming eyes up to Violet's face. "It's only been a few days since we arrived here. I don't have the right to miss him, do I?"

"You most certainly have the right. I wish you could be with him now; I truly do. Yet I am still selfishly happy that you're here with me."

"I want to be here. I want to support you as you always support me."

"I know you do. Your presence is invaluable to me."

"Truly?"

"Most truly," Violet admitted, her thoughts drifting again to the feel of her betrothed's warm, strong arms wrapped around her. "In all honesty, everything about this adventure I'm on now feels like a blissful daydream. You are the only thing still grounding me to reality."

"Oh, but it's all real, dearest. Christopher cares for you. I know he does. I see it in his eyes each time he glances in your direction. I hear it in his voice each time he speaks to you. He is as affected by you as you are by him."

Violet smiled with that reassurance, since she wanted to believe it was true. After all, it certainly felt true. And she knew her feelings for him would only deepen as their time together continued.

～

As it turned out, Violet was right. The more time she had with Christopher, the more she grew to care for him.

They spent the next few days simply enjoying each other's company. Nothing happened physically between them to rival the intensity of their sword fighting lesson, yet he eagerly maintained some form of contact with her whenever possible. He kept her hand wrapped around his arm every time they walked in the gardens, and entwined their fingers as they sat in the gazebo each afternoon.

During those precious moments alone together on the iron bench, they traded thoughts on nothing and everything. Christopher told Violet stories of his youth, of the joy he'd known when his mother was still alive and how his life had changed each time he'd welcomed a new sister into the world. Violet told him all about her childhood in London, how she'd loved to run wild in the streets and was rarely without mud in her hair.

He'd laughed at her raucous stories and she'd melted with the sight of his joy. Then she'd continued to speak on and on: about her family, about the books she loved, even about her belief that women should be free to hold their own land without being forced to marry. She'd expected Christopher to frown upon that particular thought, but he'd only nodded and said he wished his sisters had those rights as well.

Each moment of each day, Violet looked on him with more stars in her eyes. She never wanted that feeling to end. But it did end.

It ended on the eighth night.

The day transpired like every other during the week: Violet had breakfast with Gwen in her room, took a glorious afternoon walk in the gardens with Christopher, and met everyone for dinner in the grand dining room. After a lovely meal, they'd all played cards together. Violet won the games again and her betrothed congratulated her with nothing but admiration in his gaze. He'd kissed her hand when he bade her goodnight and her heart fluttered as she returned to her bedchamber to await the late hour when she could sneak out to the balcony to watch him practice his sword.

Violet had watched his swordplay every night since she'd first discovered his custom. Christopher never acknowledged her presence on the terrace above him. Not once. But she liked to think he knew she was there, watching the forceful push and pull of his muscles in the moonlight. She also liked to think he would approve of her voyeurism, as she accustomed herself further to his body.

On the eighth night, Violet made her way to the balcony with the same degree of anticipation she felt every night. However, for the first time, Christopher wasn't there. She looked and looked, her eyes searching every inch of the gardens, but she could not find him.

With a deep V etched between her brows, she exited the balcony. She knew she should return to her room, but she would have no rest with this mystery hanging over her head. She descended the stairs to the foyer instead, wandering aimlessly while considering her options.

That's when she heard the unsettling noise: the distant barks of Uncle Gilroy's hounds. Violet flinched, since the dogs never barked unless alarmed. Her stomach twisted while she stepped to the main window and looked out to the far stables.

Darkness abounded, but she could still discern the form of a man mounting a steed in front of the stable door. She knew the horse, and she knew the man. Christopher climbed barebacked onto his stallion, clinging to nothing but the mane, and rode out around the side of the stables into the wooded path surrounding the Wilmington estate.

Violet stood before the foyer window, staring out at the blackness into which he'd disappeared, wondering where he would go. As her mind grasped for explanations, every fear she'd ever had – from the moment Lord Wellington Chaney looked past her in order to see her sister – came crashing down in the worst possible way. She could only think of one possible reason for her betrothed to leave alone in the middle of the night, and the prospect ripped a hole in her chest.

He's going to see another woman. Christopher has a mistress.

Hot, salty tears pricked Violet's eyes as she stared after him, even though she already knew many husbands were unfaithful. In truth, Papa was the only man she could think of who remained entirely committed to his wife. Even

Uncle Gilroy, in all his stuffiness, probably had mistresses during his lengthy travels in Africa, and Violet imagined she had dark-skinned cousins that she would never have the privilege to meet.

She shook her head over and over, unable to imagine assuming her aunt's placid acceptance of her husband's indiscretions. The thought of Christopher sinking his flesh into another woman – of him finding release and comfort in the arms of another – was more than Violet could bear. The image tore through her brain like the fiercest of storms, forcing sharp, biting acid into her throat. Her hand flew to her mouth, pressing into her lips to prevent herself from vomiting on the floor, as she flew back up the stairs to her bedchamber.

CHRISTOPHER WOKE to the sound of knocking on his bedchamber door. He sat up and looked around, trying to recall exactly where he was. The knock came again, heralding the arrival of his breakfast tray. He cursed under his breath, since he normally awoke well ahead of the butler. Scampering up from the ground, he quickly mussed the sheets on his mattress before rushing to the door to allow the servant to enter, deposit the tray, and exit.

He sat before his meal the moment the butler left, staring blankly at the bountiful food. Christopher wasn't sure why he'd slept so late this morning, except perhaps for the fact that he felt much more at peace after his horseback ride. He'd needed that sense of freedom and escape last night, although not because he desired freedom from his betrothed.

On the contrary, when he was with Violet, he felt light and young and joyful. When he was with her, he understood what it meant to be alive. It was a gift he'd never dared dream of having again.

But when he had to leave her in the evenings – when he had to bid her goodnight with only a kiss to her hand, and stare after her in longing as she glided up the stairs to her bedchamber – the darkness crawled back into his heart so rapidly. Last night, practicing swordplay had not been enough to salve his scars. He'd needed the outdoors. He'd needed to ride through the night air, mapping the stars in his mind while flushed with fresh air on his face.

He felt much better this morning. Not only because he'd ridden, but because he knew he would get to see his Violet again in just a few hours. He would be allowed to go for another walk in the gardens with her, and bask in her light, and cling to that brightness for as long as possible.

With one hand, Christopher reached for a bite of sweet bread from his tray. With the other hand, he raised his oval locket from the table, eased the gold lid apart, and looked to the photograph inside. A peaceful smile spread his lips, for now he could match the smooth appearance of Violet's skin with the memory of how soft her flesh actually felt beneath his fingertips.

As he ate, he allowed his thumb to drift over the curves of her cheek. He wondered what sort of dress she might wear for him today. He swore her bodices sank lower each time he saw her, and even though that was probably all in his mind, he still found it difficult to not stare.

His eyes couldn't help but feast on the sinfully tight gowns that gripped her corsets day after day, yet he honestly didn't need her to go through all of that fuss. He didn't want Violet to be uncomfortable in her clothing, especially since he would be quite satisfied to see her in a simple gown with no lacings underneath. In truth, he would be very satisfied to see her wearing nothing at all.

He chuckled at the impropriety of his thoughts, forcing himself to close the locket so he could concentrate on finishing his meal, since he was now hungry for more reasons than one. Mr. Rodchester had a bathing tub brought into the room after breakfast, as had become the custom here, and Christopher tended to his hygiene before dressing. The moment he pulled on his dark brown jacket over a white, high-collared shirt with tan breeches, he slipped the gold oval into his coat pocket. He smiled with the knowledge that Violet's photograph remained with him at all times, even during the hours when she could not be by his side.

Precisely at noon, he proceeded out of his bedchamber door, his black boots clicking steadily on the marble flooring. He refused to take the time to approach the foyer in a stealthy manner today, because he needed to be with her. He simply needed her, and he didn't care who knew it.

With his heart thumping against his ribcage, he ran down the back staircase and hurried through the long hallway before turning the corner. Then Christopher saw her there. Violet stood in the foyer, waiting for him.

He knew instantly that something was terribly, terribly wrong. It wasn't just the fact that she wore a dark dress with a high neckline, long sleeves, and heavy skirts, hiding her body entirely from his view. It wasn't just the way her shoulders hunched as she stared at the floor. It wasn't just the sallow paleness of her cheeks. It was all of these things and more.

"Violet?" he breathed, his chest caving as he rushed forward. "What has happened? Are you well?"

Christopher reached for her the moment he could, cupping her elbow.

She cringed at his touch. "I...I couldn't sleep," she answered, the words breaking in her throat.

He stepped fully in front of her. "Violet, dearest, please look at me."

Her eyes rose, their pale blue edged with the redness of crying. "Oh, God, Christopher. Did you just call me *dearest*?"

"I did, for you are so dear to me. I must know why you couldn't sleep."

A little sob escaped her lips.

"Talk to me. Please," he begged.

"It's just...I just..."

He could see she was close to bursting into tears, and knew he must get her alone so she could divest her mind of her plaguing thoughts. "Can you walk? Through the gardens to the gazebo?"

She sucked in a shaky breath and nodded.

"Come with me," he urged, pulling her hand around his arm and holding it tightly in place as he guided them both through the foyer, out of the back doors, and onto the stone pathway. He barely noticed his surroundings, feeling only the unusual coldness of her fingers beneath his palm. "Take deep breaths, Violet. Just keep breathing."

She whimpered with his instructions, yet she still followed them.

His footsteps quickened, pulling her along with him as he navigated the garden path all the way to the gazebo. As soon as they stepped inside, he led her to the bench and helped her rest onto it. He seated himself beside her, although he didn't touch her any further, unsure at this point if it would help or hinder. He focused solely on her face. "All right. We are entirely alone now. You can talk to me about anything."

Violet grimaced. "I – I want to talk to you. But I also do not, because I need to ask you a question and I fear the answer you will give me."

His brow furrowed. "I never want you to fear anything about me."

"Then please be truthful with me, Christopher."

"About what?"

"About whether or not there is another woman in your life."

He cocked his head. "Another woman? I do not understand."

"It's just...I saw you. I saw you last night, riding your horse out from the stables. And if you have another woman, if you have a – a *mistress* you visit, then I would like for you to be honest with me about her." Violet's hands clasped together on her skirts, clinging so hard that her knuckles whitened. "Although, would she still be considered your mistress if you and I are not yet married? I don't know what the proper term would be for her right now, but I do know married men often have mistresses, and..."

"Violet!" Christopher commanded, loud and firm, stopping her in her tracks. "I swear to you, there is no other woman. There never will be. I am not that kind of man. At least, not anymore."

She looked into him for painstaking seconds, her eyes huge and glassy.

He sat still, staring into her, needing her to see this truth.

Eventually, she hung her head. "Oh, thank God."

Christopher reached for her, certain that touching her now would do no harm. He ran his fingers across her knuckles until she released her fearsome fists, then tangled one of his hands into both of hers. "There is no other woman for me, Violet. There is only you."

A tiny smile tugged at her lips. "Thank you. Thank you so much for being such a generous and genuine man."

"Of course. I just want to make sure you believe me in this matter."

She lifted her eyes back to his. "I do. I believe you entirely, and I must now beg your forgiveness. You have been nothing but kind since the day we met, yet I assumed the worst thing in the world the moment I was tested. I allowed my insecurities to conquer my rationality, and my behavior today has been appalling. I wish I had some better excuse, but after I saw you..." Her voice trailed off as her lips quivered.

"Please do not beg my forgiveness," he told her, desperate to prevent any more of her tears from falling. "I should not have left here, even briefly, without making you aware of my intentions."

A spark of hope lit her eyes. "Then may I implore you to extend your kindness further, and ask why you rode your horse out during the night?"

Christopher looked on his Violet then – a woman so pure and innocent that she believed his possession of a mistress would be the worst thing in the world that could happen to them – and considered not answering her. Not because he didn't want to be honest, but because he didn't want her to know the ugly truth. He didn't want her to see the blackness inside him. Not even a shadow of it.

He watched as she pushed back her shoulders and clenched his hand, working hard to be brave for him. She'd promised not to press him about his time away and she wasn't pressing him now. His betrothed simply cared for his wellbeing, far more than she rightly should.

Christopher wanted to reassure her of his health. Regrettably, he could not tell her he was altogether well, since that would be an unforgivable lie. But he could at least tell her he'd reached a place in his life where he could manage his past, even if the methods he employed might seem unusual.

He inched closer to her on the bench. "The truth of the matter, Violet, is that I go out at night to practice my sword and ride my horse because I have trouble sleeping. I have nightmares nearly every time I close my eyes, and the fear of having to endure them has led me to dread the thought of getting into bed. Any bed. I often end up falling asleep on the floor, if I sleep at all. Sometimes, I feel trapped inside the walls themselves and cannot even remain in my bedchamber. My only recourse is to go outdoors, since it feels more like home. It feels safer, in a way."

One of the tears she fought back earlier now rolled down her cheek. "Are your nightmares because of your time lost at sea?"

He reached out to touch her tear with his fingertip, smoothing the wetness from her skin. "Yes."

Violet searched his eyes. "Does sleeping on the floor feel better to you?"

"Better? No, I wouldn't say better. But there were a few years, when I was away, in which I was forced to sleep on the ground. I suppose I became used to that, and it remains familiar, even now."

She whimpered. "I'm so sorry."

"Why are you sorry? None of this is your fault."

"I'm sorry I cannot take your pain away."

Christopher allowed his hand to drop from her cheek, since now that he'd dried her tear, he couldn't think of a good reason to continue touching her face. Other than the fact that he wanted to touch her. So desperately.

"God, Violet, you do take my pain away. Please accept those words as utter truth, because every second I spend with you is precious to me. When I'm with you, I don't think constantly about my time at sea. I don't even think about how tired I am. And that is an impressive accomplishment, believe me."

She didn't move. She barely breathed for an eternity. Then she eased away from him and looked down to her skirts, straightening the wrinkles in the fabric by smoothing her palms across her thighs.

He figured she'd retreated because she needed to put some space between them after the confessions he'd made. He imagined she now questioned her decision to pick him as her husband. Perhaps she even reconsidered her option to choose the lethally boring Duke of Dunworthy.

Christopher resigned himself to his bitter, hopeless thoughts. He shifted back on the bench, allowing her distance. That is, until Violet spoke again.

"You know, I've been told that I have an excellent lap."

His brow rose. "Excuse me?"

"My lap. I've been told it is excellent."

"Excellent?"

"Yes," she confirmed, smoothing over her skirts once more before drawing her eyes back to his. "Gwen tells me all the time. 'You have the best lap in the world,' she says, and then she lays her head down on me."

Her words sucked all the air from his chest. "Violet, are you...are you telling me that I may lay my head in your lap?"

"Well, yes. But I promise I don't mean anything untoward. I just thought, since I've been told my lap is quite good, and you seem to be in need of some-place soft to lay your head, that maybe you could use it to rest. If you want to. Because you said you're tired, so I figured..."

Christopher may or may not have dived into her lap. All he knew was that one minute he sat beside her on the bench, watching her cheeks pink as she rambled her glorious invitation, and the next minute he lay down on her with the side of his face pressed to the silk of her skirts. He also wrapped his arms around her – one behind her back and the other across both of her thighs – in the same instant he flopped onto her legs. He basically claimed the lower half of her body as his very own bed, and fully expected her to rescind her invita-tion straightaway.

He tensed against her body, waiting for an admonishment to come from her sweet lips. But Violet didn't speak a word in recrimination. She simply reached her hand to his head, smoothing her fingers across his scalp.

The feel of her playing with his hair was more soothing than any sensation in the whole world. Christopher allowed his shoulders to fall and his eyes to close. Her scent of sweet cream and honeysuckle filled his lungs and he inhaled steeply, wanting as much of her as he could get. She was just so warm and soft and gentle and he didn't know if he'd ever felt safer in his entire life.

"Gwen's right," he whispered. "You have the best lap in the world."

Violet's fingers shifted to his ear, easing around the curve before slipping down to caress the line of his jaw. "I'm glad you think so. Now just quiet your-self, Christopher. Be still, and let me take care of you."

Let me take care of you.

God, he'd never heard better words. Ever. In this moment, he didn't know fear or worry or regret. He allowed himself to sink into the softness of her body. To let her warmth surround him. To let his heavy heart and over-wrought mind rest. Even if only for these few precious moments.

VIOLET KNEW the exact moment Christopher fell asleep, because the ever-present tension in his muscles finally relented and his body collapsed into hers. Her own body relaxed then, although not as much as his, since she still bore much shame. He had undoubtedly suffered through many horrors during his time away – and yet he'd been nothing but a perfect gentleman since the moment they met – and the fact that she'd doubted his faithfulness now felt like the worst of sins. Violet fully intended to apologize to him again the moment he woke. But for now, she chose to bask in the feel of his body taking refuge in hers.

She allowed herself to keep touching him, drawing her fingers from his forehead to his jaw before repeating the path. After many minutes, she drew an alternate path through his hair, over his ear, and along his neck where his stiff white collar rested. She silently admitted her desire to feel the skin beneath his clothes, as well. She worked hard to resist her indecent urge, but apparently not hard enough, because her desires swiftly overcame her sensibilities.

Violet eased her fingers below his collar, just to the edge of his hairline. Her heart pounded in her ears with the simple action, since it didn't feel simple at all. Her hand being under his clothes implied an exceptional intimacy between them: an intimacy she wanted to explore profusely the moment they were married. And when he was fully awake.

With a shaky inhale, she skimmed her fingers further below the edge of his collar. She allowed herself just a little more touch. Just a little more warmth. Just a little more contact with the man who would one day be her husband.

But then she felt something she did not expect. Christopher had a scar on his neck. From the sensation on her fingertips, it felt quite deep.

Fear overtook her in an instant. Without a moment wasted in second-guessing her actions, Violet grasped the fabric and pulled it away from his skin. His scar was indeed deep: a gashed line across the back of his neck, only an inch or two in length but most definitely fearsome. Her throat constricted as she stared, wondering who had put the scar there, and if their intentions were as gruesome as she could imagine, and how long it had taken him to heal.

She thought of Christopher's fear of fire and how he reacted so sharply to any snap of ember in the hearth. She wondered if he had burn marks on his body as well. She wondered what other scars were hidden beneath his clothes, and just how much pain he'd endured in his time away.

Violet sat there, staring at the back of his neck, questioning how deep his scars ran. Not because she found her betrothed frightening in any way, but because she wanted to help. She wanted to relieve some of his burdens and carry them herself, since she believed she could. If only he would let her.

She stared at the marred area of skin for the longest time, but didn't touch the scar further. Such an action felt too personal, especially with him currently unaware of his surroundings. When the time came for her to fully explore that scar, she wanted it to be with Christopher's unreserved consent.

Violet settled his collar back in place. She returned her hand to his hair, ruffling her fingers through the short, light brown strands. She found herself humming as she touched him, her mind drawing to the comforting tunes her mother sang to her as a child. She eased her fingers over his jaw, again and again, memorizing the feel of his prickly scruff against her fingertips as she'd already memorized the sensation on the back of her hand.

She touched Christopher continuously as he slept, since it seemed to soothe him. It soothed her, too. Honestly, she could have remained here on this bench with him forever. But she could tell by the movement of the sun across the glass ceiling that much time had passed as they sat together, and eventually someone would come to look for them.

With fathomless regret, Violet placed her hand on his shoulder and gave a gentle shake. "Christopher," she whispered, increasing the strength of her voice when he did not stir. "Christopher. It's time to wake now."

He moved sluggishly, releasing a deep groan from his throat as his eyes opened. He blinked several times before dragging himself up to sit beside her. His gaze drew to her body, examining her head to toe, before he slipped his hand back onto her thigh. "I didn't hurt you, did I?"

"No, of course not. You merely slept."

His eyes searched hers before he nodded. "Thank you, Violet. I cannot remember the last time I rested so peacefully. It's a bit...disorienting."

She placed her hand over his. "You were safe with me. I promise."

He gave her a soft smile. "I know."

"I'm glad. Please also know that my lap is yours to use. Anytime."

"And I thank God for it."

Violet stared into his adoring eyes, with her guilt eating ravenously at her soul. "Christopher, will you please..."

"It is unnecessary to ask my forgiveness again."

"How did you know I would ask your forgiveness again?"

Reaching out, he traced his fingers around the curve of her ear. "I know you, my dearest. I realize it has only been nine days since we met, but I already know your heart. I don't want you to ever feel shameful for being honest with your feelings. You have every right, with the past I've had, to question my actions. I'm very sorry I frightened you by riding my horse out in the middle of the night. I'm just grateful you shared your fears with me, and I would ask that you continue to tell me what is on your mind, always. Whether it is good or bad."

Violet nodded. "I promise I will."

"Wonderful. Then the matter is settled. You are the only woman in my life and that will not change once we're married. If anything, my vow of faith to you will only grow deeper as we move forward. Agreed?"

The grin pulling up her lips nearly caused her pain. "Agreed."

"Perfect," Christopher announced as he stood and held his arm out to her. "Now, unfortunately, I must return you to the manor. For I believe even Lady Wilmington will notice how long we've been alone today."

Violet stood beside him, wrapping her fingers around his forearm. "Yes, she actually might. Although I doubt she could ever be upset with you, as you have worked yourself quite firmly onto her good side."

"Thank goodness, for if your aunt ever tried to tell me I could not be here with you, I fear I would have to snatch you up in my arms and steal you away."

Violet gazed at him in giddy wonder. "Somehow, I do not think I would mind such a thing."

Her admission brought a perfectly dark, desirous grin to Christopher's lips, just before he tucked her hand to his chest and led her back to reality.

CHAPTER 6

A Little Something Different

Christopher stood in the foyer of the Wilmington manor, adjusting the cuffs on his sleeves for the hundredth time, as he awaited Violet's arrival for their daily walk. Today's walk would be different for them, because today was special. After all, it had been exactly three weeks since they'd first laid eyes on each other in this very room.

He could hardly believe they'd spent only these few short days together, since he truly felt as if he'd known Violet forever. She'd become a part of his life so quickly and easily that he wasn't quite sure what to think of it. Which is why, for today, he decided to not think at all. He would simply allow himself the joy of being with her.

Stepping toward the main widow of the foyer, he looked out of the tall glass to the distant stables where Mr. Rodchester stood, preparing Christopher's horse. He smiled as he watched the old caretaker pack the saddlebags with the items he'd requested, wanting his plans for today to be a surprise for his betrothed – one he hoped she would thoroughly enjoy. He fiddled with his sleeves again, ensuring his white shirt and navy jacket set well on his body. He wanted to look nice for her because she always looked beautiful for him. And because he was nervous as hell, even though he shouldn't be.

Christopher knew he had nothing to fear with Violet. Not since that day in the gazebo, when he'd confessed to not sleeping in a bed due to his recurrent nightmares. At that moment, he'd been terrified of her realizing how damaged he was and shrinking away from the bond forming between them. But instead, she'd listened to him with the most open heart, straightened her skirts, and offered him her lap to rest his weary head upon.

Since then, they'd only grown closer. Each day, she'd moved a little nearer to him on the gazebo bench. Each day, she'd held tighter to his fingers, looked deeper into his eyes, and smiled even more beautifully – until the mere thought of being in her presence made him crave her beyond reason. He craved her brilliance, her joy, her light. He craved her in every way, which he knew should terrify him. And yet, somehow, it didn't.

The gentle clicks of footsteps caught his ear and he turned to see her appear at the top of the staircase. Violet wore a bright pink dress today, with short sleeves, full skirts, and a low-cut bodice that gripped indecently to the cinched corset beneath. His heart leapt as she descended, his mind unable to fathom the reason he'd been given this fortune.

His eyes fastened to hers as he approached the steps. "Good day, dearest."

Violet sighed when she reached the marble floor. "I'll never tire of hearing you call me that," she confessed, giving him her hand.

He captured her fingers, guiding them to his mouth as he'd done so many, many times. He allowed his lips to linger gratuitously on her skin, just so he could watch the flush that lit her cheeks whenever he dwelled too long with his mouth on her body. Even if he'd only ever dared to kiss her hand.

"I shall call you that forever, if you like," Christopher offered when he finally straightened. "Although I reserve the right to choose other endearments for you in the future, provided they meet your approval."

"How gentlemanly of you to offer me approval for terms of endearment. I suppose I shall have to offer you approval for my endearments, as well."

"Honestly, you can call me anything you like, except for 'my lord'. As long as you promise you'll one day call me your husband."

A tender smile eased over her lips. "My husband," she breathed.

Those two words, spoken so genuinely, affected him much more than they should. Especially since they weren't the truth. Yet.

Christopher could hardly wait for the day he could call her his wife. Every single time he stood in her presence, just like now, he felt her reaching toward him with her hands and her heart. Violet pulled him to her, using only caring, attentiveness, and affection, and he did not have the desire to fight that summons. Not at all.

Keeping her fingers firmly planted in his, he eased his free hand to her face. Her lips parted when he caressed her cheek, her eyelids falling to half-mast as he traced a tender path all the way down her neck. "You wore your hair loose today," he noted, adoring the way the blond curls rested across her bare shoulders with such beckoning softness.

"I did," she admitted, melting into his touch. "Is that all right?"

"It's more than all right. You look like an angel."

God, he sounded like a lovesick fool. Even to himself.

Violet squeezed tight to his hand. "Goodness, Christopher. Perhaps we should go for our walk in the gardens now, before Tildy catches us fawning over one another and forces us apart."

He blinked away the disastrous image. "She would never do that."

"How can you be so sure?"

"I'm just finally certain I've worked my way entirely onto her good side."

"Really? How do you know?"

Christopher took another step closer. "Because if I were not entirely on your aunt's good side, she wouldn't have agreed to my plans for us today."

Violet's brow rose. "You have plans for us? Other than a garden walk?"

"Yes. I thought you might enjoy a little something different. To celebrate."

"Is today a special occasion?"

"It is. Today is our three-week anniversary."

Violet burst into joyous laughter. "Oh, my. Are you actually suggesting we celebrate our three-week anniversary?"

"I am. What do you think of that?"

"I think it's the most delightful, adorable thing I've ever heard."

"Funny, that is exactly what Lady Wilmington said when I told her."

"Did you really charm my aunt into letting us do something different?"

Christopher grinned, quite proud of himself. "I did."

"And what do we get to do?"

"Come with me and I'll show you," he encouraged, entwining their fingers and urging Violet toward the front door.

She stepped to his side immediately, holding close as he guided her out of the manor and onto the path toward the stables. "Is that Mr. Rodchester I see, preparing your mount?" she questioned while they walked.

"He is, indeed. I thought you and I could go for a horseback ride and have a picnic in the field past the woods. How does that sound?"

Her eyes drew to his. "It sounds incredible. But I still cannot believe you got Tildy to agree to it. Please tell me how you accomplished such a feat."

"I think her exact words were, 'Only because you are egregiously endearing, Lord Kastle.' Although, I did also have to promise that I would remain a perfect gentleman with you."

"Well, that's unfortunate," Violet said, her eyes widening the instant her brain caught up with her mouth.

Christopher laughed before lowering his lips to her ear. "It is, isn't it?"

She whimpered as they arrived in front of the stables.

"I've your horse all prepared, Lord Kastle," Rodchester informed him.

"Thank you, my good man."

"Anytime."

Christopher patted the saddlebags resting on the steed's hindquarters. "Is everything in here that I requested?"

"Everything's in order, and I'll await your return to help you unpack, too."

"Wonderful. Thank you again."

"Yes, thank you, Mr. Rodchester," Violet added, her warm palm still nestled into Christopher's as she smiled at the kind, aged man.

"You enjoy yourself, Miss Violet." Rodchester encouraged. "And you take good care of this dear woman, Lord Kastle."

Christopher nodded. "I will. Always."

Rodchester gave them each a smile, obviously satisfied by Christopher's promise, before he shuffled into the stables where the hounds bayed for food.

"That man loves you," Christopher realized once the caretaker departed.

"He's like another father to me," Violet agreed, turning to face the large creature beside them. "This is your steed?"

Christopher reached out to stroke the horse's muzzle. "He is. I bought him the night I returned to Nightingale."

"You had money with you the night you returned?"

"Only a few coins I'd managed to scrape up," he answered with a shrug. In truth, he would have brought home a treasure chest full of gold, if he'd been aware of the pallid state of his family's fortunes. "I had just enough to buy this horse and to help buy food when I reached home."

She offered him a soft smile. "Well, you chose a magnificent steed."

"Actually, he was skin and bones when I acquired him," Christopher explained, running his hand up the horse's head to scratch between his ears. "But I fed and exercised him well, so he's quite fit now."

The steed huffed out a breath of contentment with his touch.

"I can see you did a wonderful job taking care of him."

"Thank you, Violet. I tried."

"Shall we go for our ride now?"

"We shall. May I help you onto the saddle?"

"Please," she said, holding her arms up.

Christopher didn't hesitate to step into her, feeling her hands rest onto his shoulders when he grasped her waist. "Don't worry. I'll have no trouble lifting you into place."

She didn't reply, but she did wet her lips as she nodded. The sight made his fingers curl tighter into the bodice of her dress. He forced himself to lift her away from him, placing her on the steed's back near the horn of the seat. He undid the button of his navy jacket for easier movement before hooking his boot into the stirrup and pulling himself up to sit behind her.

This saddle was longer than most, but it still urged them quite close together. Violet sat sideways, her hip now pressed firmly between his thighs. She shifted herself the moment he settled.

"Are you comfortable?" Christopher asked, reaching for her waist to steady her. "I know we don't have much room up here together."

"Yes, it's, um...it's good. It's so very, very good."

He grinned while he grasped the horse's reins and pulled them around either side of her. "Then I suppose we should be off on our adventure."

With a gentle snap of the reins, he started the horse toward the woods. Violet squealed with the first shift of movement, trembling despite the fact that his arms formed a secure cage around her body. Or perhaps because of it.

He bent his head to press his lips to her hair. "I've got you. But you can always put your arms around me, if it makes you feel safer."

"Thank you," she said, immediately wrapping one arm around his back and setting the other on his chest. She rested her hand over his heart, spreading her fingers out over his shirt. Her tender touch made his pulse bound.

Christopher took a deep breath, filling his lungs with her sweet cream and honeysuckle. He had to close his eyes, just for a moment, to accustom himself to the delightful yet dangerous feel of her body pressed to his. Not that this was the first time she'd been so close to him – far from it. Honestly, Violet always felt close to him now, especially when they were in the gazebo and she allowed him to rest his head on her lap.

She'd offered him her lap many times since that first time. Some days, he would lay his head on her skirts and fall fast asleep. Other days, he would rest his head on her thighs and gaze up at her face, watching as she spoke to him of many things, gifting him with a view into her marvelous mind. In those perfect moments, he'd had to work like hell to witness the movement of her lips without succumbing to his overwhelming urge to kiss her.

Reopening his eyes now, Christopher made sure his horse walked well onto the path through the woods. As the overhanging boughs enveloped them, dimming the sunlight through the branches and shrouding them in peaceful silence, he tightened his hold on the reins. He told himself to not look down at the woman in his arms, fearing his body's reaction to her proximity. But alas, he could not prevent his curiosity. He allowed himself a glance, which was a terrible mistake.

Violet stared blatantly at his chest, to where her fingers rested on his shirt, her eyes glassed over as if she'd had one too many cups of rum. Her breaths came in short, staccato pants, betraying her indelicate thoughts. Christopher tried very hard not to notice how the unsteadiness of her inhalations, coupled with the steady movements of his steed, made the flesh of her breasts bounce above her bodice. He failed miserably.

Her hand slipped over his clothing as the horse carried them forward. At first, he believed the shifting of her fingers involuntary. But then they moved more purposefully, her inquisitive touch stirring his body to life.

While he guided the steed along the dirt path through the trees, Violet's hand roamed across his chest, becoming bolder as the minutes passed. Her fingers dipped into the outlines of his muscles, tracing the definitions through the fabric of his shirt. Christopher stiffened, fearful she might discover the scars carved into his flesh, yet she focused solely on his hardened shape. He figured the thickness of his shirt hid his imperfections – or she simply wasn't concerned with his imperfections – so he allowed his tension to ease, giving himself permission to enjoy her deliberate and intoxicating exploration.

As Violet memorized the ridges of his chest with her fingers, she moistened her lips. He could barely repress a groan while watching the slow, steady movement of her perfect pink tongue against her mouth.

"You...you are also quite fit," she finally managed to say. "Just like your horse. Perhaps even more so, I think."

Christopher worked to focus. "That is because I exercise myself even more than I exercise my horse. Everything does better with exercise."

She gazed up at him beneath heavy eyelids. "And do you plan to exercise me also, Christopher? After we're married?"

His brow shot up with her question. He fully expected her to tense in anxiety and withdraw her words in a rambling fit of mortification. But she didn't. Violet merely sat with her chest pressed recklessly onto his and her gaze drifting lazily between his eyes and his lips.

He didn't know how to answer such a question, so he decided to simply speak the truth. "You have no idea of the things I plan for us to do once we're married, Violet."

She released a shaky laugh. "Oh, well, I...I suppose I cannot possibly know, can I? But I'm happy to rely on you to teach me." Then she grinned, and it was gorgeous, and he had to tear his eyes away from her to focus on the path.

Violet leaned fully against him, resting her head on his shoulder, even if her body remained constrained by her rigid corset. "Mmm. I enjoy riding with you," she hummed, her warm breath brushing over his neck.

Christopher cleared his throat. "I'm glad."

"However, I should probably admit that I am rather accomplished at riding a horse. I could certainly have ridden beside you on another steed."

"I see. Perhaps we'll do that next time."

"Or perhaps not," she amended. "I like this form of travel very much."

He chuckled with her admission, until she wrapped both her hands entirely around his back, linking her fingers together over his spine. His laughter dimmed in lieu of the pounding of his heart. Christopher brought his arms in closer, encasing her as securely as possible while maintaining his hold on the reins.

She kept herself wrapped around him even when the horse stepped out of the woods and into the vast green field beyond. Sunlight streamed down on them again, but she just tucked her face further into his neck, not looking at all where they were going. Eventually, they arrived at their destination and Christopher pulled the horse to a stop. He dropped the reins to move his hands to Violet's back.

"We're here, my dearest."

"Mmm. Where?"

"It's a lovely old tree I found the night I went for my horseback ride. I thought we could lay a blanket out beneath it and have a picnic on the grass."

She finally lifted her head from his shoulder, turning her face to see the sheltering elm. "My heavens. This is a wonderful place."

He smiled with her praise, shifting back on the saddle in order to dismount without disturbing her. The instant his feet hit the ground, he reached up to her waist, grasping tight to help her down from the horse. Violet grinned at him when he set her feet on the grass, yet that grin fell the instant he stepped away.

"I only need to spread the blanket out and get the food ready," he explained his absence. "Then we can sit together. Does that sound good?"

Her grin returned. "Sounds perfect to me. May I help you?"

"No, no. I want to do this for you. It's our anniversary, after all."

"That's right, it is. Three whole weeks."

"Three whole weeks," he repeated while reaching into the saddlebags to pull out his treasures. He grasped the blanket first, spreading the thin green fabric out beneath the tree. Violet plopped down onto it, her copious pink skirts billowing out over her legs. She rested back against the tree trunk as he pulled out the sack of food Rodchester had packed for them. "Here are some grapes and finger sandwiches. Oh, and some rum."

"Rum?" she questioned when he set the flask on the blanket.

"Yes. Do you not like it?"

"I like it fine, actually. I just get a bit tipsy if I drink too much."

Christopher chuckled. "Then don't drink too much, or I will certainly find myself in trouble with Lady Wilmington."

"I suppose we can't have that, can we?"

"No, we cannot," he confirmed, turning his back as he removed the last few items from the bag. "I've brought something else to help us celebrate today, Violet. Something I truly hope you'll enjoy."

"What have you brought?"

"Books," he announced, feeling giddy as a schoolboy while turning to place two volumes in her grasping fingers.

"Goodness, Christopher. I absolutely love books."

"I know you do. You told me so the first night we met. I also remember asking you to read to me, which we have never gotten to do before now."

"Oh, well," she hesitated, setting the books down beside her, "I would love to read to you, but I would need..."

"Your spectacles?"

"Unfortunately, yes."

His chest puffed with pride as he reached into his jacket pocket, pulled out the wire-rimmed glass lenses, and handed them to her.

Violet's lips parted. "But, how did you..."

"Gwen acquired them for me."

"Really? Are you telling me you charmed my aunt into letting us take a horseback ride *and* charmed my sister into giving you my spectacles?"

"I am. I did."

She gazed up at him from the blanket. "Those are very dashing accomplishments, future husband. Your sisters would be impressed."

Christopher locked her eyes with his. "As long as you are impressed, future wife, that is all that matters to me."

"Oh, I am most impressed. I am also beyond thrilled, for I can honestly say I've never looked forward to the future more than I do right now."

"I understand that sentiment all too well," he admitted. Then he stared at her, engrossed by the simple shifting of her body as she breathed, for a blissful eternity. His anticipation of hearing her read to him finally broke him from his trance. "Violet, do you mind if I take off my jacket and boots, to be a bit more comfortable for our picnic?"

She stretched her legs out on the blanket, the tips of her laced suede shoes peeking out beneath her skirts. "I don't mind at all," she said, placing her spectacles on the books before resting back on the tree trunk to observe him.

Violet popped a few grapes into her mouth as Christopher shrugged off his coat and pulled off his boots. He swore he heard her hum in approval at the sight of him undressing, which made him smile rather wickedly when he sat down beside her wearing only his white shirt and tan breeches. Reaching for the flask, he took a swig of rum before holding it out to her. "Would you like some?"

"I would."

She took the flask to her mouth and tipped it back, the long column of her throat shifting with several lengthy swallows. He observed her in curiosity when she handed the silver container back to him, since her cheeks were now flushed and her lips pressed together in a firm line. It appeared as if she were fortifying herself to say something very bold. A moment later, he discovered what that was.

"Christopher, can I...can I remove my boots as well?"

"You wish to remove your boots?"

"Yes. I want to be comfortable, too. Is that all right?"

"Certainly. Far be it for me to say you cannot be comfortable."

"That is very kind," she offered. "Thank you."

Violet bent forward to reach for her shoes. However, the stiffness of her corset made it impossible for her to lean over entirely. The more she tried, the more her flesh strained against the top of her bodice, giving him the disastrous concern of having to watch her breasts pop fully out of her dress. It would be a sight he'd not recover from anytime soon.

"Um, Violet. It appears you are having difficulty reaching your boots."

She slumped back onto the tree trunk, her hands falling on the blanket beside her. "Oh, you have no idea. These corsets are like cages. My sister normally takes my shoes off for me."

Christopher didn't hesitate to speak his next words, although he probably should have. "I can certainly help, if you'd like."

"You'll take my shoes off for me?"

"If you want me to, I will."

"Yes. Please."

He didn't miss the glow of excitement in her eyes. For a brief moment, he wondered if she'd made a show of difficulty with removing her boots just so he would offer his assistance. In the next moment, he decided he didn't care.

She'd afforded him a perfect excuse to touch her, and for that he felt grateful beyond measure.

Shifting his body toward her feet, he sat on the lower edge of the blanket to face her. He straightened his spine in a display of formality, attempting to convince them both that his desire to remove her shoes had nothing at all to do with his desire to remove every last stitch of her clothing. Violet sighed when his fingers reached for the laces of her boot.

Christopher pulled on the strings slowly, enjoying the action much more than he should. He tried not to fantasize that these laces were actually on the back of her corset. He tried not to imagine how undoing the ties on that corset would reveal the line of her spine, from her shoulders all the way down to her bottom. He tried like hell not to dwell on the thought of how stunningly soft her skin would feel when he ran his calloused fingertips over the length of her bare back for the first time.

The moment he finished loosening the strings, he steadied himself with a steep inhale. He had to circle Violet's calf with his hand now, in order to remove the boot, which meant curling his fingers around her thin stocking. It also meant enduring the sound of the tender gasp that would escape her lips with that touch.

He circled her calf with his hand. The ensuing gasp that escaped her lips came out more like a groan. Christopher cursed beneath his breath.

Once he'd removed her shoe and placed it on the grass beside the blanket, his gaze drifted to the cream-colored stocking covering her foot. He licked his dry lips as he stared at the teasing glimpse of what she wore beneath her skirts, urging his mind to concentrate on the task at hand. Repeating each of the motions on the next shoe – from the untying of her laces to the circling of her calf – was nearly torture. As soon as he finished the onerous task, he returned Violet's feet to the blanket and began to shift away, retreating solely for the sake of safety.

She stopped his escape with a breathy inquiry. "Um, Christopher?"

He forced himself to look back to her face. "Yes, Violet?"

"Will you take off my stockings now?"

"Dear God. You want me to remove your stockings, too?"

"Please."

"But aren't they the kind that go all the way up above your knee?"

"Yes, they are. They do."

"And you...you want me to remove them entirely?"

"If you would be so kind. I would love the freedom to wiggle my toes."

Christopher barely heard her words over the blood rushing through his ears, yet he still didn't hesitate. "Well, if that is your desire, then I suppose I've no choice but to oblige you. As it would be the gentlemanly thing to do."

"W-wonderful," she said, her quaver betraying her bold request.

He watched her bravado falter further as he reached back to her, sliding his fingers over her thin stocking from her toes up to her ankle. He refused to dwell on the perfection of her warmth and softness, since he needed to ensure his betrothed could manage this sort of contact. Violet's lashes fluttered when he curled both his hands around one of her ankles. She trembled when he situated his body closer, so he made certain to move slowly while drawing her foot over to rest against his thigh.

Christopher searched her eyes as his fingers wandered further beneath her skirts, moving gradually up her calf. He took great care to ensure the hem of her skirt remained down, so as not to reveal any of her skin, while his heated palms forged a steady upward path. He studied her the entire time, making certain his touch did not disturb her.

Despite his best efforts, his touch did disturb her – quite apparently. Violet stared hard into his eyes, appearing to not take a single breath. She hardly moved at all until his fingertips skimmed across her knee, causing her to giggle. He couldn't help but take pride in discovering this ticklish spot. He wanted to spend the next several hours right here, skimming his fingers over her sensitive skin and drinking in her laughter. Unfortunately, he knew he must complete the task at hand as quickly as possible, for both their sakes.

Pushing past that tempting place, Christopher reached up to where the edge of her stocking rested above her knee. The instant his roughened fingertips came into contact with the bare flesh of her thigh, a flash of desire shot down his spine. And once his besieged mind realized what this contact meant, his jaw clenched.

"Good Lord, Violet," he growled through gritted teeth.

"Is – is something wrong?"

"Yes, something is definitely wrong. You are not wearing knickers."

"You can tell that?"

"I most certainly can. Knickers come below the knee and I feel nothing here but your soft, flawless skin."

"Thank you for the compliment. And you're right; I have no knickers on."

"You're welcome. But why on earth are you not wearing knickers?"

"Because I do not care for them, as they are scratchy and irritating. Also, my mother told me all ladies must wear them when I was but twelve years old and first moved to Pennyshire. At the time, in my rebellious London state, I refused. And I still refuse, to this very day."

"Bloody hell. Are you telling me that every time I've laid my head in your lap these past days, you've had no knickers on beneath your skirts?"

"That is correct."

A strangled noise left Christopher's throat, like that of a cornered beast fighting for survival. "So, you never wear knickers?"

"No, I do not. Except for..."

"Except for when?"

"Well, it's just..." Violet's words trailed as her cheeks flushed. "I have to wear them when I have my monthly woman's time, for obvious reasons. And I honestly cannot believe I just spoke to you about that."

He cocked his head. "Why would you not speak to me about that?"

"Because I've never spoken to a man about such a thing. Never, ever. Since it is terribly untoward and severely embarrassing."

"You do not need to be embarrassed with me, I assure you. I grew up in a house full of women and am well aware of the process. Besides, becoming husband and wife means we'll need to discuss many things. The fact that you bleed each month is a reassurance that your body is fertile, and I believe your ability to bear children is something that could please us both one day."

"Yes, that certainly will please me," she said with her sky-blue eyes lit as bright as the sun. "I will be so happy to bear your children."

Violet smiled gloriously when she finished speaking. Christopher merely sat and basked in her joy, allowing himself to imagine the child they would have. He saw a little girl with soft blond curls and big blue eyes, staring up at him with this same smile on her lips. Perhaps their daughter would be just as brilliant as her mother. Perhaps she would fold her arms across her chest, and pout her lips, and tell him she would not wear knickers, either.

The desire to see that child overcame him, gripping his heart in a vice. His fingers clenched in response, which made Violet whimper as he squeezed tight to her thigh – her very indecently bared thigh. His gaze fell to her skirts, to the outline of his arms beneath the pink fabric. He shook his head, realizing they'd just had an entire conversation about her bearing his children while he'd had both his hands pushed underneath her dress. It was probably the least gentlemanly thing on earth, so he forced his fingers to ease their grip and reminded himself that he was supposed to be removing her stocking, per her request.

He closed his eyes when he gripped the edge of that thin material. A little sigh escaped her lips the instant his skin curled against hers. Violet pushed her thigh more firmly into his fingers, which made his jaw clench so fiercely that he feared breaking his teeth. He began easing the stocking down her leg, foolishly thinking that pulling his hands away from her would lessen the intensity of this moment. He was incredibly wrong. Taking a piece of her clothing off – any piece of clothing – conjured images of her lying naked before him, begging for his touch. It was nothing short of sheer torment.

Christopher shifted away from her in order to remove the rest of the airy fabric. He took a deep breath before reaching back under her skirts to remove the second stocking. Only this time, he didn't allow his fingers to dwell on the smooth flesh of her thigh or to relish the heat of her skin. Much to his dismay, Violet still giggled when his thumb brushed over her knee. The sweet noise she made punched him squarely in the chest.

He hurried to complete the arduous chore while struggling to keep a certain part of his anatomy from rising to the occasion. Once he'd survived his mission, he set her feet back down. "There. Your toes are free to wiggle now," he assured, escaping quickly to the other side of the blanket.

"Hooray," she replied, the word so breathless he almost didn't hear it.

With the unsteady sound of her voice, Christopher looked back to her face. It was yet another mistake, as it forced him to drink in the delicious wetness of the lips she'd obviously been licking. "Goddamnit," he muttered.

"Wh-what was that you said, Christopher?"

"Nothing. It was nothing."

"Oh. Well then, I guess..."

A little squeak escaped her throat.

His body stilled. "Violet, did you just hiccup?"

"Yes, I believe I did."

"Are you tipsy from the rum right now?"

"No, no, of course not. I assure you I am in complete control of all my faculties," she promised with a toothy grin.

He chuckled. "If you say so."

"I do. And now I suppose that I, um, that I think I should probably read to you. Would you like for me to read to you?"

"Well, I'm certain that is the proper thing for us to do."

"Mm-hmm. Very proper, indeed. However, I wonder if you'd like to lay your head in my lap while I read?"

Christopher's shoulders slumped. He couldn't imagine suffering through that intimacy right now, especially knowing she wore no knickers beneath her skirts. Yet he couldn't imagine refusing, either. "I would very much like to lay my head in your lap. If you'll allow it."

Violet straightened her legs on the blanket, pointing her bare toes to the grass while smoothing over her skirts. "I'm ready for you, Christopher."

He groaned as he ignored all the possible implications of that statement.

Adjusting his body to the edge of the blanket, he lay on his back so he could look up to her face when he rested his head against her thighs. She gazed down at him the moment he'd settled.

"What are the book selections we have to choose from?" he asked, desperate to divert his mind from the lack of knickers beneath him.

"Do you not know which books you brought for us?"

"No, I just asked Rodchester to pull a few selections from the library."

"Oh. Let me see, then," she said, placing her spectacles on the bridge of her nose and pulling the first book up to her eyes. "This one is *Tales of the Grotesque and Arabesque*, by Edgar Allen Poe. My heavens! What is Tildy doing with a collection of this nature?"

Christopher grinned as he looked up to Violet's eyes, their blue shining even brighter behind the glass lenses. "Perhaps your aunt has a dark side we do not know about."

Violet laughed. "I highly doubt that. And I hope our other selection will be lighter than this one." Placing Poe's stories down, she lifted the next book.

"What is it?" Christopher asked when her lips curved into a smile.

"It is Shakespeare. The complete sonnets."

"Well, I believe we should definitely choose those, don't you think?"

"Absolutely. Sonnets are much more fitting for an anniversary celebration," she agreed, opening the volume with one hand while her other hand drifted into his hair. "Although I find it amusing that Mr. Rodchester would give us two such different works to choose from."

"Perhaps he wanted us to decide if we are either enraged or elated by the arrangement we find ourselves in," Christopher considered, his eyes closing with the soothing touch of her fingers against his scalp.

"Goodness, there is no question of that. We are deliriously elated," Violet stated, the forcefulness of her words drawing his gaze back to hers. He watched as a hint of doubt darkened her eyes. "What I mean to say is that *I* am deliriously elated, at least."

Reaching up to ease her hand from his hair, Christopher threaded their fingers together and urged them down to press her palm against his heart. "You must know that I feel the same as you do, Violet."

She rewarded him with a giddy smile. Her gaze wandered over his face, soaking in the honesty he knew was written all over him. Eventually, she nodded, turned her eyes back to the book, and began reading.

Christopher held her arm against his chest as she spoke, listening intently to each word. Sadly, the more she read, the harder he found it to concentrate. Violet's lips were just so pink and full and lush, and he'd never wanted to kiss her more than he did right now. Which spoke a great deal about his current desire, since he'd wanted to kiss her from the very first moment he saw her.

You're not allowed to kiss her lips yet, he reminded himself, even though that truth was painful beyond measure. *However, you have both agreed to hand kissing. Therefore, you can kiss her hand all you wish.*

Christopher grinned as he tugged her fingers up to his mouth and pressed his lips to the back of her hand. He kissed her in a very gentlemanly way, as he always had before, which didn't cause Violet to skip a single beat in her reading. Her attentiveness to the written word bothered him far more than was respectable. After all, he shouldn't desire to have an illicit effect on her senses – not until they were married, at least. Yet he still couldn't resist the urge to make her gasp, so he pushed his mouth harder against her, scraping the stubble of his beard across her skin.

"Oh," she said, pausing right in the middle of a verse. She took a second to catch her breath. But then she merely returned to her reading, as if he'd done nothing untoward.

Christopher scrunched his forehead when her words continued. He stared up at her, watching her eyes shift over the page and realizing just how much the sonnets captivated her. He honestly found her concentration quite irksome, since he didn't wish to share her attentions with some book. He wanted her attentions all to himself.

God, you're being an idiot. These are the thoughts of a child.

Still, that realization wasn't enough to stop him from goading her further. He surged forward, pressing another deliberate kiss on the back of her hand. Then another, and another. He didn't even stay in one place. He moved higher each time, easing his mouth slowly up her arm. Which he knew was wrong, because he was only allowed to kiss her hand.

But her arm is a part of her hand. Or, at the very least, it is an extension of her hand. Consequently, I should think I have the right to continue.

Christopher continued. Violet read without fail while he kissed his way tenderly yet purposefully up her forearm, but he did not miss the impact of his actions – the change in her breathing, the tremble in her voice, the shifting of her thighs beneath his head – which were all grand reactions to his rather lurid taunts. But he desired even more of a response, so he pressed his chin down to pink her skin with the coarseness of his stubble.

Violet whimpered in between her words. When Christopher's mouth reached her elbow, she finally ceased reading. She huffed out a breath, set the book onto his chest, and stared at him.

He stilled, pulling his lips from her skin to look up to her face. "Why did you stop?" he questioned, attempting a look of pure innocence.

"Because you do not seem interested in listening."

"Oh, no. That's not true at all. I love listening to you."

"You do?"

"Absolutely," he stated, tightening his fingers in hers. "When I hear your voice, I know that everything is right with the world."

She smiled down at him. "You want me to keep going?"

"I do. Very much."

"Then shall I move on to sonnet eighteen? It is one of my favorites."

"Yes, I would like that. Please."

She kept smiling while glancing back to the page, until Christopher lifted her fingers to his mouth and placed another kiss on the back of her hand. Violet bit down hard on her lip before reading. "'Shall I compare thee to a summer's day? Thou art more lovely and more temperate.'"

He stared at the marks her teeth left on her mouth. Damn, that sight was terribly unfair. It was too tempting, too torturous, since he still could not kiss her there. But he had to kiss something of her. Something...a little different.

Disentangling their fingers, he took her hand in both of his and turned it over to face her palm up. He encircled her wrist to feel her pulse, pleased by the fact that the blood bounding through her veins matched the wild cadence of his own. Christopher pressed his mouth directly into her palm. He took his time covering that surface in tender kisses, humming deeply with the sensation of this new, unexplored part of her body.

Violet cleared her throat. "'R-rough winds do shake the darling...'"

He kept going, slipping his mouth across her palm all the way to the end of one finger. After pressing his lips firmly to that fingertip, he proceeded to kiss each of them in turn. He worked gently and leisurely, lingering obscenely on each one, in order to savor the feel of her flesh.

"'The...the...d-darling buds of May,'" she fumbled.

He smiled against her skin. Then he nipped at the tip of her thumb.

"Good God, Christopher!"

The force of her voice actually startled him, causing him to drop her hand and bolt upright on the blanket beside her. He adjusted himself over to sit a good distance away. "I'm sorry, Violet. I apologize for..."

"Please don't apologize. You have nothing to be sorry for."

"Oh. Very well," he said, relaxing when he saw the genuine assurance in her eyes. But then he watched her chew another indentation into her lip –

which he tried like hell not to stare at – and shook his head. "Something is wrong, though. I can tell."

Violet set the book of sonnets down before matching his intent gaze. "I wouldn't say anything is wrong."

"Then what is it? I know you have something on your mind."

"You're right; I do. It's just that I…I want to, um…" She paused to run a trembling hand through her hair. "May I kiss you, Christopher?"

His jaw unhinged, rendering him speechless for lengthy seconds, before he could get anything out at all. "You wish to kiss me?"

"Yes. A kiss on the lips, I mean. If that wasn't already obvious."

"You wish to kiss me on the lips?" he repeated, just to make sure he hadn't imagined it.

She heaved out a sigh. "Heavens, yes. I'm terribly curious as to what it will feel like. I mean, I've pecked my mother and sister, so I know what a touch of the lips entails. But I've never kissed a man before, unless you count kissing my father on the cheek. I've certainly never kissed a man I'm so ridiculously attracted to. Honestly, I just want to feel you close to me in this way. I desperately want to know what it feels like to kiss my husband."

Christopher's fingers dug into the blanket. "God, Violet. Please tell me this isn't the rum talking."

"The rum? Oh, no. I'll admit the rum may be giving me more courage than usual, but I've actually wanted to kiss you forever. Well, not *forever* forever, obviously, since we've only known each other for three weeks. But I've definitely wanted to kiss you since that day in the gazebo, when you taught me to swordfight while holding me so tightly against your body. And every day since, I've been hoping you would choose to kiss me first. Yet you never have."

"Well, in my defense, we both decided to stick to hand kissing only."

"I know we did. But I want to change that rule. If you don't mind."

His heart lodged into his throat. "I would love to change it. Unfortunately, as much as I hate to say this, I did assure your aunt that I would remain a gentleman with you today. And the two of us kissing would probably overstep those bounds most egregiously."

Violet's face fell entirely.

Christopher couldn't help but grin. "However," he added, "since you asked to kiss me in such a kind and polite manner, I think it would be even more ungentlemanly of me to refuse your request."

Her eyes filled with hope. "Yes, I believe that's true. It would be most ungentlemanly to refuse, wouldn't it? Therefore, I think you should definitely let me kiss you."

He nodded. "Yes. Definitely."

She paused to stare at him, as if she wasn't certain they'd actually decided to do this. Slowly and carefully, she scooted closer to him on the blanket while her gaze shifted to his mouth. She concentrated hard on his lips, causing Christopher to hold his breath when she came to sit mere inches before him.

Just as Violet started to lean forward, she jumped back and startled them both. "Wait! I almost forgot about these," she yelped, pulling her spectacles from her face.

"You can leave them on, if that would be better for you."

"Really? Are you sure they would be to your liking?"

"I like everything about you," he confessed. His compliment lit her eyes further, and Christopher would have lauded himself for the stylish praise, except that he'd merely spoken the truth.

"Well, I think I'd rather my spectacles be off. If that's all right."

"It is entirely all right. This is whatever you want it to be."

Violet smiled with his assurance, folding up the wire rims and placing the lenses on the book beside her. She lifted her gaze back to his and began moving toward him again. Christopher forced himself to remain still as a statue, keeping his arms firmly at his sides, until he could feel her warm breath against his face. He closed his eyes, drinking in that sweet cream and honeysuckle scent he knew so well, and waited in eager anticipation.

Violet pressed her lips to his. The kiss was short, tender, and lovely. He knew he shouldn't want for anything more than this moment, with her mouth sealed softly onto his, however briefly. But the instant she eased away, he had to fist his hands to keep from lunging for her.

He opened his eyes immediately to gauge her reaction. Her eyes remained shut for some time, her face softened as if she were in the midst of a daydream. When she finally lifted her weighty gaze back to him, he swallowed hard.

"How was that, Violet? Everything all right?"

She nodded. "Yes. That was...yes."

"Then can I kiss you now?" he asked before he could stop himself, even though he knew full well the risk he took.

She fidgeted with the blanket beneath her. "Well, it's, um, good. I mean, I think it would only be fair to grant your request, since you allowed me the same kindness. Therefore, I believe you should...you should absolutely kiss me."

"Absolutely," he agreed.

He waited through many beats of his overly rapid pulse to see if she would rethink the situation and rescind her invitation. Mercifully, she did not. Her intent gaze darted between his eyes and his mouth as Christopher shifted toward her. He observed her closely, making sure she didn't appear hesitant or afraid, satisfied when he saw only excitement and anticipation.

He reached for her then. He grasped her face with both hands, cradling her cheeks in his palms in order to steady her. And to steady himself.

Violet gripped onto him, curling her fingers around his forearms as she closed her eyes and stilled her body. She waited with only tiny pants escaping her throat. Slowly and gently, Christopher slipped his mouth onto hers.

Warmth and pleasure engulfed him the moment her full lips melded with his. He breathed in deep, happy to drown in her intoxicating scent. He had to remind himself that he intended to keep this kiss chaste – a firmer kiss than hers had been, yet still chaste. But then Violet sighed into him, and the action parted her mouth, and he couldn't help himself. He had to taste her. He simply had to.

Christopher slipped his tongue past her lips, just far enough to touch the tip of her tongue. She tasted like grapes and rum and *her*, and his heart leapt at that carnal knowledge. He pressed his eyelids shut, struggling to keep his hands still against her face. Unfortunately, their wet, heated contact caused Violet to moan quite indecently, and to dig her fingers into his arms, and he forgot himself.

He forgot himself just enough to taste her further, to run his tongue more aggressively over hers. He forgot himself enough to push one of his hands into her hair, and wrap her curls up in his fingers, and hold her exactly the way he wanted her. He forgot himself enough to swallow her next moan, and urge her even closer to him, and shift his mouth over hers, exploring her without thought of recrimination. And it took several long, deliberate, delicious minutes for Christopher to remember himself again.

When he finally pulled back, Violet whimpered in distress. He looked to her face to find her eyes frantically searching his.

"Good God, Christopher. My heart feels like it's going to beat out of my chest. Is that normal?"

"Well, since my heart is doing the exact same thing, I'm going to have to say it is. Although I've never felt anything quite like this."

"Truly?"

"Truly," he admitted.

He let his hands fall back to the blanket, painfully aware of the disappointment in her eyes when they lost contact. He wanted to reach for her again, but before he had the chance, Violet surged forward. She slipped her hands onto his face, her fingers easing up his jaw to run over the stubble on his cheeks.

"Can we do it again?" she whispered. "Please?"

Christopher had never heard a sweeter plea in his life. He found himself unable, and quite unwilling, to refuse. He nodded and Violet sighed.

He didn't wait another second. Grabbing her by the waist, he pulled her to him. Not forcibly enough that she sat in his lap, but powerful enough to press her chest to his. The swell of her breasts strained against his shirt, the sensation eliciting a groan from his throat the instant his lips met hers. He hesitated to deepen the kiss for a moment, making sure she approved of his actions.

Violet definitely approved. She wrapped her arms fully around his neck and pushed her body harder into his. Her eagerness was both encouraging and endearing, but Christopher could tell she was still unsure of her actions. Therefore, he chose to do the exploring for both of them.

He moved his tongue over hers with expert precision, tasting and teasing as he went along. Violet responded in greater fervor with each passing moment. Her breaths came in soft little bursts, her arms tightened around his shoulders, and her fingers threaded greedily into his hair. The next instant, she pulled her legs up to drape over his thighs, curling herself into his embrace.

Christopher's palms flattened against her back when he felt the silk of her dress covering his trousers. The thought of being beneath her skirts heated his flesh in a way he could barely comprehend, making his fingers twitch against the ties that laced over her spine. The urge to pull those ties free, and undress her right here on this blanket, set his body ablaze. He knew she wore no knickers beneath her skirts, and he could sink himself between her legs so easily, and that perfect agony caused him to growl into her mouth. Violet moaned, matching his sinfully needy sounds, opening wider to the exploration of his tongue while pressing her breasts fully to his chest.

Her eager, wanton actions confirmed how deeply and boundlessly his wife desired him. Christopher basked in that knowledge as he continued devouring her mouth. He reveled in the beauty of her yearning, in her undiluted need for his touch, wanting nothing more than to fulfill all of her body's demands.

He wanted to make Violet shiver and sigh in pleasure as he worshiped her with his tongue and fingers. He wanted to slide his bare flesh onto hers, to run his rough lines across her soft curves, to warm every inch of her with his heat. He wanted to bury himself deep inside her, again and again and again, until he felt her come apart beneath him as she screamed his name in pure, raw passion.

Christopher wanted his wife beyond measure, and with the heady feel of her tongue currently tangled with his, those desires overtook him. He clamped his arms around her back and dug his fingers into the stiff boning of her corset, far rougher than intended. The harsh desperation of his touch made her cry out, her anguished noises wrenching his mind back to reality.

He loosened his hungered grip that instant. "I'm – I'm so sorry," he breathed against her lips. "Did I hurt you?"

She shook her head almost violently. "No! Heavens, no. I love having your hands on me. I love it when you hold me so fiercely against you. The way you make me feel is just...it's quite simply...incredible."

Christopher smiled with her generous acceptance. He pressed his mouth to hers again, as softly as he could, before drawing back. "I cannot tell you how pleased I am to hear that."

Violet stared into him with a million questions swimming in her eyes. The brief respite allowed him much needed time to calm his consuming desires. Then the most marvelous thing happened: she kissed him. It was only a simple press of her lips to his – but it wasn't shy or tentative at all – and his insides warmed with her ease in their newfound intimacy.

"Mmm," she murmured as she eased away. "Will it be our rule now that we can kiss whenever we want?"

"I should think so. As long as that sounds good to you."

"Oh, yes. Most definitely. I actually want to do this all day. Do you think we can stay right here and kiss for the entire day?"

He chuckled, tracing his hand up her spine to curl his fingers into her hair. "As much as I treasure that offer, I do believe we would eventually be missed. At which point, Lady Wilmington might decide I'm a horrid lothario and finally send the hounds after me."

"Well, I imagine it will take her some time to reach such a conclusion. Therefore, I think we can stay here and kiss for a little while, at least."

Christopher tightened his grip on his wife's body. "That sounds like a perfect plan to me," he said, just before claiming her mouth again.

RODCHESTER AWAITED THEM, just as promised, when they returned to the stables. Christopher dismounted from his steed, his body already yearning for Violet's warmth as soon as they were parted. He reached up to help her from the saddle, gathering her hand the instant her feet hit the ground.

"Thank you for everything you packed for us today, Mr. Rodchester," she offered the caretaker. "And just so you know, we chose to read the sonnets."

The elderly man smiled at her. "Very good, Miss Violet."

She giggled, the sound of her joy settling deep in Christopher's chest. He tugged her closer to his body as he guided them back to the Wilmington manor. Once they walked through the front door and into the grand foyer, his footsteps stopped altogether.

Violet turned to search his eyes. "Is everything all right, Christopher?"

He drew his fingers down the side of her face. "Everything is perfect. Except I don't wish to leave you, no matter how much time we've had today."

"I don't wish to leave you, either," she sighed. "But I do need to change clothes for dinner, as I must look a fright after our horseback ride."

"You look more gorgeous now than ever before. I promise you."

Violet beamed up at him. "Thank you for that. And thank you for all my surprises today. For the celebration of our anniversary, for the picnic, for the books, for taking my shoes and stockings off, and for putting them back on again. And, of course, for all the kissing."

"You are most welcome. Although I should confess something to you."

"What is that?"

"I have wanted to kiss you from the very first moment I saw you, standing here in this foyer."

"Truly?"

"Truly."

"Then have you been waiting all this time for me to ask you for a kiss?"

"I have, actually."

"I see," she considered, her gaze falling to his chest before dragging slowly back to his face. "In that case, will you grant me a favor?"

"Anything at all."

Her eyelids fell to half-mast. "Please do not ever wait for me to request things of that nature again, Christopher. For I am terrified of missing out on some incredible sensation you could make me feel, simply because I do not know enough to ask you for it."

With her perfectly scandalous plea, a roguish smile curved his lips. "Then I promise to keep you informed, from this moment on, of every sensation you might want me to provide."

She whimpered with his vow. Arching up on her toes, Violet pressed a quick kiss to his lips before turning away. "I'll see you at dinner," she sang over her shoulder as she hastened up the staircase.

Christopher watched her ascend until she vanished around the corner of the upper hallway. He stood, lingering in place, desperate to hold onto this feeling. He didn't want to be without her, not even for the few hours left before dinner, and wondered how indecent it would appear if he simply remained in the foyer to wait until she returned.

He shook his head as he loitered, silently admitting his amazement with his current situation. If anyone had told him a year ago that he would be betrothed to such a wondrous woman -- and staring after her with his heart this open and raw -- he would have assured them they were delusional. Yet here he stood, and he could not deny his yearning. He could not deny his hunger. He could not deny his connection to her. To his Violet. To his wife.

Christopher smiled softly, shifting on his feet as he settled into place. He fully intended to remain in this exact spot for the rest of the afternoon, right up to dinnertime. Until the sound of horse hooves and wooden wheels rumbled in the distance, finally wrenching his attention from the staircase.

Taking the few steps over to the front window of the foyer, he peered out with weary interest at the carriage journeying up to the manor. Two magnificent, mahogany steeds pulled the coach to where Mr. Rodchester waited at the entryway. The moment Christopher could see into the window, he spied a younger man inside.

Rodchester opened the door of the carriage the instant it came to a stop, allowing the visitor to step out onto the gravel path. This new person came dressed in London finery, and was definitely a grown man, yet his face was boyishly handsome and altogether too smiley. Christopher's spine stiffened as Rodchester gave the newcomer a cordial bow and directed him toward the manor with a wave of his hand.

The visitor patted the old caretaker on the shoulder before his lanky legs carried him to the door. As soon as he stepped into the foyer and saw Christopher standing there, he nodded in greeting. "Hello there."

Christopher held his ground. "Hello to you."

The younger man grinned. "It is a beautiful day, is it not?"

"Quite," he agreed. "I am Lord Christopher Kastle, by the way."

"Yes, right. I knew that. You're the heir to the Earl of Nightingale."

"That's correct. And who might you be?"

The boy's fingers twitched beside his finely tailored trousers. "Oh. I'm, um, I'm Welly. Lord Wellington Chaney, if you prefer formality."

Lord Wellington Chaney.

Every nerve ending in Christopher's body caught fire all at once.

This is the heir to the Earl of Centreville. The man Violet rejected as a suitor, who continues to pursue her against her will. The man who caused her to earn the title of Picky Princess. The man who has now pursued her all the way to the Wilmington without her consent.

In this moment, in the face of the person who had done such harm to his wife, Christopher's blood boiled over. He stalked toward the creature, driven by rage alone, his vision blurred in the darkest shades of red.

"What the hell do you mean by coming here, Chaney? Haven't you done Violet's reputation enough harm by pursuing her constantly at her home in Pennyshire? The woman rejected you, man! You need to learn to live with it!"

Lord Chaney stumbled as he backed away, his boyish grin faltering. "No, it's…you don't understand…"

"I understand perfectly!" Christopher bellowed, moving ever forward, unnoticing of the flurry of footsteps on the stairs behind him. "You've come for her again! Despite the fact that she does not want you! And now I shall personally remove you from her life!"

"Christopher!" Violet screeched from the staircase as his fist gripped the collar of Lord Chaney's shirt, his brutal grasp forcing the young man's thin body up against the wall. "Please don't hurt him, Christopher! Please!"

The sound of fear in Violet's voice unsettled him. He hesitated.

A second later, Gwen appeared at Lord Chaney's side, clutching his hand in an effort to pull him away.

Violet rushed to Christopher's other side, her fingers resting over the arm that held the man in place. "Please let him go," she whimpered. "This is truly not what you think it is. Please give me a chance to explain."

With his wife's distraught words, he released the boy's collar. Gwen pulled the offender several feet away, far from Christopher's reach. When Violet wrapped her hand around his fist, he finally met her wide eyes.

His breath caught in his chest, not only with the realization of the fury he'd felt to defend her honor, but with her ability to extract him from those fiery depths with only the sound of her voice. "What is this?" he questioned. "What is going on here?"

She gave him a little smile before glancing to her sister. "Gwen, why don't you and Welly go for a walk in the gardens? It will be lovely. And settling."

Gwen nodded, tugging a still-stunned Lord Chaney with her toward the back of the foyer, maintaining a wide berth around Christopher.

Violet's eyes lifted back to his. "Will you come with me, please?"

"Violet…"

"Please, Christopher. Just come with me."

He sighed, finally releasing his fist to allow her to entwine their fingers. He followed along as Violet led him up the staircase to the double doors leading onto the second-story balcony. Christopher knew this was her late-night perch, where she watched him practice his sword in the darkened gardens, and that realization confused him even further.

"Will you please tell me what is happening?" he begged.

"Wait just a moment," she whispered, urging him toward the railing. "Just wait here with me and watch."

He nearly growled at her, since he didn't want to wait. He wanted Violet to tell him what all of this meant, and it took every bit of his willpower to not demand obedience. But instead of regressing to his old habits, he forced himself to inhale and exhale, staring down at the gardens as she did.

Within moments, Gwen and Lord Chaney emerged on the stone pathway.

Christopher held entirely still, watching the two of them interact. He saw Gwen's fingers curl around the man's sleeve as he pulled her closer to his body. He saw the boyish creature grin down at Gwen and lean in to whisper something in her ear. He saw her giggle wildly in response, beaming up at him as if she'd never heard anything better.

Christopher observed the couple for several minutes, but it didn't take that long to understand the feelings they shared. They acted just like he and Violet did: entwining their bodies and gazing into each other's eyes, every moment they could. That realization hit him like a punch to his gut.

"Oh, sweet hell," he breathed. "They're in love with each other."

Violet rested her head against his shoulder. "Yes. They are."

His mind worked to grasp the multitudinous implications of his discovery. "My God, Violet. Are you telling me that you gave him up for her? You refused Lord Chaney so your sister could be happy?"

"I didn't give him up, really. I didn't own him."

"You know what I mean. Your father picked him for you, not her. You could have demanded him as your husband. You could have had a sturdy marriage to a kind young gentleman of good societal standing. You could have had a simple, easy life."

"But, Christopher...you should have seen the way they looked at each other the first time Welly came to court me. You should have seen how their eyes lit up the moment they met, how Gwen's cheeks turned pink and Welly's fingers trembled. You should have *seen* it."

Violet lifted her head from Christopher's shoulder, looking out to the gardens with a serene smile. He stared hard at the side of her face. "But you let people think the worst of you. You let the gossipers believe you were cold and fickle while Welly continued coming to your home to visit your sister. You let them call you the Picky Princess and didn't say a word in your own defense."

"I couldn't say anything, for I would never risk harming Gwen's chance at happiness," she explained, still looking to the couple walking in the gardens. "Although, I must admit, I didn't know I was going to earn such a terrible title. When Papa spurned me for refusing Welly, it felt like I'd made a rash decision. But now..." Her words trailed off as she lifted her eyes to his.

"Now?" Christopher asked, holding his breath.

"Now that life has led me to you, it feels like the best decision ever."

With her blissful assurance, the air rushed back into his lungs. He reached for Violet's hand, drawing it gently to his mouth to place a kiss on her soft skin. Then he ran the scruff of his chin across her fingers, just a little, to watch her eyes brighten as she giggled.

"You know, Violet, I remember the first time I met your sister. Shortly after you and I said our hellos, she came to stand beside you in the foyer. You looked terrified, and I thought it was because you were nervous about meeting me. But now, I wonder if you were nervous that I would prefer her to you."

Violet flinched. "I – I will admit that the thought crossed my mind."

"Well, I hope you are more certain than ever now of the truth."

"What truth?"

"That I have no eyes for any other woman. I never will."

She gave him a brilliant smile. "Thank you, Christopher. Thank you so much for being you."

"Please don't thank me, for I am in awe of your generosity already. I can hardly believe you gave up everything for your sister's happiness."

"I think you give me too much credit."

"I think you deserve more credit than I can give. If I had been even half the sibling to my sisters as you are to yours, all our lives would have been better."

Her forehead crinkled. "I don't understand. What would you have done differently?"

Christopher tensed with her query. "If I'd been a better brother, I would never have taken the coward's way out and run off to join the Royal Navy."

"The coward's way out? How can you say this of yourself? You joined the Royal Navy to serve God and Country."

"No, I didn't. I joined to get away from my lush of a father, and the memory of my lost mother, and the needs of seven younger siblings."

Violet turned fully toward him. She slipped her hand onto his face, searching his eyes in earnest. "I can see you punish yourself for that decision."

"Yes, I do punish myself. As I should."

She traced her fingers down his neck and onto his chest, her palm coming to rest over his heart. "I'm afraid I cannot agree with you on that. But even if I did, I would say five years lost at sea was more than enough punishment to endure. Don't you think?"

Christopher huffed out a laugh. "I – I suppose. Perhaps."

"Then perhaps you can forgive yourself for making that mistake. Perhaps you can free your burdened mind and allow happiness into your life again."

He rested his fingers over hers, pressing her palm more firmly onto his heart. "Don't you see, my dearest? I've already allowed happiness into my life again. By being with you."

"Good," she said, awarding him with yet another luminous smile. "You make me happy, too, you know. So very, very happy."

Christopher kissed her then, because he had to. Because kissing her was something he could do now, and something he never wanted to stop doing, ever. Violet responded instantly to the touch of his lips, shifting her body closer, and he had to use all his strength to keep this chaste. He wanted to make sure she knew this kiss was a sign of reverence and gratitude. Not that he didn't wish beyond reason to kiss her in other ways – in deep and passionate and desirous ways – but just not right now. Not until the time and place were exactly what they needed to be.

When their lips eventually parted, he rested his forehead against hers. "I don't know what I ever did to deserve you, Violet. But I thank God for it, every day."

With his words, her hand curled up over his heart. "My husband," she breathed, the title warming every part of his body, inside and out.

VIOLET WASN'T sure how long she and Christopher stood in silence on the balcony with their bodies pressed so closely together. She couldn't be bothered to concern herself with the passage of time right now. Not when she wished nothing more than to remain with this man, anytime and anywhere, for the rest of her days.

When Welly and Gwen finally returned from their walk, passing beneath the balcony where Violet and Christopher stood, Violet huffed. "I suppose we should go speak to them," she sighed, pulling back to see her husband's face.

He gave her a soft smile as he leaned down for yet another kiss. The moment their mouths fused, she felt that bizarrely flawless buzzing sensation in her chest again. It didn't seem to matter that this kiss was nowhere near as passionate as the ones they'd shared out in the field earlier today. Each time Christopher's lips met hers, her entire being responded to him, infinitely and intoxicatingly. Violet hoped these feelings were normal, although she didn't exactly care if they weren't.

"I suppose we should," he admitted when the kiss ended. "I do believe I owe Lord Chaney an apology for my foul behavior today."

"Well, in your defense, you thought you were protecting my honor. And I do greatly appreciate that sentiment."

Christopher gathered her hand in his, wrapping it around the sleeve of his coat. "I would do anything for you, my dearest."

Her mouth fell open with those words, spoken so nonchalantly, as he guided her off of the balcony and down the hall. She had to concentrate solely on putting one foot in front of the other just to make it down the staircase without tripping over her own tongue.

Gwen and Welly stood by the main window, speaking in hushed tones.

"Is everything well with you two?" Violet asked as she and Christopher spanned the foyer floor.

Her sister turned to her with bright eyes. "Everything is grand. Truly."

"Wonderful."

Christopher pulled Violet closer to his body before clearing his throat. "I would like to take this opportunity to apologize to you, Lord Chaney."

Welly's brow quirked. "Oh, well. There's no need, really."

"Yes, there is a need. I should not have acted toward you with such ferocity. My only excuse is that I was not fully informed of the situation."

"And now you are informed?" Gwen questioned, her eyes shifting from Christopher to Violet.

"Yes, now he is," Violet answered.

Gwen nodded. "I'm glad to hear that, because Welly came here today to announce a ball being held at the Chaney estate in Centreville next week."

Violet dug her fingers into Christopher's arm. "A...a ball?"

"Yes," Welly confirmed. "It should be a grand affair and I wish you all to attend. Actually, Lord Kastle, I would love to extend an invitation to your whole family, if that is agreeable to you."

"That is a most gracious offer," Christopher accepted. "I'm certain my sisters would jump at the chance to dance at such an affair."

"That's perfect, then. It is all settled."

Gwen turned to Welly. "Do you mind if I speak alone with Violet?"

"I don't mind at all."

She walked over to Violet. "May I borrow my sister, Christopher?"

"Certainly," he replied, loosening his arm to release her.

Violet didn't particularly want to be away from him, but she still managed to smile as Gwen pulled her from the foyer. She looked back only once, to see Welly's face fall the moment he stood alone with Christopher.

"I, um, I think I'll wait outside for Gwen," Welly fumbled.

Christopher nodded just before the other man escaped through the front door. He stepped to the main window to look out over the Wilmington entryway. Violet watched him as long as she could, until her sister tugged her around a corner and into the back hallway. Once they were out of earshot, she refocused her attentions.

"All right, Gwen. What do you wish to speak with me about?"

Gwen grasped her hands. "Oh, Violet, please do not be cross with me."

"Why on earth would I be cross with you?"

"Because after I received that letter from Welly, saying how much he missed me, I wrote to Mama and Papa. I told them you and Christopher were enthralled with one another and would desire to wed without question."

"Oh. I see. Well, that is actually true, so why should I be cross about it?"

Gwen grimaced. "Because I did it for selfish reasons. I wanted Papa to allow Welly and I to wed right away. And I...I got my wish."

Violet's brow shot to her hairline. "What? What are you saying? Will Papa allow you and Welly to wed now?"

"Yes! Welly went to him and begged him to allow us to be together and Papa actually agreed! We are going to announce our engagement at the ball!"

"Oh, God, that's wonderful!" Violet squealed, grabbing her sister and pulling her into her embrace. "I'm so happy for you! For you both!"

"Thank you, Violet. For everything. I owe you all my happiness."

"No, you don't," she insisted as she pulled back, swiping a tear of joy from her eye. "You just owe it to yourself to be happy."

Gwen grinned at her for another moment before her face fell. "But there is something else to consider."

"What is that?"

"The ball is in just a week and I must prepare ahead of time. Welly has offered to take me back to Pennyshire today, so Mama and I can plan for a gown to be made. Which means I must leave you alone with Christopher."

Violet stared at her sister as the words swirled in her brain. *Alone with Christopher.* "Well, that...that is fine. Do not concern yourself with me."

"But I promised to remain with you throughout your courtship."

"Circumstances change, dear sister, and these are wonderful circumstances to find ourselves in. I insist you go home to prepare for the night of your big announcement. I also insist you do not worry over anything, especially not me. I shall be fine here with my husband. I mean, my future husband."

Gwen searched her eyes. "You're certain?"

"Quite certain."

"Oh, goodness!" Gwen exclaimed, breaking into nervous giggles. "I have to go inform Aunt Tildy now! Please wish me luck in my endeavor!"

"I wish you all the luck in the world," Violet answered, smiling as Gwen pecked her on the cheek and scurried away to dash up the staircase.

Violet's smile sank as she stared after her sister. Her heart lodged into her throat while she stepped back into the foyer to see the man who waited for her by the window. *Alone with Christopher. You'll be alone with him from now on. And there is going to be a ball. In just one week.*

She shivered as she walked back to him. Some of her shivers were in anticipation of the time they would be able to spend with just each other. But some shivers were in fear – fear she could not control at this moment.

Christopher turned to her. "Violet? Is something wrong?"

"Not really," she answered when she came to a stop before him.

He skimmed his hands down her arms. "But you're trembling."

"I suppose I just have a lot of information to absorb."

"Like what?"

"Like my father has agreed to allow Gwen and Welly to wed, and they shall announce their engagement the night of the Centreville ball."

Christopher stilled. "I see. Does that news sit well with you?"

"Of course. I'm thrilled for her, for them both. She leaves tonight, actually. Welly is taking her back to Pennyshire to prepare."

"Oh," Christopher said, dropping his arms to his sides. "Then are you trembling because you are concerned Gwen will not be here to chaperone us, and you will be alone with me more often than not? If that is the case, rest assured you do not have to worry. For I will still remain a gentleman with you, and I will..."

"Christopher. That is not why I'm trembling."

"You do not fear having so much time alone with me?"

"Goodness, no. I never fear being alone with you. Honestly, I crave time alone with you. Much more than is proper, I know."

A smile spread his lips. "Thank God, because I feel just the same."

She attempted to smile in return, although it didn't work entirely.

His head tilted. "If you are not concerned about a lack of chaperoning, Violet, then what are you concerned about?"

Worrying her hands together in front of her stomach, she forced a deep breath. "It's just...it's the ball. I haven't been out in society in such a long time and I don't particularly wish to return to it. I don't want to hear the whispered remarks behind my back. The moment we step into that ballroom, I will be the Picky Princess of Pennyshire again. And honestly, I've so enjoyed being here with you, away from all that gossip."

Christopher gathered her hands inside his. "You know, you'll be with me at the ball. I'm sure the gossipers will want to talk about the broken sailor who was lost at sea for five years, much more than they'll want to talk about the fickle princess."

She huffed. "That does not make me feel any better."

He stepped closer. "Violet, listen to me, please. We can do this."

"Do you really think so?"

"I know so. After all, you and I are going to be with each other from here on out. The people of society will have to learn to accept that fact, since I plan for us to be married all our lives and have many children who will hopefully be proud to carry the Nightingale title. I see a bright and glorious future ahead of us, therefore I know we can go to this ball together and show all those people just how happy we are to have found each other."

"God, Christopher, I am happy. I'm so very happy with you."

"Well, then. I have heard that happiness is the best revenge."

"I suppose it is," she considered, feeling her smile return. Violet squeezed onto his fingers and threw her shoulders back. "You're right. We can do this. We'll take them all on together."

"Together," he agreed, leaning in to press a kiss of promise to her lips.

CHAPTER 7

On Stage

Violet stared at her reflection as she sat in front of the vanity in her bedchamber. Birdie – the handmaid Aunt Tildy assigned when Gwen left for Pennyshire a week ago – stood behind Violet, working furiously to place each curl of blond hair into a spiral on her head. The older maid had been employed at Wilmington forever, and always did Tildy's hair, but many years had passed since she'd needed to fashion a look fit for a ball.

"It's a good thing your aunt did not desire to travel so far in order to attend this affair," Birdie remarked while pinning up the last curl. "For it would have taken me all day to make you both look beautiful. Not that you don't already look beautiful, Miss Violet, even without all this ado. However, your aunt would have required a good bit more attention. Although please do not tell her I said so."

Violet giggled at the reflection of the woman standing in attendance behind her. "I promise I will not say a word, Birdie. Truly, I cannot thank you enough for your assistance in preparing me today."

"Oh, there's no need to thank me. I'm excited for you. Lord Kastle seems like a fine man, and you should have a splendid time together at Lord Chaney's gathering."

"Lord Kastle is truly wonderful. I certainly hope we'll enjoy our time at the ball...with all of society there."

Birdie's weary brown eyes darkened with concern. Violet appreciated the maid's sympathy, for she did not wish to be seen as the Picky Princess tonight. She only wished to be a woman attending a ball with her betrothed.

"There you are now, Miss Violet. I'm all finished with your hair."

Violet took one more look at her pinned-up curls and gave Birdie a smile. "Thank you again. It is so very lovely."

"You're welcome. Shall we pull on your crinoline form?"

"Yes, please," Violet agreed, even if she despised this part of dressing as a lady. Nevertheless, she had to admit the gown Tildy had commissioned for her this week was the most beautiful she'd ever seen. She also had to admit she was pleased Mama had packed a bell cage to wear, just in case.

"Lift your outer skirts and petticoats," Birdie instructed while shifting the large hooped form in her hands.

Violet did as told, hoisting the yards of silky fabric up into her arms, leaving only the thinnest gossamer slip against her bare skin. Birdie set the hoops on the floor and Violet stepped into the waiting circle of the cage, sucking in her breath until the band at the top of the crinoline was fastened to her waist with a few tight but simple ties. When finished, Violet released her held breath as much as her clothing allowed before assisting Birdie to arrange the outer skirts into place around the crinoline form.

The older woman stood back then, looking her over. "Oh, Miss Violet! Don't you paint the portrait!"

Violet glanced to her reflection – to the soft white silk, ribbon, and lace hugging her corset and swooping out over the wide bell around her legs – and marveled at the sight. Despite the fact that every woman present tonight would be dressed in white, she still felt astounded by how much this resembled a wedding gown. She looked precisely like a bride, and could hardly believe her courtship with Christopher was already half over. In just another month, they would announce their own engagement.

"You are most generous with your compliments, Birdie."

"And you are more lovely than you know. Now go and enjoy your party," the handmaid instructed as she exited the bedchamber.

Once alone, Violet reached for the long silk gloves that matched her dress. She tried to entertain only good thoughts as she pulled the fabric over her hands, because tonight should be about her sister's big announcement. It should be about her meeting Christopher's family and him meeting more of hers. It should be about the two of them together, united in the face of society, just as he'd assured.

The moment she'd donned her gloves, with the slick white material pulled up to her elbows, she took a deep breath, moved to the door, and stepped out into the hallway. She rubbed her concealed fingers against each other while she walked, accustoming herself to the odd sensation. Violet actively dreaded her inability to feel Christopher's skin against hers tonight. His touch was something she did not even know a month ago, yet now she couldn't fathom enduring an entire evening without it.

When she arrived at the top of the staircase, she glanced down to the foyer to see Christopher waiting for her. The sharp black suit Tildy had commissioned for him fit his large body like Violet's glove fit her hand. Her flesh heated further with the sight, since his shoulders were too broad, his arms too thick, and his thighs too muscular to be lawfully showcased in such a snug manner. The only part of his suit that did not cling to his powerful form were the tails of his coat, which hung halfway down the backs of his long legs.

Her hand flew to her chest, attempting to contain the wild pounding of her heart, as she soaked in the vision of her husband. She knew for certain that no man in history had ever looked more devilishly desirable, and felt thankful for the slight bit of lace that peeked up from the edge of her bodice, covering a bit more of her corset-pinched flesh than usual. She did not wish to be caught panting at this ball, with the tops of her breasts heaving out of her dress, while she gawked at the man by her side.

Once she gained a modicum of control, she began to descend the staircase. Christopher turned to see her and his jaw unhinged. He didn't move at all, not even when her feet hit the marble and carried her toward him. He only stared in stunned silence, with his gaze drifting mercilessly over her body, until the moment she stood in front of him.

"Violet," he breathed, his voice caressing her name in sheer reverence.

She curtsied. "Christopher."

"My God, you are a vision. As always, of course, but this dress...this dress looks like a wedding gown."

"Yes, it does," she agreed, searching his eyes for approval. He didn't say anything in response. He simply smiled with utter, brilliant joy, and she'd never seen anything better. "You look very fine, as well."

"Oh. Thank you," he said, his fingers moving to adjust the black cravat against his throat. "Lady Wilmington's tailor did a remarkable job."

"Well, I'm certain she paid him well. Honestly, it amazes me that my aunt insisted on having a fresh suit created for you for the ball. You have truly won her over in every way."

Christopher leaned forward. "But have I won you over, Violet?"

His proximity unglued her. "Do you honestly have to ask?"

"No, I suppose not," he admitted, grasping her hand and entwining their fingers. "Hmm. You are wearing gloves, I see."

"Yes, unfortunately. They are proper for the occasion."

His gaze narrowed. "Quite proper, indeed. But please be advised that I intend to take them off of you as soon as this ball is ended, so I may feel your skin against my own."

"Yes, I – I rely on it."

A spark lit his eyes as he lifted her hand and pressed his lips to her glove. When Violet's fingers trembled, he stiffened. "You're shivering. Are you cold? Or are your nerves still giving you difficulty over tonight's affair?"

"I'm never cold when I'm with you, Christopher. But I'll admit I am still nervous to go out into society again."

He took a step closer, as much as her wide skirts allowed. "I'll be with you the whole time, my sweet. I shall not leave your side. You know that, right?"

"I do know. And did you just call me 'my sweet'?"

"I did. What do you think of it?"

"I think it is a lovely new endearment, dear husband."

A tempting smile slid across his lips with her own endearment. He tugged on her hand to wrap it around his sleeve. "We should go now, Violet, for I'm certain your sister desires your company. Please rest assured that there shall be much for us to enjoy tonight. This I promise you."

She tried to smile, although her fingers still knotted into Christopher's arm while he guided her from the manor entrance, down the steps, and onto the gravel entryway. "Mr. Rodchester has already pulled the carriage around," she mentioned, witnessing the fine dark coach standing before them, pulled by two strong black stallions. Violet knew this was Tildy's grandest carriage, although it still had only one sitting bench inside and would probably feel cramped for the two-hour journey to Centreville.

"We shall arrive in grand style," Christopher added, nodding to the coachman who sat on a separate front bench directly behind the horses. The driver started to dismount to open the door for them, but Christopher waved him off and pulled on the door himself, sweeping his hand toward the private inner chamber. "In addition, Lady Wilmington has deemed me worthy of traveling alone with you."

"Further proof that you have won her over entirely," Violet mused as she looked through the door to the single bench awaiting them inside. "Although it does concern me that people may find it untoward when we arrive alone together."

"I do not think it untoward at all, since we are betrothed. Also, it will be nighttime and quite dark when we reach the Chaney estate. I imagine everyone shall be occupied with their own carriages and coachmen, so our means of arrival should not merit any interest."

"You're right; I'm sure," she granted without further protest, since she actually loved the idea of sitting beside her husband in such a confined space, no matter how untoward the circumstance. In truth, she felt certain that the rides to and from the ball would be the best parts of her night. That is, if her gigantically impractical dress would even fit inside.

Violet stared at the innards of the coach, and then at her copious skirts, and sighed. "Regrettably, I do have one further concern."

"Oh? What is that?"

"I do not believe my hooped skirts will fit through that door."

"Hmm," Christopher considered, looking from her gown to the carriage and back. "Will the cage beneath your petticoats collapse somewhat?"

"Somewhat, although I do not think I can manage the task by myself."

He leaned down to press his lips to her ear, lowering his voice away from the coachman. "Well, my dearest, as I have previously helped with your shoes and stockings, I can certainly help with your dress, too."

Violet knew she shouldn't notice how Christopher's warm breath slipped across her skin when he spoke, especially not with this problem at hand. And she definitely shouldn't imagine him removing her dress as slowly and purposefully as he'd removed her shoes and stockings. "I shall truly appreciate your help, husband. In any way you deem fit."

He gave her a mouthwatering grin, and she had to tear her eyes from that scrumptious sight in order to step safely toward the carriage. She lifted her skirts, assuring she did not reveal any more than her ankle, while she placed her foot on the doorstep. Violet felt him move in behind her, his hands coming to the hem of her dress to tilt the lower hoop sideways. His assistance enabled her to step into the coach, although not in any graceful way. She hoisted herself inside the cramped space and collapsed onto the cushioned leather bench, her inelegant actions forcing the base of the cage up nearly to her chin.

"Oh, good heavens!" she protested, pressing down on the unruly hoops while Christopher climbed into the carriage on her heels.

He struggled to sit beside her without crushing any of the abundant silk, ribbon, and lace now consuming the bench. Once he managed to close the door behind them and rap his hand against the hood to signal the coachman, he turned his body toward hers. "What can I do to assist you?"

Violet shook her head as the horses began pulling the coach down the gravel path. "I don't even know. All of this finery is quite overwhelming," she grumbled, trying to stuff the lower circle of her cage down to the floor.

Her forceful movements caused her skirts to puff out on the sides, billowing fabric onto Christopher's trousers. He shifted closer to her, attempting to control the jutting of the crinoline by placing his hands on either side of the cage. Sadly, the more he tried to tamp down the ample material in some areas, the more it popped up in others.

Violet expected him to be irritated by the fabric's unwillingness to cooperate with his efforts. But Christopher did not give up. He merely tried harder, spending each passing moment tackling a different unruly section of her petticoats, only to have the dress continuously fight back.

This untamable conundrum apparently frustrated him in the most gleeful way. He grinned as merrily as a jester in court, and Violet watched him in utter adoration. She never imagined her imposing husband being so joyously playful while performing such an odd task. His large body shifted and jostled beside her, his solid chest coming ever closer, the heat of his skin filtering through the nearly nonexistent space between them. He laughed as he wrestled further with her dress, batting at her skirts like a kitten pouncing on a ball of string.

The look in his eyes was truly radiant, which brought a calming smile to her lips and infinite delight to her heart. "Are you having fun, Christopher?"

He stopped his pouncing, with both fists still full of fabric, and glanced to her eyes with more than a little guilt in his own. "Yes. I daresay I am."

Violet giggled, drawing his attention to her mouth.

"God, I love to hear you laugh," he confessed, releasing one hand from her skirts to reach to her face. The instant he allowed the dress leeway, it sprang up again. He chuckled as he drew his fingers down her cheek. "You know, my sweet, if you invite me to lay my head in your lap, I shall be able to keep your skirts at bay until we arrive at the Chaney estate. I shall also be able to feel the warmth of your body on mine throughout this journey, which will make me very happy, indeed."

She whimpered. "Will you please lay your head in my lap?"

Christopher gave her a wicked grin. "I thought you'd never ask," he said, his gaze dragging willfully down to her mouth. His fingers moved from her cheek to her chin, holding her in place while he shifted forward.

Violet held her breath in aching anticipation of his kiss. He leaned in just enough to fuse their lips in the most gentle, simple fashion. She melted into that sensation, so accustomed now to the feel of his strong mouth and prickly scruff. Her fingers slipped up to curl around his shoulder, trying to pull him closer and urge him to kiss her more deeply, like he had the day of their picnic.

Much to her dismay, Christopher only offered a tender yet firm pressure of his lips on hers. This was all he'd permitted them since that first time: just soft, easy kisses that became more and more familiar as the days passed. Violet figured his actions were purposeful, giving her time to become accustomed to the act itself before he taught her anything more.

She appreciated his noble intentions. She truly did. But now, after a solid week of these pleasurable little kisses – a torturous week of feeling her husband's lips melded tenderly with hers whenever he could steal the opportunity – she wanted more. More mouth, more tongue, more skin, more...him.

After lengthy moments, Christopher eased away from her. He held her gaze while he inched back on the bench, and Violet wracked herself with guilt over her desire to thrust her arms around his neck and drag him fully onto her. After all, her flagrant yearnings went directly against the grain of society's rules. The same society she must face tonight.

Once he'd shifted enough to bend at the waist, Christopher flopped his upper body down across her thighs. Her dress puffed out forcefully to the sides beneath his weight. The hooped hem of her cage quickly admitted defeat, resolving itself to rest on the floor.

"Mmm," he hummed when her dress had finally bowed to his command. "Isn't this better? To have me close to you as I conquer your unruly dress?"

"It is always better to have you as close to me as possible," she assured. "And as for the dress, you are my hero."

Christopher curled his arms around her waist and legs, hugging onto her lower half. He closed his eyes, smiling warmly while snuggling his cheek into her skirts. "You're perfect," he told her, his shoulders easing on a contented exhale. "Everything about you is perfection."

Violet watched his smile for the longest time, until his face relaxed along with the rest of his body. She watched until he fell asleep directly on her, which she did not mind at all, since she knew his reprieves were few and far between and she loved being one of them. She worked hard to concentrate on the steadiness of his breathing and the strength of his body, and to not think about the nerve-wracking event that lay before them tonight.

CHRISTOPHER HEARD his name called from a great distance. He didn't wish to leave the comforting fog of his slumber, yet he knew he must. As much as he cherished the warmth and softness currently surrounding him, he could sense that something was wrong.

"Christopher. *Christopher*. Please wake. We're nearing the Chaney estate."

Rising sluggishly on the carriage bench, he ran his fingers across his eyelids, becoming accustomed to the dark night sky he could now see through the small window. "How long was I asleep?"

"I, um, I don't know. Almost two hours, I suppose. I'm not sure."

Violet's restless voice hit him like a bucket of ocean water dumped over his head. Christopher straightened on the seat beside her, examining his wife's body in the dim light. He witnessed the furrow of her creased brow, the teeth marks on her swollen lower lip, and the ferocity of her clenched fingers. His heart sank instantly into his gut.

"Bloody hell, Violet. I'm sorry. I'm so sorry I fell asleep on you."

She shook her head. "Don't be sorry. It was all right."

He reached out, covering both of her tight fists with one of his hands. "No, it was not all right. I know how anxious you are about tonight, and I should have stayed awake to soothe your nerves. Instead, I took my rest, leaving you alone to worry while I allowed myself peace in your arms."

Christopher cringed with his admission, since the fact that he could find such comfort in this woman, especially at such an untimely moment, made him question everything. It made him question every assumption he'd made in his entire existence. Because Violet Bell was never supposed to become *this*.

She was never supposed to be his refuge. She was never supposed to be his salvation. She was never supposed to be his light and his happiness, all wrapped up in one beautiful little body.

"Please forgive me," Christopher begged, edging closer to her. "Please say you forgive my atrocious behavior, or I will never be able to forgive myself."

Slipping one hand from under his, she eased her gloved fingers up his jaw. "There is nothing to forgive. I am grateful to be able to give you peace."

Violet granted him the softest smile as she caressed his cheek. His heart swelled so painfully in his chest that he spoke his next words just to relieve the crushing pressure. "I swear to you that I am yours," he vowed, leaning in to rest his forehead onto hers. "I swear that I am yours from this moment on. I shall never leave you alone again. I am beside you for as long as you desire."

Her fingers threaded into his hair, fastening him to her. As their warm breaths mingled in the darkness, he worried she might release her hold on him. He feared she would pull away from the rawness of his promises, since he was painfully aware of how thick and heady they sounded. Still, he couldn't bring himself to regret speaking his vows. Especially not with her this close to him, dressed in a gown fit for a bride.

"And I swear that I am yours," Violet whispered, instantly soothing his anxieties. She lifted her eyes to his. "I am beside you for as long as you desire. I shall put my faith in you, Christopher. Always and completely."

The swelling sensation returned to his chest, even more pronounced than before. He nodded to her in acceptance, knowing that no matter what happened from here on out – no matter where life's bizarre twists and turns might take them – his mind would always seek her thoughts, his heart would constantly reach for the shelter of her own, and his body would forever find a home beside hers. And that understanding didn't scare him nearly as much as it should.

He could have sat here, staring his promises into her eyes, for the rest of the evening. But eventually, the carriage stopped moving and the coachman stepped down from his perch to open their door. Christopher forced himself to pull back so no one would see how close he and Violet were to each other. Although he honestly didn't know if he could conceal that truth from anyone, even if he never touched her once all night.

The moment he stepped out of the coach and onto the gravel entryway, he reached for her hand. She placed her fingers into his, maneuvering herself and her dress out of the carriage door. They took a few steps toward the manor, allowing the coachman to direct the horses to the side of the estate.

Once alone, Christopher waited patiently for Violet to straighten her skirts, standing guard as he surveyed their surroundings. The Chaney estate was gigantic, twice as big as the Wilmington and Kastle estates combined. The lawns were plush and exquisitely manicured, showcasing marble fountains flowing in the light of oil torch lamps spread across the front of the manor.

He had never witnessed anything quite so grand, and could not imagine how many servants it took to maintain such a home. "I see the Earl of Centreville is quite wealthy," Christopher mentioned, trying not to dwell on the fact that Violet could have had all of this, if not for her determination to make her sister happy.

"Oh, yes, very wealthy," she confirmed, running her hands across her petticoats one more time. "Their family fortunes go back generations. Welly's father, Henry, is a surgeon and a member of the Royal College of Physicians. He trained at Oxford."

Christopher sighed. "My father is a lush who gambled away our fortunes."

Violet shrugged. "And my father is a ruthless businessman and just shy of being a criminal."

He looked to her with a smile tugging at his mouth. "Well, then. We do make quite the pair, don't we?"

"That we do," she agreed, attempting to return his smile before biting her lip. Her fingers twisted into the skirts she'd just straightened as her eyes assessed the polished bodies stepping out of other carriages on the front path.

Christopher's chest constricted, knowing his wife feared the societal judgment they would face tonight. He couldn't truly assure her that there would be no condemnations over their union. Still, he didn't want her anxiety to cloud her enjoyment of the time they would have here together.

"I suppose we must go inside," she mumbled.

He gathered her hand, guiding it to wrap around his sleeve. "Violet," he said, looking ahead to the entrance while pressing his palm firmly overtop of her fingers. "Stay close to me always."

She gripped onto his arm. "God, I wish we could be even closer than this."

With those words, Christopher's eyes darted to hers.

"Oh!" she gasped. "I – I didn't mean that in an immoral sort of way."

He relished her wide-eyed stare before leaning down to whisper in her ear. "Damn, I hope that's not true, for I have all sorts of immoral thoughts of you running amok in my brain right now."

Violet moaned with his words, confirming that he shouldn't have said them. In truth, he'd been working like hell all week to keep their physical affections at an acceptable level. Partly because he'd wanted to give her time to acclimate to their newest intimacies. But mostly because – as soon as they'd agreed to kiss whenever desired – he struggled constantly with the requirement of maintaining a virtuous relationship with her.

He'd had to remind himself, each and every minute of the past seven days, that she was not actually his wife yet – no matter how much his mind, body, and heart disagreed. He'd tried to keep their kisses chaste, even if he put no limit on their number. He'd also tried to keep his hands mostly to himself, and not overly partake of the feel of her soft, sweet flesh.

Consequently, Christopher now dreaded seeing the result of the scandalous words he'd just spoken. He could already envision Violet's blown pupils, flushed cheeks, and entranced gaze, and knew he should feel shameful about his deliberate choice to make her body react sinfully to his. However, when he eased back to witness the blatant proof of what he'd foreseen, he couldn't make himself regret anything. The fact that he'd become her entire focus at this moment meant she'd forgotten her anxiety over this party, at least for a little while. It felt like his best accomplishment ever.

"Come now," he encouraged with a seductive grin, listening intently to the sigh that escaped her lips before he led her up the enormous staircase.

Gratefully, Violet made it to the entrance without tripping over her copious skirts. Christopher held her as close as her dress allowed while he drank in their surroundings. The inside of the manor reeked of as much wealth as the outside. Gold inlay laced the trim of every door, priceless artwork decorated the walls, and fine porcelain vases stood proudly at the entrances to the many vast rooms lining the elongated hallways. Sharply dressed servants ushered the two of them into a receiving line the moment they entered. He saw Welly and Gwen, in addition to an older couple he assumed were Welly's parents, standing in a row to greet each new guest.

"Are you with me?" Christopher asked while inching closer to their hosts.

"Always," Violet assured, clinging to his arm.

He smiled, tucking her hand into his chest as they waited in line.

A few minutes later, they reached the first host. Christopher looked to the young heir's face as he turned to them. Welly startled a bit before plastering on a grin and extending his hand.

"Lord Kastle, it is a pleasure to have you in our home."

"The pleasure is mine," he replied, grasping Welly's hand in a firm grip.

Christopher felt the boy's fingers twitch beneath his own and figured he should be remorseful about the heir's nervous state, considering the ferocity with which he'd nearly strangled his future brother-in-law up against a wall in the Wilmington foyer. Yet he couldn't bring himself to be entirely sorry, since Lord Chaney was still the man who'd looked past Violet in order to see her sister. He'd made her doubt her own beauty and desirability, which would always be a travesty in Christopher's mind.

He nodded formally to the boy once he'd released him. Welly returned the nod with an uneasy smile. It was probably the best they could achieve for now.

"It is good to see you again, Welly," Violet spoke from Christopher's side. "We appreciate the invitation to your home."

"Of course," Welly offered her with a more genuine grin. "You are welcome here anytime."

The young heir glanced to Violet's gloved fingers, yet he did not reach for her hand in greeting. The fact that he didn't attempt to touch her was honestly best for everyone involved, as far as Christopher was concerned. He gave the boy another nod before guiding Violet to the next host in line.

"How are you, Gwen?" he asked once they stood before her.

"Oh, Christopher, I'm so good! Especially since the two of you are here!" Gwen grasped for her sister, throwing her arms around her neck, even though both women had to bend at the waist in order to hug around the widths of their skirts.

Violet returned Gwen's embrace with one arm only, keeping her other hand fastened to Christopher's sleeve. "I've missed you so much," she spoke beside her sister's ear. "And you look just beautiful."

"As do you," Gwen confirmed, glancing over Violet's dress the instant they parted. "Did Tildy have this made for you?"

"Yes. Did Mama fuss over you and your clothes all week?"

"Good heavens, you have no idea. I think she missed having two daughters to preen. I'm certain she'll find you at some point tonight."

Violet glanced up to Christopher's eyes. "Yes, I'm sure she'll want to meet my future husband."

"I look forward to that moment," he assured.

"I wish you both luck with it," Gwen added with a quick kiss to Violet's cheek. "Please do enjoy yourselves tonight, for I cannot tell you what it means to me to have you here."

"We'll try," Violet said as her fingers gripped harder to Christopher's arm.

"We shall see you later in the evening, Gwen," he promised, garnering a smile from both sisters while he led Violet to the next person in line.

The Earl of Centreville stood tall and straight to Gwen's left, glancing over both Violet and Christopher as he spoke. "So, this is Lord Christopher Kastle. You are the Royal Navy sailor who was lost at sea, are you not?"

Christopher bowed to their host. "I am, indeed."

"I'm happy you've returned to England," Henry Chaney offered with fatherly pride. "I thank you for your service to God and to Country."

Christopher tensed as stiff as a board, until Violet's fingers stroked his arm. "Thank you, Lord Chaney," she spoke in Christopher's silence. "My husband-to-be is a brave and wondrous man indeed."

The earl offered Violet a deep bow. "Such a pleasure to see you again, Miss Bell. I am happy you finally found someone to stand beside you."

Violet tensed as stiff as a board, until Christopher tugged her closer to his body. "She certainly has," he confirmed, giving the older gentleman a tight smile. "Thank you again for the invitation to your lovely home."

"Certainly. Please partake of all the food, drink, and dance you desire, for these festivities are intended as a joyous celebration."

"Quite joyous," Christopher echoed, easing Violet away from Welly's father and on to his mother, who stood quietly beside her husband. The Countess of Centreville was pleasant and amenable, shaking their hands with gentle assuredness. She invited them inside the estate without any further ado.

Christopher felt a sense of accomplishment when stepping past the receiving line, since they had faced the entire Chaney family without incident. Unfortunately, they must now face the rest of society. Holding Violet's hand close to his chest, he escorted her across the foyer and down the extensive hall, following the sound of music. His eyes widened when they entered the vast main ballroom beneath multitudinous gold chandeliers and mural-painted ceilings. At least a hundred couples stood before them, centered around a short stage in the front of the room where a full orchestra played.

Despite the melodic music filling his ears, Christopher still heard the tone-deaf whispers accompanying their arrival. He worked to ignore the foul sounds while his eyes shifted across the room, soaking in the river of finery. All ladies bore lavish white dresses and all gentlemen donned black coat-and-tails. Heavy jewelry draped across every female neckline in sight, while the men stood with spines as hardened as their jaws.

Christopher refused to cower as the gossip rose in swells around them. He urged Violet forward, skirting the outer edges of the room where every person looked down their noses at the two of them walking past. He understood now that his wife had been right; this was a hostile environment. Not openly lethal, like those he'd experienced in the jungles of Africa. But the hairs on the back of his neck still rose with the deeply laden animosity surrounding them – simmering just below the surface of the glittering room, pristine lace, and starched suits – because this environment felt even more threatening.

Painfully aware of the hollowness in this world of wealth and snobbery, Christopher stared in wonder at the lack of color in these poor souls. As his eyes scanned the strangers, he saw only black and white everywhere, in every-one. Until his gaze finally settled on the woman at his side.

The instant Violet focused on him, he could see no color in the room at all – except for the pink of her lips, the blue of her eyes, the gold of her hair. Christopher pulled her as close to him as her dress allowed. He gave her a soft smile, and watched her smile in return, and his heart finally settled.

"Bloody hell, if it isn't Lord Kastle," a voice came from behind them. The sound pulled his attention immediately, for this was a voice nearly as familiar to him as his own.

"Nick Marlow," Christopher stated, securing Violet's hand while turning toward the man.

"One and the same," Nick agreed, coming to stand before them dressed in his best London finery. His gaze landed on Christopher for only a second before moving decidedly to her.

Christopher bristled when his oldest friend looked on his wife. Honestly, as much as he loved this man like a brother, he found it difficult to be in his presence right now. Nick reminded him of all the things he'd done during his years at sea, and all the pieces of his soul he'd lost along the way, and he didn't want to acknowledge any of that. Not with Violet here, standing so innocently by his side.

After surveying her for a moment, Nick looked back to Christopher and held out his hand. Christopher grasped onto him for a brief handshake. "What are you doing here, Nick?"

"I was invited. By your sister, Daniela."

"Daniela invited you?"

"She did."

Christopher's shoulders bunched. "And just how much time have you been spending with my sister in my absence, Marlow?"

Nick huffed out an exasperated breath.

Christopher felt Violet's fingers smooth up and down his arm.

"Will you introduce me, please?" she requested.

The bright sound of her voice pulled him back. "Oh, right," he said. "I'm sorry. I forgot my manners."

Nick snorted. "God knows I'm used to that."

Christopher glowered before taking a deep breath. "Violet, my sweet, this is Mr. Nicholas Marlow, my oldest friend. And Nick, this is Miss Violet Bell, my future wife." Christopher looked to her after making his introductions, watching her eyes light up with her title.

She gazed at him before turning her attention to the other man present. "It is a pleasure to make your acquaintance, Mr. Marlow."

Nick's discerning eyes shifted between the two of them. "My heavens, Miss Bell, I must insist that you call me Nick. Since Mr. Marlow is my father," he announced with a roguish grin.

That mischievous smile made Christopher's hand tighten over hers.

"Very well, then. I shall call you Nick, if you will call me Violet."

"Violet," Nick addressed, offering a graceful bow. "I would ask to kiss your hand, but Lord Kastle appears to be gripping it rather fiercely. I fear having my own hand bit off if I were to attempt such a thing."

Christopher growled. "Go with your instincts on this, Marlow."

Violet giggled. "Goodness, Christopher. You are so funny."

"Christopher? Funny?" Nick questioned.

"Oh, yes. He makes me laugh so often. It's quite wonderful."

Nick stared incredulously at her. Christopher couldn't help chuckling.

"Now, would you be *the* Nick Marlow?" Violet clarified. "Of the prosperous Marlow Merchant Company?"

"Yes, that is my family's business. How do you know of us?"

"I used to see your family's ships all the time in the waterways of London when I was younger. I see them now in Nightingale Port whenever we travel there for shopping. I believe your main operation runs out of Nightingale, does it not?"

"It does. We've transferred away from London almost entirely."

"I think that's wise. London has become clustered with so many merchant ships. I believe your expansion into Nightingale makes your family a pioneer of future business throughout the country. And the world, for that matter."

"I couldn't agree more with you, Violet," Nick said before glancing back to Christopher. "I believe your betrothed has a mind for business, Kastle."

"She has a mind for many things. You should see her play cards."

"Really?" Nick asked, looking back to her. "Do you play well?"

"Passably so," she offered. "Just let me know if you ever desire to play and I shall try to keep up."

Laughter erupted from Christopher's throat. "Don't let her fool you. Play cards with my Violet, and she'll empty your pockets before you can blink."

Nick grinned. "Bloody hell. That's wonderful, isn't it?"

She returned his grin. "I think you and I have much in common, Nick."

"Oh? How so?"

"Well, you are from a sailing family and I am from a gambling family. And last I checked, sailors and gambling go together like biscuits and tea."

Nick chortled even as he shook his head. "Damn, you're a lucky bastard. Aren't you, old mate?"

Christopher pressed his palm onto her gloved fingers. "That I am, Marlow. That I am."

"Is this where the festivities truly are?" Daniela questioned, her voice carrying ahead of her body as she emerged from the crowd to join them. Christopher shifted toward his eldest sister with a smile on his face. Yet his brow furrowed as soon as he looked her over, soaking in the radiant new dress of white silk and lace she wore over her own crinoline cage skirt.

"Lady Daniela Kastle," he announced once he could tear his gaze from the unexpected finery of her clothing. "I wish to introduce you to Miss Violet Bell, my future wife."

Daniela and Violet locked eyes and curtsied simultaneously, but it was Violet who spoke first. "It is lovely to meet you, Lady Daniela. Christopher often speaks of how amazingly strong you are, keeping the Kastle manor to such high standards in the absence of your dear mother."

Daniela's eyes glossed with the mention of Miranda, but she recovered quickly. "It is a pleasure to meet you, as well. And I assure you, I only do what is expected of me."

"Well, according to your brother, you go above and beyond. It is a remarkable quality, to be sure. And may I also say your dress is gorgeous."

"Thank you, Violet. It was newly made just this week, after we received the invitation to this grand affair. It has been forever since we were asked to attend a function of this caliber, so all the girls had new dresses made."

"Really?" Christopher probed, his eyes darting to Nick.

"Are all of your sisters present tonight?" Violet asked.

"All but the two youngest," Daniela replied. "Constance is only twelve years old and Octavia only nine, so I did not find it suitable for them."

"I completely understand. I have only one younger sister, but I feel the need to guard my Gwen at all costs."

"I am glad you understand."

"So, dear sister, exactly how much time has Nick been spending at our home this past month?" Christopher interrupted the women, unable to prevent his hackles from rising with the offensive thought.

Daniela stared him down. "Quite a bit of time, actually. Nick has been helping me with the household chores while you're away."

Violet stiffened. "Oh, heavens. I'm so sorry, Lady Daniela. I did not mean to steal your brother from you for such a length of time."

"There's no need to apologize, Violet. Every woman deserves a proper courtship," Daniela insisted, turning to the dark-haired man at her side. "Isn't that right, Mr. Marlow?"

Nick's eyes brightened the moment she focused on him. "Yes, that is definitely correct. And with that being said, I very much hope you'll grace me with a dance, Lady Daniela."

She gave him a tender smile. "I would love to dance."

Nick nearly fell over his own feet before turning back to Christopher and Violet. "Will you both excuse us now?"

"Of course. Go enjoy yourselves," Violet encouraged.

Christopher managed to nod, still giving Nick a stern glare as the man led his sister to the dance floor.

"Goodness, Christopher," Violet spoke once the couple escaped. "How long has your best friend been in love with your eldest sister?"

He groaned as he looked to Violet's eyes. "Forever."

"I take it you do not approve of him being with her?"

"I – I don't know anymore," he admitted as much to himself as to her. "I've never approved before, but now..."

"Christopher!"

He turned his head with the shout of his name, only to see Cora sprinting toward him through the parting crowd. His heart filled to bursting, as it always did, the moment he saw his fierce little warrior of a sister. The second she reached him, she grabbed hold of his arm and arched up on her tiptoes to peck his cheek.

"My God, it's good to see you," Cora gushed, taking a step back to shift her bright green eyes to the woman at his side. "And should I assume this is Miss Violet Bell?"

"She is," Christopher confirmed, his chest swelling with pride. "Violet, I wish to present my sister, Cora. And Cora, I wish to present my wife."

Cora's eyes shot to his. "Your wife? I thought she was still your betrothed."

"Oh, well, I ..." he fumbled, knowing he shouldn't call Violet his wife yet. At least, not in public. But he didn't get a chance to rescind the title he'd given the woman beside him – not before she started squealing.

"Cora! You're Cora!" Violet exclaimed, bouncing on her heels. "It's so wonderful to finally meet you! Christopher speaks of you so often that I feel like we are best friends! I hope we will be, for you are brave and fearless and positively perfect! I cannot wait to spend time together and learn even more of each other! I'm so excited that I just want to hug you! May I hug you?"

Cora's eyes widened while Violet's words tumbled from her lips. She smiled wholeheartedly as soon as the speech ceased. "You may, indeed."

Violet released her grip on Christopher for the first time all night, which made his arm instantly cold. He wanted to complain, but he couldn't bring himself to be quite that selfish – not while watching his wife pounce on his sister with such voracious fervor. Their wide skirts billowed out behind them when Violet's arms flew around Cora's neck.

His sister returned the embrace in good measure, even as she glanced up to him with a quizzical expression. He couldn't help grinning in response to her unspoken queries. His smile widened further when the hug ended and Violet returned to his side to wrap her hand around his arm once again.

"My heavens, you give the best hugs," she spoke to Cora in earnest. "Of all the things Christopher has told me about you, he neglected to mention that you give such marvelous hugs."

"I do apologize, my sweet," he offered, glancing to his wife's vibrant eyes. "I should have reported the value of a Kastle sister's hug the second we met."

Violet scrunched her brow in playful displeasure. "Yes, you should have. But since you are glorious and adorable, I shall forgive you. Just this once."

Christopher chuckled with her teasing words, unsure if she could be any more precious to him. "I thank you for your kindness, as always," he said, settling his fingers over her hand to press her palm securely onto his arm.

She beamed up at him and he beamed right back. Afterwards, he turned to

Cora and met the gaze of an utterly shocked woman. Her mouth hung open, her forehead crinkled into a bow, and her arms hung flopped at her sides.

He laughed again, having never before seen the little warrior so speechless. It was a perfectly new experience and one he enjoyed beyond measure. Christopher didn't know if Cora would have ever snapped out of her stupor, if not for the arrival of three more Kastle ladies.

"Here come my other sisters now," he informed his wife, pulling her closer as he took in the sight of the women walking toward them, each in a brand new and beautiful white dress of their own. "The one with light brown hair and blue eyes, who looks most like me, is Juliette. The twins have dark hair and eyes, and are identical, as you can see. They more resemble Daniela."

"We do not look like Daniela," Ruby protested when the three of them arrived beside Cora. "We look like each other, and like ourselves."

"Yes, quite like ourselves," Pearl agreed, turning her big brown eyes to Violet. "And I must assume this is what our future sister-in-law looks like."

Christopher nodded. "May I present Miss Violet Bell," he announced.

Ruby, Pearl, and Juliette all curtsied as Cora still stood in stunned silence. Although she did manage to shut her gaping jaw, at least.

Violet curtsied in return. "What a grand pleasure it is to meet you all."

"It is a pleasure to meet you, as well," Pearl said. "I am Ruby. And this creature beside me is Pearl."

Ruby offered a sly grin. "Yes, I am Pearl Kastle. So good to meet you."

"Ladies," Christopher growled, disappointed but not shocked by their trickery. "Please behave yourselves."

With his grumbly admonishment, Violet burst into giggles. The sparkling sound drew all eyes to the woman standing beside him. Even Christopher stared at her, utterly confused by her delight.

"What on earth are you laughing about, Violet?" Cora inquired.

"I just figured, since Christopher used his growly voice, that Ruby and Pearl must have told me their names incorrectly. Which is quite funny."

Cora's jaw dropped again. "My God. Did you just acknowledge that Christopher has a growly voice? And then *laugh* in spite of it?"

"Well, yes. I suppose I did. Is...is that a bad thing?"

"No," Cora insisted, her eyes shifting back to her brother. "No, not at all. That is actually a very wonderful thing."

Christopher smiled as his wife's body relaxed beside his.

"Thank goodness," Violet breathed, looking to the twins. "And just so you know, I completely understand about not wanting to behave as a lady."

Ruby's brow rose. "You do?"

"Very much. My parents have demanded I act as a lady for the past ten years, since we moved from London to Pennyshire. It's exhausting."

"It is," Pearl agreed. "Daniela makes us act like ladies all the time."

Violet sighed. "Well, I'm sure she's only trying to be supportive of you, as my parents were of me. Although, now that I think of it, I once put a frog in my father's boot just to prove that I could act in any manner I chose."

Ruby and Pearl giggled uproariously with that account, making Violet stiffen again. "Oh! I certainly didn't mean to suggest that you put a frog in Daniela's shoe," she amended.

Christopher chuckled as the twins honed in on her with wide smiles.

"My goodness, please do not do such a thing," Violet continued, "for I fear that Daniela finding a frog in her boot would not place me on her good side at all. She might also be upset with you, and then she might not let the two of you climb the twisty tree in the gardens at Kastle manor. That would be an awful occurrence, for I know what the tree means to you both."

Ruby gasped. "Did Christopher actually speak to you of our family tree?"

"He did. He said you like to climb the branches whenever possible. I'm hoping you'll teach me the best way to climb them when I come to live with you. That is, if you don't mind sharing the tree with me. I do so love to climb, and I promise I will try to keep up. I also promise I shall work very hard to learn how to tell the two of you apart, although you are both lovely, beautiful, and sparkling, so I fear it may take me a long while."

"That's Pearl," Ruby admitted, pointing to her twin. "You can tell because she has a little scar on the side of her neck."

"I do," Pearl agreed, tilting her head to show off the pale line just above her collarbone. "I fell out of the twisty tree as a child and was cut on a branch. It's the only difference you can see between the two of us, from the outside."

"Oh, thank you for that," Violet breathed. "Although I'm certain I'll be able to tell deeper differences once I get to know you each better."

Ruby huffed out a laugh. "My heavens, you're perfect. Aren't you?"

"You are. Utterly perfect," Pearl agreed. "We look forward to having you come live with us."

Moisture edged Violet's eyes. "You are too kind to me. I appreciate it more than I can possibly say."

Christopher turned toward her, the action pulling her watery gaze up to his unwavering one. "I do look forward to bringing her home with me," he spoke to his sisters, even though he stared solely at the woman by his side. "More than I can possibly say."

Violet matched his intent gaze, a sweet grin overtaking her lips as she blinked away her tears. He nearly kissed her, right here in front of his family and all the rest of society. Honestly, he'd grown quite used to kissing her whenever he damn well felt like it, so he could barely control his impulse.

"Well, we can certainly see that truth," Cora broke the moment of silence, pulling his attention back to the people in front of them.

Christopher searched each of his sisters' faces, absorbing their tender, affectionate expressions. Then he looked back to Violet, whose smile lit up the room with rays of sunshine. His wife had charmed his whole family tonight – just as she'd charmed him from the moment he laid eyes on her – and he couldn't feel more thrilled or more humbled.

"We shouldn't simply stand around here all night," Cora added. "There will be plenty of time to learn about our new sister when she comes home to Nightingale. But for now, there is a very fine dance floor to be explored."

"Oh, yes! Let us dance!" Ruby insisted, grabbing hold of Pearl's hand and pulling her toward the crowd. "I hope to see you out there, Violet!"

Violet waved to the twins as they departed. Christopher took that moment to look at Juliette, who would be the one Kastle to struggle the most in such a social situation. "How are you tonight, my little star?" he asked, using an old, private endearment to pull her big blue eyes to his.

Juliette gave him a shy smile. "I am well, Christopher. Thank you."

"I wanted to let you know that my Violet shares your love of books."

"She does?" Juliette asked, turning her gaze to the woman on his arm.

"Yes, I do. Very much," Violet assured. "Any books. All books. I especially love stories of adventure and romance."

Juliette blushed. "I enjoy those, as well. Although a good science text can be riveting."

"Quite riveting, indeed. Perhaps you and I could read together at the Kastle manor, after Christopher and I are wed."

"I – I would like that."

Violet nodded to her. "Wonderful."

"It is wonderful," Cora said, taking the little wallflower's hand in her own. "And now you shall come with me, Juliette, so we can show our fine dance skills to the world."

Juliette glanced to the floor before allowing Cora to pull her away. Christopher stood in place, watching his sisters sweep into the crowd. He watched them pass the bejeweled and starched onlookers, who turned on them with sour gazes as they began to dance with each other instead of with men. He wondered if any gentleman here would even dare to court the dowry-deficient Kastle women.

"We do not have to dance, if you do not care for it," Violet offered, her melodic voice drifting gently across his skin.

"I would very much enjoy dancing with you," Christopher assured. "Although I haven't done it in some time, so I must beg forgiveness if I do not remember the steps entirely. Yet I shall try my best, as I will take any excuse to hold you near me."

"I'd love that. But only if you're certain, for you seem a bit hesitant."

"That is because it is hard to watch my sisters out in society like this. I want to protect them, to keep them safe from prejudice and harm."

Violet ran her hand down his sleeve to capture his fingers. "And that is why you are a wonderful brother, and why they all love you with such ferocity."

Christopher turned to her, trying to understand for the millionth time how he'd gotten so fortunate as to have her look at him like he'd hung the moon. "You know, Violet, you have officially managed to charm every member of my family here tonight. In truth, you've charmed Constance and Octavia as well, since I'm sure their older sisters will offer reports of how wonderful you are the moment they return to Nightingale."

"Do you really believe all your sisters find me wonderful?"

"I am certain of it, especially since the twins never admit to that scar of Pearl's. They never want anyone to know the difference between them. They would much rather play tricks on unsuspecting victims."

"Then I suppose I can rest assured that they approve of me."

"They most definitely approve of you, which does not surprise me at all, since you are perfectly irresistible to everyone."

"Does that include you, my husband?"

He gazed down at her. "Do you honestly have to ask?"

Violet nibbled against her lip, the sight of which nearly caused him to groan loudly and unsuitably in front of every person at this ball. "No, I suppose I do not," she admitted, although she still appeared uncertain.

Christopher shook his head, truly unable to comprehend her continued insecurity, especially in regard to his need for her. The thought that Violet could doubt her irresistibility struck him as an absolute travesty — one he intended to fix tonight.

With a devilish smile, he leaned down to whisper in her ear. "Let us dance now, sweet wife, since I fear where my hands may choose to travel on your body if they are not formally occupied." He listened intently to the whimper that escaped her lips before he continued. "For due to the untold number of people surrounding us, I am painfully aware that I cannot fulfill my indecent craving to touch you in every way I want. But please believe me when I say that my desire for you is a powerful, aching, and ever-present need. And so very, *very* improper."

Christopher lingered a bit after he finished speaking, letting his breath fan across her neck and watching the tiny hairs rise across her nape. When he finally pulled back, he looked immediately to her face. He drank in the glorious color that spread across her cheeks, flitted down her shoulders, and sank beneath the collar of her bodice where the tops of her breasts strained with her stuttered pants.

Unadulterated lust shot down his spine with the wanton picture Violet painted. He cursed beneath his breath as he straightened beside her, taking her fingers gently in his to guide her to the dance floor. He honestly didn't know how he would live through their carriage ride home tonight without running his hands over every inch of her body. And he sure as hell didn't know how he would survive until their wedding night without claiming her entirely.

Christopher felt grateful for the three waltzes they danced in succession, since it allowed him to hold Violet close enough to breathe in her sweet cream and honeysuckle scent. He did not care as much for the more formal promenades that followed, as they necessitated them forming a line across from each other, keeping arms' length apart and stepping in time with everyone else on the floor. To be fair, those dances did offer them the opportunity to promenade beside Nick and Daniela, and Cora and Juliette, and Ruby and Pearl. Christopher could see firsthand the joy in his sisters' eyes, which brought him more happiness and contentment than he thought he would ever know again.

In truth, the best part of dancing was how Violet squealed and giggled as they all moved together. He could rest assured that she wasn't concerning herself with the more fearsome aspects of society right now, since the only people in her immediate surroundings belonged to his family. He hoped she could sense the solidarity she would have with them. He wanted her to understand – no matter how far the Kastles had fallen – that they would always shield one another. He wanted her to know that she was a part of this family now and always would be.

After a good hour of dancing, Christopher finally led his wife away from the crowd to the refreshment tables. They partook of the feast of foods present, as well as several glasses of wine. They also stood entirely too close to one another, and grinned and held hands like lovesick fools, and simply ignored the looks and whispers of unknown spectators.

Only when he was certain his wife had filled her belly with food and drink did he dare to lead her away from the tables and back toward the dancing bodies. Yet before they could return to the ballroom floor, they were intercepted by an older couple stepping forward through the crowd. The tall, reedy, silver-haired man held himself with poise and purpose as he escorted the stylish blond woman at his side, both sets of eyes scrutinizing Christopher with obvious uncertainty before fastening onto Violet.

"Mama and Papa!" Violet called, reaching her free hand out to grasp her mother's arm and stretching her neck to press a kiss to her cheek. "I am so happy to see you both!"

Christopher stood firm beside his wife, pushing his shoulders back and puffing out his chest as he took in the sight of the people in front of him. Violet's mother warmed to him instantly, offering a generous smile, but her father did not. Noah Bell wasn't a large man, nor was he physically intimidating, yet he had an unmistakable keenness in his eye. Christopher knew better than to think him any less than the criminal mastermind of report.

"Mama and Papa, this is my Christopher," Violet announced, her voice pitched higher with excitement. "I mean, he is Lord Christopher Kastle, heir to the Earl of Nightingale, of course. Which you both already knew, but here he is. My future husband."

He smiled with Violet's rambling introduction as he bowed deeply to her parents. "I am beyond thrilled to meet you."

Her mother took a step toward him. "Lord Kastle, it is a pleasure. I am Lady Liza Bell of Pennyshire. And this is my husband, Mr. Noah Bell."

"Yes. Violet has told me so much about you both."

"Only good things, I hope," Noah interjected, his brow quirking as he looked to his daughter.

Violet laughed. "Oh, Papa! There are only good things to tell!"

The man's steely eyes warmed in an instant. Truly, everything in Noah Bell's body changed the moment he heard his daughter's laughter. The harsh coldness of his entire being turned peaceful and still, and Christopher understood that transformation all too well. He now felt a far more kindred connection to his future father-in-law than he ever imagined possible.

"Thank you," he breathed, desperate to show his gratitude. "Thank you so much for arranging this marriage, Mr. Bell."

Noah's gaze narrowed. "Are you indeed thankful, Lord Kastle?"

"I am profoundly thankful; I promise you. I believe myself the most fortunate man in the world to stand here beside your daughter. For she is a brighter, kinder, better person than I could ever hope to be, and I am humbled to know I shall one day call her my wife."

The older man studied him for a long moment, the intensity of his gaze as sharp as any blade. Eventually, he gave a curt nod. "Well, then. I trust you'll work to deserve her."

Christopher bowed again. "I assure you I will. Every day."

Violet's father seemed to take solace with those words, even offering a brief smile before Gwen scurried up to their group and linked arms with her mother and sister.

"Look at all of us, here at a ball!" Gwen gushed with bright eyes and a toothy grin. "I'm so excited for us to celebrate tonight!"

"We are excited for you, dear girl," Liza assured.

"How wonderful," Gwen replied. "And now, I must pull you all to the back room, where the Chaneys have a photographer waiting to take pictures with the Bell family."

"Are the pictures with all of us?" Violet asked, grasping Christopher's arm.

Gwen's gaze shifted between them. "Oh, well, um, I suppose it's..."

"That is all right," Christopher stated, not wishing to create any conflict. "I do not need to be in the photographs. At least, not until Violet and I can have an engagement party of our own."

"Thank you for your understanding," Gwen sighed, the relief apparent in her eyes. "I promise I won't keep my sister from you for long."

Violet continued clinging to his arm, so he lowered his voice for her ears only, even if everyone could still hear them. "I can come with you, if you like. I'll wait in the back of the room until the pictures are completed."

She smiled up at him with her usual warmth. "No, Christopher, that is not necessary. I shall be with my family and able to manage. Why don't you enjoy your own sisters' company for a while, and I will come find you later."

"Only if you're certain," he said, having sworn that he would not leave her side tonight, and neither intending nor desiring to leave her at all.

"I'm quite certain," she assured, giving his arm a squeeze before detaching herself from his side.

He felt instantly cold after she took one step away. He had to press his mouth shut, fighting back his overwhelming urge to lean down and capture her lips with a kiss. After all, as inappropriate as that act would have been in front of his sisters, it would be even more so in front of her parents. "I look forward to your return, Violet," he offered as he straightened his spine.

She nodded to him. "Christopher."

He heard her say a thousand different things with just the whisper of his name. She disappeared into the crowd with her family, swallowed up in a sea of black and white. His heart fell the moment he could not see his wife's colors, so he remained right where he was, concentrating on the memory of her face. He nearly reached into his coat to grab hold of the gold locket that held her portrait, but then a voice filled his ears.

"Are you going to stand here and stare after her for the rest of the night?" Cora questioned, emerging from the crowd to fill the empty space at his side.

Christopher smiled while turning to her. "I might."

Cora shook her head even as she matched his grin. "Good Lord, dear brother. She's brought you back to life, hasn't she?"

"Yes," he admitted without hesitance. "Yes, she has."

"Well, then. I think I love her already."

"You should, Cora. She is very easy to love."

His sister looked him up and down. "I can see that. And I thank the heavens for it, because this means I will not have to threaten you again."

"Threaten me? What are you talking about?"

"I'm talking about the fact that I thought our meeting at this ball tonight would transpire very differently. I believed before I arrived here that I would look at you and see the urge to run in your eyes. I thought I would have to remind you of the promise you made me: the promise to take me with you if you ever set sail away from Nightingale again."

"Hmm. I don't believe I ever promised you that."

Cora pivoted toward him and folded her arms across her chest. "Then promise me now, Christopher. Promise you'll never sail away without me."

He shrugged. "Actually, I can promise you that. Quite easily. Because I'm not leaving. I am not leaving ever again."

His sister scrutinized him before her face finally softened. "You know, for the first time since you came home, I honestly believe you when you say those words. God bless that woman."

His heart thudded deep. "You have no idea how much of a blessing she is."

"I suppose I don't. Not yet. But I look forward to finding out just as soon as you bring her home."

"And when exactly will that be?" Nick Marlow asked, butting into their conversation as he staggered up beside them.

Christopher surveyed his old friend. "Soon, I hope, Marlow."

"The sooner the better for you, I imagine," he mused with slurred words.

"Where is Daniela?" Christopher inquired, watching Nick widen his stance to keep his balance.

"Off to the powder room with the twins. Apparently, the Chaneys have indoor plumbing and it is all the rage. While the women fawn over toilets and bathtubs, I figure you and I should get a drink."

"I think maybe you've had enough to drink, old mate."

Nick laughed, but it held no joy. "I don't think I have, Lord Kastle."

Christopher looked back to Cora, who smiled sympathetically at the man beside them. "Why don't you go with your friend, dear brother, and I will see you later," she offered.

He nodded to her before she slipped into the crowd. Then he turned to the sad, soused man beside him. "All right, Marlow. Let's go have a drink."

"Perfect," Nick said, pulling his shoulders up as he led them around the outskirts of the dance floor.

Christopher expected to be directed toward the refreshment table, where food and drink lay in abundant supply. But his friend cut a path to the back of the room instead. "Where exactly are we going?"

"Toward the parlor rooms down the hall. There's one with a full bar."

"And how are you such an expert on the Chaney estate?"

Nick's eyes found his. "Because I familiarized myself with the layout of the manor as soon as I arrived. Old habits die hard, you know."

Christopher nodded, since his inclination would have been the same had he not been intent to remain by Violet's side. "Lead the way, then."

When they arrived at the back corner of the vast ballroom, where several doors to the hallway stood side by side, he caught sight of Juliette sitting alone in a chair. Christopher strode toward her, meeting her blue eyes with his own. "What are you doing here all by yourself, my little star?"

Juliette smiled up at him. "Just taking a much-needed rest."

"Are you well?" he wondered, glancing at the jutting bell of her wide skirt, which forced her to sit at the very edge of her seat.

"I am very well, dear brother. Simply resting my weary feet."

"I understand. But if you need me, do not hesitate to ask. I shall be with Nick in one of the parlors just down this hall."

"Thank you for the assurance," Juliette told him, holding his concerned gaze until he followed Nick through one of the back doors.

Christopher refocused on his friend as they walked the stretched corridor lined with entrances to other rooms. "All of my sisters have on brand new dresses, Marlow. You wouldn't know anything about that, would you?"

"Yes, I would. I know everything about it."

Christopher's hands fisted at his sides. "What do you mean by buying them clothes? When I've already told you I will not accept your charity?"

"Bloody hell, man. I couldn't let them show up to the ball in their old rags. Have you not read the fable of the cinder girl? As it is, they may all drop glass slippers on their way down the steps at midnight. And that will be an inordinate number of shoes on the staircase."

"And I suppose you clothed them all in silk and lace to impress Daniela?"

Nick led him into a large, wood-paneled room with a well-stocked bar. "Everything I do is to impress Daniela. I'm certain you know that."

Christopher's shoulders bunched to his ears with that confirmation, even though he was well-aware of his friend's desires. He probably shouldn't care about it as much as he did, but the fact remained that he did not think Nick worthy of Daniela. He'd seen all the depraved things the man had done in his youth, and knew all that happened to him in their years at sea, and couldn't imagine allowing a lout like that anywhere near one of his beloved sisters. Which made Christopher the biggest hypocrite to ever walk the earth, because he'd been right beside Nick for every bit of it, and had committed more sins than Nick ever did.

In truth, Christopher knew he was completely unworthy – of any woman, let alone one as vivacious and faultless as his Violet – but that could not change anything. He needed her beside him, to make him feel whole and alive. Soon, they would be husband and wife, and he could hardly wait. Hell, he'd basically said his vows to her in the carriage earlier, and he'd meant every word.

I may be a sinner and a wretch, but that woman is my salvation, he acknowledged as he looked on the deep lines of worry etched across Nick's face. *Violet is my salvation. Just as Daniela is his.*

Nick reached for two glasses and poured them full of brandy, pressing one of the drinks into Christopher's hand. "So, do you have anything else to say on the matter of me and Daniela right now?"

"No. Not right now," Christopher grumbled, painfully aware that he might never have the right to judge his friend in that regard ever again.

"Well, then. If we are not going to talk about your sister, can we address another issue?"

"What issue is that?"

"The issue of the pirate Blackheart."

The pirate Blackheart. Holy fuck.

Christopher's body pulled tight as a bowstring with the mention of that name, his fingers clenching the glass in his palm. "I've told you a hundred times since we returned home: I have no interest in discussing that issue."

Nick took a long swig of his drink. "Have you at least paid attention to the most recent newspaper reports?"

"I heard he's moved out of China," Christopher admitted, recalling the night Lady Wilmington had spoken of the pirate at dinner – causing Christopher to nearly choke on his soup – and how Violet had thrust her body across the table in an attempt to save him. "I heard he's sailing toward Africa."

"That's right. The most recent reports speak of him raiding villages in India along the way. And do you know what he is doing to those villages, once he is done raiding them?"

Christopher swallowed a gulp of brandy. "What?

Nick looked him dead in the eye. "He's burning them. *Burning* them."

Acid crawled from Christopher's gut into his throat.

"You know what that means," Nick breathed. "What the fire means."

Memories of sky-high flames pushed against the inside of Christopher's skull. "No, I do not know what that means. It could mean nothing. Nothing at all."

"Or it could mean everything."

Christopher looked away, revolted by the thought. He didn't know what Nick hoped to achieve with this line of conversation, but he could imagine the endgame. He envisioned Nick demanding to set out on some foolhardy quest that would take them both across the seas and most likely get them killed.

Christopher wouldn't be doing any such thing. He'd just assured Cora that he wasn't going anywhere, and he'd told Violet earlier tonight that he would be beside her for as long as she desired. Therefore, Nick's words could not mean anything to him at all.

"Just tell me you're at least a little worried about him," Nick huffed. "Tell me that Maxwell Taylor enters your thoughts, even once in a while."

"Damn it, man! Of course, he does!" Christopher bit back, working to keep his voice to a low roar as the memory of the young sailor's face lit his mind. Max, the kind, funny boy who had emulated Christopher from the moment he'd stepped foot on that Royal Navy ship. The orphaned lad who'd followed him straight into the lion's den – and a depraved life of piracy – the instant their ship was captured.

He honestly couldn't remember how many times in the past year he'd seen Max in his nightmares, but Christopher was trying hard to forget what had happened during his many years lost at sea. Now, with Violet, he'd finally succeeded in granting himself some reprieve. He refused to go backwards.

"Not a day goes by that I don't think of Max. But I'm trying to move on, Nick. Just as you should."

"But how the hell can you move on? I most certainly cannot. I can't stop thinking about any of it, and you've got to be as worried about him as I am."

Christopher ran a rough hand through his hair. "I am worried. But Max made his choices, and we have to live with them. We told him we would live with them. We *swore* it."

"I know we did, but the reports I heard..."

"How can you even be sure what you've heard is true? Maybe the tales of Blackheart's vengeance are just tales. No truer than that of the cinder girl."

"Bloody hell, how can you dismiss this so easily? How can you just chalk all of this up to tales and falsehoods?"

"Because I've made vows!" Christopher bellowed, watching his brother wince. He felt the guilt of his ferocity immediately and worked to calm his voice. "You do not understand, old friend. I have made promises. I promised Cora I will not leave again. I swore to Violet I will stay with her, to be beside her for as long as she desires. And I shall keep my vows."

Nick glared at him. "What about the vow you made to Fan Cheng?"

The muscle in Christopher's jaw twitched. "Do not speak that name to me. Not here. Not now."

"Then who else am I supposed to speak to about all this? You and I swore we would never tell another soul what happened to us out there. We swore we'd never talk of the atrocities we had to commit in order to survive. But I have to speak of it to someone, because it eats me alive. It eats at my very *soul*."

"You do not think it eats at me? Good Lord, I've barely slept at all in the year we've been home. And even if I thought I still had a soul when we returned to Nightingale, it would have been slowly eaten away every dark night since. But now, I've finally reached a place where I can see some light. I can actually see a *future* for myself, and I'm not about to give that up because of some goddamn rumor."

Nick tossed back the last of his drink, then stared at his empty glass as if it held all the answers. "I need you to understand something, Kastle. I need you to understand that I've spent the last month in hell without you. I've felt entirely alone with these tales of Blackheart festering and rotting inside me, and then I see you tonight with your betrothed at your side. I see the way you are with her and I'm...I'm happy for you. I swear I am. I'm happy you've found a future for yourself and I envy your ability to decide that these tales are just tales and nothing else. But I cannot simply let this lie. I need to either confirm or refute these rumors. I have to know."

Christopher studied Nicholas Marlow, witnessing the pain and regret harbored in his dark eyes. Looking at his friend now was like looking at his own reflection, before her. Before Violet. Honestly, he pitied the man for not being able to see the bright and blissful promise of tomorrow.

After taking his final bitter taste of brandy, Christopher rested his glass on the table. "Look, I understand where your mind is. I really do. If you feel you must pursue the truth about Blackheart, I won't stop you. And I promise to be available if you need to discuss your findings further. But in the meantime,

I will do as Max has asked us and live my life. I want to focus on the fact that I am at a ball with my future wife. I want to focus solely on her, because Violet is...she is everything to me. She is all I want."

He knew he'd gone too far in his speech when Nick's jaw unhinged.

"Damn, Christopher. I thought you said this marriage was a business arrangement. I thought you said you weren't going to fall in love."

"I know what I said. I just..."

"You just what?"

"I just..." he floundered, pinching his eyelids shut before looking back to the man who'd journeyed through life beside him. "Hell, Nick, you met her. You can see with just one look, you can know with just one conversation, how incredible she is. Violet is everything I could have ever hoped for. She's kind and joyful and bright and so, so beautiful and I'm..."

"In love with her," Nick finished his sentence.

Christopher stopped talking. He couldn't confirm that statement. He couldn't deny it, either. In truth, he'd thought for years that his heart was too broken to love. Yet here he was, with a woman he wanted more than anything in the world within his grasp, and he didn't know what he might actually be capable of feeling.

Nick pried Christopher's cup from his hand. "I've known you since before we could walk, Lord Kastle. Therefore, I know these feelings you have for Violet are overwhelming you entirely." Nick set their empty glasses on the bar. "So, if you ever realize you're in too deep, and you need a little time and space to clear your head, feel free to use my spare room in Nightingale Port."

Christopher stiffened. "You keep a room in Port?"

"Yes, for those nights when I can't make it home after one too many rounds of drink. The room is on top of the tavern on Wharf Street – the one closest to the docks. Just tell the barkeep you're a friend of mine and he'll let you use it anytime."

"A room on top of a bar is quite convenient for you, I suppose."

Nick chuckled darkly. "You have no idea."

Christopher could imagine his friend too drunk to even scale the steps to that spare room, as they had both been in such states in their debauched youth. Yet he was not that man any longer, and never wished to be again. "Thank you for the offer," he forced himself to say, since he knew it was only polite. "But I will never have need of your spare room. I don't have any desire to run away from Violet. Not ever."

Nick sighed as his shoulders fell. "I understand," he said. Then he poured them both another drink.

CHAPTER 8

Behind the Scenes

Violet felt a bit strange at the moment, posing beside Mama, Papa, and Gwen to take photographs. Her discomfort was not due to the fact that she stood in one of the many private parlors of the Chaney estate, attending her sister's engagement party – which would have been her own party, had Welly chosen her. On the contrary, she felt strange standing in front of the camera because the last time she'd posed for a picture, she'd been quite angry about taking a photograph intended for her betrothed.

Now, the pain she'd felt back then seemed ridiculous. Violet still vividly recalled why she'd been upset at the time, of course, and she also still wished the decision to wed had been in her control all along. But knowing what she knew today – and being perfectly aware of how her heart, body, mind, and soul all pulled toward Lord Christopher Kastle – she could not deny the joy that had come from Papa forcing her to choose a husband.

After the snapping flash of the camera, the Chaney photographer ushered Violet and her parents to the edge of the room in order to summon Welly to Gwen's side for an engagement portrait. Violet watched Gwen smile radiantly as she grasped Welly's arm. The sight filled Violet's heart with joy, not only because she loved seeing her sister so happy, but also because she felt the exact same way whenever she was with Christopher.

Dear heavens, what if I'd chosen to marry the Duke of Dunworthy? What if I'd agreed to be a place card at his dinner table, just to watch him fall asleep in his soup bowl? What if I'd decided to spend my days confined to the Dunworthy library, reading stories filled with emotions I would never experience firsthand?

She shivered with her harrowing thoughts, pulling her mother's attentions from the photographer's work. Mama drew her arm around Violet's shoulder, urging her a few steps away to speak more privately.

"What is wrong, my dear girl? Why do you shiver?"

Violet shook her head. "It's nothing."

"It does not seem that way. Are you certain you are well?"

"I am. I'm better than well. I'm…" Violet paused, trying to find the right words. "I'm ecstatic. Elated. Enlivened. Enraptured."

"He really is lovely, then? Your Lord Kastle?"

"Christopher is absolutely wonderful, Mama. He is everything I could have ever hoped for."

"And you should see them together," Gwen chimed in, stepping into their little bubble while Welly and his parents posed for more photos. "You should hear the way Christopher's voice changes when he speaks to her. You should see the way his eyes sparkle when he looks at her."

Liza grinned wildly as she looked back to Violet. "So, you are happy, little one? You are truly happy with your betrothed?"

"Oh, yes," she sighed. "Happier than imaginable."

Mama threw her arms around Violet's neck, hugging her as closely as their skirts allowed. "Then I am thrilled, for all I have ever wanted is your happiness and security. The fact that Lord Kastle can give you both fills me with joy."

"Speaking of Lord Kastle," Gwen said, "I hoped you could go find him."

Violet eased from her mother's embrace to look to her sister. "Oh? Why?"

"Because Welly's father is going to make the big announcement for us soon. I would like you to be there, near the stage. If that is all right."

"I will be there for you, front and center," Violet promised, even though she knew all eyes would travel to her once the engagement was announced.

"Thank you so much, dearest sister."

"Certainly. I shall go find Christopher now."

The mission to search out her husband granted Violet instant solace, since she needed him with her in order to endure the events to come. Mama and Gwen offered gentle smiles before Violet slipped out of the private parlor and headed down the hallway toward the main ballroom. The orchestra still poured music into the air, bathing the glamorous bodies with flowing notes, but she kept her eyes forward and her footsteps purposeful while sweeping along the edge of the crowd.

She tried to hum with the music, so as not to hear the murmurs from the people around her. Sadly, the words "picky" and "princess" still found their way to her ears, making her crave the serene feeling she'd had earlier on the dance floor when she'd been surrounded by the Kastle family. Daniela, Cora, Juliette, Ruby, and Pearl had all given her a sense of protection and made her feel at home. And then there was Christopher, standing right beside her through everything.

Violet craved Lord Kastle most of all. She craved the warm comfort of his arms. She craved the peace of his calm, strong presence. She craved the beauty of the infinite emotions she witnessed each time his eyes locked with hers.

Skirting around the dance floor, Violet sought out her husband's broad form, knowing he should not be difficult to spot in this crowd. Or in any crowd, for that matter. Yet she still could not see him, which only increased her longing. After several more minutes of fruitless searching, she discovered Juliette sitting in the very back of the room, resting quietly on a chair with her eyes closed. Violet's heart skipped a beat while she approached the young woman. "Juliette? Are you well?"

Her eyelids popped open. "I'm quite well, Violet. How are you?"

"I'm fine. But what are you doing sitting all the way back here?"

"Well, I am a bit tired from all the dancing," Juliette admitted. "But mostly, I am mapping the stars in my mind."

"Mapping the stars?"

"Yes. Christopher taught me to do it when I was little. He said you could plot a course to anywhere in the world, just by looking at the stars. When he left to join the Royal Navy, I would stare at drawings of the night sky and wonder if he could see the same stars as me. I memorized all the patterns, and if I close my eyes, I can still find them in my mind."

Violet stared into the bright blue eyes of the woman who shared such striking features with her brother. "You know, I memorize drawings in books all the time. I can see almost anything in my mind, if I choose."

"Truly?"

"Truly. It is a special gift, Juliette. Be sure to value it."

"I shall. Thank you."

"There is no need to thank me, for I am very excited to learn all I can about you and your sisters, especially when I come to live with you. But for now, I must ask you to excuse me, since I need to go find your brother."

"If you wish to find him quickly, you'll want to travel down that hall," Juliette offered, pointing to the second door on the back wall. "He went there with Nick a while ago, to visit one of the parlors."

"Oh, thank you for that. I appreciate your help."

"I really do look forward to you coming to live with us, Violet."

"I look forward to that as well."

She touched Juliette's shoulder before pivoting toward the hall. Violet stepped through the second door, striding silently across the ornamental wool carpeting, glancing into random doorways as she searched for her husband. Only a few more seconds passed before she heard Christopher's voice.

The sound of his deep, rich tenor caused her whole body to hum with excitement...until she realized that he actually sounded quite disturbed. Violet's soft footsteps slowed while her blood raced through her veins. When Christopher's words drifted out to the hallway and straight into her ears, she froze entirely.

"Hell, Nick, you met her. You can see with just one look, you can know with just one conversation, how incredible she is. Violet is everything I could have ever hoped for. She's kind and joyful and bright and so, so beautiful and I'm..."

"In love with her," Nicholas Marlow finished his sentence.

Violet's throat constricted, halting her breaths while she stood just outside the door. She knew she shouldn't be here, lurking noiselessly in the hall and listening in on their conversation, even if Christopher had once told her she was the loveliest spy he'd ever come across in all his travels. Yet she also couldn't force herself to leave, since she desperately wanted to hear his reply.

Violet closed her eyes and strained her ears, needing to know if her husband would confirm or negate his friend's statement. But he did not say anything in response. Not before Nick spoke again.

"I've known you since before we could walk, Lord Kastle. Therefore, I know these feelings you have for Violet are overwhelming you entirely."

Her face fell with those words, since she didn't wish to believe his feelings for her could ever cause him harm.

"So, if you ever realize you're in too deep," Nick continued, "and you need a little time and space to clear your head, feel free to use my spare room in Nightingale Port."

"You keep a room in Port?" Christopher questioned.

"Yes, for those nights when I can't make it home after one too many rounds of drink. The room is on top of the tavern on Wharf Street – the one closest to the docks. Just tell the barkeep you're a friend of mine and he'll let you use it anytime."

"A room on top of a bar is quite convenient for you, I suppose."

"You have no idea."

Violet whimpered. She didn't want to think of her husband running away from her to stay in some room over a bar. She couldn't bear to think of him running away from her at all, and prayed he wouldn't choose that option, even as a mere possibility.

"Thank you for the offer," Christopher replied, which made her heart plummet to her feet. "But I will never have need of your spare room," he told his friend in the next moment. "I don't have any desire to run away from Violet. Not ever."

She nearly fell over in the hallway, her whole body sagging with relief. She had to flatten her hand to the wall in order to keep herself upright. And as her legs wobbled, she realized quite painfully just how attached her entire being had become to this man.

"I understand," Nick replied before the room fell silent.

Violet waited a while longer in the shadows, working to gain control of her wits as she focused on the distant sound of liquid being poured into glasses. Once she could think clearly, she shifted a few steps back from the door and called to her husband. "Christopher? Are you here?"

"Violet? I'm in here."

Forcing her unsteady legs forward, she rounded the corner to the room. "I'm glad I found you," she said as she entered, moving toward the bar where the two men stood.

Christopher's bright eyes lit even brighter when he saw her. "I was just having a drink with Nick. Do you need me, my dearest?"

"Yes, I do. We just finished with the photographer and then I searched for you in the ballroom. I found Juliette there and she told me you came this way," Violet admitted, although she wouldn't admit to anything else.

She wouldn't admit to the conversation she'd just overheard – at least, not anytime soon. She didn't think it would be right to corner Christopher about his feelings for her, especially if he wasn't ready to put a name to his emotions. Still, she refused to believe her affections could ever do him harm. As far as she was concerned, love could never be harmful.

Love could never be harmful.

Love.

Violet nearly tripped over her own two feet while she strode across the room toward her husband. For she understood, just now, that she loved him. She loved Christopher Kastle fully and completely, without shame or remorse. And she could not bring herself to fear that truth, no matter how imprudent the rapid formation of her feelings may be.

He reached out to touch her. "Is everything all right?"

"Everything is perfect," she realized, placing her gloved fingers in his palm.

Christopher searched her eyes. "Are you certain?"

She stilled herself as she stood beside her husband's strong, heated body, gazing into the fathomless blue she knew so well. Violet felt her heart reach for his without bounds. The sensation was beautiful, wondrous, and beyond compare, and she did not wish to give it up for anything in the world.

"Quite certain," she assured.

I love you, Christopher. I love you with all that I am.

He didn't hear her decree, since she did not speak it aloud. But he still smiled, entwining their fingers to pull her closer. "I'm glad all is well, my sweet. Shall we return to the ballroom now?"

"Oh, right. That is actually the reason I came to find you. Gwen asked that we be present near the stage for her announcement."

"Very well," he agreed, tightening his grip on her hand.

"What announcement?" Nick questioned.

Violet turned to the other man in the room. "You should come with us and see," she invited, trying to give Mr. Marlow the benefit of the doubt. She did not wish to judge him too harshly for offering his friend a room above a bar where he could escape her, even though the thought of that offer stung fiercer than she could fathom. She could only soothe her sting with the knowledge that her husband did not desire such a reprieve.

"Yes, do come with us, Marlow," Christopher encouraged as he urged her fingers onto his coat sleeve. "It is a happy occasion tonight."

Nick finally set his drink down. "All right."

Christopher focused solely on Violet while he guided her through the door, down the hallway, and back to the ballroom. Her heart pounded in her chest as she gazed at him, gripping his arm for purchase while her newly named feelings rushed like wildfire through her body. Yet the intensity of her love only strengthened her backbone, keeping her head high when they reemerged into the enormous room filled with society's judges.

She tore her gaze from her husband in order to glance around the dance floor, noting that Juliette no longer sat to the back of the crowd. A second later, Violet realized no person sat at all. Everyone stood throughout the room, looking to the center stage where Welly and Gwen formed a united front with Lord and Lady Chaney before the now-silent orchestra.

"Should we move nearer the stage?" Christopher whispered.

"Yes, please. Gwen desires us to be as close as possible."

He led Violet away from Nick, swerving deftly around the other guests before coming to a stop at the front of the room, directly before her sister. Gwen caught her gaze and offered a nervous grin. Violet answered with her bravest smile, which seemed to lessen Gwen's anxiety.

"Greetings, ladies and gentleman," Lord Henry Chaney announced. "We wish to thank you all for your attendance tonight. And now, we have some truly lovely news to share." The Earl of Centreville absolutely beamed as he turned toward Welly and Gwen. "Wellington Chaney, my son and heir, has chosen a bride. He will wed Miss Gwendolyn Bell, daughter of Mr. Noah and Lady Liza Bell of Pennyshire, at the end of the season. You shall all be invited to help us celebrate this wonderful union."

A raucous round of applause filled the ballroom. Violet saw Gwen's face light up gloriously – almost as gloriously as Welly's. The two of them radiated sheer bliss, and for a moment Violet thought of nothing but her sister's happiness and the freshly-minted couple's ability to move on with their lives now.

Christopher slipped her hand from his arm in order to wind their fingers together. Violet glanced up to him, watching him smile down at her from his place by her side. She watched his eyes shine with barely contained radiance – reflecting a depth of emotion she'd witnessed building each day since the moment they met – and the sight stole the air from her lungs.

Is that love? Does Christopher love me as I love him?

God, she wanted it to be true. She even believed it might be. She felt the emotion in his body whenever he touched her, whether that touch came in tender reverence or wanton desire. She saw the emotion in his eyes whenever he looked at her like he did now, as if his entire world existed inside her. She heard the emotion in his voice whenever he spoke her name, as if it was the best name he'd ever known.

Acknowledging that her husband might feel the same for her as she did for him made this moment nearly perfect, allowing Violet to swim in her sister's joy while nearly drowning in her own. She almost forgot her current situation, standing amidst this crowd of gaping onlookers. But then she felt their slicing glances shift toward her, gauging her reaction to her younger sister's engagement to her ex-suitor. This was the moment she'd dreaded all week, because it pulled the focus from Gwen's joyful news and soured the whole occasion. Yet now, as Violet stood beside the man she'd chosen to take a chance on loving – the man she already loved, who quite possibly loved her, too – she simply glowed with contentment.

Christopher grasped her fingers as they endured the scrutiny around them. He didn't recoil at all when they became the center of attention. He merely pulled her hand up to his face and pressed his lips to the back of her glove.

Violet focused entirely on her husband as he created a rather sinful display: lingering with his mouth attached to her hand for much longer than necessary, all while keeping his eyes pinned on hers. She knew his actions were a show of devotion and solidarity in the face of so many naysayers. Yet he also managed to make it feel like a moment between just the two of them, with no other soul in sight, and she loved him all the more for it.

"Now, let us all continue with the dancing and merriment," Henry Chaney announced, pulling everyone's attention back to the stage. "For this is a grand night for the Chaney family, as we welcome our newest member wholeheartedly, and we desire as much celebration as possible!"

Tears sprang to Violet's eyes with their host's declaration, because Gwen could finally move forward. Lord Henry Chaney's acceptance of her meant that Gwen's happiness would never again be dependent on the choices of her older sister. Those ties were cut forever, and while Violet felt some degree of pain with that understanding, she also knew Welly had a good soul. He would keep Gwen close and safe always, which allowed Violet an unparalleled sense of relief.

"Please tell me you are well," Christopher whispered when the orchestra music filled the room again. "For I see tears in your eyes, and that sight shall cut right into me if I think you are in any way unhappy."

The raw ache in his voice pulled at her insides. "My heavens, how could I ever be unhappy, Christopher? When you stand beside me as you are, and look at me as you do?"

A perfect smile lit his face before he brought her hand back to his mouth to press another kiss to her glove. When he finished, he leaned in close. "I hope you are imagining that kiss on your hand was actually placed on your lips, since my desire to feel your mouth on mine is absolutely crushing me and I cannot bear to endure the agony of it alone."

Violet gripped hard to his fingers. "I do feel your lips on mine. And I promise that you shall never have to endure agony alone, ever again. Not so long as I have breath in my body."

He stared at her after she finished speaking, searching her eyes intensely and meticulously. She wanted nothing more than to tell him she loved him. She wanted to sing it at the top of her lungs and shout it from the rooftops, all at once. Yet she did not. If Nicholas Marlow was correct, and Christopher's feelings for her were overwhelming him entirely, then she did not want her words of love to cause him undue pressure.

Nevertheless, Violet still stood solidly beneath his probing gaze. She did not wish to overwhelm him, yet she also refused to cower away from her feelings. If he witnessed the conviction of her emotions within her eyes, and understood the depths of her love without her actually speaking the words, then she was prepared to live with those consequences.

After many thick moments, Christopher set her hand back on his arm. "Come dance with me again, my sweet. I am in great need of holding you close, and this is the only way I can do so, given our current location."

Violet raised her chin. "I'd love to feel you close to me, dearest husband."

He matched her passionate gaze as he led her into the crowd.

They danced together forever. At least, it felt like forever. Time simply stopped while they held onto each other and swept over the floor, removing everyone and everything else from the room. Violet saw only him. She felt only the heat of his body. She knew only the security of his embrace.

No one disturbed them as they moved blissfully together. She wasn't sure why, but she also didn't care. She appreciated the opportunity to be in his presence, letting the melodic sounds of the orchestra carry her away, right into the deep blue of his eyes. She lost all track of time, so when Cora tapped on Christopher's shoulder and urged them to separate, Violet was genuinely surprised to find that nearly everyone in the room had vanished.

"I just wanted to say goodnight," Cora explained her interruption, giving Violet a soft smile before turning her eyes to her brother. "In case you didn't realize that it is quite late now, and definitely time to leave."

Christopher chuckled as he took Violet's hand. "I appreciate the information, Cora. I don't know if I would have realized these things on my own."

"I am aware of that," she said, shaking her head even while smiling. "And since the rest of our sisters are already in the carriage Nick provided for us, and are all thoroughly exhausted, I assured them I would bid you both goodnight on behalf of everyone. Until we see you again."

"Please tell everyone how much I enjoyed meeting them," Violet entreated, releasing her hold on Christopher in order to throw her arms around his blessedly embraceable sister.

Cora returned her hug with vigor. "I will. And please know that we truly loved meeting you, as well."

Violet nodded ardently as she eased back, feeling the wildest leap of joy.

"Brother," Cora addressed while arching up on her tiptoes to peck his cheek. "Do come home soon."

"I shall," he promised, tugging Violet back to his side. "And I shall bring this wondrous woman with me."

"That is perfect," Cora agreed. "Goodnight to you both."

"Goodnight," they spoke in unison, watching together as Cora exited the ballroom, passing the last few couples still roaming across the floor.

"Hmm," Christopher contemplated. "I suppose we should leave now."

"Yes, that is probably..."

"Violet!" Gwen squealed, rushing toward them. "You're still here!"

"I am, indeed. Do you need me?"

Gwen skidded to a stop in front of her. "Just for a moment, if that's all right. Mama and Papa plan to whisk me back to Pennyshire to begin arrangements for the wedding, but I wanted time alone with you beforehand."

"Oh. Certainly," Violet agreed, glancing to her husband.

"Why don't I go outside to wait for you?" Christopher offered. "I shall ensure our carriage is brought around to the front."

"That is lovely. I'll only be a moment."

He released his hold on her, huffing with the loss of their contact before composing himself to smile at Gwen. "Thank you again for inviting us here tonight. And please do offer Wellington and his parents our gratitude, also."

"I shall," Gwen promised while linking her sister's arm.

He looked back to Violet, capturing her eyes. "I will wait for you on the front steps, my sweet."

"Oh, yes, that's...mmm. I mean, very good. I shall meet you there shortly."

Violet laughed at her own nervous speech, unsure how she could still feel so flustered by a man she'd be in such close proximity to throughout the night. Christopher grinned before walking away, and she could barely keep her jaw from hanging while gaping at the fluid movement of his large form beneath the tightly cut fabric of his coat and trousers. Honestly, no man should ever have the right to wear clothing that well, especially when she could still smell his scent on her own clothing.

"You're drooling, sister," Gwen whispered.

"Am I?" Violet gasped, her fingers flying to her lips.

Gwen giggled. "I didn't mean that literally. Although I may as well have."

"My goodness! Do not scare me in such a way!" Violet admonished, sharing her sister's laughter as they both watched his retreating form.

"Come with me," Gwen encouraged. "You must need to tidy up before your journey back to Aunt Tildy's, and I do so wish to speak with you."

"Is anything wrong?" Violet questioned while Gwen ushered her toward yet another door along the back wall of the immense ballroom.

"No, not at all. Everything is perfect, actually. Except for the fact that you and I will both be married soon, living in different homes that are hours apart from one another, and I am going to miss you so much."

Violet pressed her hand over her sister's. "It will be all right. We shall always be in each other's hearts, even if we cannot be in each other's sights."

"I know. It is just difficult to think upon."

"It is," she admitted as they walked down the back corridor.

Gwen led them both inside the Chaney's large powder room. Violet's eyes widened as she glanced around at the private facilities. "My goodness, Gwen! Look at this room! I've heard of indoor plumbing, but I've never actually seen it!"

"I know!" Gwen exclaimed, running her hands across the edge of the deep bathing tub built into the floor. "Welly's home is so lovely. It has everything anyone could ever want. I honestly cannot believe I get to call it my own," she said, smiling with her words. Seconds later, her eyes clouded with guilt. "Although, I'm sure the Kastle estate will be just as lovely. Or, at least, quite fine. I mean, I hope it will be fine."

Violet reached for her sister's gloved fingers, taking them inside her own. "Gwen, please listen to me. I want you to know – no matter what happens from this moment forward – that you and I are exactly where we need to be, with exactly the men we are supposed to be with. I need you to understand that I believe this with all my heart, and do not regret anything that happened to bring us here. Love works in mysterious ways, but it does find a way."

"Sweet heavens, Violet. Are you saying you love him? Do you actually *love* Christopher?"

Violet pressed her lips together. She hadn't wanted to admit this truth to anyone, since she hadn't yet told her husband. But she also couldn't lie, not when asked this blatantly. "I do, Gwen. In truth, I am madly in love with him. And perhaps I shouldn't be. Not so soon. Perhaps I should guard my heart more prudently, but I have never known feelings like this before and I want desperately to experience them. I want to learn all I can with him, to know myself entirely by understanding all that I am capable of feeling."

When she finished her confessions, Gwen remained silent. Violet tensed, expecting the same warning she'd heard weeks ago about the rashness of taking Christopher's scars and burdens onto herself. She held still as stone as she looked into her sister's eyes, awaiting censure.

Gwen merely threw her arms around Violet's neck. "Oh, goodness, I am so thrilled for you! I am so thrilled for us both!"

Violet grabbed hold of her, not even caring how their skirts jutted wildly out behind them as they embraced in a full-body hug. For her heart had never been so full and she'd never been so happy. Never, ever.

BY THE TIME Violet finished visiting with her sister – and employed Gwen's assistance with her dress in order to use the indoor facilities, and checked on her appearance in the looking glass, and stepped back into the ballroom – only a dozen couples remained. Violet gave her sister one last hug goodbye before moving through the hall to the grand entry foyer and proceeding out of the front door into the cool night air. When she reached the top of the stairway, Christopher stood in wait for her. Her body hummed the instant she saw him.

"Is everything all right with Gwen?" he asked while extending his arm.

Violet wrapped her fingers around his coat sleeve. "Oh, yes. She simply desired time together before we must start living our lives apart."

"I see," Christopher considered as he guided her down the staircase. "Please rest assured that we can invite the Chaneys to the Kastle estate whenever you desire. I do not wish to think of you being sad without her."

Violet gazed up at him in the dimming glow of the manor torches. "Thank you for that. I do look forward to visits with her in the future. But for now, Gwen and I will be fine. I assured her that she and I are in exactly the right places, with exactly the right men beside us."

His footing faltered. "You truly believe that?"

"I do. I know it absolutely," Violet assured with a smile.

Christopher stared at her with a look of sheer incredulity, as if he did not understand her words at all. But then he returned her smile, securing his hand over hers while they stepped onto the gravel path heading toward the line of waiting coaches. He steadied her beside him as they moved, the heat of his body easily combating the chilled air.

Her husband's permeating warmth reminded Violet of the hours they'd spent pressed together while dancing. "You were right, you know," she conceded to him while they approached Tildy's carriage.

Christopher's brow quirked. "What about?"

"You said earlier that there would be much for us to enjoy at this ball, and I'll admit I didn't really believe it. But you were quite right."

His smile deepened. "I'm glad you had fun. What was your favorite part?"

"Oh, I adored many things, especially the many dances. However, my favorite part must be meeting your family. I love all your sisters already. Including the two I have not yet met."

He guided her to a stop in front of their waiting coach, looking to her eyes as he brushed his fingertips across her cheek. "And they love you, Violet. Everyone loves you."

Dear God, does that include you, Christopher? "I – I am glad you think so."

"I know so," he confirmed, skimming his fingers over her pinned hair before his hand fell away. "I suppose I should open the door for you now."

Violet nodded, although she despised being away from him for even the moment it took him to pull on the door. She frowned as she stared into the cramped inner carriage chamber. "Bloody hell," she muttered.

Apparently, she didn't curse quietly enough. Christopher shook his head as he turned to look on her. "My, my, Violet. What language."

Her gaze shifted sheepishly to his face. "I'm sorry for swearing. I just...I can't imagine stuffing this dress back into that coach again." *No matter how much I'll enjoy being alone with you for the next two hours.*

"I was teasing about your language," he assured while striding back to her side. "You can always say anything you want to me. Always." He came to a standstill when his shins hit the lowest hoop of her abundant skirts. "Also, I have an idea about making you more comfortable for our return trip."

Violet held her breath as his gaze drifted leisurely over her face, stroking the curves of her mouth. "Really? What is your idea?"

He glanced around them, at the few scattered couples still filing out of the Chaney manor. "Why don't we get inside where we can be alone," he suggested in a rough whisper. "Then I'll tell you all about it."

Her palms dampened when he looked to her with eyes as dark as the surrounding night. "All right," Violet agreed without thought, even though she should definitely question his intentions. After all, questioning his intentions would be quite prudent. But she did not desire to make prudent decisions right now. She only desired to be with the man she loved.

Gathering her skirts in both hands, she lifted them a few inches from the ground while stepping toward the coach. Christopher moved in behind her, assisting discreetly with the shifting of her cage so she could climb the single stair and finagle her way inside. The moment they both sat on the cushioned leather bench – along with her innumerable petticoats and stiff crinoline – he pulled the door closed and rapped on the roof to signal the coachman.

As the horses began to shimmy the carriage wheels over the gravel, Violet began to fuss with her dress. She bent entirely forward, straining against her tight corset while struggling to keep the lower circle of her cage pressed to the ground. She expected Christopher to assist her, helping her tame the unruly hoops like he did on their journey here. She would be very happy to see him pounce on her skirts like a kitten again, since his actions had been adorable, even if ultimately ineffective.

Alas, he did no such thing. Her husband did not assist with her struggles in the slightest. He merely stared out of the window, watching the lights from the party fade into the distance. "Will you tell me your idea about my skirts?" Violet prompted, hoping to reclaim his focus.

Christopher finally turned toward her. Even in the dim light of the carriage, he still managed to seize her gaze. "I will tell you my idea. But first, I must warn you that you may consider it indecent."

Her heart thudded erratically. "You can always say anything you want to me, Christopher. Always."

A tempting smile teased his lips. "Very well, then. My idea is to remove your crinoline hoops entirely for the trip back."

"*What?* Remove my cage? How on earth would we manage that?"

"Actually, I think we can do it without too much fuss. That is, if you're willing to lift your skirts and allow me to help you with it."

Violet's jaw dropped.

Christopher chuckled before glancing out of the window again. "I've been waiting for us to be far enough away from the other coaches before we attempt such a thing. I do believe we are quite alone now, and shall remain alone for the next two hours. Therefore, if you'd like to remove your cage for our journey, I'll be happy to assist."

"But...it's...I..." she stammered, her mind struggling to grasp the highly unsuitable thought, as well as all the implications surrounding it. "I mean, I suppose the idea does have some merit. Unfortunately, as difficult as it will be to remove the atrocious thing, it will be absolutely impossible to reattach it while we're still riding. I will surely arrive back at Wilmington tonight without any crinoline form beneath my skirts. And then what will Aunt Tildy say?"

His gaze returned to hers. "Violet, your aunt can barely manage to stay awake through dinner. I highly doubt she'll be up in the dark hours past midnight when we return to the estate. And the servants who see you upon our return may gossip amongst each other, but I don't think they will inform your aunt of anything, for fear of recrimination."

"Hmm. You are probably right about that."

"I do believe I am. But please know that it is perfectly acceptable to refuse my suggestion. If you do not feel comfortable enough to do this with me, I promise I'll understand."

Violet shook her head immediately. "No, it's...that's not it. I am utterly and entirely comfortable with you."

"Good. I want you to be."

"I know that," she said, blowing out a frustrated breath. After all, his quest for her comfort was the reason why he always acted so properly, and why he reined in her desires whenever she ventured too far, and why he'd only kissed her softly and chastely this whole past week. Christopher was a perfect gentleman, and in truth, his politeness was becoming rather maddening. Now that she knew she loved him, and that she wanted him in every possible way, she wasn't at all concerned about how untoward things would appear when she stepped onto the Wilmington entryway with no form beneath her skirts. What she was concerned about was if her husband would actually do anything with her once he released her from her cage.

Violet focused on his eyes in the darkened chamber, lit only by the pale moonlight filtering through the window. She attempted to steady her mind, working to channel the same courage she'd possessed the day she entreated him to teach her swordplay in the gazebo. "I wholeheartedly accept your suggestion," she began. "But before we proceed, I need to make sure you understand certain things about this finery I'm wearing. You must realize that I will have to lift my skirts in order for you to detach my crinoline, and that I will have only a single thin slip remaining underneath."

Christopher's eyes narrowed, but he didn't look away. "All right."

She shifted a bit closer. "I also think I should impress upon you that my lowest slip, the one touching my skin, is very, very thin. To be honest, it's basically see-through. And, of course, I am not wearing knickers."

A stifled groan erupted from his chest. "All right."

"In addition, I shall have to stand as best I can in this cramped space, in order to lift my skirts. I'll have to angle my body so you can reach the ties of the crinoline on my lower back, which means I'll have to bend over to push my hips into your hands. At that point, my bottom will be rather brazenly in your face, and as I mentioned before, my lowest slip is see-through. There shall be nothing beneath it but my bare skin, so you'll definitely be able to see my..."

"Damn it, Violet. *Stop talking.*"

She sealed her lips the instant he growled at her. She also whimpered, although not because she was upset by his command. She simply couldn't believe the depth of hunger she saw in his eyes with just the few sentences she'd spoken.

Christopher sat up straighter on the bench. "I – I apologize for my forceful words. Please do not stop talking to me. I never want that."

"All right," she said, moistening her lips with her tongue and watching the muscle in his jaw twitch at the sight. "I just want to make sure we are both on the same page about what is going to happen now. Since I imagine this will be a difficult task."

"Yes, it will be," he agreed, his voice so low that it sounded like the gravel scraping under the wooden wheels. "But we'll manage."

"Very well, then. I guess I'll stand up."

His eyes never left her body. Not when she moved to the edge of the bench, nor when she turned her back to him. Violet could feel his gaze on her skin as she attempted to stand, hunching over to prevent her head from hitting the roof. She continued to feel his stare as she reached down to grab hold of her skirts, gathering them in her fingers, pulling them up and up and up until they all sat bunched at her waist. She definitely felt his eyes boring into her now, with only the cage and thin slip remaining on the lower half of her body. And with her bottom most definitely in his face.

Violet held her breath, rather involuntarily, as she struggled to keep her chin tucked to her chest and her arms full of fabric. With her lung sounds stilled, she could hear the rotation of wheels, the clipping of horse hooves, and the rapid beat of her own heart. She listened in painful anticipation as the bench leather creaked with the shifting of Christopher's weight.

Only shallow breaths escaped his throat while he brought his hands to her hips. He moaned as his fingers grasped the base of her corset. Once his palms rested against her – and his warmth seeped straight through the stiff herringbone and into her skin – she released a needy little noise of her own. His grip on her tightened almost painfully.

"Can you, um, can you see where the ties come undone, Christopher?"

"Mm-hmm," he murmured, although his hands didn't move for several seconds. Then he started pulling at the strings, undoing the laces holding the crinoline in place. The amount of time that lapsed while his fingers tugged against the base of her corset became languid and torturous, even though he had the cage ties open in mere moments. When he finished unlacing the strings, his fingertips curled into the loosened upper band.

"I'm going to take this off now, Violet."

"Mm-hmm."

He pulled straight down. But he took his time. Christopher dragged his knuckles determinedly against her body the entire way, skimming the gossamer fabric of her lowest slip. He traced over the curves of her bottom, across the backs of her thighs and knees, all the way down to her ankles. He drew his clenched fingers over her barely concealed flesh with leisurely precision, until he finally pushed her crinoline entirely to the floor. She felt his hot breath puffing across the skin of her bottom, soaking through the single thin layer of clothing still concealing her lower half from his eyes. Although, to be honest, she knew her sheer slip wasn't really concealing anything.

Violet chose to not move at all, even after Christopher freed them both from her cage. She just stood there, holding her skirts up, letting her husband look on her. She wasn't in the mood to hide from him. She wanted him to look. She wanted him to touch.

She intended to wait forever for that touch, even though she wasn't sure it would come. Now that he'd completed his task, he had no reason to continue touching her. Yet she did not let that fact deter her. She stood her ground, with her skirts bunched about her waist and her heart pounding in her ears.

A hundred years elapsed before Christopher's hands drew back to her body. When he finally reached for her hips, and his fingers came in contact with the airy slip beneath her corset, she gasped. Violet regretted the unseemly noise instantly, since it made him pause his actions. She bit into her lip to contain her voice as she waited impatiently for him to continue.

He did continue. When she made no further noises or any protests, he eased his hands across her waist, tracing over the curves of her hipbones slowly and intentionally. His palms were wickedly hot and just a little damp, and she could feel that slight moisture seep through her gauzy slip. She teetered a bit with that sensation, losing some of her balance – not because she couldn't support the weight of fabric in her hands, but because the world spun all around her.

At that moment, one of the carriage wheels hit a hole in the ground, slanting the coach harshly to one side. Violet yelped as she fell straight back onto Christopher's lap, her thinly clad bottom landing on his hard thighs with a decided bounce. He grabbed hold of her in an instant, banding his arms around her waist and pulling her into a sideways position on the bench, securing her to him with lightning-fast reflexes.

Violet wasn't sure how he'd gotten his hands out from under her skirts and overtop of her dress that quickly. Nor did she know how her own arms had wrapped around his broad shoulders without her knowledge. All she knew for certain was that she now sat on him, with only the thinnest material separating her bare bottom from his trousers. And with the side of her bodice indecently close to his chest. And with her lips nearly pressed to his.

Their heated breaths mingled while Christopher's fingers twitched against the stiff lines of her corset. The cloth waves of her skirt poured over the side of the bench and pooled onto the floor. Only a small bunching of fabric separated her hips from his, and she couldn't help but want it gone.

"I swear to the heavens that I did not fall into your lap on purpose," Violet insisted the moment she could find her voice, feeling the need to defend her very recent, very treacherous actions.

He stared directly into her. "I know you didn't."

"Oh. Well, good. Although, I suppose I should move off of you now."

"Do you want to move off of me?"

"No. Not at all."

"Then don't."

Christopher's words were simple. The look in his eyes was anything but.

Violet didn't move a muscle. However, she did wish to verify their current understanding. "So, you desire me to remain here, sitting on your lap?"

"*Yes*," he growled. Then he stopped speaking. At least, he stopped speaking with words. But his ravenous gaze spoke volumes.

She held entirely still. On the outside. On the inside, her blood bounded through her veins and her lungs stuttered in her chest.

He studied her for extensive moments, with every second torturous to her entire being. After forever, he eased forward and pressed his lips to hers. Slowly. Tenderly. Gently.

Violet knew this kiss very well. It was the same one he'd given her over and over for the past week, ever since they'd left the sanctuary of their picnic blanket in the Wilmington field. This was a safe kiss, a comfortable kiss, and it frustrated her beyond reason.

Christopher kept the kiss exactly like this: just a simple press of their lips together. But she wanted so much more. She reached her hands to his face – running her gloved fingers over his jaw, grasping at his stubble, and tilting her head – trying desperately to deepen their actions.

He groaned and wrenched his mouth from hers. "Violet."

The gruff sound of her name on his lips caused her physical pain. "Yes?" she asked, waiting in dread for his admonition of her desires.

"Let me see your hands, please."

Her brow rose. "Very well," she agreed, letting her arms drop down while still maintaining her balance on his thighs. She held her cloth-covered fingers in front of his chest with the backs of her hands facing upward.

Violet couldn't help but flinch at her current situation. She recalled having to hold her hands out like this as a child, to have a ruler rapped across her knuckles by her governess as punishment for her mischievous deeds. Not that Violet believed her husband would ever strike her; she knew he was not that kind of man. Yet the position she now found herself in felt like one of scolding, inciting her guilt for grasping onto him as lasciviously as she had.

He kept one arm around her waist, securing her on his lap while bringing his other hand to hers. Christopher circled his fingers around her right wrist, easing across her pulse point before flipping her hand over to face her palm upward. He dragged one finger across the center, tracing a path all the way to the tip of her thumb. The next instant, he began to tug on the silk fabric concealing her lower arms.

"If you intend to grab hold of my face again, as you just did, then I want these gloves off," he explained, eliciting chills across every surface of her body.

"You see, this fabric is quite soft, yet it feels coarse as sand compared to the touch of your skin. And I have despised my inability to feel your flesh on mine throughout this entire night."

Violet heaved a sigh of relief, her muscles easing as her fears of condemnation evaporated. She watched with unbridled anticipation while he took his time tugging the silk material away from each and every one of her fingers before pulling the glove off altogether. As soon as he'd discarded the offending fabric on the floor, he pressed his bare palm into hers. She moaned with that simple yet perfect contact. He smiled at the wanton sound, and then repeated his actions with her other glove.

Once both her arms lay bare, Christopher stroked the ring finger of her left hand. "There were so many jewels on the women at the ball," he reminisced, his gaze focused on the sight of his fingers caressing hers. "The ladies were draped in every gem imaginable, and all I could think of was my desire to give you at least one. I want nothing more than to place a wedding ring on this finger. Although no jewel could ever match your brilliance."

Violet grinned even as her heart clawed to reach his. "I appreciate that thought, but I truly do not care about jewels. I only care about you."

His eyes drew back to hers. "And I care for you. So deeply."

Her breath caught. He didn't say he loved her. But she'd nearly heard it.

Christopher's fingers continued smoothing over hers. "What ring would you want, my dearest? If you could have any in the world?"

"I haven't thought about it, actually."

"I could get you an emerald snakehead ring, just like Queen Victoria's. Would you enjoy something like that?"

Violet crinkled her nose. "Goodness, no. I do not think a snake should be a symbol of love, no matter how much society clings to the idea because it's Queen Victoria's ring. Besides, when I look at you, I do not think of a snake. A snake is a slithery little creature, and you are anything but. You are big and brave and strong, like a lion. Or a panther, even. You move like a panther, I think, especially when I watch you practice your sword at night. Your actions are so gorgeously feral and agile, and your hands are big like paws, engulfing me whenever I feel your touch. And all of your muscles are so perfectly broad and defined and..." She ceased speaking, struggling for air beneath the onslaught of his dangerously darkening eyes. "And I should probably stop talking about your body now, shouldn't I?"

Christopher brushed his hand across her cheek. "Please don't stop talking to me. Not ever."

She nodded slowly, unable to tear her eyes from his. "All right."

He eased his fingers upward, skimming over her pinned curls. "I want you to know how grateful I am that you like my body so much, Violet. Since I am most desirous of yours."

"Y-you desire my body?"

"God, yes. You have no idea."

She whimpered with his unashamed confirmation.

Christopher's fingers drifted over her hair, his touch steady even as his voice quavered. "Do you – do you remember that day we spent together on the picnic blanket, my sweet?"

"Remember? Good heavens, I think of it constantly."

"Mmm. As do I. Do you also remember what you said to me when we returned to the manor afterwards? How you asked me to keep you informed of any sensation I could give that you might enjoy?"

She swallowed hard. "Yes. I remember."

"Well," he continued, his gaze shifting up to her curls, "I think you might enjoy the sensation of me removing your hairpins."

She stared at her husband's mouth. In truth, those weren't the exact words she'd expected to come from his excellently sculpted lips. To be honest, removing her pins was a simple act of care she'd experienced nearly every day of her life and not at all sensual. Nevertheless, Violet trusted that she would like anything he did to her. "I suppose, since Aunt Tildy isn't going to be awake when we arrive at Wilmington, and we've already gone so far as to remove my cage, that it won't matter if my hair is down, too."

"Your logic is sound," Christopher granted, his eyes still roaming across her fastened curls. With Violet's consent, he traced her hairline with his fingers. The motion encouraged her eyes to close, allowing her to revel in the feel of his skin on hers. When he finally reached into her hair, found the end of a pin, and began pulling it slowly downward, she moaned without censure.

"This is going to take a while," he informed, his warm breath fanning across her cheek. "Because I want it to."

Violet was a bit confused by his current desire. But then he pulled the first hairpin all the way out, dragging her single freed curl down to her collarbone while tracing over her skin with his fingers, and she realized exactly why he wanted this to last forever. It felt like he was undressing her. It felt like he was deliberately and languorously removing pieces of her clothing, making her whole body shiver as he persisted.

Christopher took his time with each pin, easing them gently down to pull the curls onto her neck and across her shoulder, his fingers maintaining constant contact with her skin. He acted as if they would be in this carriage for all eternity and he therefore had nothing better to do than drag out each unhurried, aching second. By the time he'd dropped every one of her pins onto the floor, and swept all the loose locks of her hair over her shoulders and onto her bare upper back, Violet panted in time with her rapid heartbeat.

She looked back to him, watching as he stared at her halo of curls for a long minute. Then he pushed his fingers up inside, running them firmly against her scalp until he cradled her head in his palm. She groaned crudely with the sensation, biting her lip in an attempt to stifle the coarse sound.

Christopher watched her teeth sink into her skin. He drew his thumb onto her mouth, tracing the lower edge before pulling it free from her bite. A moment later, he returned that hand to the base of her spine, securing her in place against him.

He stared hard at her mouth – so hard that Violet swore she could already feel his lips on hers. Then he kissed her. It wasn't a soft, simple kiss, like the ones he'd been peppering over her mouth for the past week. This kiss was fierce and hungry and possessive. Christopher clutched her body tightly to his, pinning her onto his chest with his large palm flattened over her back. His fingers coiled in her hair, fisting her curls almost painfully. Yet it didn't hurt at all, since she now realized that he'd taken her pins down in order to hold onto her exactly the way he wanted when he kissed her. That comprehension of his forethought sent a wave of heat crashing over her skin.

When he slipped his tongue past her parted lips, Violet thrust her upper body onto his, winding her arms around his neck to grip him just as fiercely. She clutched at his collar, desperate to have him even closer. But she was careful to not run her fingers beneath the fabric, since she knew the scar he bore on his neck and didn't wish to draw attention to it. Not now, when she desired his full focus to be here, with her. With them.

She breathed in deep as Christopher kissed her, saturating her senses with the soap and leather scent of his skin. He tasted like the brandy he'd been drinking, and his tongue felt thick and wet and hot in her mouth, and she opened herself up to him entirely. This was her only current means of accepting a part of his body into her own, and she craved it beyond reason.

The ferocity of her husband's kiss brought with it the tempting promise of *more*. Violet threaded her fingers into his hair, gripping him to her, wanting to know all he could make her feel. He ran his tongue over hers again and again, angling her head to control and deepen his actions, setting her flesh on fire. The intensity of her desires made her quite angry when he eventually tore his mouth from hers. She growled at him for breaking their contact, even after so many moments of lustful perfection. And she wasn't even ashamed of herself.

With her disgruntled noise, Christopher huffed out a laugh. He eased his grip on her bodice and uncurled his fingers from her hair, holding her in a much kinder fashion. He waited patiently until she raised her eyes to his.

His deep blue sparkled more profoundly than ever. "Please tell me, Violet. Do you like it when I slide my tongue into your mouth?"

The question sent a tremor straight through her, making her nipples pebble and her breasts ache. She rubbed her bodice against his chest to feel some form of relief, her instinctive action eliciting a groan from his throat. "Yes," she admitted, barely recognizing her own voice. "I love it when you slide your tongue into my mouth."

Christopher's fingers slipped down from her hair onto her spine. "Well, then. I think you might enjoy doing the same to me."

"Oh. You – you want me to slide my tongue into your mouth?"

"I do. I want it very much."

"Well, I guess that's...yes, of course."

Her husband smiled with her approval, even as he held his breath.

Violet relished the anticipation written across his face. Yet she still hesitated, not because she didn't wish to fulfill his desire, but because she wanted to choose the best possible way to proceed. She decided to begin by framing his face in her hands and gliding her bare fingers over his prickly stubble. Next, she leaned forward to ease her chest onto his. She savored the yearning look in his eyes before finally pressing their lips together.

Christopher's arms tightened around her the moment she initiated their kiss. His fingertips stroked up and down the back seams of her bodice, encouraging her with his touch. She smiled before darting the tip of her tongue out to trace over his lips. His responding moan fueled her courage, so she pushed herself harder against the wall of his body as she sought entry into his mouth.

When Violet slid her tongue inside, seeking the heat and wetness awaiting her, he opened himself instantly. She sensed the tension growing in his muscles while she explored, knowing her husband struggled to restrain himself. Yet he was giving her this time to experiment as she desired, so she greedily accepted his kind offer.

Violet tried tasting the tip of his tongue, then brushing deeper across it, then tangling it against hers. She practiced for lengthy moments, changing the position of her lips on his and playing with the speed and tempo, to see what tempted him most. She felt him slowly lose his control while she learned, yet she kept going, charting this new territory for as long as he allowed.

Once she curled her body into his lap in order to rub her chest fully onto his, Christopher finally snapped. He moaned against her mouth as his arms enveloped her. His tongue matched the fevered movements of hers, their kisses enduring for lengthy, frenzied minutes, until they pried themselves apart for the sole purpose of dragging air into their lungs.

Violet panted with both nervousness and excitement. "How did I do, Christopher?"

"Perfectly," he praised in a low rasp, his eyes dragging slowly open. "You did so perfectly. Did you enjoy it?"

"I did. Immensely."

"Wonderful." His drunken gaze shifted to watch his own fingers as they drew over her hair and down her neck. "You know, my dearest, I think there is another sensation you might enjoy."

"Good God, what is it? Tell me. Please."

"I think you might like it if I kiss you here," he answered, his fingers trailing over the column of her throat. "I honestly believe you'll enjoy the feel of my mouth on your neck."

"Oh, heavens. Yes, definitely," she agreed, tilting her head back to give him as much access as possible.

Christopher chuckled with her eagerness, but his laughter was not in ridicule. On the contrary, the sound was dark and delicious, sending perfect little shivers over her skin as he lowered his lips to her body. The moment his mouth settled against her flesh, just below her jawline, Violet nearly came unglued. "Sweet hell," she whimpered. "Do more. I beg you."

She felt his lips pull into a smile. Then he did exactly as instructed. He kissed up her jaw, all the way to her ear. He caught her earlobe in his teeth and bit down, enflaming her body to the point of delirium. Violet found it impossible to sit still. She arched her back and shifted her bottom over his thighs, despising the bunches of skirt fabric keeping their hips separated.

Christopher groaned with her restless movements. He released her earlobe to return his mouth to her neck, kissing decisively down her throat and onto her shoulder. He pushed her loose curls a bit too roughly to the side, removing them from the path of his lips, but Violet didn't mind his ferocity. She matched it by yanking on his hair, urging him closer by any means possible.

His teeth latched onto her shoulder, nipping greedily at her skin before he kissed across the line of her collarbone. The stubble of his chin raked over her flesh with every movement of his mouth, creating bizarre sounds from deep in her throat. Violet knew she looked like a brazenly lustful creature, with her hair strewn wildly across her back and her skin scratched to a bright pink from the scruff of his beard. Yet somehow, that image didn't bother her. It only made her want more.

"Does this feel good?" he questioned, his heady words scraping over her flesh as surely as his whiskers. "Are you enjoying it?"

"Dear Lord, Christopher. Please tell me my enjoyment is obvious to you."

Her words stopped his delicious assault on her body. When his eyes drew back to hers, she matched his intense, probing gaze. He stared into her for the longest time, absorbing her undiluted craving for him, as she gripped the short strands of hair at the base of his neck. He reciprocated by reaching his hand back into her curls and tightening his fist.

"Bloody hell, you're beautiful, Violet. You're so damn beautiful, and I want you with a ferocity I can barely fathom."

Her lashes fluttered. "I want you, too. So desperately that I can feel it beneath my skin. And it...it hurts."

"God, I know that feeling. But I think I can ease your pain somewhat. If you'll allow me to kiss another part of your body."

"Where?" she asked, all her muscles tensing in anticipation.

He held her eyes while slipping his fingers down from her hair to ease over the neckline of her gown. Christopher dragged his hand along the edge of her dress, running his fingertips over the lace trim of her bodice slowly and intently, tracing the tops of her breasts where they strained above her corset. "Here," he said.

Violet emitted a strangled groan before she spoke. "Y-yes. Yes, please."

He didn't move his mouth to her breast right away. He just watched her in the dark light, with his fingers leisurely caressing the rounded swells of her cinched flesh. Violet had never felt any such touch before, and his tender, tempting movements caused her teeth to sink into her lip.

Christopher's eyes flared as he leaned in to press his lips to hers. She opened her mouth to accept his tongue, but he didn't deepen their kiss in that way. Instead, he captured her lower lip in his own teeth, biting down on her flesh to redefine the indentations she'd made.

Violet whimpered with his actions, even though he didn't hurt her. Her need for him had simply reached fiendish proportions and she could not contain her untoward noises. Once he released his teeth, and slid his tongue across her lip to soothe the skin he'd abraded, she moaned loudly and lustfully.

His eyes drew back to hers. "Did my bite cause you any pain, Violet?"

She couldn't find her voice. But she did manage to shake her head.

He gave her a dark smile. "Good, because I would like to do that again. I would actually like to do that quite often, in the future."

Violet still couldn't form words. But she could nod. A lot.

Christopher absorbed her silent agreement as his fingers dragged back and forth over her low neckline, causing her nipples to tighten painfully beneath her bodice. He pressed his lips to hers once again, yet stayed there for only a moment before easing his mouth downward. He kissed her chin, and then her jaw, and then her neck, and then her collarbone.

He granted her time to become accustomed to the sensation of his mouth moving tenderly and gradually down to her chest. Honestly, it was the most ridiculous thought Violet could imagine. She didn't know how anyone could ever get used to the feel of scratchy whiskers on sensitive skin, scraping lusciously downward moment by moment. She didn't know how anyone could take for granted the heat of panted breaths caressing the swell of flesh above a corset, or the firm, perfect pressure of masculine lips edging toward a feminine neckline.

When Christopher finally pressed his lips to the top of her breast, with more care and control than she could even comprehend, she arched her back in an attempt to meet his mouth. She grabbed hold of his hair and tugged him down, wanting him closer still. He groaned with her wicked encouragement, slipping his fingers just below the edge of her laced bodice.

His lips parted as he kissed her strained flesh and the feel of his wet mouth so near to her pebbled nipple fueled a raging inferno inside her body. Heat pooled between her legs, forging a decisive ache low in her belly. Violet discovered quickly that she could only relieve that ache by rubbing her thighs together, yet that friction soothed only the tiniest portion of the hollow sensation now swamping her body. All she knew for certain was that she needed more of him. She needed as much of Christopher as she could possibly have.

Reaching down, she grabbed hold of the bunched fabric still separating her hips from his. She yanked the clustered material up and out of the way so she could push her thigh fully against his hips. That's when she felt him – that very specific part of him – hard as steel and barely restrained inside his trousers. The thick ridge of his manhood pulsed against her leg, making her fingers clench like claws against his scalp.

Violet had already grasped the anatomical concept of lovemaking for quite some time. She'd been spying on her maids' conversations long enough to understand which body parts went where, and logically, it made sense. But she never knew that a hollow feeling could actually originate from deep inside her, or how desperately she would want her husband to fill that emptiness.

Good Lord, based on the size of the shaft currently pressed into her thigh, he would fill her quite completely. Violet wondered if his sex would even be able to fit inside hers, and a part of her feared her smaller body wouldn't accept his large one at all. Yet she still wanted to give it a thorough try, even if she could only imagine the degree of pain she would feel upon the attempt.

She thought to worry herself over that pain now, but then his thumb brushed across her bodice. He raked over the ridged peak of her nipple, making her eyes roll back in her head. "Holy hell, Christopher. Please kiss me."

He moaned with her cursed plea, seeking her mouth out to sink his tongue inside her. He bent forward on the bench to drag her even closer to his chest. Violet pushed against him, rubbing her barely covered thigh against his thick, rigid length. He growled like a madman, centering his thumb over her nipple and pressing down hard, sending bolts of lightning from her breast straight to the juncture of her thighs.

She cried out into the air, but he merely swallowed the sound against his lips. One of her hands flew to his, her small palm trying to envelope his fingers, urging him to repeat the motion. Violet wanted his thumb pressed even more urgently to her breast. She wanted to feel that shock of lightning again, to verify the origin of the wetness now pooling inside her sex.

With the impatient fervor of her grasp, Christopher gripped the neckline of her dress, curling his fingers beneath the laced edge to reach the aching flesh concealed by her bodice. Sadly, the material was just too snug. The more he tugged, the more it strained against her back. He paid no attention, fisting his hand tighter over her breast, until the fabric eventually made a popping noise. Violet gasped with the realization that one of her back ties had snapped.

Christopher sat back the moment he heard the sound, releasing her dress and wrenching his lips from hers. But that just wasn't acceptable. She didn't need less; she needed more. She thrust her arms around his neck and plunged her tongue into his mouth. He accepted her challenge without hesitation, banding his arms around her waist, his hungered grasp on her body more needy and frantic now than ever before.

Their tongues warred, pushing and pulling, tangling and twisting. She forced her thigh up onto the ridge of his manhood and he growled into her, running both his hands through her hair to grab a harsh hold on her curls. He tilted her head as he desired, chasing her tongue into her mouth, tasting her deeply and thoroughly while she arched and clawed her way closer. He wound her body until it vibrated beyond measure and she wasn't sure how much more of this she could endure without some method of release.

Regrettably, that release came in the form of another huge hole in the earth, which shook the ever-moving carriage wheels entirely. The bench rocked wildly to one side, forcing her teeth to clamp down right on his tongue. Violet bit him quite hard, making him grunt in pain.

She pulled back that instant, her hands flying to his face. "Oh, my heavens! Are you injured? I didn't mean to bite your tongue. Is it bleeding?"

"No, no. You did not draw blood," he assured, shifting his jaw while easing his voracious hold on her body. "It was only a moment of discomfort."

"I'm so sorry. It's just that the carriage bounced and I..."

"All is well, my dearest. I'm quite fine."

Violet shook her head even before she met his gaze. She figured the look inside his deep blue would no longer be lustful, and she was right. Christopher now observed her with only soft understanding, and she knew the spell of this carriage ride had been broken. Her gallant husband would most certainly temper their actions and become a proper gentleman once again.

"Honestly, this little accident is probably for the best," he said, easing his hand from her hair to trace over her cheek. "It reminds me of the impracticality of our current location, not to mention the impropriety of my actions. After all, I am well aware that we should not get so carried away with each other before our wedding night."

"But I like getting carried away with you," Violet whispered, not wanting to let this moment slip through her fingers.

"And I like getting carried away with you. But this is not the right place. Nor the right circumstance. Not yet." He brushed his thumb across her lips when she frowned with his sensible words. "I promise you it will be the right circumstance one day, my sweet. But today is not that day."

Violet nodded, knowing he spoke with reason and wisdom. She also knew she should agree with his logic, even if a huge part of her didn't agree at all. "I suppose I should get off of your lap," she conceded, shifting against his thighs.

His arms tightened around her. "I do not think that is necessary."

"But didn't you just say we shouldn't get carried away with each other?"

"I did. Yet the thought of letting you go is too atrocious to bear."

Her shoulders fell. "Unfortunately, you must make up your mind. Either you want to get carried away with me or you don't."

"God, Violet, there is no question as to what I *want* to do. Please know that practicing restraint in your presence is egregiously difficult for me. But even more pressing than my desire for your body is my desire to do everything the right way. I want to give you the experiences you deserve, as they are meant to be experienced."

She sighed with his earnestness. "You are such an honorable man, and now I must apologize, since my desire for you makes me do things that are terribly wanton and entirely inappropriate. And I don't even know all of the things I want to experience. I only know I want to experience them with you."

"Do not apologize for desiring me, my dearest. Not ever. For I shall never apologize for desiring you."

Those words laced over her flesh like fingers. Violet worked to stay motionless and simply stare into his eyes, relishing the heightened need she witnessed in his brilliant blue. It shook her to her bones to know how desperately he fought his urges in order to maintain her innocence. Especially since she would give him her innocence, most freely and without limitations, if he simply asked for it.

"May I say one more thing on the topic of our desire, Christopher?"

"Certainly."

"I just want you to know that I think every moment we share is perfect. No matter when or where they occur."

"Thank you for that," he offered as he caressed her face. "And I must say I agree completely, since every moment we've had together is beyond anything I'd ever hoped for. But that is precisely why I need to do right by you. I've just...I've made so many mistakes in my life. Time and time again, in nearly every situation I've found myself in, I have made the wrong decision. Sometimes those decisions led me to do foolish things. Sometimes they led me to do dreadful things. And I want all of that to stop. Here. With you. With us."

Violet sat on his lap, speechless and still.

He traced the curve of her ear, across her neck, and down her arm, to smooth over the pulse point at her wrist. "You are a part of me now, Violet. You are the best part of me, honestly. And you will be my wife." Christopher smiled as he gathered her hand in his. "I must also assure you, beginning the night we are officially wed, that I shall make love to you thoroughly, completely, and exhaustively, every chance I get for the rest of our lives."

"God, that sounds wonderful," she breathed.

"It does sound wonderful, doesn't it? It sounds incredible, actually. But until then, we must wait to fulfill our desires. We must wait until everything is right, and when we are finally able to make love for the first time, it's certainly not going to be on a bench in a carriage. You deserve better. You deserve a bed with silk sheets and pillows, with candlelight and romance."

Her brow furrowed. "I appreciate that sentiment, most sincerely. But it also makes me worry about you, for I thought you could not lie in a bed anymore since your return to England. I thought you only felt comfortable sleeping on the floor."

He pulled her hand to his mouth to press his lips to her skin. "For you, I shall make an exception."

"Are – are you saying you'll sleep in bed with me?"

"I shall sleep in bed with you every night we're together. I promise."

Violet sank onto him, resting her forehead against his and closing her eyes. She brought her fingers to his chest to spread them out over his heart. "You are too good to me, Christopher."

"On the contrary, I shall never be good enough for you. But I am going to try like hell to be the man you deserve."

"Just be you, please. For you are all I want."

He didn't reply to her words. But he did pull her closer, flattening his hands onto her bodice to run his palms over her spine. He held her as close as possible, with their breaths mingling in the dark carriage, until his fingers found the tiny gap in the back of her dress. "Damn it. I think I tore one of your bodice ties."

She laughed. "I think you did, too."

"Can it be repaired?"

"Oh, yes. I'm actually quite skilled with a needle and thread, since Mama insisted Gwen and I both learn the womanly art. I can fix the dress as soon as I return to my room and no one shall be the wiser. Well, except for Birdie, who will have to help me remove the gown. But I shall simply tell her I caught the fabric on a branch, and I'm sure she'll be satisfied."

"I'm so sorry I broke it."

Violet pressed her face into the side of his neck. "Please don't be sorry. I'm certainly not," she insisted as she collapsed fully against his chest.

"Are you tired, my sweet? I know it's been a long night."

"Mmm. I am a bit tired."

"Then why don't you take your rest on my lap for once?"

"But aren't you tired, too?"

"Not since you allowed me to sleep on you during the carriage ride to the ball. I think it's only fair that you sleep on me for the return trip."

"That sounds lovely, Christopher."

"It does. Just close your eyes and rest, and I shall hold you the entire way."

Violet nodded, burrowing even further into the solid wall she could feel beneath his shirt. She honestly wasn't sure how someone so hard of muscle could also feel so soft and warm and perfect. But he did, and she couldn't be happier about it, for she would spend the rest of her days snuggling up to this chest. The most solid chest, which housed the kindest heart. "My husband," she sang as the soothing darkness began to overtake her.

Violet remembered only two things before edging into slumber: the press of his lips to her forehead, and the sound of his deep, loving voice.

"My wife."

CHAPTER 9

Wants, Needs, and Obligations

Rain drizzled onto the glass roof of the Wilmington gazebo, creating tiny rivers and seas in the clear panes. Violet's eyes rose to watch the water stream down as she sat on the iron bench, cradling Christopher's head in her lap. He'd been napping on her for a long while and she would have to wake him soon. She just hoped to wait until the rain stopped.

The clouds had opened up over the Wilmington estate every day for a week now, ever since she and Christopher returned home from the ball. Such inclement weather had confined them to the inside of the manor for the past seven days, preventing them from being alone. Instead of their daily walks in the garden, they'd been forced into Aunt Tildy's library each afternoon, with Violet reading to him as they sat in separate chairs. It really wasn't too terrible, except that each time her husband reached out to her, to steal a kiss on the lips or even just on the hand, a new person suddenly appeared in the room. Sometimes it was Mr. Rodchester, sometimes Birdie, sometimes Tildy herself...each showing up at a most inopportune moment.

Violet hoped the untimely interruptions were coincidental. She didn't want to believe the residents of Wilmington distrusted her being alone with Christopher after the Chaney's ball. Having returned home with no cage beneath her skirts, a torn tie on the back of her bodice, and her hairpins scattered about the floor of the coach, she imagined some talk had occurred amongst the servants. However, she didn't think their gossip had reached Tildy's ears yet, since her aunt still seemed quite taken with Lord Kastle.

As far as Violet was concerned, the worst thing about this past week wasn't the suspicious disruptions of the servants. The worst thing was being forced to watch Christopher suffer without his daily rests on her lap. His face grew wearier with each passing hour, and she feared he hadn't slept at all. Her only consolation was that he still practiced his sword in the gardens each night, soothing his soul while soaked to the bone in the cool rain. Sadly, she could only watch him through the water-drenched window, catching mere glimpses of his powerfully magnetic movements.

By noon today – after a solid week of being unable to touch each other the way they truly needed – Violet's exasperation had grown as painful to her as his exhaustion obviously was to him. Therefore, she informed her aunt that they would take their walk in the gardens this afternoon, despite the inclement weather. She didn't wait for a reply before grabbing an umbrella, along with her husband's arm, and dragging him to the gazebo.

The instant they'd arrived inside the ivy-coated glass walls, hidden from the outside world, Violet flopped down on the iron bench and straightened her skirts. Christopher collapsed onto her that very second, pressing his cheek to her thighs while hugging her lower body in his arms. She'd felt his muscles relax for the first time since their carriage ride.

Now, as she sat and stared at the striking features of his softened face, she struggled to not act on her selfish desire to kiss every inch of him as he slept. In truth, she'd wanted to do just that ever since their time alone together after the ball. She knew full well that they should have been more careful with their actions in that cramped carriage, but at the time, she hadn't cared. She'd only felt her body's pull to him – after realizing he already owned her heart – and wanted nothing more than to show him her love in any way she could.

With a deep sigh, Violet slipped her fingers through Christopher's hair. She indulged in the recollection of the heated moments they'd shared on that shifting leather bench. She remembered all too well the feel of his mouth on her lips, her neck, and her breast. She could still see his stark look of hunger as he'd gripped her to his chest while she squirmed on his thighs and grasped at his body. She could still feel the hard length of his manhood throbbing against her and quickening her pulse. She could still recall wondering if he would even fit inside her when the time came for them to be together as husband and wife.

She'd thought almost nonstop about their lovemaking since that night. She'd thought about how Christopher promised to make love to her thoroughly, completely, and exhaustively, every chance he could once they were married. She'd thought about how much she wanted that – about how much she wanted him – and her wicked, reckless desires had filled her mind to the point of bursting nearly every moment since.

Violet struggled to remain motionless now, her breathing turning strenuous and heavy with the mere consideration of all the sensations awaiting them. She tried not to move at all, lest she disturb her husband's peace. Yet he still stirred beneath her hands.

Christopher adjusted himself against her skirts, snuggling the side of his face further into the silk fabric as his arms tightened around her waist. She looked down to watch her fingers smooth the hair back from his forehead, drinking in the smile now pulling at his lips. He was nearly awake, and she wondered if her labored breathing had drawn him from his slumber.

It was bizarre to think he could be so in tune to her that he comprehended the sinful nature of her thoughts even in his sleep. However, it did not surprise her. She simply understood that her husband knew her completely. Violet held no secrets from him, nor did she want to. She enjoyed being an open book in his presence, her pages laid out entirely, eagerly awaiting his eyes. She only wished he would open himself entirely to her.

The clawing desire to know every single part of Lord Christopher Kastle took hold of her body the moment it entered her mind. Her fingers moved over his skin of their own volition. They drifted from his forehead down across his cheek, coming to rest against the collar of his shirt.

Her heart stumbled against her ribs, for she knew what lay beneath his collar: the scar that remained hidden from her view. She'd never mentioned her knowledge of the scar to him, nor had she touched it again. Not from the moment she'd found it, the first time he ever laid his head on her lap.

Now, Violet wanted to touch it. She wanted her husband to feel the softness of her caress as she explored that roughened skin. She needed him to understand that she didn't care about his scar, or scars, as they may be. She only cared about the man beneath.

With a fortifying breath, she eased her hand under the stiff white edge of his shirt and glided her fingertips over the ragged flesh on the back of his neck. Christopher's entire body braced in an instant. Violet ceased her movements, holding still as stone, with her fingers resting on the old, tattered wound. She waited in painful anticipation to see what he would do.

Time slurred as she watched his eyes open to stare blankly at the rain-fogged glass walls. She was tempted to retreat, but refused to give in. She did not remove her touch from his scar in the slightest.

Eventually, Christopher drew his arm up from her legs to reach for her hand. Violet expected him to pull her fingers away from his torn flesh. He didn't. He settled his palm on the back of her hand instead, guiding her movements so she traced the scar over and over.

He winced with her constant touch, even though he directed it, and she could barely draw breath into her lungs. "Does it still hurt?" she whispered.

"Not physically," he said, his answer as thick as the humid air.

Christopher removed his hand from hers to settle his arm back onto her legs. He didn't pull away from her, so she didn't stop. She drew her fingers across the scar again and again, until his face softened once more. She watched him constantly as she caressed his skin, ensuring his body felt entirely calm against hers, before daring to ask another question.

"Is this the only scar you have?"

He flinched before answering. "No. It's not the only one."

"Are there many?"

"Yes."

"H-how many?"

"More than you can imagine."

Violet swallowed hard, since she could imagine quite a lot. Still moving her fingers over his raised skin, she pushed her voice past the constriction in her throat. "Will you tell me how you got this one?"

His body tightened against her legs. His hands twisted into the silk of her skirts. The full contracture of his muscles made her heart clench.

"Never mind, Christopher. Please forget I asked. I do not ever wish..."

"It was a sword," he confessed, cutting off her protests with determined words. "A man held his blade to the back of my neck."

"And this man, he...he meant you harm?"

"Yes, Violet. He meant me great harm."

Tears sprang to her eyes as she pulled her hand away from the scar to rest on his shoulder. When Christopher grimaced with her actions, she smoothed her palm up and down his coat sleeve. "I'm so grateful he did not harm you," she said, thinking the words would soothe him further. She was wrong.

He jumped up, snatching his body from hers to stride toward the ivy-coated walls before them. Violet whimpered with the rapidity of his withdrawal. She clenched onto the edge of the bench, holding on for dear life as her husband paced a rut in the floor.

CHRISTOPHER COULDN'T STOP MOVING. His feet kept shifting back and forth across the stone ground. He could feel Violet's eyes on him the entire time, and he wanted to stride back to her, pull her up into his arms, and kiss her senseless. He wanted to forget anything in his life ever existed prior to their courtship. He wanted to believe nothing else would ever exist in the future except the two of them and their happy life together.

But he knew reality was never so kind.

In reality, this entire past week had been hell – being stuck inside the Wilmington manor as rain poured over the estate – keeping the two of them apart. For the first few days, Christopher had managed his needs rather well. He very much enjoyed sitting in the library with his wife, listening to her sparkling voice as she read to him. But as the rain wore on with no end in sight, he started to suffer without their time alone in this gazebo.

He needed time alone with his Violet. Not just to take his rest on her lap. Not just to feel her skin beneath his fingers. Not just to absorb the smiles she reserved solely for him. He needed her in every possible way he could imagine.

Regrettably, she also needed him. Violet relied on his strength, craved his touch, and savored his affections. Her attachment to her husband was as natural as his attachment to his wife. Yet her need for him still sickened his stomach, since she only comprehended a mere part of who he truly was.

Violet only knew the Christopher Kastle he'd shown her these past five weeks. She understood nothing of the other life he'd led while he was away – of the other person he'd become in order to survive those years lost at sea. He couldn't tell her the truth of it, either, since he and Nick had sworn never to speak to anyone else about what happened out there.

But that oath to his friend felt terribly wrong now, when Christopher stopped his pacing and stood before her. As he absorbed the deeply caring, concerned look in her eyes, he acknowledged the fact that he was keeping an entire side of himself away from her. He didn't want that, even if it was a side he wasn't proud of, and one he hoped to never see again.

"Violet, I – I need to tell you something."

She gave him a tremulous smile. "All right."

"The thing is," he began, raking a hand through his hair, "I was not shipwrecked all those years ago, as people believe. As I've told them."

Her fingers clenched harder to the iron bench. "You weren't?"

"No. I was living on an island for a time, but my ship was not destroyed by a wild storm or rocky crag. It was attacked."

"Attacked?" she echoed, her eyes widening. "By whom?"

"By a...a band of pirates."

"My God, Christopher! *Pirates*?"

"Yes."

"And that is how you got the scar on the back of your neck? A pirate held you beneath his blade?"

"The day my ship was captured, I was forced to kneel down on the deck. One of the pillagers held his blade on me."

Violet's body recoiled in horror. "Great heavens, I'm so sorry. I don't even know what to say to you. I don't know what I could ever say."

Christopher worked to calm the twisting tension in his muscles. "You don't have to say anything. I just don't want to lie to you about the scar. I want you to know the truth of how it came to be."

She nodded slowly, her eyes locked to his. "Is there anything else you can tell me about your time away? If it doesn't hurt too much to speak of?"

His gut fell to his feet with her words, since she had every right to ask him for more. Yet this was the trickiest of all trick questions, because he knew he should tell her everything and also knew he never would. A huge part of him wanted to end this conversation right now, to lock the memories away again this instant. However, much to his surprise, another part of him wanted to continue – to give her just a little more – even when he knew the shame of his admissions would be nearly unbearable.

"There were a few of us who survived the attack," he offered, his voice so low that she strained forward to listen. "One was an orphaned lad named Maxwell Taylor, who was just a year older than Cora. Max had followed my every footstep for the three years prior. He was young and sometimes fool-hardy with his emotions, but he had a good mind and a strong back. He was eager to learn and would do anything I asked of him. And then there was Nick, standing directly by my side. Max and Nick both made it off that ship and onto the island with me, except Nick made it all the way back home to England and Max didn't."

"I'm so sorry," she offered. "I'm sorry Max did not make it home."

"Thank you, Violet. It's just...I wrack myself with guilt over it. I have every day since the moment I returned."

"I wish you wouldn't, as I'm certain you did all you could for Max. And for Nick, as well."

"I honestly don't know that I did."

She studied him with a furrowed brow. "If you don't mind me asking another question, Christopher, there is something I do not understand."

"What is it?"

"I don't understand why you felt the safety of those men was your responsibility at all, since you were just another sailor lost at sea along with them. I mean, I know you are an honorable man and a loyal friend, and I can understand if those qualities made you feel a certain sense of duty. But I still do not think that makes you responsible for their lives."

Christopher shook his head, glancing to the floor before meeting her steadfast gaze. "Do you know why Nick was out on that ocean with me?"

"No. I do not."

"It's because he followed me. He'd always been by my side, every day of our lives, and when I made the rash, selfish decision to run away from my family, Nick came along. He came to be with me, as my brother. Therefore, everything that happened to him – to both of us – is my fault. And I will forever owe him a debt that cannot truly be repaid."

Violet shuddered. "But surely, you must take some solace in the fact that you brought Nick back home."

"You're right; I did. But what about Max? What about all of the other sailors who were on that ship with me the day we were overtaken? What about the men who never made it home? I cannot bear the thought of it sometimes. And even worse than that is the fact that I...that I..."

"That you what?"

Christopher shifted on his feet. "I did things, Violet. When I was lost. I made choices no one should ever have to make. I committed acts no good person should ever commit. I did so many terrible things in order to survive. To ensure I would find a way home to my family."

He stopped speaking then, just to look on her, even though it burned his insides to tell her these truths. Yet she did not look back on him with disgust or pity or fear. When she replied, he heard the same sweet voice as always.

"I understand now, Christopher. I understand the origins of your guilt and the thoughts that keep you awake at night. But I do not believe you need to torture yourself over this. We cannot know why life leads us in one direction versus another, or why it favors one person to live while another dies. All we can do is treasure what we have, each and every day we have it. And I do treasure what I have. I treasure *you*."

His heart caved in with her words, struggling to absorb her acceptance.

"Do you wish to speak any further of your time at sea?" Violet asked. "For I shall listen to anything else you wish to tell me. I'll always be here for you."

"I know that. I also appreciate it more than I can say. But I do not wish to speak any further right now, if that is acceptable."

"Certainly," she agreed, staring into him with fierce determination. "I just want to say one more thing on the matter. If you'll allow it."

"I shall."

"And may I be brutally honest with you in my speech?"

"Always."

"Very well, then. The brutal truth is that I don't care what you had to do to survive during those years you were lost. I don't care about the terrible acts you committed so you could make it back home. And I realize that is wrong of me. I realize it is ungodly and immoral. But I cannot bring myself to feel guilty, for I only care that you did survive. I only care that you came home to your family. I only care that you came home to *me*. Because I needed you to come home. I needed you to be here, to be my husband." Her head tilted as she studied him. "Will you please forgive me for my selfishness, Christopher?"

He blinked back his tears. "God, of course. I forgive you unreservedly."

"Good. Then I want you to know that the scars on your body will not bother me to look upon. I mean, they will bother me, because you were hurt and I detest the thought of your suffering. But they will not deter my touch, nor will they alter my overwhelming desire for you."

Violet whimpered with her admission. Christopher struggled to draw air into his lungs, since the look in her eyes was so unflinchingly raw, and the need he felt for her in this moment shook him to his depths.

"Although," she continued, her fingers clenching the bench until her knuckles whitened, "if you do not want me to see your scars, I promise I'll understand. I will not push you to allow that particular part of our intimacy, even after we are married. As I understand it, the act of lovemaking can be achieved with most clothing on. I know that only certain parts of our bodies need to connect, and that we do not have to be entirely naked in order to..."

"Stop right there," he growled. "We are going to be naked. We are *both* going to be *entirely* naked."

She fidgeted beneath his sharp, hungered gaze. But she didn't look away. Not even with his next statement.

"When I have you in bed with me, Violet, I will want all of you open to my touch. I want you bared to me – every part of you – mind, body, heart, and soul. When you are my wife, I shall expect everything from you. In return, I shall give you all that I have left to give."

A needy little noise escaped her throat. "In that case, I will want to see your scars. Every one of them. Not because I will look at you any differently, but because I want to look at you. I want to see all of you."

Christopher grinned wickedly with her scandalous confession, making her blush beneath his unapologetic stare. He nearly swallowed his tongue with the glorious color that lit her cheeks and sank down below her cinched bodice. Her body's heady response reminded him that he was actually grateful for the rain that fell this past week, keeping them confined to the Wilmington library since their return from the ball. The time he'd spent with her at that party, and especially during their carriage ride home afterwards, had been altogether too tempting. He'd promised his wife, as he'd held her on his lap on the shifting coach bench, that he would not make love to her before their wedding night. Yet his vow by no means lessened his desires. If anything, it did the opposite.

"That was untoward of me to say, was it not?" Violet questioned him, filling the gap left by his utter lack of speech. "I suppose I should apologize for saying I want to see all of you."

He shook his head. "I've told you before that you should never apologize for desiring me. Especially since I want to see all of you, as well."

Her eyes lit up for the first time since they'd arrived in the gazebo today. "Good heavens, Christopher. I so look forward to our wedding night."

"As do I," he confirmed, trying like hell to not let his mind dwell on all the things he wanted to do to her, and for her, just as soon as he could.

The very next moment, Violet's bright eyes cast down to the iron bench. "I – I want to thank you for it, in advance."

Christopher cocked his brow with her sudden shyness. He strode to the bench, mad with curiosity. Once he'd reclaimed his seat beside her, he took her hand and entwined their fingers. "What are you thanking me for, in advance?"

She clenched onto him. "For taking care of me when we make love."

"I will take care of you," he vowed. "I will always take care of you."

"I know that. I just..."

He watched her eyelids close as her words trailed. "Violet, you do realize I'm here for you, right? Just as you are always here for me."

"Oh, yes, I do. But this is not necessary."

"What is not necessary?"

"Me asking you any more questions today. It's unnecessary, especially after all you've already shared. It feels wrong to ask for more."

Christopher reached for her face, catching her chin in his fingers to lift her eyes to his. "Ask me what you will, my dearest."

"But it is a very indecent question."

"Ask. Please."

A shaky laugh escaped her throat. "H–have you ever had a virgin before?"

He winced. "Yes," he admitted. "A few."

"I see. And can I ask you something else about your past? Although you certainly don't have to answer if you don't..."

"You want to know if I was a rake in my youth. Don't you?" he surmised, releasing her to let his arm fall to his side. He figured she would want less contact with him, given the current topic. As it turned out, he was wrong.

She moved eagerly toward him, crowding him on the bench as she regathered his hand in both of hers. "Well, it's just that I heard rumors. My maids spoke of your conquests when I was spying on them back at my home, but I shall not believe any of their idle prattle if you tell me it isn't true. After all, I know from personal experience how false and unfair gossip can be."

"I know you do, and I wish I could tell you this gossip is false. I wish I could say I'd been a pious man when I was younger, but in truth, I was not. I did have a lot of women, although I assure you my atrocious behavior was the result of my idiotic venturing as a thoughtless lad and is not who I am anymore. Please believe me when I say I am not the same person I was before I joined the Royal Navy all those years ago."

Violet scooted closer, pressing their thighs together. "I know you are not an idiotic or thoughtless person. Most definitely not. However, your level of experience does make me curious about something else."

"What is it?"

"How, um, how did you keep from getting any of them pregnant?"

Christopher sighed. "There are ways," he offered, not wanting to go fully into the explanation of every time he'd pulled out of a woman before spilling his seed. He figured Violet didn't really want or need that much detail. "It's rather simple, honestly, if you know what you're doing."

"Rather simple," she echoed, gripping his fingers as she processed his words. He could practically watch her mind churn behind her eyes. Then her gaze drifted to his mouth, staring blatantly at his lips while she wet her own. He felt her mood shift from questioning to craving in an instant.

"I guess it's a good thing you know what you're doing," she surmised. "Because, I mean, you obviously do know. And I certainly don't have any demeaning intentions when I say that. I intend it quite as a compliment, in fact, for I am well aware that I'm currently reaping the benefits of your proficiency in such matters. Especially since I can tell, based on my own experience, that you definitely know what you're doing when it comes to all of that."

Christopher couldn't help chuckling with her convoluted explanation. It amazed him to think he could laugh now, when they'd been discussing such troubling memories just moments ago. But then again, this was simply his life with Violet: joy in the place of sorrow, acceptance in the place of damnation, light in the place of dark. "All of what, exactly?" he prodded, succumbing to his desire to tease his innocent wife.

"Oh, I'm just saying it's...well, you must know what I mean...since you're so incredibly good at that."

"I'm not sure I do know what you mean. Can you be a bit more specific?"

"Well, um, *that* meaning *all* of that – that which you do to me – which is so very entrancing."

He reached his hand back to her face. "Entrancing?"

"Mm-hmm. Entrancing. Exciting. And rather breathtaking, to be honest."

"Breathtaking?" he questioned, easing forward to skim his lips over hers.

Violet moaned at the feather-light touch. "Very breathtaking, indeed."

He rubbed their noses together. "I never wish to steal your breath."

"But you do, and it's quite wonderful."

Christopher skimmed his mouth across hers again, barely touching her lips before pressing their foreheads together. "So, you enjoy all of that?"

"Oh, yes. All of it," she declared, wrapping her arms around his neck to pull him closer. "I want all of it."

"I want all of it, too. Unfortunately, since we've decided not to get carried away with each other yet, and since this has been a long and rather emotional trip to the gardens, I think it best that we head back to the manor now."

She groaned with his words. He huffed out a laugh as he reached to her arms, unwinding them from his neck to press them down onto her skirts. Rising from the bench, he stood and gave her a tender smile.

"Come now, my sweet. I'm certain we've been gone entirely too long. Someone shall come to find us soon if we do not return."

Violet looked up to him with pleading eyes. "Good Lord, Christopher. I know we cannot get carried away with each other, but please do not make me leave this gazebo today without a single proper kiss."

He stared the words out of her mouth. Then he reached down, grabbed her by the shoulders, and pulled her straight up off the bench and onto his chest. He sank his mouth onto hers, slid his tongue past her parted lips, and tasted her for languorous, lengthy minutes.

When she collapsed against him with a feverish moan, Christopher couldn't help the satisfaction he felt. He drank her in, teasing and tempting her further with his tongue, as her body sagged beneath his hands. It nearly killed him to finally pull back from her, to steady her legs while he struggled to solidify his own.

"Violet?"

"Hmm?"

"As long as you concede that I've given you a proper kiss, I really do believe we should head back to the manor."

Her eyes finally dragged opened. "Oh, all right. If we have to."

Christopher smiled while he gathered her fingers in his, wrapping them around his forearm. "You make it very hard for me to keep my vow of being a gentleman," he told her while guiding them toward the rain-soaked gardens.

Her hand curled into his sleeve. "I would say I'm sorry for my behavior, but you've told me twice now to never apologize for desiring you."

He paused when they arrived at the gazebo entrance, turning to pin her eyes with his. "You know, my dearest, the day is going to come when I no longer have to control myself around you."

She wet her lips. "That day cannot come soon enough for me."

"Nor for me," he agreed, reaching for their umbrella and holding it up to shelter them both from the rain.

~

VIOLET LAY in bed with her sweltering velvet duvet thrown back and her shivering body resting overtop of her sheets. She wore nothing but her thin nightgown, the ivory fabric gauzy and nearly see-through, yet she didn't shiver because her scant clothing made her cold. Violet shivered because she knew Christopher could see the rose peaks of her tight nipples, as well as the dark juncture between her thighs, while he sat beside her on her mattress.

She wasn't entirely sure how he'd gotten here. One moment, she'd been watching him practice his sword in the gardens – listening to him grunt and groan as he thrust his sharp blade into the dense night air – and the next moment, they were both in her room. On her bed.

Violet knew she should be quite concerned that he was in her bedchamber and they were alone together in the dark. But truthfully, she did not care about those things at all. She only cared about how goddamn gorgeous he looked. Her husband wore nothing but tight black breeches and a loose white shirt. A thin sheen of sweat made his clothes cling indecently to his heated skin while his bright blue eyes fastened to her face.

"Why are you here?" she asked, her fingers digging into the sheets.

Christopher moved then, crawling toward her on the mattress. He slung one long, muscular leg over her body, so his knees rested beside her waist and his hands bedside her shoulders. She gazed up at him as he held himself suspended over her without actually touching her at all.

"I'm here for you," he whispered, lowering his lips to pepper soft, coaxing kisses across her face. "Do you want me to touch you, Violet?"

"Yes. Please, yes," she begged without shame or remorse.

"Where do you want me to touch you?"

"Anywhere. Everywhere."

He pulled back just enough to give her a devilish grin. Balancing himself on one hand, he drew his other over her loose hair, across her flushed cheek, and down her arched throat, until his fingers eased onto the neckline of her nightgown. Violet gasped for air while he traced the laced edge with expert precision, his fingers inching ever closer to the painfully tight peaks of her chest. The moment he cradled the rounded swell of her breast in his large palm, Christopher pressed down on her taut nipple, sending a feverish frisson of lightning straight to her sex.

Violet cried out, trying desperately to arch her body up to meet his, yet he merely continued hovering over her. She could feel him, but not nearly in the way she needed. "Touch more," she pleaded, practically crying from the sharp ache of her desire. "Touch more of me, Christopher. I beg you."

He gave her another smile, a dark one this time, as his hand eased over the curve of her breast before slipping farther down her body. His fingers skimmed across her ribcage and onto the swell of her stomach, swirling over her bellybutton until she smiled in return. He studied her face while his hand pushed further down, his fingers dipping slowly but intently between her legs to push the gauzy fabric of her nightgown up against the wetness pooling inside her sex.

She didn't think twice before spreading her knees apart for him. "God, yes. Touch me there. *Please* touch me there. Christopher!"

Violet awoke abruptly, panting and whimpering with her heart in her throat. She lay in her bed with her sweltering velvet duvet lying atop her. The cover felt altogether too heavy, so she threw it back to reveal her nightgown-clad body to the cool morning air.

Her eyes darted about the room, just to see if her husband was actually here. Sadly, he was not. He had never been here at all.

"Oh, if only that wasn't a dream," she sighed, wanting those sensations to be as real as they seemed. She could almost still feel him: his heat, his strength, his lips, his fingers. The intensity of the images left her deliriously lustful and conjured an unusual wetness between her thighs.

"Damn it," Violet grumbled into the morning air as her tender sex thrummed and ached. She could feel that hollowness inside her body again – the same one she'd had in the carriage when Christopher ran his mouth and hands across her skin – and she didn't know what to do about it. Part of her wanted to touch herself, since her pulsing sheath begged to be soothed in some manner. Yet she couldn't do that, fearing the act would be far too wrong.

Violet pinched her eyes shut in utter frustration. What she needed right now was someone to talk to about all of this: someone willing to teach her how to cope with the unbridled desires of her flesh. She just had so many questions, and no one to answer them.

She couldn't reveal her licentious inquiries to Aunt Tildy, obviously. Nor to her handmaid, Birdie. And most definitely not to Mr. Rodchester. Violet couldn't ask any of the servants, especially with them watching over her and Christopher like hawks. There were also no books in her aunt's library, or in any library she knew of, that could teach her what she wanted to know.

Which just left Lord Kastle himself. He was the only person Violet could ask her questions of, yet she had no idea what he would think of her if she did. She imagined he would be open and kind in his responses, as he always was, but she didn't know if she possessed the courage to ask about everything she yearned to understand.

With a harsh groan, she tamped down the urges of her body as she rose out of bed. Stepping over to the window of her chamber, she looked out to the gardens. "Oh, thank the heavens. It has finally stopped raining," Violet sang, feeling blessed that the sky was now blue after two full weeks of gray. "Christopher and I shall be able to walk in the gardens again."

The two of them hadn't been back to the gazebo since the day she'd touched his scar, and that was already a week ago. Tildy had simply refused to allow them back out into the rain again. "You'll both catch your death of cold!" she'd scoffed, insistent they heed her warning.

Violet had been forced to content herself with sitting beside her husband in the library for another seven whole days – reading to him while he played incessantly with her fingers and stared longingly at her mouth – only to return to her room each evening barraged with immoral thoughts. She honestly didn't know what to do with her overpowering desires. Especially now, when her wicked contemplations had evolved into vivid fantasies that accosted her whenever she struggled to sleep.

A knock came at her door, heralding the arrival of her breakfast tray and startling her nearly from her skin. Violet huffed at her own nerves while stepping away from the window. She told herself to stop dwelling on the dream of her husband's body suspended above hers in bed. After all, her ardent craving to have that experience would definitely lead to no good.

CHRISTOPHER LEFT his bedchamber precisely at noon, intent on meeting his wife in the foyer to guide her out to the gardens for the first time in so long. Two weeks of constant rain had wreaked havoc on their routine and allowed them only one afternoon in the gazebo, which had been seven lengthy days ago. He fiddled with the sleeves of his navy jacket and straightened the high collar of his white shirt as he descended the back staircase and proceeded down the extensive hallway. The moment he stepped around the corner into the sunlit foyer, his heart tripped in his chest. Violet already stood in wait for him, looking more radiant than he could fathom.

She wore a stunning, ocean-blue dress with a cinched bodice and long skirts that flowed around her legs like waves. Even more exquisite than her outfit were the long, loose curls of her hair and the bright pink flush of her cheeks. He watched as she swayed back and forth while staring at the floor, her fingers shifting incessantly over her gown. If he didn't know better, he would assume she was nervous, or perhaps even embarrassed. Yet those emotions made no sense, since she had no reason to be either.

"My dearest," he addressed as he began walking toward her, eagerly watching her eyes rise to his.

"C-Christopher," she stammered.

His footsteps slowed. Now that he could see her face fully, he could tell something was wrong. However, *wrong* wasn't entirely the right word. He'd seen her distraught before – the day after he'd ridden his horse out at night – but that wasn't how she appeared at this moment. She didn't look hurt, angry, or sad, and yet she was obviously bothered.

Violet's lips parted when he came to stand before her, with her tongue darting out over that lush rose, and Christopher took a moment to drink her in. Her pupils were wildly dilated. Her breaths came shallow and rapid to her chest. Her fingers fisted into the silk of her skirts.

Good God, she looked like she did in their carriage after the ball, when he'd held her on his lap and run his hands over her body. She looked as wanton now, in the full light of the sun, as she had when he'd kissed her lips and neck and breast in the dark of that inviting night. He'd thought back then that she could never look more gorgeous, but that was before today, before witnessing her desire for him on blatant display at high noon.

His body leaned toward hers of its own volition, making Violet groan with his proximity. His teeth clenched at the sound, the muscle in his jaw twitching while he struggled to understand his wife's current state. Bloody hell, she simply vibrated with need. He could practically hear her flesh humming louder as the seconds passed, and the sight of her in such a bold state of arousal made his cock ache in sheer desperation.

Christopher didn't dare reach for her, fully aware that a lack of contact was for the best right now. She didn't reach for him, either. Even though she always reached for him.

"You, um, you wore your hair down today," he said, unable to think of any other topic of conversation, since the blood normally in his brain had shunted itself to another part of his body.

"Yes," she breathed, glancing anxiously up at him. "I...I couldn't sit still long enough to have my curls pinned."

"Oh? Is there a reason why you could not sit still?"

Her eyes widened with guilt. Her mouth opened, but no words came out. Christopher barely had a second to think before her gaze shifted to his lips, staring in shameless longing.

When a strangled groan escaped her throat, his entire being responded to the indecent sound. He inhaled steeply, swearing he could smell her thirst for him, even though her skin danced only with the scents of sweet cream and honeysuckle. He leaned in closer, wanting as much of her as he could have. "I think we should go for our walk now, Violet."

"Mmm," she hummed, her eyelids falling to half-mast with his closeness. "That sounds good. That sounds so, so good."

He nearly reached for her hand, but knew his touch might intensify her cravings and incite her to action. As much as he wished to experience the full force of her current desires, he knew he most certainly should not. Instead, he dug his fingernails into his palms as he walked beside her across the foyer, through the stained-glass doors, and onto the path of the gardens.

Violet did her best to not look at him while they strolled. Her eyes darted from the pathway stones to the blossoming flowers to the marble sculptures as her fingers took turns raking through her hair and fisting at her sides. The intoxicating vibrations radiating from her skin drove him nearly to madness. Christopher wanted nothing more than to relieve her flustered, frantic body. He wanted to take care of her carnal needs as only he could. He just wanted someone to give him the goddamn permission to soothe his own wife.

But he did not yet have that permission, and could only offer himself to her as a sounding board. "Is everything well with you?" he asked, hoping the ability to speak about her emotions might grant her some reprieve.

Violet's gaze drew to his mouth before shifting back to the flowers. "Yes, it's...I'm fine. I merely had trouble sleeping last night."

"I'm so sorry you didn't sleep well. Do you know why you had trouble? Bad dreams, perhaps?"

"Bad dreams?" she resounded, her fingers sliding over the tight waist of her bodice. "God, no, they weren't bad at all. Although I really, probably, certainly shouldn't discuss them." She bit her lip when she finished her speech, her eyes glazing while she licked the indentations her teeth had made.

Christopher's simmering body jolted as he deduced the truth from her answer. *My Violet had an erotic dream about the two of us together. And she awoke ravenous with need.*

"I see," he said, his mouth watering with that delicious knowledge. Knowing she'd spent the entire morning hungry for him made him all the more famished for her. His gaze drifted from her fiery cheeks to her tangled hands, watching her fingers fidget against each other. He wondered idly if his wife had touched herself with those dainty hands while she dreamed of him. Unfortunately, the thought only remained idle until the moment it entered his mind. Once that perfectly sinful idea bludgeoned his brain, he could think of nothing else.

Christopher could only imagine Violet spread out on her bedsheets, completely naked, with her fingers roaming over her breasts and down between her thighs. The image lit with perfect clarity in his mind's eye, as if it were happening here in this very garden. Holy hell, he needed to watch her do that. He needed to watch her touch herself. Then he needed to join her. He needed to see her come to completion with nothing but the caress of his hands on her breasts and her wet, throbbing sex. The mere thought of it made his own sex throb as he studied each movement she now made.

Every sigh that escaped her lips while she glanced at the surrounding flowers sent a bolt of lightning through his body. Every brief, awkward contact her eyes made with his caused his muscles to stiffen further. Every time her gaze wandered over his chest, and her fingers twisted against her waist, his cock pulsed and swelled.

Eventually, Violet gave up pretense and stopped looking away. She focused in, utterly and completely, on his face. Her footsteps barely carried her forward as she struggled to walk beneath the burden of his heavy glare.

Christopher's nerves rubbed themselves raw with every stumbled step they took. He definitely should not act on this. They'd already agreed to not get carried away with each other before their wedding night, and it was a good decision. It was the right decision.

Yet now – forced to watch the delectably swelled tops of Violet's breasts heave against her corset while she drank him in – he honestly didn't give a fuck about anything but their desire. Her desire for him and his for her. His desire to touch her, hold her, kiss her, taste her…

Christopher reached for his wife. He grabbed at her hands, urging them apart from one another so he could tangle them with his. The instant they made contact, Violet moaned outright. He gnashed his teeth as he tugged her closer to his body and pulled her forward. She worked to match the strides of his long legs, clenching onto his fingers and running to keep pace.

As soon as they reached the gazebo entrance, he banded his arm around her waist and lifted her up the three stairs. He didn't make it over to the bench. He couldn't. He just spun her around to face him, seizing her by the shoulders to push her up against the nearest glass wall, before crushing her lips beneath his own.

Violet dove onto him. With her mouth, her hands, her chest, her legs. She grasped and pulled and thrust, tangling their bodies and winding their tongues, giving and taking in time with his hungered movements.

Christopher encased her completely, wrapping his arms around her twice over. He clung as tight as he could to her perfect little body, reveling in the sensation of her lush, strained breasts pressed fully against his chest. When her fingers lunged into his hair, fisting the short strands to clamp his mouth onto hers, he drank her in more deeply, dragging her scent into his lungs with every grasping breath of air he took against her lips.

She writhed and wriggled in his severe embrace, arching up on tiptoes to meet his demanding mouth, yet her smaller stature still prevented their bodies from being entirely aligned while they stood. His aching shaft could only run against the lower edge of her cinched stomach, frustrating him to no end. Christopher reached down, smoothing both hands over the back of her skirts to outline the upside-down heart shape of her bottom, before he grabbed full hold of her ass and wrenched her up onto him.

Violet gasped into his mouth, but she didn't hesitate to respond. She fought to encircle his hip with her leg, battling the weight of her dress. The feel of her body opening so willingly to his caused his vision to blur, even with his eyes closed. He slid one hand down the length of her thigh, grasping onto her leg through the silky layers of her burdensome skirts, pinning her between his chest and the glass panel at her back.

The air in her lungs puffed out over his lips when he fastened her tighter to the wall, yet Violet stayed with him. She stayed with him eagerly, trying her damnedest to circle her leg over his. Christopher dug one hand into her skirts and the other into her hair, gripping onto her with everything in his power.

His body took over entirely then, with a will of its own. He thrust his rigid shaft over her tiny belly, lunging his hips into the hard lines at the base of her corset. He dragged her leg up higher, shifting his position to aim his painfully stiff cock between her thighs. Violet's foot may have come off the floor when he tugged her upward, but neither of them took notice. At least, not until he managed to run his rock-hard length directly against the juncture of her sex. Despite the many layers of fabric separating them, such a distinct connection could not be ignored.

Violet tore her mouth from his and cried out into the air, her anguished sounds stopping his movements instantly. He stilled his body while looking to her face. She matched his intense stare with eyes dark as night.

"Are...are you all right?" he asked, the words coming in broken pants.

Her fingers remained fisted in his hair while she nodded. "Yes, I – I'm fine. I mean, except for the insane pounding of my heart. And the bizarre swooping sensation in my belly."

"Are those the reasons you stopped kissing me?"

"No. They are not."

Christopher forced himself to ease his grip on her so both her feet could rest back on the floor. He set his hands on her waist, holding her carefully in place. "Will you tell me why you stopped?"

"Well, it's just, um..." she fumbled, her words ending in awkward silence.

"You can always speak to me," he assured, knowing she'd needed to talk with him since they met in the foyer today. He should have tried harder to discuss her feelings, instead of selfishly dragging her in here to act on them.

"I know I can speak to you, Christopher. But this is terribly hard to speak about. Because it's just, it's so very hard."

His brow rose. "What is so very hard?"

She blushed deeper than before, which he didn't think was possible. "You. You're so very hard. Your manhood, I mean. It's quite, quite hard."

He smiled despite himself. "Do I need to apologize for that?"

"Heavens, no. I'm flattered you are in such a state because of me."

"It is because of you," he insisted, easing his hand to her face to trace over her cheek. "Everything pleasurable in my life is because of you."

"It will be pleasurable, won't it?" Violet asked, her forehead crinkling in concern. "I mean, when we are finally able to make love?"

"Yes. God, yes. It will be most pleasurable. I promise you."

"Then you are sure that, um...that your manhood will fit inside me?"

Her hesitant question hit him like a brick. Christopher took her face in both hands, holding her steady to pin her eyes. He hated the doubt and insecurity he witnessed inside her. He hated that he had to wait so long to show his wife what would happen in their marriage bed. Especially since all he wanted in the world was to bury himself inside her right now.

He wanted to sink so far inside her that he wouldn't know where he ended and she began. He wanted to spill his seed as he never had with any woman before – deep within her soft walls – while her bare legs circled his waist and gripped him to her. He wanted to make her ripe with new life, to kiss her belly as it swelled day by day, to feel their unborn child move beneath his lips while he smiled into her skin. And he didn't want to wait another second to have any of it.

"Violet," he whispered, caressing her name with his tongue. "I am quite certain that I will fit perfectly inside you."

She nodded slowly. "And will it hurt? The first time we're together?"

Christopher grimaced with her question but didn't look away. "You will feel some pain, I am sorry to say. That part is inevitable and beyond my control. But the discomfort will be brief, and when it subsides, I swear I will make everything in your body feel good." Leaning down, he ran his nose over the side of hers. "In all honesty, I will make you feel a hell of a lot better than just good. I will make you feel things you cannot possibly imagine. I will give you so much pleasure that you will beg me to go on and on and never stop."

A tortured whimper escaped her throat as Violet gripped onto his shoulders. "That sounds wonderful. I would like that very much."

He grinned against her mouth. "I'd like it, too. I'd like it right now."

"Yes," she breathed. "Now is perfect. Now, now, now."

Christopher ran one hand back into her hair to grip the gold in his fist. He ran his other hand down the side of her body to curl against her hip and pull her forward. Violet mewled when his hard shaft pressed into her belly again. He growled in response, forcing his next words past the constriction of his throat. "It is very unfortunate that we have to wait, isn't it?"

She tilted her head to nibble his jaw, darting her tongue out to taste his skin. "It's so incredibly unfortunate."

His hand moved from her hip to the back of her skirt, grabbing her flawlessly round ass through the layers of fabric to wedge her body against his. "It's fucking horrible, if I'm being brutally honest."

Violet shifted her hips, rubbing herself onto his stiff cock with brash determination. "God, yes. It's so fuck–"

Christopher plastered his mouth to hers, swallowing the foul word on her sweet lips. Her arms flew around his neck as she returned his fevered kisses. She chased his tongue with her own, pushing her chest onto his while she whimpered and panted and writhed.

The friction of her uninhibited actions made his already painfully rigid shaft even harder. The strength of his need rendered her body weightless as he lifted her clear off the floor to pin her spine against the glass wall. Violet spread her legs beneath her dense skirts, inviting him inside her thighs. He wedged his hips between hers to grind his full length into the folds of fabric.

"You feel so good," she moaned into his mouth, battling her dress to wind her legs around his waist. "You belong here."

"I do," he agreed, pulling her thighs more securely around his hips. "I belong right here."

"*Christopher.*"

"*Violet,*" he growled, biting down on her lower lip and sucking it into his mouth. She arched her back to push her breasts into his chest. His pulse tripped as he imagined how hard her pebbled nipples would feel against his tongue, if he could just get his mouth around them. That wicked image fueled his raging hatred for every complicated piece of clothing currently keeping them apart.

The instant he released her lip, Violet pushed her tongue inside him, sliding it willfully into his mouth as her fingers gripped his hair. Her bold, demanding actions sent a shock of desire racing across his skin. The blood rushing through his ears made it impossible to hear his name being called.

"Lord Kastle? Lord Christopher Kastle? Are you in the gazebo?"

Violet responded to Mr. Rodchester's voice first. She wrenched her mouth away and pushed against Christopher's shoulders. But it still took several seconds for him to realize what was happening.

"Quick! Go sit!" she ordered in a frantic whisper. "He's nearly here!"

Christopher moved with lightning speed then, releasing her body from his licentious grip so he could scramble over to the bench. He sat down and crossed one leg over the other knee, shifting his coat in a pitiful attempt to hide the insidious length of his cock. He barely managed to situate himself before Rodchester arrived in the gazebo.

"Here you are," the elderly caretaker announced. "Here you both are."

"Yes, we're here. We're both here," Violet confirmed, her words winded as she stood beside the glass wall.

Christopher made the mistake of looking back to her. The sight stole all the air from his lungs. His wife's hair lay mussed about her shoulders from the manipulation of his fingers. Her skin glowed bright pink from the burn of his jaw stubble. Her lower lip sat pouted and swollen from the pull of his teeth. There was no way in hell Rodchester wouldn't know what they'd been doing.

"What do you need?" she asked the man, trying to stiffen her spine while she looked him in the eyes with more than a little guilt in her own.

"Oh. Lord Kastle just received a message," Rodchester stated, holding out a letter in his frail fingers.

Violet stepped toward him. "That is wonderful. I shall take it."

He handed her the envelope, his eyes shifting from Christopher back to her. "Are you well, Miss Violet?"

She nodded a bit too violently. "Yes, Mr. Rodchester. I'm quite fine."

"Are you certain?"

"I'm certainly certain. And I've got the letter now, so you...you can go back to your other duties. Thank you so much."

Rodchester eyed them both before turning and walking away. Violet stood in place until the caretaker was gone. She stared after him even longer, until she finally spun toward the bench.

"Oh my God," she gasped.

Christopher flinched as he met her eyes. "Are you truly well?"

"Yes, yes, I'm fine. How are you?"

"I'm fine, too," he assured her.

The next instant, they both burst into fits of laughter.

"Good heavens, that was close!" Violet exclaimed through her giggles, stumbling to the bench and collapsing down beside him.

He rested back against the wrought iron as he chuckled. "It certainly was. If your aunt had been the one to discover us, we would have been eaten by the hounds for sure."

Violet grinned. "Oh, well. I imagine we'd make a fine snack, at least."

Christopher shook his head at her reckless nonchalance, yet he still ran his fingers across her shoulder and down her arm, contenting himself with touching her as he pleased. But when he reached for her hand, he stopped short. He took a good look at the envelope she held, recognizing the wax seal with the scrolled letter "M" pressed into it.

"I almost forgot about this," she realized, offering the paper to him. "I guess you should read it, since Mr. Rodchester delivered it so urgently."

"I guess I should," Christopher conceded, forcing himself to take the letter and break open the seal. He scanned the brief message before informing her of the contents. "It's from Nick Marlow. He wishes to speak with me."

"When?"

"Tonight, after dinner. He wants to meet me in Nightingale Port." *At the same tavern where he maintains his spare room.*

Violet's entire body tensed with his words. Christopher's eyes darted to hers, catching a glimmer of fear before she cleared her throat. "I suppose you should go to see him, since he is your oldest and dearest friend."

He set the letter down on the bench. "I suppose."

She bit into her lip, worrying the flesh beneath her teeth.

"What is it, my sweet? You seem upset."

"I guess I'm just not quite over what happened earlier. Given that Mr. Rodchester interrupted us when we were so...intricately entwined."

"Intricately entwined – that is one way to put it," Christopher mused, draping his arm over her shoulders. "I'm sorry we were nearly caught."

"I'm sorry, too. Good Lord, I honestly cannot wait until we are married. Then we can touch each other as much as we want, whenever we want."

"Damn, that sounds too good to be true."

"It's not, though. We can be married very soon."

"How soon?"

"A couple months, perhaps?"

"*Months?*" he grumbled.

"Well, we still have two more weeks of courtship here," she explained. "Then I'll go home to Pennyshire to make plans for our engagement party. But after that announcement, it should only be another month or two for my parents to arrange a proper ceremony."

"Bloody hell, a couple months sounds like a lifetime right now. Please tell me we do not have to wait for Gwen to be married, because her ceremony isn't scheduled until the end of the season."

"Oh, no, we shouldn't have to wait. I've never played the elder-sibling card before, but in this case, I will make an exception. We have every right to get married before she and Welly do. Besides, I do not think our wedding needs to interfere with theirs at all."

"Thank the heavens for that. Although, if you need more time, I promise I'll understand. If you desire a big engagement party and a grand wedding, I know these things take great planning and effort."

"I do not need anything of the sort," Violet insisted. "I only require you."

Christopher grinned with her proclamation. "And I only require you. Although two months still seems like forever to wait."

"It does. But do you want to hear something even more dreadful?"

His arm tensed across her shoulders. "What is it?"

"Before I came here, I asked my father for a six-month courtship."

"My God! *Six months?*"

"It sounds preposterous, doesn't it? Thank goodness Papa refused me."

"Can you imagine waiting half a year to be together? I'd never survive it."

"Me neither."

"I'm barely surviving now," Christopher confessed, reaching down to trace his fingers over her wrist. "For all I desire is to touch you, every moment of the day."

She grasped at his hand. "I want that, too. So very much."

He sighed in defeat. "I am fully aware of your desires, my dearest, for they mirror my own. But as much as we both want the same thing, I think it's important that we do not..."

"I know; I know. We must not get carried away with each other."

"And yet we still do. As evidenced by what happened here before Mr. Rodchester's rather timely intervention."

"You're right," Violet admitted, unable to hide the dejection in her eyes. "I'm sorry I couldn't control myself around you today."

"No, no," Christopher corrected. "Today was my fault. Entirely my fault. And I don't regret it."

Her gaze softened. "I'm glad you don't regret it."

"I shall never regret a moment we spend together. However, I must try harder to slow things down between us, and I need your help to do so. For you see, the more we touch, and the more we kiss, and the more I feel your body pressed to mine, the more difficult it becomes to maintain my control."

"I know what you mean," she seconded, her eyes traveling brazenly down across his chest. "All I have to do is look at you, and my will is gone. Truly, I don't even have to look at you. I just have to think about you. I only have to think about you taking me in your arms, and wrapping me up in your big, strong embrace, and holding me against your thick, hard..."

"*Violet*," he groaned.

She bit into her lip, ceasing her untoward speech.

Christopher stared at her mouth. "I don't want you to stop talking," he clarified. "I told you before that I know all is right with the world when I hear your voice, and I meant it. But listening to you speak of your eagerness for my body is causing me actual physical pain. Therefore, I must ask you to change the subject."

"I never meant to cause you pain. Please forgive me."

"There is nothing to forgive. I just need you to help me slow things down. Can you help me slow down? Just until our wedding night?"

"Yes, Christopher. I promise I can."

His shoulders fell. "Thank you."

"You're welcome," she offered, stealing another glance at his chest. "Although, do you think it's still allowable for me to hug you?"

"You can always hug me. I only ask that you do it gently, please."

She grinned. "Gently. I can do gently."

He returned her smile as she pressed closer, easing her chest onto his. He wrapped his arm across her back while she nuzzled her face into his neck. Violet inhaled deeply and sank against him entirely.

She remained unmoving in their tender embrace for several minutes. Then she slipped one hand onto his chest and spread her fingers out over his heart. He felt his steadily thrumming pulse beneath her palm and wondered if she felt it, too.

Christopher nearly fell asleep, sitting bolt upright on the iron bench, just from the heavenly warmth of her flesh. But when her hand skimmed farther downward, running over his shirt in a tentative exploration, he forced himself to stay awake. He almost asked her to stop her provocative touches, seeing as they went directly against his need to slow things down, yet he couldn't bring himself to say the words. Her fingers slid across his coat, making him stifle a groan, until her actions ceased of their own accord.

"What is this in your pocket?" she questioned, her hand settling on the oval outline beneath the fabric.

"Oh," he said, barely keeping his eyes open. "It's my photograph of you."

She lifted her head to meet his drowsy gaze. "You mean the locket my father sent you before we met?"

"The very one."

"Why do you have it with you now?"

Christopher reached under her fingers to pull the trinket out and cradle it in his palm. "I keep it with me always."

"Always?"

"Every moment of every day."

Violet's breathing quickened. Her gaze drifted to his lips while she licked her own, which made his arm tighten around her back. Once she tore her eyes from his mouth, she refocused on his hand. "I've never actually seen this," she said, reaching to touch the gold oval nestled in his fingers. "May I look on it?"

He had to steady himself before he could speak. "Of course."

She took the locket and opened the lid, watching as the halves parted. When she saw the picture inside, her brow furrowed. "Dear heavens, Christopher. I'm surprised you even agreed to meet me after seeing this photograph. I'm positively melancholy."

He huffed out a laugh that fanned her hair. "I've always wondered what made you look so sad in this picture. Do you remember what it was?"

"I do. My father had just told me I would have to marry. He said I only had two choices in my life: you, or the Duke of Dunworthy. I didn't want that. I didn't want to be forced to give up my life to a man."

Christopher swept a loose curl behind her ear. "How do you feel now?"

Violet's eyes rose back to his, filled with more emotion than ever before. "I don't feel like I'm giving up anything at all. On the contrary, I've gained an entirely new and wondrous life." She looked back to the photo with a soft smile. "I have no reason to be sad anymore. Not when I'm with you."

"Good. For all I ever want is your happiness. Ever," he assured, just before pressing his lips to her forehead.

~

CHRISTOPHER SPENT the rest of the afternoon with his wife, holding her as gently as possible while they rested together on the gazebo bench. He spent the evening sitting across from her at the dinner table, trying not to gawk at her like a lovesick schoolboy. After dinner, he escorted her back to the foyer and bid her goodnight with a slow, serene kiss.

Once she ascended the staircase and glided around the corner on the second floor, he stared at the empty space she'd just occupied. He kept her ethereal image fresh in his mind while he strode from the manor to fetch his steed from the stables. He held onto that image as he rode away with his heart in his throat.

The journey from the Wilmington estate to Nightingale Port took less than half an hour by horseback. Before Christopher even had the chance to settle his nerves, he found himself jockeying down Wharf Street toward the tavern nearest the docks. His destination stood close to the harbor, where the Marlow Merchant Company anchored many vessels. His horse's hooves clipped across the cobblestone while he directed the steed to the side of the tavern. He dismounted and secured the reins to a wooden post, stroking the animal's muzzle as he glanced out to the clipper ships in the near distance.

The mastheads of several vessels rocked up and down with the soft ebb and flow of the water, matching the cool breeze generated by the ocean itself. Christopher listened to the faint swoosh of waves splashing across the wooden slats of the docks, surprised by how the lulling cadence still soothed him despite the pain he'd endured in his time at sea. In an odd way, he imagined the ocean would always be his home away from home.

With a shake of his head, he patted his horse one more time before making his way to the front of the tavern. Dread filled his gut as he approached the entrance, forcing acid into his throat when he opened the door. The first thing he saw inside the main room was a hearth glowing with fire. He struggled to not cower at the sight. Instead, he nodded to the beefy man behind the bar before glancing over the sparse patronage. When he did not find Nick lying in wait for him, Christopher stepped to the far side of the room to take a seat at a small wooden table beside a window.

The moment he settled onto the creaking slatted chair, he reached into his coat and pulled out his locket. He opened the gold oval to look on his Violet, his thumb moving to her face to drift over the curve of her cheek. *Nick just needs to talk*, he assured himself as he gazed at her likeness. *I told him at the ball that I would be available to talk, and now I merely need to listen.*

Christopher wanted to believe that assurance. He truly did. But deep down, he knew this meeting would involve rumors of the pirate Blackheart and what Nick desired to do about them. Honestly, that was the last thing in the world Christopher wanted to think about. He only wanted to think about his Violet, and about how soon he could make her his wife.

"Is this what you do when you're not with her?" Nick's voice came from behind him. "You just stare at her picture and wish you were with her?"

Christopher didn't bother to look away from the photograph, even after Nick took a seat beside him. "I'm not here to discuss Violet. I'm here because you asked for me, Marlow. What do you want?"

Nick chuckled as he unbuttoned his coat to settle into his chair. "You certainly do get straight to the point, don't you? Can't a man get a drink, at least?" he asked, signaling to the barkeep with two fingers.

"Have your drink. Then tell me what you want."

"I think we should both have a drink," he contended when the barkeep stepped over and set two glasses before them, along with a full bottle of rum. Nick nodded to the furry, portly servant. "Thank you, my good sir."

"Anytime, Mr. Marlow," the barkeep replied before lumbering away.

Nick poured both glasses, raising his in the air. "Toast with me, old mate."

Gripping Violet's photograph in one hand, Christopher took his glass in the other. "What are we toasting to?"

"To brothers," Nick declared, his voice echoing in their small corner of the tavern. "Those we have lost, and those sitting here at this table."

Christopher nodded solemnly, clinked the glasses together, and took a sip. As he set his rum down, he met his brother's eyes. "All right, we've had our drink. Now, tell me what you want."

Nick finished his glass before resting his arms on the table. He leaned forward, pinning Christopher's determined gaze with his own. "This isn't about what I want. This is about what I *need*. It's about what *you* need."

"You know nothing of what I need."

"That's fucking shit. I know everything about you. You are my brother, and I know you inside and out."

Christopher's fingers clenched around his locket. "Bloody hell, please tell me this isn't about Blackheart again. Because I cannot...."

"Of course, it's about Blackheart," Nick growled, barely keeping his voice out of range of the other patrons. "Who else would it be?"

"I'm not doing this with you. I am not having this conversation again."

"Yes, you are."

"No, I'm not. I'm..."

"Yes, you are!" Nick hollered, slamming his fist on the tabletop. Rum sloshed from Christopher's cup onto the wooden surface. He felt all eyes in the room boring into his back until Nick resettled in his chair. "You will listen to me, Lord Kastle, because you are my brother."

Christopher shifted in his seat, his needy gaze searching out Violet's face for a brief moment of reprieve. "Fine. Speak what you must."

Nick exhaled slowly, his shoulders easing from the level of his ears. "I've done what I told you I would, on the night of the ball. I sought out the facts about all those rumors I'd heard. And now, I can tell you precisely what is happening across the world. Because I know it's all true."

"What is true?"

"All those unnerving reports about the pirate Blackheart. That he's traveling from China to Africa. That he's raiding villages in India along the way. That he's setting those villages on fire. It's all true."

Christopher gritted his teeth. "And?"

"And? Is that all you have to say to me? *And*?"

"What the hell do you want me to say to you, Nick?"

"I want you to say that you see it! I want you to admit the fire is a sign!"

"A sign of what? That Sid Bishop is alive and well and hell-bent on revenge?"

"Exactly! That's exactly what this means!"

Christopher snatched his rum, downing the sickly tart remainder before clanking the empty glass on the table. "Do you honestly believe Sid Bishop has survived, and is now sending us smoke signals from across the world?"

"I do. I believe it wholeheartedly. And I know you do, too."

"I – I don't know what to believe," Christopher lied, pressing his fingers against his eyelids. "I just don't know."

Nick's voice softened to a whisper. "Yes, you do. You don't want to believe it, but you do. You also know this means Max is in danger. He needs us, Kastle. Max needs our help."

"Hell, Marlow. If what you say about the pirate Blackheart is true, then Max is already dead."

Nick shook his head. "No. That doesn't make sense. Sid wouldn't just kill him. He would consider death too easy. He would keep Max alive to torture him. And he would set wild, blazing fires to make sure you and I know all about it."

Christopher groaned. "Good God, what do you want from me, then? What do you see happening here? Do you expect me to drop everything in my life? Do you expect me to leave everyone I love here in England, so I can travel across the world in search of a half-dead boy and a lunatic? Is that what you've come to ask?"

Nick stared at him with his face fallen. But when he spoke, his words rang clear. "Things are burning, brother. The world we lived in all those years is on fire. The *friends* we loved are on *fire*, while we sit in this cozy room and drink our rum. I can't do it any longer. I can't stay here for one more goddamn minute, knowing what is happening out there."

Christopher wrenched his eyes away from his old friend's distraught face to look down at the photograph in his hand. He didn't want to hear these sharp, strident words. He only wanted to hear her. He only wanted the sound of Violet's sweet whispers and whimpers in his ears.

He knew what his brother was saying to him now. Nick was telling him they needed to go save Max, and to defend all the innocent people they'd left behind. But the only thing Christopher truly heard was that he had to give up his Violet. All he understood was that he couldn't have her, and that realization ripped his heart from his chest.

He drew his thumb languorously across the curve of her cheek.

Nick exhaled. "Damn, you really do love her."

Christopher didn't reply. He merely poured himself another drink while he studied her picture. A long minute later, he spoke the raw truth.

"You do know what you're asking of me, don't you, Marlow? You're asking me to travel back to the place that took my soul. You're asking me to return to the horrors of the life I led for all those dreaded years. You're asking me to become the same hollow, wretched man I was before...before..."

Before her.

Nick sat in deathly silence as he listened. He refilled his own glass and tossed it back. Once he'd returned his empty cup to the table, he inhaled steeply. "You do know that I'm in love with your sister, right?"

Christopher's eyes cut to his, sharp as daggers.

"You and I have never addressed this topic openly," Nick continued despite the lethal glare, "but I know you know. I began to love Daniela when we were all just children, playing in the gardens behind your home. I grew to love her more and more as the years went on, as I watched her become a strong, astonishing young woman. But I was a foolish idiot back then – you and I both were – and the careless things we did made me look irresponsible and untrustworthy in her eyes."

Nick paused to suck in another steep breath. "You joined the Royal Navy to escape your burdens, Kastle. But I joined to prove to Daniela that there was more to me than what she'd seen. And all those years you and I were away, in those dark, desperate nights when we dreamed of how our lives would be once we returned home, she was the only person I thought of. I wanted to return for Daniela alone."

"And now you're here. You and she are both here."

"Yes, we are. But I don't deserve her yet, do I? I am not a whole man, you see. I am nothing more than a broken, haunted creature."

Christopher huffed at the frighteningly familiar words.

"I know why you don't want me to be with your sister," Nick admitted with a sad smile. "You're right to refuse me as a suitor, of course. I am not good enough for her. I wake with nightmares almost every night. And during the day – whenever I cannot be by her side – all I think about are the vile choices you and I were forced to make. I think about the heinous crimes we committed. I think about the poor, innocent people we left in our wake. I think about all of it constantly, unless I'm with her. She is my only solace from the insanity in my mind, and I want nothing more than to cling to her."

Nick stopped to run a rough hand through his dark hair. "But the more time I spend with Daniela, the more I question my actions. Because it's not fair to her, is it? It's not fair to offer her a broken creature to spend her life with. It's not fair to expect her to one day call me her husband, to sleep beside a man who wakes screaming in the middle of the night. It's not fair to take all of her warmth and kindness and caring, just to purge the demons I cannot rid myself of on my own."

Christopher bowed his head as every word hit him like a hammer.

"But now I can purge my demons, Kastle. We both can. If we take this opportunity to make things right, we can absolve all our sins. And when we return home again, we can be with the women we love without guilt or fear."

When Nick finished speaking, Christopher could hardly breathe. He clenched onto the gold oval in his hand as he forced his words from his throat. "Well, then. I must say that sounds quite lovely, Marlow. But just what do you think the odds are that we make it home alive a second time?"

"Slim. The odds are slim. But there is a chance – a chance for us to come home to Nightingale as whole, complete men – to give Daniela and Violet the husbands they deserve. I want so much to be a proper husband. I want a cozy, peaceful life. I want a home and children and the ability to grow old by

Daniela's side. But not if it means abandoning innocent people to the hands of a madman. Not if it means abandoning Max to a fate worse than death. I can't do that. Can you? Can you leave that boy – and everyone else we grew to care about during those years – out there, unprotected and suffering, when you know we can help them?"

Christopher glared hard at his brother before looking back to his locket. He soaked in the sight of his wife, basking in her comfort and peace.

"Good Lord," Nick scoffed. "Are you truly questioning your decision here? Are you still considering staying in England, just to be with her?"

"Yes. I most certainly am."

"Bloody hell, Christopher. You've only known Violet for six weeks. You've wanted her for mere *days*. I have longed for Daniela my *entire life*."

"And that makes your feelings more valid than mine?" he bit back.

Nick stilled. "No. No, it doesn't. But it does mean I fully understand how agonizing it will be to leave her behind."

Pain sliced through Christopher's brain, stabbing at the innards of his skull. He slammed his eyes shut, working to fight the fierce, pounding ache.

"I do understand why you don't want to leave her," Nick added in his silence. "But there is something I need you to understand, as well."

"What is that?"

"Even if you don't come with me on this journey, I'm going anyway."

Christopher's jaw unhinged. He looked back to his brother with sheer incredulity. "What the fuck are you even talking about, Nick? You'll never survive out there without me. You and I both know I'm your only chance at returning to Nightingale alive."

"Yes, I'm well aware of that. Why else do you think I brought you here?"

Christopher glowered at him, trying with all his might to hate Nicholas Marlow. But he couldn't. He recognized the pain trapped behind the man's haunted eyes, and he couldn't bring himself to hate his own brother.

"I need to be the man Daniela deserves," Nick insisted even as his shoulders drooped. "As such, I shall make this trip with or without you. You don't have to come with me. You can stay right here and watch me leave."

"And just how am I supposed to do that? How am I supposed to watch you sail away, knowing you'll die without my help? Daniela loves you more than life itself, and you know it. How can I ever look my sister in the eyes again after her heart shatters with your loss?"

"I don't know, old friend. But staying is still an option for you, I guess."

Christopher shook his head in pure disbelief as the walls of the tavern closed in around him. He looked back to his locket, to the face of his wife, wanting only to be with her. He wanted to rest his head in her lap, to feel her fingers ruffling through his hair, to settle against her body as everything cruel in his life faded into the background.

"Don't you see what you need to do here, Kastle? I can see it clear as day. The answer to all of your problems is so simple."

"I think that rum has addled your brain," Christopher barked. "Nothing about this is simple."

Nick leaned forward on the table. "Yes, it is, because you know you're coming with me. Deep in your heart, that decision is already made. All that plagues you now is the desire you have for the woman in that picture. But the answer is simple."

"And what is the answer?"

"If you want Violet that badly, then just marry her before you leave."

Christopher nearly fell off of his chair. "What the hell, man?"

"Oh, please. Don't act like you're shocked by the idea. You forget that I've seen the way she looks at you. I've seen the way she acts in your presence. Your betrothed is madly in love with you."

Christopher's heart wanted to soar with those words, yet it remained chained to the ground. Violet had never said she loved him, although every movement of her body and every look in her eyes screamed to him of her love. He yearned to hear her say the words, even while knowing full well that he didn't deserve them.

"Violet loves you," Nick reiterated. "At least, she loves the Lord Kastle you've allowed her to see. If you ask her to marry you now, and to wait for your return, I'm certain she'll do it. In fact, having said it, I think it's a brilliant idea. If the thought of returning home to your eagerly waiting wife gives you purpose on our journey, then we shall all be better off."

"Damn it, Nick. I cannot possibly do that. I can't marry Violet one day and leave her the next."

"Why not? If she wants you and you want her, then why on earth not? She won't deny you. Just tell her you've been called away on urgent business and you'll be gone for a time. Then marry her, bed her, and leave with the knowledge that you've got a wife to come home to. Hell, perhaps she'll have a babe waiting for you upon your return, to place right into your arms."

The mention of a child with Violet pulled at every deep desire in Christopher's body. He fought against the pain of longing that threatened to spill tears from his eyes. To be a father – to have children with this woman who shone brighter than the sun – was a gift he wanted so badly he could taste it.

But would he ever deserve that gift? Would he ever deserve such a wholesome future if he let innocent people suffer as they were now? Would he ever be able to look his children in the eyes and feel worthy of their adoration if he remained here to bathe in his own selfish needs? Would he ever earn the love of his angelic wife if he used her heart and body to quench the thirst of his demons while allowing the rest of the world to burn?

Bloody fucking hell.

He should have known his life with Violet was too good to be true. He should have known his need for atonement would seek him out, all the way across the oceans, and force him to pay for his sins. He should have known he would only end up hurting her.

Christopher hung his head as he looked to her photo once more. He relished the blissful softness of her face, of every gentle curve he knew by heart. He drank her in long and hard before asking the inevitable question.

"How fast can you get a ship together?"

All the air whooshed from Nick's chest. He worked to compose himself before replying. "If I throw enough money at it, and tell my father enough lies, I can do it in two weeks. Maybe less."

Two weeks. Goddamnit.

Christopher struggled to focus. "We'll need a crew."

"There are plenty of men toiling about the docks who'll come with us if we promise gold and glory. They'll be a grisly lot, but they'll learn to obey."

"We'll need to track down Dorian Stonewall if we're going to have any chance at finding Max."

"That shouldn't be a problem. I'm sure Stone is right where we left him."

"We'll also need rations onboard for at least five months."

Nick nodded. "Aye, Captain."

Christopher's lungs seized. *Captain.* He'd never wanted to be called that again. He'd never wanted this day to come. Yet here it was.

He poured himself another glass of rum. "There is something else I need you to do for me before we leave, Nick."

"Name it."

"Cora. Go to my sister and tell her everything."

Nick's eyes grew as big as saucers. "*What?*"

"I want you to tell her everything," Christopher repeated in no uncertain terms, tossing the burning liquid down his throat.

"You cannot possibly mean to tell her *everything*."

"I do. I need Cora to know the full truth about our time at sea."

"But why in the world would you want her to know the truth? I mean, unless you..." Nick's words trailed off when his mouth dropped open. "Oh, dear God! You don't intend to take her along with us, do you? You don't intend to take your little sister on a five-month voyage across the seas, with Lord-knows-what waiting for us on the other side. Do you?"

Christopher filled his glass again. "No, I most certainly do not. Cora will *not* be coming with us."

"Well, thank goodness for that, although I still don't understand your logic. Why do you want her to know so much of our perfidious past?"

"Because I've sworn to her, since the night I returned home, that I would remain in England. Yet Cora never believed me, no matter what I said. She made me promise that if I ever sailed away again, I would take her along."

"But if we're not taking her along, then why tell her?"

"She just...she just deserves to know, Nick. If I must break my vow to her, then she should at least hear why. Hopefully, when she learns the whole story, she'll understand my purpose for leaving. Hopefully, she'll forgive me and I will not have to lose a beloved sister over this."

"Hell, I think you'd be more afraid to lose her over the truth."

Christopher glowered at his brother, despite the validity of his statement.

"Fine, fine," Nick withdrew. "I'll tell her everything. Although, if she must know, I'm certain she'd prefer to hear it from you."

"You're right; I'm sure she would. But I cannot do it, because I need to get back to Violet." Christopher drained his rum again before setting the cup back on the table. "And because I don't think I can look Cora in the eyes and tell her the whole story. I simply cannot."

Nick didn't say anything in response. Christopher merely stared at his empty glass. Eventually, Nick straightened in his seat, buttoned his coat up, and nodded. "Very well. I'll do it. But I hope you're aware that you will have to speak to Cora at some point."

"I am fully aware. And Nick?"

"Yes?"

"Only tell Cora. Not any of my other sisters. Definitely not Daniela. Swear to me that you will only tell Cora."

A tempest of emotion tore through Nick's eyes at the mention of Daniela, but he recovered quickly. "I swear it. However, if I do this for you, then I want you to allow me something in return."

"What is it?"

"I want you to let me give your sisters a nest egg of money. I don't want any of them to suffer again in our absence. And yes, I know you haven't wanted to accept my money before. I also know, if you marry Violet, she'll bring a dowry with her. But I want to help them myself, and I want your permission to do it."

Everything about Nick's offer hurt Christopher, and not just his pride. Still, he would not allow his sisters to suffer this time around. "All right. You may leave them a nest egg."

"Good. I shall make the arrangements."

Christopher nodded, unable to bring himself to reply, even though he should definitely thank his friend for offering to help his sisters. He simply couldn't bear to thank Nick for anything right now. Not when the man had just robbed him of all that was good in his life.

Nick studied him, not saying a word.

Christopher shifted in his seat. "What is it, Marlow?"

"I just...I have one more thing to ask of you."

"Good God. What now?"

"If we make it back home, I'm going to ask Daniela to marry me. And if she'll have me, I want your blessing."

Christopher stared his friend straight in the eye, seeing nothing but the utter conviction of his emotions. For the first time ever, he knew he could give the man what he wanted. "If we ever make it back home alive, you'll have my full blessing, Mr. Marlow."

A smile tugged at the corners of Nick's mouth when he stood from his seat. "I'll keep you updated on the ship's progress," he vowed before pivoting on his heels and walking away.

Christopher watched his brother's retreating form until it disappeared from sight. Then he turned back to the locket in his hand. His eyes instantly sought the face of his wife.

Violet, my love. I have no choice but to leave you.

He sighed, collapsing further into his chair. In the most regrettable way, this turn of events made perfect sense to him. Christopher had always known, from the moment he'd laid eyes on her, that she deserved better. She deserved a man who had not run from his responsibilities at the first opportunity, a man who did not wake screaming in the middle of the night, a man who did not cling to her as his sole source of peace and comfort.

Violet deserved a whole man. One who was not scarred and broken. One who could love her with all his heart. One who would willingly fall to his knees for her. And as much as he wanted to be that man, he couldn't. Certainly not now. Probably not ever.

Yet all Christopher could hear were the words Nick said moments ago.

If you want Violet that badly, then just marry her before you leave.

CHAPTER 10

Best Laid Plans

Violet paced the floor of the Wilmington foyer, keeping to the shadows of the dimly lit section in the back. She'd hidden in this alcove once as a child, concealing herself in order to listen to Mama and Aunt Tildy argue over Papa. She distinctly remembered her mother telling her aunt that love was not a fate – it was a gift.

Violet still believed that. Love was indeed a gift, and her love for Christopher was more precious than anything she'd ever known. Which is why she now paced the floor so late at night, awaiting her husband's return.

Christopher had left Wilmington after dinner, intent to meet Nicholas Marlow in Nightingale Port. Violet had reassured herself that it was simply a gathering of two friends who desired to drink and laugh together. Yet her mind had not been able to clear the stinging sound of Nick's invitation to Christopher at the ball: *if you ever realize that you're in too deep, and you need a little time and space to clear your head, then feel free to use my room in Nightingale Port.*

She shivered with the thought of her husband seeking sanctuary in some dank, dark room above the Wharf Street tavern. The chilling image had haunted her all evening, keeping her from changing into her nightgown after dinner or even attempting to sleep. Instead, she'd crept back downstairs to wait, unable to imagine enduring until morning without seeing him again. Especially since she feared that being out of sight meant being out of mind.

"God, don't be so dramatic," Violet chastised herself in a firm whisper as her feet moved incessantly over the marble. "Christopher only went to the tavern because Nick asked to meet him. He did not run away from you."

She made herself nod in acceptance of her words. However, her fingers still twisted over the tight bodice of her ocean-blue dress, her heart still beat at a frenzied pace, and her teeth still nibbled firm indentations into her lower lip. That is, until the front door finally opened.

Christopher stepped stealthily into the foyer, slipping the door shut behind him before turning on his heels. The instant Violet saw his blue eyes sparkle in the oil lamplight, she sighed in relief. "You're back," she breathed, her turbulent pulse now coming to a near standstill.

He froze the moment he heard her voice. She wasn't sure why he remained so far away, but she didn't take time to ponder it. She strode toward him, faster and faster, nearly running by the time she launched herself into his arms.

Christopher caught her to his chest, encasing her in his heated embrace. Violet buried her face into his collar, filling her lungs with his scent while digging her fingers into his coat. He didn't discourage her attempt to merge their bodies. He only held her to him, pressing kisses into her hair, without a word of protest.

She gripped onto him with fierce resolve, never wishing to release her hold. But her guilt eventually became too much to bear, and she eased back to see his face. His eyes fastened to hers as he brushed an errant curl from her cheek.

"What are you doing still awake, Violet?"

"I was waiting for you."

"Why?"

She whimpered with the expected question. "To be perfectly honest, I was worried about your return. I tried to prepare for bed, but I couldn't prevent my unease with your absence. The only explanation I have is that I've never been separated from you for this long, not since you first came to court me, and I suppose I simply missed you. Do you find that silly?"

Christopher shook his head. "Not at all. I missed you, too."

His tender admission allowed the anxiety to seep from her bones. "I'm sorry about the fierceness of my embrace, especially since I promised you earlier that I would only hug you gently," she apologized while settling back on her heels. With a bright smile, she released her fists from his coat. "At least until our wedding day, when I shall earn the ability to hug you as frequently and fervently as I desire."

He returned her smile, albeit his was a struggled attempt. She eased her fingers over his tight jaw, absorbing the weariness in his eyes. "Are you well, Christopher?"

"Yes, I'm...I'm quite well."

Violet knew it was a lie. She hated that he felt the need to shield his weaknesses from her, especially since she understood why he'd concealed the truth. "You know, I realized something after you left to see your friend this evening."

His brow rose. "What is that?"

"I realized you probably hadn't slept all week, since the rain kept us from returning to the gardens until today. I should have let you sleep on my lap in the gazebo this afternoon, so you could have some much-needed rest. But instead, we found ourselves...otherwise occupied."

"Otherwise occupied," he hummed, leaning in closer.

"Yes," she whispered, contentedly drowning in the memory of his body pinning hers to the ivy-coated glass wall.

Christopher's breaths turned shallow as he stared into her, obviously sharing the recollection. The hunger in his eyes was nothing new to Violet, yet it never failed to surprise her. Her body drifted nearer to his, stopping only when the tops of her cinched breasts rested onto his chest.

He inhaled steeply. "You're right," he admitted, easing his hands down her arms to shift her slightly back from him. "I haven't really slept. But that is nothing new for me, and nothing you need concern yourself with."

"I know it is nothing new. But it is definitely my concern, for I always desire your health and happiness. To that end, I think I've discovered a solution for you. Possibly. Hopefully."

"What sort of solution?"

"Well, you could, um..." Violet paused to fight back the butterflies in her stomach. "You could come to my room and lay in bed with me. I mean, you told me once before that you would lay in bed with me every night we're together, so I just thought we could start tonight. And I swear I'm not suggesting anything untoward, since I promised I would help slow things down between us and I intend to keep that vow. All I am proposing is that we lay down together. You could rest with me until early morning and then return to your room before anyone discovers your whereabouts. You could lay with me and simply sleep."

Christopher studied her as she spoke, the longing in his gaze making her blood bound. She wanted to take his hand, lead him up the stairs, and bring him to her bed. She wanted to pull him onto the mattress and gather him in her arms, pressing his body to hers from head to toe. She wanted him to relax in the warmth of her embrace and allow her to protect him as he slept.

He exhaled heavily. "Thank you for the kind offer, my dearest. I truly appreciate your concern. But I cannot come to your bed tonight."

"No? Why not?"

His gaze slipped from her eyes to her mouth, staring at her lips as he wet his own. Then he wrapped his arms around her waist, dragged her fully onto his chest, and kissed her without any semblance of restraint. The moment their tongues entwined, Violet clawed at his shoulders. Her fingers burrowed into his coat while his mouth shifted relentlessly over hers. Her body lost all balance, yet he merely held her upright when she sagged against him. He tasted her with deep and desperate need before finally pulling back to rest his forehead onto hers.

Christopher continued supporting her weight, with his arms like steel bands, while his warm breaths brushed over her lips. "*That* is why I cannot come to your bed," he answered, his words rough as gravel.

"O-oh. I understand," she said. Except she didn't really understand at all. The only thing Violet currently comprehended was how much she wanted her husband with her.

He held her for one more minute, ensuring the stability of her wobbly legs, before he took a step back. When the cool night air crept beneath her skin, she shivered. "Are you cold, Violet?"

"Yes, I am. But in truth, I feel cold anytime I'm not in your arms."

Christopher grasped her face in his hands. "God, I never want you to be cold. I never want you to be anything but warm and happy. I...I just think..."

Violet stilled, waiting for him to continue. He searched her eyes long and hard, with his lips parted. It looked as if he wished to ask her an important question, or tell her an eager secret, or share a provoking thought. Yet no further sound came. "What do you think?" she asked, eager to know his mind.

After a moment of deafening silence, he dropped his arms to his sides, breaking all contact between them. "I think it's late. I think we should go to our bedchambers now. Our *separate* bedchambers."

"I see. But we'll still have our walk in the gardens tomorrow, won't we?"

"Yes, we will. Tomorrow."

"Tomorrow," she repeated, forcing herself to smile as he strode away from her. She watched him take three full steps toward the hall before reclaiming his attentions. "Um, Christopher?"

He stopped short, pivoting back to her. "Yes?"

"My bedchamber is the fifth door on the left, after you reach the top of the staircase. In case you change your mind."

His jaw clamped shut. "Thank you," he replied through gritted teeth.

She could find no words to respond, so she merely nodded. Then she stood stiff as a plank while he slipped away from her.

Violet sat alone in front of the looking glass in her bedchamber, awaiting dinnertime. Birdie had already fixed her hair and assisted with her dress, so waiting was all that remained. As Violet studied her reflection, she saw her welcoming bed in the background, primly made with freshly laundered sheets. Ten days had passed since she'd given Christopher directions to her room, offering him to sleep in this very bed with her, but he'd never come.

Shifting her attentions back to her face, Violet watched the movements of her own hand as she stroked her forehead and skimmed over her pinned curls. Everything beneath her fingertips felt soft and inviting, yet her husband had barely touched her in the past ten days. He did still touch her a little, at least. He still offered her his arm when they walked in the gardens. He still held her hand as they sat on the gazebo bench, while she rambled to him about anything and everything. But his touches grew ever more polite as the days passed, with no sense of urgency or appetite. Violet understood that they'd agreed to slow things down between them, but this slug's pace was far worse than she'd imagined.

She hadn't felt his lips on hers since the night he'd returned from Nightingale Port. The only time of day in which he kissed any part of her was when he walked her to the staircase after dinner each night. Christopher stood there with her, lingering at the bottom step, and pressed his lips to the back of her hand. Then he searched her eyes long and hard, just as he had the night he'd returned from Port, as if he needed to say something of great importance. He stared into her with rapt intention and obvious words on the tip of his tongue. But he never said anything. Ten full days had passed, and the time for their courtship was coming swiftly to a close, yet all he did each night was kiss her hand and walk away.

Violet's brow furrowed as she considered what might vex him so much that he could not bring himself to discuss it. Perhaps he was upset by the conversation they'd had on that rainy day in the gazebo, when he'd admitted his ship had not been wrecked, but rather attacked. By pirates, no less. She didn't want to believe Christopher could regret any confidence he gave her, but she could also understand how discussing his past might cause him undue stress. On the other hand, perhaps he actually wished to tell her more of what had happened during those fateful years but didn't know how to begin.

She wanted to help her husband, yet she was at a loss on the topic. Violet understood very little about pirates, except for what she'd read in the newspapers and overheard from the gossiping of her maids. The reports Harriet and

Beatrix gave for the pirate Blackheart had been outrageously different and difficult to accept. According to them, he was either a stringy black-haired old man who ate the limbs off of children for breakfast, or a flowing black-haired Adonis who bedded a dozen wenches a night.

Violet knew neither rumor could be entirely true, but she did understand that Blackheart was a cruel destroyer and a wanted criminal. She even recalled sitting beneath her favorite tree on the Bell estate, dreaming about conquering the dastardly pirate and avenging the world. In truth, her dreams had not changed. She still wanted to conquer Blackheart, along with every other pirate in existence. Except now, she didn't yearn to avenge the world. She only wished to avenge her husband. She wished to avenge each and every scar on Christopher's body.

Christopher. Dear God, how she loved him. Violet loved him in every way imaginable, making the thought of leaving him in mere days – to go back to Pennyshire to make arrangements for their engagement party and wedding – quite unimaginable. Instead of feeling ecstatic about her ability to plan such desired events, she felt sick with the prospect of being apart from him for the weeks those preparations would take. Especially in light of the distance she'd felt between them over these past ten days.

Her chest constricted beneath her cinched bodice. "Good Lord, there is no distance between you," she chastised herself. "And even if there were, it's not like you can say anything about it. You can't tell him that he doesn't gaze at you quite as fiercely as he used to, or that he doesn't thread your fingers as tightly in his, or that his chin doesn't scrape as enticingly against your skin when he kisses your hand. Voicing any of those concerns will make you sound like a crazy person."

Violet hung her head, hoping beyond hope that Christopher still craved her as much as ever, and that he only subdued their mutual yearnings for the purpose of maintaining her virginity until their wedding night.

"You should be pleased to have a husband who cares enough to preserve your innocence with such conviction," she told herself before standing and stepping toward the door. "He's a wonderful man who very much wants to have you for his wife. Go to dinner with him now and you'll see for yourself."

~

CHRISTOPHER SAT on the chair in his bedchamber, staring at the bed he'd never slept in. He'd already prepared for dinner, dressing in his best pinstriped gray coat and trousers, awaiting the moment he would leave his room to meet

Violet. Part of him couldn't wait to see her again – to watch her eyes light with unfettered emotion as they looked to his – but another part of him dreaded that vision even more. Ten days had already passed since his life-altering meeting with Nick, and Christopher now felt the weight of the world collapsing his chest.

Since the moment he returned from Port on that fateful night – to find Violet anxiously waiting for him in the foyer – he'd thought of nothing but her. His entire being yearned to make her his wife. Every night since then, he'd guided her to the bottom of the staircase after dinner, kissed her hand, gazed into her eyes, and opened his mouth to say the words:

Marry me, Violet. Now. Tonight. Marry me so we can be together entirely, if only for the few days I have left before my honor dictates that I return to the sea. I shall be forced to leave you all too soon, my dearest, and I cannot bear the thought of never truly knowing you as my wife. I need to believe you shall be here, awaiting your husband's return after a long and perilous journey across the oceans, if I am to have even the smallest chance of making it back home alive.

Every night, Christopher opened his mouth to say those words. And every night, he closed his lips again without speaking a word. For in truth, he knew nothing about this was right.

No matter how much the thought of claiming Violet as his own tempted him in every way, shape, and form, the deed was far too selfish. Acting on this desire would only create more problems for her, not the least of which would be the defamation of her honor. Her reputation would be egregiously defiled by a quick, middle-of-the-night marriage, even to her betrothed. If she did not wait the required months to arrange a proper wedding ceremony, society would assume she'd allowed herself to be compromised by him and that he was merely making up for his mistakes by marrying her in such a deviant fashion. With as much disdain as she already received from the ranks of the upper class, he could not fathom saddling her with more. Especially when he would have to leave her almost instantly, to face all of that judgment by herself.

Violet deserved better than that. She deserved better than him. Christopher understood that truth without question, but the understanding in his mind did not lessen the longing in his heart.

His heart belonged to her, fully and completely. Spending these past ten days in her presence had been utter torture: knowing he must leave her; knowing they could never truly be together; knowing he had no right to touch her any further. He honestly should not touch her at all now, yet he couldn't find the will to stop. He still offered her his arm when they walked in the gardens each day. He still wound their fingers while they sat together on the gazebo bench. He still kissed her hand in parting every night.

Christopher assured himself that being pleasantly affectionate with her was appropriate at this point. After all, Violet needed to believe everything was still well between them. He could not risk her suspecting otherwise, and potentially jeopardizing his impending voyage, since too many lives depended on him making it across the oceans once again.

However, if he wished to be completely honest with himself, Christopher knew he remained affectionate with her these past days simply because he was greedy. He was a covetous, greedy bastard who wanted her in his life as long as possible. Because all he truly desired was to grab hold of her and never let go.

"Lord Kastle?"

The sound of his name called through the door wrenched his thoughts back to the present and expelled him from his seat. "Come in."

Mr. Rodchester shuffled into the room with a letter held in his weathered fingers. "A message arrived for you, my lord. Just now."

Christopher reached out to take the missive. "Thank you, my good man."

The caretaker nodded cordially before taking his leave.

Once Mr. Rodchester pulled the door closed behind him, Christopher looked to the envelope with the familiar "M" pressed into the wax seal. The last letter he'd received with this seal had directed him to Wharf Street, where his world was spun on its axis. His stomach lurched as he collapsed back into his chair and read Nick's message:

Christopher – Our ship is nearly prepared and will be ready to set sail by midnight in three days' time. I have spoken to Cora as you asked and she now knows everything about our past. I'm sure you are aware that your sister can be quite frightening at times. This is one of those times. Cora has informed me most directly that she shall accompany us on our journey, come hell or high water. I assured her there would be both on this voyage, but her fortitude did not falter. Consequently, I am making preparations for her to join us aboard the ship. Please do try to convince her otherwise, because I could not. – Nick

Christopher's hand shook by the time he finished reading, the anger and fear in his heart mixing so caustically that he barely knew what to do with himself. All he knew was that he had to get to his sister. He had to go home to face Cora, and to find a way to dissuade the fierce little warrior from this ludicrous idea of accompanying him across the sea.

He reread Nick's message at least a dozen times, then burned the page using the candle on his bedstand. Christopher watched the wretched fire destroy the words while their memory nearly destroyed his heart. He knew he must return to the Kastle manor right away, which meant he must leave Violet even sooner.

Standing from his chair, he straightened his coat while fortifying his determination. He proceeded out of his bedchamber, down the far staircase, and through the hallway. Christopher held his breath when he rounded the corner to the foyer, knowing Violet would already be waiting for him. She did not disappoint. She stood by the great window in a fitted emerald gown with loosely pinned gold hair.

Every muscle in his body tensed when her gaze drew to his. His heart thudded against his ribcage when her eyes lit with excitement. His fists clenched when a glorious smile pulled up her lush lips. He nearly fell over when she spoke his name.

"Christopher," she sighed, gliding toward him.

He couldn't be sure if her feet touched the ground or if she merely floated. She drew to him with the pull of a magnet, and he could not have moved away from her even if he wished it. "Violet. You look beautiful. As always."

Her hand wrapped around his coat sleeve the instant she reached his side. "Well, you are certainly the most handsome man I have ever seen. And I do not think I am speaking from bias, even if you are my husband."

He felt the sting of salt behind his eyelids. "Let us go to dinner, shall we?" he asked, pulling her closer.

"I would be delighted."

She moved easily beside him, step for step. Honestly, it felt as if she were born to walk with him, and he with her. He could hardly breathe, let alone speak, while guiding her to the dining room.

Lady Wilmington already sat in the head chair when Christopher and Violet entered the grand space. "Come join me, you two," the elderly matron instructed. "The cook has made us a wondrous meal tonight."

Christopher nodded his agreement, forcing a smile as he seated Violet to her aunt's right before moving around the table to take his own chair. The servants descended upon them, presenting mouthwatering foods for their delight, while the women discussed the upcoming nuptials of Gwen and Welly. The meal was indeed delightful, with its tender steak, spring greens, and fresh potatoes, and Christopher reminded himself to enjoy the quality of food that he would no longer have access to in three days' time.

God, only three more days. He had to leave Violet in just three days. And their time together would be even less than that, since he must now venture back to the Kastle manor to dissuade Cora from her absurd plans.

Gulping down one last bite of steak, Christopher drew his gaze across the table to where Violet sat. He'd spent the evening trying not to look at her, because it simply hurt too much. It hurt to see the bright glow of her eyes as she glanced at him over her wine glass. It was sheer agony to witness the loving smile on her lips when she caught him unconsciously staring at her. It killed him to know she still believed they would one day marry.

Perhaps taking a trip home now is for the best, he thought as he watched his betrothed take another sip of wine. Perhaps she would benefit from spending some time without him. Perhaps his ultimate departure would cause her less pain if she hadn't been in his presence immediately beforehand. Perhaps he could return from the Kastle manor in three days' time, and tell her he could no longer marry her, and then walk out of her life without hurting her in the least. And perhaps he could accomplish all of this without turning to dust along the way.

Christopher set his fork and knife down on the table, took a very long drink of his wine, and straightened in his seat. "Lady Wilmington. Violet. I must tell you both some news."

Violet's eyes latched to his while Tildy wiped her mouth on a napkin.

"What is your news, Christopher?" Violet queried.

He fiddled with the stem of his glass. "Well, I have realized that I need to go back home for a few days. To the Kastle manor."

Tildy's brow rose. "Oh? Why is that?"

"I've just...I've been gone for a long time now, and I need to check on my sisters. I also need to check on my father, and on the grounds, and..."

"How splendid!" Violet shouted. "I cannot wait to see your sisters again! I've already met five of them, and now I'll get to meet the youngest two, as well!" Spinning in her seat, she addressed the woman at the head of the table. "Can I accompany Christopher to his home, Aunt Tildy?"

Tildy's eyes locked with hers. "You mean *unchaperoned*?"

"But I won't be! There are seven Kastle sisters and I'm sure they will all be there!" Violet returned her bright, expectant focus to him. "Won't they, Christopher? Won't your sisters be there?"

He wasn't entirely sure of what had just happened. In the span of mere seconds, he'd gone from escaping his betrothed to the possibility of having her with him constantly for the next three days. He could barely wrap his mind around the thought.

In his bewildered silence, Tildy reinforced her niece's question. "Well, Lord Kastle? Will your sisters be present at your manor?"

"I, um, I suppose they will be," he admitted.

"See?" Violet squealed, looking to her aunt with gorgeous, pleading eyes. "I'll be quite chaperoned! I'll get to see my future home and spend time with my future sisters! It will be brilliant, if only you'll allow it! Please do allow it, Aunt Tildy! I shall be eternally grateful to you!"

Bloody hell, Christopher grumbled in his head. Violet had never looked more adorable or bubbly or perfect than she did right now. He knew no one stood a chance against such a sight. Not even Lady Wilmington.

"Hmm. I suppose it will be suitable," Tildy agreed.

Christopher's shoulders bunched to his ears.

Violet's shoulders fell on a contented sigh. "Thank you so much," she sang to her aunt before turning eagerly back to him. "When will we leave?"

He shifted in his chair. "Oh. Well, I – I thought tomorrow at noon."

"Perfect. How long will we stay? I only ask so I know how to pack."

Christopher stared at her, trying to think of any legitimate reason why she could not accompany him. But he couldn't conjure anything, especially not with her looking as if he'd just offered her the best gift ever. He couldn't bear to tell her that the Kastle manor would never be her home. He couldn't imagine saying that his sisters would never be her sisters. And he couldn't possibly fathom how he would tell her goodbye when they returned to Wilmington in three days' time.

"Two nights," he answered her. "I shall bring you back on the third day."

"Wonderful," Violet agreed, her eyes glinting like the stars.

THE FOLLOWING NOON, Christopher waited for Violet in the foyer as he knew he should. Still, he couldn't help pacing, or clenching his jaw, or fisting his hands, since this was going to be one hell of a trip to the Kastle estate. Not only did he have to convince Cora that she would not be going out to sea – which would be a treacherous feat in itself – but now, he must also withstand Violet's presence at his side in the place he called home.

"Damn it," he muttered, staring at his black boots while they clipped across the marble floor. "Damn it, damn it, damn it."

"What was that, Christopher?" Violet asked, her sparkling voice pulling his attentions as she stepped off the staircase.

"It was nothing," he dismissed, bracing himself for her approach.

She stopped directly before him, running her hands over the crimson riding cape she wore to match the gown beneath. "Do you think I'm dressed properly? I did not bring gloves, but I did remember to put my spectacles in the pocket of my cape, in case Juliette desires to read books with me."

A smile tugged at his lips as he imagined his betrothed reading with his little star. "You are dressed perfectly. As always."

"Thank you. Do you think your sisters will be surprised to see us?"

"No, actually. I sent a message ahead this morning to tell them of our visit, so our arrival would not cause any undue pressure."

"That is splendid thinking. I would hate to intrude on anything."

"You could never be an intrusion," he assured, the words leaving his mouth before he could stop them.

Violet stepped to his side and wrapped her hand around his arm, smiling up at him in glorious fashion. "You are too kind to me, dear husband."

Christopher averted his eyes to the door. "Why don't we move to the carriage to begin our journey?"

"Yes, please. That sounds wonderful."

He escorted her out of the Wilmington foyer and onto the gravel entryway. The same coachman and carriage awaited them now as on the night of the ball. The coachman had already placed her trunk on the back of the carriage, opened the door to the inner chamber, and taken his seat on the bench behind the horses.

"Thank goodness I do not have a cage beneath my skirts this time," Violet whispered while they stepped forward. "Although, removing that blasted thing turned out to be quite an enjoyable task."

Christopher glanced to the woman at his side just in time to see her cheeks pink. He watched in aching silence as she nibbled her lip, fully aware that he shouldn't reply to her inflammatory comment. He should not tell her how much he loved removing that cage from her body. He should not admit to how often he'd dwelled on the memory of her hipbones as he'd traced their curves with only her thin slip to separate their skin. He should not confess to how perfectly her rounded bottom fit on his thighs when she'd fallen in his lap, or how much he'd wanted to fully grasp that flesh in his hands. He should not say a single word, so he bit his tongue, offering only a pained smile as he swept his hand toward the door.

Violet stepped up into the coach. She took her seat and he followed suit, closing the door behind them and rapping on the hood. He sat stiffly beside her on the cushioned leather bench while the large wooden wheels began to shimmy with the clip of the horses' hooves. He stared straight ahead as the memories of what happened the last time they'd sat here – of untied cages, dropped hairpins, heated kisses, and wicked moans – badgered his mind in rapid succession.

"How, um, how long until we reach the Kastle manor?" Violet inquired, her trembling voice and twisting hands betraying her own illicit thoughts.

"Only a half hour, at most," Christopher answered, struggling like hell to compose himself while her luscious body jostled beside him. "It is not far from the Wilmington estate."

"Oh, good," she said, her voice turning as bright as the sunshine filtering through the window. Violet untwisted her fingers in order to reach for his. "I'm so excited to see your sisters. Excited, and a bit nervous."

He met her eyes when their hands entwined. "Why are you nervous?"

"Because there are two I have not yet met."

"Constance and Octavia will love you. Everyone loves you."

Tears sprang into her eyes and he immediately regretted his words. It felt cruel to tell her such truths when it would all be taken away in so short a time. He hated himself for the pain he must inflict on her in a mere two days.

Violet's palm shifted against his and Christopher glanced down to where their hands lay interwoven on the bench. Her fingers looked so soft and small wrapped inside his larger ones, and the serene image sent knives of guilt slicing into his heart. He shouldn't allow them these perfect little moments together. He should begin to distance himself from her, in order to lessen the pain she would feel with his loss. And yet he honestly didn't know if he could.

He continued to hold Violet's hand throughout their journey, until the Kastle manor came into view in the distance. His home appeared just as he'd left it – with the crumbling parapets at the entryway and the surrounding barren fields – except the vines he'd worked to remove from the front of the manor had already started to grow back, making the white walls green with ivy. He wanted to be happy about being so close to his ancestral home, yet all he could think of was how Violet must see it. He could only imagine her disgust at witnessing such vicious weeds and trampled dirt, especially after she'd seen the Chaney estate's manicured lawns, indoor plumbing, and armies of servants.

Christopher felt ashamed for her to be here now, since she deserved more than his crumbling home. He could only temper his shame by assuring himself that she would have more. Violet would have so much more, just as soon as he was out of her life. Once her marriage to the heir of Nightingale was no longer an option, Noah Bell would send his eldest daughter off to marry the duke. The Duke of Dunworthy, with his one ball, and his extensive properties and wealth. Violet would become the Duchess of Dunworthy. She would live in a fine home and have all the fine things she could ever want. She would be surrounded by gilded doorframes, priceless artwork, and servants who waited on her by day and night.

Christopher tried to convince himself, as he watched his decaying home come closer and closer, that he would feel good about sending her off to live such a life. He tried to assure himself that Violet would actually be happy as the well-kept fourth wife of a lethally boring old man. But he knew, deep in his gut, that it was nothing but a lie.

"This is your manor?" she questioned, drawing him from his thoughts.

He looked to her with his heart in a vice. "Yes."

She stared into him with an unearthly light in her eyes. Then she gave him the best smile in the entire world. "It's beautiful, Christopher. Just beautiful."

Goddamnit.

"I love you, Violet," he said.

Except he didn't say it out loud.

"I'm glad you think so," Christopher offered instead. "I love it here."

She nodded. "I can see why."

He squeezed her hand so tightly that it must have caused her pain. Yet she neither flinched nor faltered. She only smiled wider as the carriage eased up to the front of the manor and six of the seven Kastle sisters poured out of the front door.

"They're here! They're here!" the twins shouted in unison, with Ruby in her ivory dress and Pearl in her cherry dress.

"Ooh, look at the beautiful horses," Constance cooed, her long, loose dark hair glistening in the sunlight as she twirled in a circle.

"Is Violet in there?" Octavia asked, jumping up and down in an attempt to see into the carriage window.

"Yes, she's in here," Christopher answered his littlest sister when the coach pulled to a stop. He glanced back at Violet, giving her a reassuring smile before opening the door and hopping onto the ground.

"Step back a bit, Octavia," Juliette instructed, pulling on the young girl's shoulders to keep her away from the shifting steeds.

Octavia pouted her lip, making Christopher chuckle. He reached back into the coach to grasp Violet's hand, allowing her to step easily to the ground while addressing the Kastle brood. "How wonderful it is to see you all!"

He recognized the looks in his sisters' eyes, so he released his hold on her straightaway. Ruby and Pearl attacked her first. Then Juliette, Constance, and Octavia. The girls all took turns hugging Violet quite ferociously, although one barely had the chance to finish before another began. Violet simply giggled through it all, accepting each of them with open arms.

Christopher watched the display with his fingers twitching at his sides. The moment the hugs were finished, Violet slid over to him and circled her hand around his forearm. Only then did his fingers stop twitching.

"It is a pleasure to have you here, Violet," Daniela offered from her stoic perch at the back of the crowd. "I prepared a room for you as soon as we received word of your visit."

"Thank you so much, Lady Daniela. I do appreciate it."

"You're certainly welcome," Daniela replied with a curtsy.

Violet curtsied in return, just as another girl leapt in front of her.

"We have not met before! My name is Constance!"

Violet grinned at the young lady with the big blue eyes. "You're right; we have not met. But I'm so glad we are meeting now, Constance."

"You may call me Stanzi, if you like. Everyone in the family calls me Stanzi, so you should, too. After all, you are going to be family soon."

Christopher tensed, but Violet only held tighter to his arm. "Thank you, Stanzi. It is an honor to be included in your family. Truly."

Octavia stepped up to tug on Violet's crimson cape.

Violet looked down to the dark-haired girl with the bright green eyes, who was a nearly perfect miniature of Cora. "And who might you be?"

The little girl straightened to her full, short height. "I am Lady Octavia Kastle, youngest daughter of Quinton Kastle, the Earl of Nightingale."

"Well, that is quite the title, Lady Octavia."

"Yes! Daniela taught it to me. I don't often get to practice saying it."

"And yet you say it so well."

"Thank you, Violet. And may I say that you have lovely hair. Juliette told me you did, but now that I see it for myself, I know it is truly spun like gold."

"That is very kind of you to say, Lady Octavia. Thank you."

"You're welcome," the youngest Kastle offered, reaching out to squeeze Violet's hand while lowering her voice to a whisper. "But you don't have to call me Lady Octavia. Honestly, I don't much care for the *lady* part."

Violet laughed as she leaned down to peck Octavia on the cheek, making the little girl's eyes light up like emeralds. Christopher watched the entire scene with a mix of joy and sorrow and more than a little pain. He tore his gaze from the sight to search out the woman he needed most to see.

"Where is Cora?" he asked Daniela.

"Oh, she is just..."

"I'm here," Cora said, emerging from the house to join the rest of the family. She didn't look to Christopher at all. She walked straight to Violet and threw her arms around her neck, hugging her tight. "It's so lovely to have you here, Violet."

"Thank you, Cora. It's lovely to be here."

When Cora pulled away, she smiled at Violet. That smile fell when she finally focused on Christopher. "Brother."

He returned her daunting gaze. "Cora."

"Good to have you home."

"Good to be home."

"Hmm."

Christopher glared at his indomitable sister for a terse moment before Violet edged closer to his side. When he met her eyes, he remembered to breathe. "We should go inside," he told his betrothed.

"Yes, do come in," Ruby encouraged. "We have many fun things planned."

"And so much to show you," Pearl added.

"Not yet," Daniela corrected when the sisters began filing back into the house. "Violet and Christopher need time to settle in."

"I suppose we can give them a minute," Ruby huffed while fluttering inside. "But we shall demand your company later!"

Christopher's ears filled with Violet's laughter as the women preceded them into the foyer. He barely noticed Cora's attempt to slip past him, yet he still managed to grasp her elbow. "I want a word with you," he commanded.

"Later," Cora insisted, yanking her arm from his grip and disappearing through the doorway.

He glared at her retreating form until he found himself standing alone with Violet at the entry to his home. Her hand shifted over his sleeve, worrying the fabric between her fingers. He looked down, focusing on her nervous actions, as he drew her forward to step across the threshold. Once they entered the large circular foyer, she smiled with pure radiance.

Christopher brought them both to a standstill just inside the door. "I must say, you look rather happy at the moment," he noted.

Violet's luminous eyes drew to his. "Oh, I am. So very happy. For I remember you telling me that the moment I stepped foot in your home, it would be our home. And I love our home."

Her words could not have struck him any harder if she'd pierced them straight into his chest. Christopher braced his weak knees as he gazed at her, wishing he could offer her this home and everything in it. He would do so without hesitation, provided he could spend his life here beside her.

"I'll make sure the coachman sees Violet's things to her room," Daniela assured him when she came to stand at his side.

"Thank you. He already knows to pick us up the day after tomorrow."

"I shall go to confer with him now. In the meantime, I think you should take Violet to meet Father. He's been waiting for the two of you forever."

"Very well," Christopher agreed. Once Daniela stepped outside again, he turned back to his betrothed. "Do you mind meeting my father?"

"Not at all," Violet insisted. "I would be honored."

Christopher nodded, even though *honored* was not a word he would use in conjunction with his father. He didn't want Violet to even see the man, in all his wasted glory, clutching his brandy as he stared forlornly out of the window. But he supposed he had no choice in the matter.

Leading her up the right side of the two grand staircases, Christopher cringed with the familiar groan of the thinning wood steps beneath their feet. He drew her to the upper landing and then down the long hallway. He said nothing when they approached the anteroom to his own bedchamber, keeping that location securely to himself. He led her swiftly past that door, as well as several others, before finally pulling them both to a stop.

"This is the anteroom to my father's bedchamber," Christopher explained. "He never much leaves here."

"I understand," she told him with a squeeze of her hand.

Christopher took comfort in her kindness as he knocked on the door.

"Come in," a raspy voice answered.

He undid the metal latch and pushed on the heavy wood that creaked with the burden of age. "Father, it is Christopher. I have brought my betrothed with me."

"That is good news, my son. Please do allow me to meet her."

Christopher kept Violet slightly behind him, entering the room first in order to take stock of his father's condition. Quinton Kastle sat in his chair by the window as always, with his decanter of brandy at his side. Christopher tried to temper his reaction when he realized the man had worsened considerably in the past two months. Quinton's skin would be pale as snow if not for the grisly yellow undertone, his belly had rounded even as his arms and legs had thinned, and his cracked lips could barely manage the effort of a smile.

Pulling Violet to his side, Christopher wrapped her fingers around his forearm before covering her hand with his palm. He wanted to say he performed the gesture in order to support her in the face of such a ghastly sight. But in truth, he simply needed to feel her with him.

"Father, may I present to you Miss Violet Bell, daughter of Lady Liza and Mr. Noah Bell, of Pennyshire."

Violet curtsied, although she did not attempt to remove her hand from Christopher's arm. "It is a pleasure to meet you, Lord Kastle," she said, her voice ever sparkling, if not a bit tremulous.

Quinton examined her from head to toe, until his eyes watered. "My God, you're as lovely as a flower. You remind me so much of my Miranda. I want you to know that she would be so pleased to have you here in our home, with our son. I'm certain she would." Quinton looked back to Christopher. "Don't you think?"

"Of course," he agreed. "Mother would have been thrilled."

Violet's fingers twitched beneath Christopher's palm as she addressed the earl. "Thank you so much, my lord, for your kind words. And thank you for giving your son to me." The moment that sentence left her lips, she stiffened entirely. "I mean...that did not come out right. I didn't mean to suggest that you gave him to me. I only meant that I am grateful to be betrothed to him. If anything, I suppose it is *I* who was given to *him*. Not that I'm at all upset by that. I'm quite happy about it, actually. I mean, I wasn't when I was first informed of the arrangement, but now, I am positively thrilled. He's just so kind and sweet and wonderful and...well, he's Christopher. But you already know who he is, since he is your son, so I suppose I should stop talking now."

Quinton's gray brows lodged firmly into his receding hairline by the time she finished speaking, and Violet's fingers dug fully into Christopher's sleeve. He couldn't help but chuckle as he turned his eyes to hers. "All is well, my sweet," he whispered, even though he knew his father heard him.

Violet gave him an anxious smile before turning back to the earl. "I'm so sorry for the impropriety of my speech, my lord. I'm a bit nervous."

Quinton glanced between the two of them before settling his sights on Violet. "There's no need to be nervous, dear child. I'm quite certain you are part of this family already. My daughters have spoken constantly of your joy and radiance since they returned from the Chaney's ball." His gaze shifted to Christopher. "And now that I see my son in your presence, I do believe he is exactly where he should be, standing beside you. Am I right about that?"

Christopher's heart constricted while he studied the man's weary eyes. He honestly didn't know how much time he had left with his father, since Quinton Kastle would most likely not be alive by the time Christopher returned home to England again, if he ever did. He didn't wish to lie to the once-proud man, especially not in the last few days they had together. Therefore, he turned to Violet, took hold of her hand, and spoke the absolute truth.

"You are very right, Father. Violet makes me happier than I have ever been in my entire life. She is the most amazing woman I could ever hope to have by my side. And she is so very, very precious to me."

Violet's eyes lit with moisture as her body lit with sun. The sight of her in this moment took Christopher's breath away. He wanted to bend on one knee here and now, in the witness of his father. He wanted to beg her to be his wife, to spend every last moment they had together in each other's arms, and to love him forever. He may have done just that, had Quinton not spoken.

"It is good to see you happy, my son. It is good to see you both so happy in each other."

Those words rang like a death toll in Christopher's ears. This happiness had no future. Not with the barren life awaiting him at sea.

"Well, I suppose you should visit with your sisters," Quinton said. "For I know they have been anxious to see you."

"Yes," Christopher agreed. "We'll go to them now."

"It was a pleasure to meet you," Violet offered.

"And you as well."

"I'll speak to you later, Father," Christopher promised before he turned away, directing Violet across the floor and back out of the doorway.

Daniela awaited them in the hall, her concerned eyes drawing instantly to his. "How is Father doing today?"

"He's still alive, at least," Christopher answered.

Daniela sighed. "Well, then. Shall I take Violet to her guest room? Her trunk has already been delivered and I thought she might like some time to become accustomed to her new surroundings."

Christopher exhaled in relief. He should be as far away from Violet as possible right now, since he wasn't sure if he'd ever needed or wanted her more. "That will be good, Daniela. She should have time to settle in."

Violet gripped his fingers. "Will I see you again soon, Christopher?"

"Of course," he said, extracting his hand from hers. "Quite soon."

She gave him a soft smile when Daniela began to guide her down the hallway. Christopher watched them for mere seconds before forcing himself to turn and walk away. As much as he wished to watch Violet stroll the halls of his home forever, he had another matter to attend.

The matter of Cora Kastle.

VIOLET STOOD by the window of her guest bedchamber, staring out at the grounds behind the Kastle manor. She could see the many overgrown gardens Christopher had spoken of, with their tenacious weeds and unkempt boxwoods. However, none of that overgrowth really concerned her. All she wished to focus on was twisty tree she'd heard so much about: the Kastle family tree, where all the girls gathered for fun and leisure; the tree out of which Pearl had fallen and earned the scar on her neck; the tree the twins had promised to share with her.

Violet stared at its fascinating trunk, absorbing the beauty of its dark knots and turns. She wondered how long the tree had stood here. She wondered if it would still be here long after her children had stopped climbing it.

"Children," she whispered, her heart latching to the sound. She felt certain she and Christopher would watch many children play in this tree, after what he'd said to his father earlier today. *Violet makes me happier than I have ever been in my entire life. She is the most amazing woman I could ever hope to have by my side. And she is so very, very precious to me.*

Her soul lit with the memory of her husband's words, and with the heartfelt look in his eyes as he spoke them. His speech settled her soul for the first time in nearly two weeks. The distance she'd feared growing between them simply evaporated when they'd stood in his father's room. She assured herself that the only reason Christopher had sent her off with Daniela after they'd left the earl's chamber was just so she could get settled into her own chamber.

"Violet? Are you done unpacking?"

She turned at the sound of her name, seeing Juliette peek her head around the corner of her partially opened door.

"Yes, I am quite done."

"Oh, good," Juliette said, at which point the door burst fully open.

Ruby, Pearl, Constance, and Octavia all fluttered into the bedchamber.

"You must come climb the twisty tree!" Ruby and Pearl shouted in tandem, each grasping Violet's hands to tug her out through the doorway.

"I want to play dolls with you," Octavia said, sidling up to Violet as soon as the twins moved up the hall. "I have a lovely dollhouse we can share."

"Well, that sounds wonderful, Octavia."

"And we must sing and dance together!" Constance added, raising Violet's hand to spin around beneath her arm. "I can also play the piano, if you like. I really want to be the one to play for you. Although we can all play quite well."

"Yes, but you are the best of us, Stanzi," Juliette amended, pulling Constance aside to free Violet from her clinging grasp.

Constance grinned. "I am the best," she whispered before scampering up to the twins, who led everyone else down the lengthy hall.

Octavia gripped onto Violet's skirt. "This is where my dollhouse is," the youngest girl explained, pointing to the right. "It's the room next to yours. It's actually the Kastle nursery."

"The Kastle nursery," Violet echoed, craning her neck for a glimpse as they walked past. "I'm sure it's lovely. May we play dolls a bit later?"

Octavia giggled her acceptance while running to catch up with Constance.

"Yes, you can do that later," Pearl spoke from ahead. "But for now, we must finish showing you the manor. This is our room – mine and Ruby's."

"I see," Violet said as they pointed to the door across from the nursery.

Juliette linked Violet's arm, pulling her closer. "The twins prefer to stay in one room together, even though they could each have their own. They do not like to be separated for any length of time."

"I suppose that makes sense."

"And this room on the right is Father's, as you know," Juliette continued while they moved toward the upper staircases. "The next two rooms are Constance's and Octavia's, both to the left. The last room in this wing is Christopher's."

Violet ogled the final door. "That is Christopher's room?"

"It is. I thought you should know the location, since I figure you will stay there with him after you are married. It has a large anteroom with a beautiful hearth and seating area, and his bedchamber lies in the room beyond that. I think you will find it all quite lovely."

Violet's mouth ran dry. "I'm, um, I'm certain I will," she said, her nerves exploding wildly beneath her skin. She would surely have said more – something to mortify her, or make Juliette blush horrendously, or both – except Violet was prevented from sticking her foot in her mouth by the boisterous, violent shouting coming from behind Christopher's door.

"My goodness!" she gasped. "What is going on in there?"

"Oh, never mind that," Juliette dismissed as they stepped past the closed entrance to his anteroom. "They're just arguing again."

"They? Who are they?"

"Christopher and Cora. They shout at each other sometimes."

Violet's eyes widened when she looked back to Christopher's sealed door, her ears pricking with the sound of his strained voice. She could not discern his bellowed words, nor Cora's shrill response, since every noise came muffled from behind the heavy wood. Violet could only imagine how loud the yelling must be inside the room. "Please tell me, Juliette, do Christopher and Cora argue often?"

"Not all the time, but they definitely find the occasion. I think because Cora is the only one of us who has the fortitude to challenge him. She was just born with that sort of bravery."

"No one else argues with him?"

"Not really. He is a lord, after all. Even if the title itself did not demand respect, Christopher has truly been the man of the house ever since our mother passed. In fact, during the eight years he was gone, it still felt as if he was head of our home. No one argued with him before he left for sea, and no one has argued with him since his return. No one but Cora."

"Oh," Violet considered, wincing when another shout came from behind the door. "Do you think we should go in there? To see if we can help?"

"Goodness, no. It's best to leave them alone when they're in such a state. They'll work it out on their own. They always do." Juliette patted Violet's hand while drawing her farther up the hall. "I realize my sisters also wish to have time with you, but I hope we can spend a few moments in the library at some point."

"You have a library here?"

"Yes. It is not a huge room, but there are many wonderful books. You said you liked to read, so I thought we could do so together."

"That sounds brilliant," she agreed, hugging tighter to Juliette's arm. Violet did her best to focus on all of the young women walking in front of her, leading her through the manor. Although part of her soul remained behind, standing before the door to Christopher's room, wondering what on earth caused he and Cora to become so angry with one another.

VIOLET AWOKE the next morning to an interesting noise. She'd been deeply asleep and knew nothing of the sunshine streaming through the window in her guest room – not until she heard giggles at her bedside. They were little girls' giggles, and they were absolutely delightful. Violet kept her eyes closed, pretending to still be asleep so she could enjoy the sounds further. She honestly had no idea of the time. She only knew she was here, in the Kastle manor, and it felt more like home than she'd ever dreamed it could.

Yesterday afternoon, the Kastle sisters had taken her on a tour of the entire house. Despite the fact that the carpets below their feet were terribly worn and the walls bare of decoration, the girls made everything warm and inviting.

Violet loved that a building so large could still feel so cozy. The manor was nowhere near the scope of the Chaney estate, nor did it rival the luxuries of Wilmington, but this home was still grand in its own way.

Violet actually loved everything about this place. She loved seeing the estate through the eyes of each young woman surrounding her. She loved hearing stories of the Kastle manor's history, told by so many different voices. She loved helping Daniela set the dinner table last night. She even loved being pulled into a seat by Ruby and Pearl, who flanked her on either side. Although, to be honest, she would much rather have sat nearer to Christopher at the head of the table, but only because she'd craved a bit of his attention.

As she'd eaten dinner with her husband and his sisters, Violet told herself that craving his attention was quite silly, considering the vast, vibrant attentions she'd received from everyone else. Yet Christopher barely glanced her way at all during their meal, and when he did, his eyes appeared edged with weariness. The worrisome sight made her wonder again what he and Cora had been arguing about.

Violet had hoped to have a few moments alone with him after dinner, but he'd excused himself the instant the meal ended, as had Cora. The two of them ventured back upstairs together without so much as a backward glance, and Violet found herself quickly pulled into the library to read aloud with Juliette while the younger girls listened. It was quite enjoyable, except that Violet could not stop thinking about Christopher and Cora. Especially since she discovered them still arguing late that night, when Juliette escorted her back to the guest bedchamber after hours of reading.

Christopher's deep, angry voice and Cora's high-pitched shrieks had resounded into the hallway, setting Violet on edge when Juliette led her past his door. Even though Juliette assured her that all would eventually be well between the two, Violet was still alarmed by their ferocity. She'd gone to bed worried about them both, and expected to wake up to the same.

But instead, she woke to the sweet sound of giggles, which put a glowing smile on her face.

"Stanzi, Stanzi, look...Violet is smiling. Do you think that means she is awake now?" Octavia asked, butchering her attempt at whispering.

"I do not know, but we must not wake her," Constance whispered back, a bit more versed in keeping her voice down. "Daniela says it is most polite to allow a guest to sleep in."

"But I have already been up forever! And Violet needs to come play dolls! She said she would!"

Violet couldn't prevent her own giggles when the youngest girl went from whispering to shouting in so short a time. She faked a stretch and a yawn, rolling over in bed to lift one eyelid. "My goodness! I did not realize the two of you were in my room! How long have you been here?"

The sisters both shouted in delight and jumped on the mattress beside her. The old bedframe creaked with even the slight addition of weight.

"We've been here for quite a while!" Octavia answered in earnest. "I could not wait to play dolls with you, Violet! Having you here is like Christmas morning!"

"Well, that may be the loveliest compliment I have ever received, Octavia."

"And it's true!" Constance seconded. "Will you come play with us?"

Violet sat up in bed. "Certainly. Just let me get dressed."

"Oh, no! You don't need to go through all that fuss so early in the day," Octavia insisted. "For we are in our nightgowns, too."

Constance nodded. "Yes, we both are. And the nursery is right beside your room. It will only take a second to walk there from here."

"Hmm. You do make fine points," Violet conceded, glancing at the girls' long-sleeved and lengthy ivory nightgowns, which looked very much like her own. "Let us go, then."

The two of them shrieked simultaneously, each pulling on one of Violet's hands to lead her from her room and into the hallway. She regretted her decision to not change clothes when a draft of morning air swept down the vacant corridor and through the gauzy fabric of her nightgown, straight into her skin. But then the girls steered her into the next room, where the natural light from the window flooded the nursery and warmed her instantly.

"This is a lovely room," Violet remarked as she stepped inside, soaking in the vision of the white walls with a dark cherry crib in the center of the floor.

"This is where all of us slept as babies," Constance explained.

"Really? All eight of you?" Violet asked while moving to the tiny bed.

"Even me," Octavia sighed. "But our mother never saw me in here."

Violet looked to the child at her side. "She didn't?"

"No. I'm told she was not able to bring me in here because she had to go be with the angels after I was born." Octavia stared down at the crib before raising her emerald eyes upward. "Do you believe in angels, Violet?"

"Most certainly. And I'm sure your mother is with them, helping to watch over you always."

"I hope you're right," the littlest Kastle said, glancing back to the small bed. "I also hope you will fill this crib again. Very soon."

"I'm...I'm sorry?" Violet sputtered.

"Well, that is what a husband and wife do, is it not? They get married, and then they bring a babe into the nursery. And since you and Christopher shall be married soon, and this is where all of the Kastle children slept, I figure your babe should sleep here, too."

Violet stared in wonder at the girl before turning to the crib. "Our babe," she hummed as she studied the small white blanket resting on the mattress.

"You do want a babe with Christopher, don't you?" Constance asked.

Violet touched the edge of the wood railing. "Yes, I do. Very much."

A noise came from behind them then – a half-cough, half-choke – and all three women turned to see the man in question standing in the doorway. Constance and Octavia both grinned and yelled, "Christopher!" But Violet could not join in, having lost her voice at the sight of him.

He leaned against the doorframe with his arms crossed over his chest, staring directly at her. She had no idea how long he'd stood there, listening to their conversation. She honestly didn't know much of anything right now – except how perfectly delicious he looked first thing in the morning. He had not dressed entirely yet, wearing only a loose-fitting white shirt that lay open at the collar and black breeches that hugged his hard thighs quite indecently. His sleeves were rolled up to the elbows, revealing the thick muscles of his forearms. And his skin was a little damp, making his shirt cling rather rudely to the planes of his chest.

Violet could smell the crisp, clean scent of his soap, which made her realize that he'd just been bathing and his flesh was most likely still heated from the warmth of the water. All she wanted to do was to close the scant distance between them, plaster herself onto his body, and breathe him into her lungs. Given the current potency of her husband's fixed gaze, she could only assume he wanted the exact same thing.

"Violet is happy to bring your babe into this nursery," Octavia assured her brother. "That shall be a splendid thing, don't you think?"

Christopher didn't answer. He kept his silent, powerful focus solely on Violet. She hadn't seen this penetrating stare in so long, not since the night he returned from his meeting in Nightingale Port. She loved witnessing it again: the yearning desire and blatant need on full display in his stunning eyes.

She smiled at her husband as encouragingly as she could. Yet he didn't return her smile. Not even when Octavia continued speaking.

"I always wanted a little sister. But since that wish cannot come true, I'll settle for being Aunt Octavia. I'll even let you bring a boy in here, if you must. Although he'll have to learn to play with dolls. There is no question of that."

Christopher held Violet's riveted gaze for a few more aching seconds, although she couldn't be certain of how much time actually passed. Everything slowed and slurred as he drank her in. She had to remind herself that she was indeed wearing clothing, albeit very little clothing, while he looked on her so nakedly. And she could not move at all, not even when he finally broke their connection to address his youngest sisters. "I know you enjoy your playtime, girls. But let Violet have some breakfast, won't you?"

"But we haven't even gotten to play dolls yet!" Octavia protested.

He shook his head. "Later, little one. Breakfast first." His eyes drew back to Violet, roaming the length of her scantily clad body for the briefest instant. "Although I think it best that you all get dressed beforehand."

With those words, he turned on his bare heels and exited the room as silently as he'd entered. Violet swore it took an entire minute just to fill the air back into her lungs. She blinked several times, unable to clear the image of him standing in the doorway.

Octavia sighed dramatically. "I guess we can play later, Violet."

"Yes," she agreed, her voice winded as if she'd run the length of a field. "We'll definitely play later."

~

CHRISTOPHER FOUND himself seated at the breakfast table before anyone else arrived. He knew he should go to the kitchen, to offer help with preparation of the meal, but his legs could barely support him. His body still reeled from the vision of Violet standing in her thin nightgown in front of the nursery crib, speaking of having his babe. The pain of that heavenly image was unbearable in a thousand different ways.

When the women finally joined him to eat, and the plates of bacon, fruit, and bread were passed around the table, Christopher avoided all contact with his betrothed. He barely even spoke to his sisters, since he couldn't trust his own voice. The moment breakfast finished, he stood from his seat and began clearing the dishes. His actions did not go unnoticed by anyone.

"What on earth are you doing?" Daniela questioned him.

"I just...I thought I might do the dishes this morning."

Her brow shot up. "Really?"

"Yes, really," he insisted. "Why don't you all go outside to enjoy this beautiful day together? I'm sure everyone will fare better with some fresh air, and I can certainly manage to clean up."

Cora stood from the table. "Our brother is right, for once. You should all go outside while I help him with the kitchen duties."

Daniela shrugged as she rose. "Well, I'm certainly not going to look a gift horse in the mouth. Come ladies, let us go to the backyard."

Christopher watched his sisters and Violet stand and exit the dining room. They all walked together through the kitchen and out of the back door, headed toward the gardens. He felt Violet's eyes on him as she strode away, even though he kept his back turned to her. As soon as the door closed behind them, his shoulders slumped in relief. Until he realized Cora remained by his side, glowering at him with all of her infuriating tenacity.

He chose to say nothing to his little sister. They'd certainly said plenty to each other yesterday afternoon, and last night, and into the wee hours of this morning. Honestly, Christopher was sick and tired of fighting with her.

He chose instead to finish clearing the breakfast plates, hauling them into the kitchen to wash them in the sink. Cora stood beside him, drying the cleaned dishes with a towel. They made quite a good team – a fact he knew thrilled her to no end, given the decision they'd finally reached.

Once the dishes were put away and the kitchen back in order, Christopher stepped to the window to watch the young women playing out in the disheveled gardens. Ruby, Pearl, Juliette, and Constance danced in a circle around Violet and Octavia, while Daniela sat beneath their family tree, watching them all with a tender glow on her face. He couldn't help smiling at such a serene sight. But then Cora came to stand beside him, making his face fall with her looming proximity.

"Did you stay behind so you could argue with me even more?"

"Of course not," she refuted his assumption, lining her small body up to his large one. "I no longer need to argue with you, since the matter is settled."

His fists clenched at his sides. "You know, Cora, just because I've agreed to take you on this journey does not mean you've won. Nor does it mean you are in charge of anything. When we are on that ship, I shall be captain. I'll expect obedience from everyone onboard. Including you."

She huffed out a laugh. "Obedience has never been my strong suit."

"Yes, I'm well aware. Which is why I need you to understand this fact, and swear it to me without question. I *will* be in charge of you and I *will not* tolerate you doing anything that could put you in harm's way."

"I can take care of myself, Christopher. I'm an excellent swordfighter and I've a sharp mind. You know these things."

"I do know. They are the reasons you are standing beside me now, even discussing this as our future."

"No, I'm standing beside you now because I wore you down with logic. You finally realized, after we screamed at each other for endless hours, that I am going to be an asset to you on this journey. I'll help you rescue your friend Max, and then I'll assist you in bringing everyone back home safe and sound."

Christopher's spine stiffened as he looked to her. "You did not wear me down with logic. You wore me down with threats."

Cora shrugged. "I said what I had to say to make you see reason."

"And threatening to run off and join a *brothel* if I left you in England was how you decided to make me see *reason*?"

She grinned brilliantly. "A woman does what she must. I knew you'd choose to leave me here to rot, rather than take me on what you believe will be a deadly voyage. Therefore, I simply came up with a fate for myself that you would consider worse than death. But that doesn't matter now. All that matters is you finally seeing reason and agreeing to take me with you."

Christopher shook his head at his sister's contented smirk. "You make it sound as if I fancy the thought of this voyage being deadly, as if it is not the truth. Men die all the time on these journeys, and I'm not even talking about the wretched evils awaiting us on the other side of the world. I'm talking about the journey *itself*. Sailors suffer from scurvy and consumption and a myriad of illnesses physicians have not yet named. Even in the best conditions, the men will be filthy, unwashed beasts almost entirely lacking in hygiene. The smell alone shall be enough to sweep your legs out from under you."

"Goodness, you make it sound so lovely. How could I possibly resist?"

"Cora!"

"God, stop yelling at me," she snorted, crossing her arms over her chest. "You yelled at me all night and I'm quite done arguing about this. Risk is inherent in life. I could die of consumption in this very house, at my ripe old age of five-and-twenty, without ever having left the shelter of these barren walls. But I refuse to remain sequestered here any longer. And before you say it again, I do not care that Nick Marlow is going to leave us money. I do not desire to have a dowry. Nor do I desire to get married."

"But you have not taken enough time to truly consider this offer. You could have a very suitable arrangement, given the benefit of Nick's wealth. You could have a stable, reliable marriage to a fine young man."

"No offense, dear brother, but the men in my life haven't exactly been stable or reliable. Father sits upstairs as we speak, poisoning himself with brandy after having gambled away our family fortunes. And you...God, you left me just when I was coming of age and needed you most. You left me standing here with little Octavia, a mere babe in my arms. And now that you are finally back home, you insist on telling me that you're leaving again – after you *swore* you would not. Consequently, you'll have to forgive me for not desiring to remain here, waiting for some random suitor to want me now that I can have a dowry. I have already helped to raise five younger sisters and have stayed in this house for as long as I'm able. I now intend to live my own life, and it may as well be a life at sea."

Cora stopped speaking only to draw a breath. "Besides, Christopher, I do believe the stench in a brothel is not much better than what you've described aboard a ship. It may even be worse. And as for diseases, I understand that most whores eventually become afflicted with syphilis, which will certainly kill them at some point, although not before they go fully insane. I imagine that's a hell of a sight to behold, let alone endure."

Christopher shook his head at her inflammatory speech, questioning his decision to bring her with him for the millionth time today. He wasn't sure if Cora would actually join a brothel if he left her in England, but he couldn't risk it. As intelligent as she was, he could still see her doing something egregiously stupid just as a means to punish him. He'd finally realized, after many relentless hours of arguing with her last night, that he preferred to have her in his sights – even on a ship traveling across the ocean into God-knows-what – rather than drive himself mad wondering if she was safe in his absence.

"Good Lord, Cora. You certainly do have a devilish side. Don't you?"

She merely smiled. "Well, I think you knew that before today. Honestly, I see it as a trait I can use to my advantage, as well as yours. After all, tomorrow I shall become a pirate."

His entire body tensed when the dreaded word left her lips so cavalierly.

Christopher lifted to his full height to glare down at her, terribly aware that he would never be able to fully contain his fierce little warrior of a sister, yet still desperate to protect her. Especially from herself.

"*Nothing* shall happen tomorrow until you have made your *vow* to me," he growled. "The rules of the sea are quite set. If you come aboard my ship with the thought of disobedience, you will be punished for insubordination. I will have no choice. A ship is only as strong as the man who commands it, and I *cannot* and *will not* continue to argue with you when I am captain. There must be order between us at all times, for everyone's safety. I know how much you want to be your own person, and throw off the shackles placed on you by womanhood, but you cannot do that on the ocean. Not if you expect us to survive. I shall require you to understand and accept my command, and swear your unquestioning allegiance to me, from the moment we leave shore until the moment we return."

Cora matched his forceful glare the entire time he spoke. He could see the defiance burning in her eyes, but he also knew she could see the determination boiling in his. After many terse minutes, she finally gave up their staring contest and dropped her shoulders.

"Fine, Christopher. I swear."

"You swear obedience to me throughout this journey, no matter what?"

She looked a bit nauseated, but still nodded. "Aye, Captain. I swear."

Her vow settled him. It didn't settle much of him. But it did offer the smallest measure of relief.

Cora turned back to the window. "We are square then, you and I?" she asked, gazing out at the women in the gardens. "And we no longer need to argue the course of action we shall take tomorrow night?"

He exhaled, long and slow. "Yes, we are square."

"Good. I'm glad our business matter is settled. However, seeing as we have not yet left shore, I would like to retain my freedom of speech with you for a bit longer. After all, it's far past time to settle your other business matter."

"What other matter is that?"

"The one currently hanging upside down from a tree branch."

Christopher followed the path of Cora's sight out of the kitchen window to the twisty tree where Violet hung by her legs. Her knees wrapped over a branch and her arms draped down to the ground, her fingertips grazing the earth along with her long blond curls. Even at this distance, he could discern the wild smile on her lips and the utter joy in her eyes. The image squeezed his chest hard enough to force the air from his lungs.

"It must be difficult to see her here," Cora surmised in his asphyxiated silence. "To watch her playing with our sisters and dangling from our family tree. To witness Violet blend seamlessly into our home, when you know you cannot stay with her."

Christopher hung his head. "It is excruciating."

"Well, then. Are you at least going to marry her before we leave?"

"Did Nick tell you to ask me that?"

"No, Christopher. I came up with it all on my own."

He didn't respond to his sister's caustic tone. He just kept staring out at the vision of his betrothed.

"You know she would marry you in an instant, if you asked her," Cora pressed on. "I mean, you do see the way she looks at you, do you not?"

"I do see it. I know Violet. I know her heart."

Cora turned toward him. "And do you know your own heart?"

He met his sister's eyes, fully aware of what she asked. He knew his answer without hesitation. "I do. I know my heart very well where it concerns her."

"Then I'll ask again. Are you going to marry her before we leave?"

Christopher looked back to the window, watching Violet laugh with Ruby and Pearl while Constance and Octavia danced around her dangling arms. The sight was more beautiful to him than anything else in the world. When he managed to speak, he asked the woman beside him one question. "Do you know how Violet earned the title of the Picky Princess of Pennyshire?"

Cora tilted her head. "Daniela said it's because she was betrothed to another heir to an earldom before you, and she refused him."

"That is correct. You know the heir in question already – Lord Wellington Chaney, whose ball we attended – and you also know Lord Chaney is now marrying Violet's younger sister, Gwen."

"I am aware. I assume he chose Gwen after Violet dismissed him."

"That is what everyone assumes, but that is not what happened. Violet did not dismiss him. Lord Chaney fell in love with Gwen the moment he laid eyes on her, and Gwen with him. Violet saw this and could not bear to separate the two. Only then did she reject him. She gave up her chance at a good marriage to a fine, upstanding young heir. She gave up a life in an expansive manor where her every whim would be fulfilled by an army of servants. She chose instead to endure the harsh derision of society, just to ensure the happiness of her sister."

"My God. Is she some sort of angel?"

"Yes," Christopher answered with a sorrowful smile. "She is an actual angel, and I've asked myself a hundred times in the past two months what I ever did to deserve the fortune of having her as my wife. The answer, I now realize, is I have never done enough to deserve such a gift."

Cora's brow furrowed as her lips parted, but he spoke again before she had the chance to argue with him.

"I do not deserve her, Cora. I very much wanted to, believe me. From the moment I met her, I tried to be worthy. I treated her as well as I possibly could, with all of the respect and admiration she merits. But then Nick came to me, to speak of this journey we must take. He reminded me that my past shall never let me rest. Violet does not deserve to be stuck with a man like me. She does not deserve to be mired by my burdens and saddled to my sins." Christopher sucked in a deep, painful breath. "Therefore, the answer is no. I cannot marry her, because an angel must be free to fly."

Cora didn't speak for a long while. Just when he thought his heart might implode with grief, she said, "For what it's worth, I think you do deserve her."

"Thank you for that," he sighed. "I appreciate your faith in me."

"Oh, I'm not finished, dear brother. Not only do I believe you deserve her, I believe *she* deserves *you*. If Violet truly is an angel, then she should get what she wants out of life. And anyone who takes a single glance at that woman can see, plain as day, that all she wants is you. Perhaps you should tell her the *truth* of why you must leave, and actually give her a *choice* in the matter."

"I hear you, Cora. But I cannot give her a choice in this."

"Why not? Because you know she'll choose to marry you right now?"

"Exactly."

Cora huffed. "I think you're making a terrible mistake."

Christopher's eyes narrowed. "Weren't you the one who told me how much pain you felt when I sailed away nine years ago? Didn't you say you could not describe the agony you experienced when you thought I was dead at sea?"

Her shoulders sagged. "I did."

"Then I think you'd understand that even if I did believe myself worthy of Violet, I cannot bear the thought of causing her that much pain."

"But she's going to feel pain regardless, because you're leaving her."

"I know that, damn it. But at least I can leave with the knowledge that I did not put selfish claims on her life. I will not doom her to wait in constant fear, for what will easily be a year or more of separation, wondering if the husband she had so little time to know will ever return to her. Especially since I highly doubt I'll be fortunate enough to find my way home a second time."

Cora examined him at length before she relented. "I suppose I can see your point of view. But our ship leaves tomorrow at midnight, so when exactly are you planning to tell her you're leaving?"

Christopher refocused on the window, at the ethereal vision of his betrothed. "I need you to understand something, Cora. When we step foot on that ship, you will see a completely different side of your brother. You shall see a man in full command, a man who can crush other men with merely a look. You shall see a man in complete control of everything."

He watched as Violet hopped to the ground and giggled, making his chest deflate entirely. "That is the man I shall become tomorrow night. But I am not that man when I am with her. Violet brings out all that is gentle and good in me, so for now, I will remain a coward. I cannot bear to hurt her and I shall wait until the last possible moment before I must."

Cora shook her head while they both watched their sisters drag Violet away from the twisty tree to lead her back toward the house. "Well, I do wish you luck with all of that. You're definitely going to need it."

He flinched with her words, knowing how true they were. Christopher stood stiff as a board when Ruby and Pearl burst through the door, tugging Violet into the kitchen as the rest of the girls tumbled in behind them.

Violet instantly sought his gaze. "Christopher," she sang, her cheeks pinking beneath his barefaced stare.

He gave her a simple nod before focusing on his sisters. "Did everyone enjoy the twisty tree today?"

"Yes! Indeed!" came the resounding cheers of all the younger Kastles.

"It was truly lovely," Violet added.

His eyes wandered to hers without his consent.

"Goodness, I believe it is already time to begin preparing lunch," Cora piped in. "Would you like to help us cook, Violet?"

"Oh, dear. I would love to, but I fear I'm a terrible mess in the kitchen. Although I'd be more than happy to cheer you on, if that is allowed."

"That's perfect," Ruby said. "I've never been cheered while cooking."

"Will you stay with us, too, Christopher?" Constance asked, turning her big blue eyes up to his. "You can stand beside Violet and cheer us on."

His mind reeled, unable to imagine standing beside Violet and not holding her hand. Or pulling her into his arms. Or kissing her senseless. "No, I'm sorry to say there will be no lunch for me today. I have much business to attend."

"Aw," Constance replied, frowning up at him.

He ruffled her dark hair. "Don't be sad, Stanzi. I shall see you at dinner."

"Very well, then. We'll see you at dinner."

With a polite bow to all the women, Christopher turned on his heels and exited the kitchen. He did not look back at Violet. He chose to remain a coward, seeking out the sanctity of his bedchamber, so he could hide for the remainder of the afternoon.

Violet had the loveliest day with all her future sisters. They cooked her lunch and cooked her dinner. In between the two meals, they told her amusing stories about each other, and played dolls with her, and played piano for her, and asked her questions about her life in London and in Pennyshire. Even Cora joined the festivities, looking warm and happy, and Violet's heart settled with the belief that Cora and Christopher had indeed worked out their differences, just as Juliette said they would. After dinner, the sisters drew Violet a bath in her guest bedchamber, bringing buckets of heated water up the stairs one-by-one, so she could sink inside the tub and relax her tight muscles.

In truth, Violet felt wanted by every person in this household today.

Except for the one person she needed to want her.

After enjoying her blissfully warm bath, she toweled off and slipped into her laced ivory nightgown. Violet cinched the delicate satin ties up her chest and made a little bow beneath her chin. As she dressed herself, she thought about the one time today when she'd actually felt desired by her husband. She vividly recalled that moment in the nursery this morning, when he'd overheard her speaking of having his babe. Christopher had looked at her like he wished nothing more than to take her in his arms and create their babe, right then and there. Yet he'd barely looked at her again for the rest of the day.

With an exasperated shake of her head, Violet moved to the window. The darkness of night blotted her view and she could no longer see the twisty tree in the gardens. But she could see her own reflection in the glass pane, highlighted by the glowing oil lamp on the bedstand behind her. Her hair lay loose about her shoulders. Her cheeks shone rose pink from the heat of her bath. Her thin nightgown clung to the curves of her body.

She wondered what Christopher would do if he were here now. Would he be overcome by desire and carry her to the bed, finally claiming her innocence for himself? Or would he turn his head from her, insisting they be prudent with their actions, before striding away without a second glance?

Two weeks ago, she wouldn't have had to wonder. She knew that if her husband had found himself in her room, with her dressed in this revealing manner, he would have taken her in a fit of raw passion. But now, she couldn't be sure of anything. He'd changed from hot to cold and back again in so many ways over the past two weeks, ever since he'd returned from his meeting in Nightingale Port. He'd kissed her like his life depended on it that night, yet he'd not kissed her lips again since. He'd told his father just yesterday that she was precious to him, then barely spoke to her for the rest of the evening. He'd looked at her as if he could devour her whole in the nursery this morning, but could hardly meet her eyes over the breakfast table.

Violet had never felt so spun around, left reeling and twisting like a top.

She understood that Christopher Kastle was an honorable man. He'd made many vows to her during their courtship – he swore himself hers, swore to remain by her side for as long as she desired him, swore to make love to her completely, thoroughly, and exhaustively as soon as they were married – and she believed he would keep his vows. Still, she feared something had gone terribly wrong between them already, before she'd even had the chance to plan their engagement party.

Violet sighed, deeply ashamed of her current thoughts. She should trust her husband and believe that all was well, yet she could not. Sadly, she knew the reason why. The fault of her mistrust lay within her own heart, because she was still the same woman who'd stood in the parlor of the Bell manor, watching Wellington Chaney look past her to see her sister. She was still the same tender girl who'd wondered what was so wrong with her that it caused the heir of Centreville to see through her entirely.

Violet could not bear to think that Christopher had come to see through her the way Welly had. Even the mere consideration that her husband might not want her made her body ache deep into her bones. Standing here now, in the home they were supposed to share together, she could not ignore or pacify her doubts any longer. Not when they must journey back to Wilmington tomorrow, and she must return to Pennyshire shortly thereafter.

She needed to see her husband. She needed to speak with him. She needed to touch and hold and kiss him, to have actual physical proof that his feelings for her had not changed. Violet needed to know, absolutely and without doubt, that Christopher still wanted her. And she needed to know *now*.

Taking a full, resolute breath, she stepped away from her window and crossed the floor of her bedroom. She pulled quietly on the door latch, opening it only far enough to squeeze her small body out. The moment she found herself in the hall, Violet looked furtively around. A single wall lantern flickered in the darkened corridor, revealing an empty hallway.

She tugged the door gently closed behind her before padding her bare feet across the worn carpet. She could not hear any noise at all, save the pounding of her own heart, while she snuck past the nursery, the twins' room, the earl's room, and the younger girls' rooms. Her skin hummed as the cool air seeped through her nightgown, her pulse sputtering wildly when she finally spied Christopher's door and saw that it stood ajar.

Violet came to a stop before the anteroom to his bedchamber. She peeked inside the small opening between the door and its frame, seeing a hearth filled with crackling flames. Woefully aware that her husband did not like fire, she frowned as she rested her hand against the door. She glanced further into his private space, taking note of a dark leather couch that sat with its back to the hearth. Past that, there were two chairs facing both the couch and the fire. Sitting in one of those chairs was her Christopher.

The instant her eyes latched to his form, Violet took a step closer. The tip of her nose pressed into the wood of the door as she peered around the edge. He sat in his high-backed, threadbare, embroidered chair, wearing the same tight black breeches and loose white shirt he'd worn all day, with his sleeves rolled to his elbows. He held a glass of pale brown liquid in his hand, staring blankly at the fire with his normally bright eyes glossed over.

Christopher looked incredibly alone. And weary. And lost.

Violet wanted to take him in her arms and hold onto him forever.

She shifted nearer, needing him so much that she didn't realize how far she'd gone. She pushed the door open by accident, making the wood creak in protest. She stopped moving immediately, but it was already too late. Christopher's head swiveled toward the doorway. His eyes locked on hers.

If she'd been breathing normally before, that would have stopped now. As it happened, her erratic breaths only became more so when she witnessed the dark blue of his eyes shift even darker. His body did not move at all as she stood frozen before him. Only his gaze shifted, drifting down over her unpinned hair and onto her gauzy nightgown.

With his silent, unhurried appraisal, Violet became overtly aware of how she looked at this moment. She knew her mouth lay parted as her tongue moistened her lips. She knew her fingers drew anxiously over the very thin material of her gown. Yet she did not desire to change her appearance. She merely stood and waited.

Christopher's painstaking gaze eventually dragged back to her face, to hold her in place with such determination that she could practically feel his hands pushing against her, preventing her from entering the room. He had every right to refuse her, since she definitely shouldn't be here. But she couldn't let propriety deter her. Not when she'd come this far.

Mustering every morsel of courage she'd ever possessed, Violet stepped inside to stand in front of his door. As soon as she felt the solid wood against her spine, she pressed her shoulders back and pinned his eyes.

He swallowed hard. "This is the anteroom to my bedchamber, Violet."

"Yes, I know."

The muscle in his jaw twitched. "Then you must also know that you shouldn't be here."

His voice was lower than ever, the words spoken raw and harsh from his chest. She swayed on her feet, shifting her nightgown across her hips and ankles. "Do you not want me here, Christopher? If you honestly desire me to leave, just say so, and I shall."

Violet fully expected him to speak up. She expected him to tell her to go now, to return to her room, to behave as a proper lady. He didn't. He simply sat in his chair, fisting his glass in his hand, watching her.

With his silence, her lips pulled into a smile. She closed the door behind her, leaving them entirely alone. Then she stepped forward.

CHAPTER 11

Sins

Christopher sat in one of the high-backed chairs in the anteroom of his bedchamber, after a long and exhaustive day. The embroidered seat he occupied had been in this room for as long as he could remember. It was nearly threadbare, but it was comfortable. It was safe. It was home.

He stared straight ahead, past the brown leather couch facing him, into the blazing hearth beyond. As the fire leapt up, Christopher forced himself to watch the crackling flames. He'd lit the hearth on purpose tonight, to remind him of all his past sins, and he stared at them now while clinging to the glass of brandy in his hand. He'd already had two drinks prior to this one, and it felt both right and wrong to hold this glass of Quinton Kastle's favorite poison while that man lay dying just a few doors away.

Christopher couldn't believe he would never see his father again after tomorrow. He couldn't believe he had to leave the home he'd returned to barely a year ago, to travel back across the world and most likely to his own grave. He couldn't believe he'd agreed to take Cora along on this wretched journey into hell.

But most of all, he couldn't believe he had to walk away from his Violet.

The fire sparked in the hearth, snapping and popping at him, so he took another drink to soothe his frayed nerves. Returning the glass to the arm of his chair, he focused on the burn of the liquid sliding down his throat. He'd spent the past two days warring with his sister, and cowering from his betrothed, and it had left him barely functional.

Christopher fisted his hand, desperate to fight this sensation of drowning beneath the ocean of his life. He needed a pleasing thought – the more lovely, the better – to keep his head above water. Without hesitation, his mind's eye drew to the image of Violet in the Kastle nursery this morning. Good Lord, she'd looked otherworldly, with the sunshine catching the gold of her hair as she stood before the crib wearing nothing but her nightgown. He'd hardly been able to control himself while he'd imagined her standing there someday, gazing down at their babe resting in that little bed. He'd barely managed to stop himself from spanning the floor in three strides, taking her in his arms, and kissing the hell out of her.

The only reason he didn't give in to his desires then and there was because Stanzi and Octavia would have been forced to bear witness. Especially since he wouldn't want to stop at kissing. He'd want to lift Violet in his arms, carry her down the hall into this very room, sweep her into the bedchamber just beyond where he now sat, and make love to her for every second they had remaining.

Christopher allowed himself to dwell on the fantasy of his betrothed laid out on his bedsheets, writhing and moaning beneath his body. The image was perfection and purgatory, and he knew he should be grateful his youngest sisters were indeed in the nursery this morning. They'd unwittingly prevented anything untoward from happening, and that was surely for the best.

After all, he had no right to touch Violet anymore. He didn't have the right to claim her in any way, let alone in all the ways he desired, so he'd kept his distance by hiding in this room. He needed to cool the flames that ignited so rapidly between them, since he had to leave her in just one day.

God, he hated that he had to abandon her. He hated that he must hurt her so deeply. And still, Nick's arguments in favor of this journey were horribly true and agonizingly right. Christopher could not stay in England to bask in his own needs while the rest of the world burned. He could not remain in this house with his Violet, burying himself over and over in the warmth of her body, while so many others suffered in his absence. His vast sins had come to collect their due, and they intended to take all that remained of his life, which meant he had nothing left to give her. Nothing...but the truth.

He knew he should give her that much – he should tell her everything about his past and why it must drive his future – yet he never would. He didn't want her to know about the wretched man he'd been before, or why he must become that man again tomorrow night. He would never confess the whole truth, so he honestly had no goddamn idea what he was going to say to her when he left. He had no fucking clue how to tell the woman he loved that he could not simply stay with her and love her. He only knew that when he told her he must leave, the pain in her eyes would rip his heart from his chest.

Christopher groaned, rubbing his fingers across his forehead. He took another swig of his brandy before setting it back down on the chair arm and gazing into the fire. He was exhausted as hell, and should definitely drag himself to bed, but he didn't have the energy to move.

His vision glossed over as he watched the flames lick the embers of wood in the hearth. He barely saw anything at all. But that didn't prevent his eyes from darting to the door the moment it creaked open.

His heart stopped when he witnessed Violet standing in the entrance to his room. Christopher locked her gaze even as he lost his voice, struggling to reconcile the fact that she was now in a place where she definitely should not be. He tried with all his might to focus only on her face, hoping beyond hope that he could ignore the rest of her body. Regrettably, his fortitude faltered in mere seconds and his eyes drifted down.

Violet's hair lay loose and tumbling over her shoulders. She wore the same nightgown as she had in the nursery this morning, the delicate fabric covering her skin from neck to ankle. The gown's tiny stripes of lace made her look pure and chaste, yet as Christopher absorbed the curves of her breasts and hips beneath, his thoughts were anything but.

He dragged his eyes slowly back to hers, pausing to drink in the vision of her parted mouth and wet lips. When he could wrench himself from his current stupor, he pinned her in place with the most fearsome glare he could muster, desperate to keep her from coming any closer. Her presence in his room was unthinkable, and he could only hope she'd gotten lost wandering the halls and merely stumbled upon his chamber by accident. He prayed she would now realize her mistake and leave as swiftly as she'd arrived.

Violet did nothing of the sort. Instead of muttering a sheepish apology and scurrying away, she stepped fully inside his room. She moved brazenly forward, until the heavy wood door rested against her spine, before stilling her feet and pressing her shoulders back.

Christopher swallowed hard. "This is the anteroom to my bedchamber, Violet," he said, offering her the excuse of an unintentional entrance.

"Yes, I know," she replied, as if the fact held no consequence.

The muscle in his jaw twitched, his next words coming out far rougher than intended. "Then you must also know that you shouldn't be here."

She swayed, shifting her nightgown over her legs. "Do you not want me here, Christopher? If you honestly desire me to leave, just say so, and I shall."

He heard her quite clearly, and he knew he should say something. He should tell her to walk out now, to retreat to her room, to get the hell away from the likes of him. But he couldn't, because telling Violet that he honestly desired her to leave would be a lie of ludicrous proportions.

Christopher remained where he was, still and silent, strangling his brandy glass to death as he watched the hem of her dainty gown dance around her ankles. With his unspoken allowance, a smile pulled up her lips. Violet closed the door softly but firmly behind her.

The moment they were alone in his antechamber, she stepped forward. She did not come directly to him. She moved nearer the fireplace instead, her sky eyes shifting quickly back and forth to assess her surroundings. She glanced at the chair he sat in, as well as its twin beside him. She looked at the leather couch that sat before him, and at the tattered rug beneath his feet, and at the door in the wall behind his back that led to his bedchamber. She seemed to notice everything at once, until her roving gaze finally settled on the far corner of the room.

Taking several more barefoot steps forward, Violet came to a standstill in front of the hearth and concentrated all her energy on that empty corner. Christopher had no idea why she now stood as stone, directing her sights to the floor. But he couldn't clear his mind enough to even question her actions, since he sat absolutely mesmerized by the vision before him.

She'd stopped directly in front of the fire flames, with her body turned sideways, which gave him a flawless view of her silhouette in the otherwise dimly lit room. The angle at which she now stood allowed the back-glow of the fire to cut straight through the slight gown she wore, turning the fabric almost entirely sheer. He opened his mouth, intent on instructing Violet to alter her current position, since he could see each of her curves as if she stood here purposefully naked.

The words of warning sat on the tip of his brandy-coated tongue. Yet when his eyes travelled unreservedly over her body, drinking in her goddamn gorgeous form, he couldn't bring himself to alert her to the sinful view she'd unwittingly offered. Guilt swamped his mind, yet Christopher remained silent in order to fully immerse himself in the stunning portrait before him.

He filled his sights with every part of her backlit body: the gentle slope of her shoulders; the perfect swell of her breasts; the tiny bow of her stomach; the firm shape of her lush bottom. She was not wearing knickers, because his Violet did not like to wear knickers. Which meant he could see her completely.

Holy fuck, her ass was so stunningly round and taut, with her gown arched out over its full curves. He remembered feeling that soft, supple form against his trousers when she fell into his lap in the carriage. He remembered tracing the upside-down heart shape overtop of her skirts the day he pinned her against the glass wall of the gazebo. He absolutely ached to feel that flesh beneath his fingers now, skin on skin, with no barriers between them at all – not even this tiny little slip of a gown.

Christopher gripped his brandy glass with all his might, legitimately fearing he might break it with his bare hand.

"What used to stand here?" Violet asked.

Several seconds passed before he could focus on her face. "I'm sorry?"

"Here," she said, taking a few more steps toward the corner of the room. Her change in position removed her body from the firelight, reversing the sight of her nightgown from sheer back to solid.

He had to pinch his lips shut to not groan in frustration.

Violet pointed to the ground, at a discolored rectangular patch in the wood floorboards. "Did there used to be a piece of furniture here?"

Christopher shifted in his seat, struggling to repress his disobedient thoughts. "An old clock used to stand there, one that had been in our family for generations. It had a dark mahogany casing and stood seven feet tall. My mother taught us all to tell time by it. All but Octavia, of course."

"I see. But why is it no longer here?"

"I'm told Daniela had to sell it two winters ago, to pay for food."

Violet grimaced. "Well, perhaps we can track down its whereabouts and buy it back. After all, my father's money should be good for something." She turned toward him, her fingers twisting over her stomach. "I mean, other than caring for your sisters. They are all so wondrous and lovely, and I'm thrilled that the funds from my dowry can help to care for each of them. It can care for this entire home, and all the grounds and gardens, and it can buy back your clock. If you want the clock, that is. If it pleases you."

He watched her worry her hands together for a time before he looked to her eyes. "You are what pleases me, Violet. Above all else."

Christopher wasn't sure why he said those words. Wasn't he supposed to distance himself from her? Isn't that what he'd been trying to do all day? Wasn't he supposed to unravel this unearthly attachment they shared, so she would not ache as much when he told her he had to leave? And yet, somehow, that wasn't what he was doing right now.

"You know I began this arrangement between us for your dowry," he continued, his heart flowing straight out of his mouth. "You know I started all of this so I could have the funds I needed to give my sisters the future they deserve. But from the moment I met you, this became something more than a mere arrangement. It became so much more, and I want to be certain you know that I'm not here now for the money. I'm here for you. Only for you."

Her eyes widened with his declaration. A second later, she rewarded him with the most radiant smile. Violet drifted forward with the glow of the hearth lighting her face. She came to a stop a few paces before him, to stand in front of the couch facing his chair. She sat down without any semblance of prudence, settling herself into the leather cushions while looking to his eyes. "You know I began this arrangement because I wasn't given a choice in the matter of marriage. You know I was only given a choice between two men. And you told me – the very first time we took a walk in the Wilmington gardens – that you hoped one day I would actually choose you. Not because I was forced, but of my own free will."

"Yes," he acknowledged. "I remember that very well."

"Then I hope you know by now that I do choose you. I choose you of my own free will, Christopher. Prince or pauper, I will always choose you."

Prince or pauper. She would take me as a prince or a pauper.

But would she take me as a pirate?

He didn't reply to her wondrous words. He took another drink instead, the smooth liquid slipping over his tongue while he held her with his eyes.

Violet endured his scrutiny for a long while before glancing down to her lap. "I'm sorry if my visit to your antechamber tonight seems untoward," she spoke to the ivory fabric of her gown, playing the lace adornments between her fingers. "Although, I must admit now that I am very happy I took the chance to come here. Because I had...I had started to worry."

Christopher watched her fingers shift mercilessly over her thighs. His own hand curled into a claw, desperate to reach out across the space between them. "What had you started to worry about?"

"About how distant you've felt to me lately. Only in the past two weeks, really. You seemed to act a bit differently than you did before, and I'd started to worry that you'd changed your mind about certain things."

He heard her concern, but he was too caught up in the sight of her sitting so close to him – in his antechamber in the middle of the night – without a single soul present who could judge their actions. His eyes wandered over her gown, from where her fingertips touched her thighs, up over her soft belly, and onto the perfect curves of her breasts, before finally settling on her face. "What did you think I'd changed my mind about?"

Violet looked up to him. "Me," she whispered, her uncertainty written deep in her eyes. "I thought, perhaps, you no longer desired me."

Christopher nearly choked on his tongue. He honestly couldn't believe those words had just left her lips. Bloody hell, if only she knew the truth of his overpowering, relentless need for her. If only she knew the things he'd dreamt of doing to her, and for her, if he ever had the right. If only she knew how he'd taken his painfully stiff cock in hand, stroking himself to completion, every night since that night in the carriage. If only she knew how he'd groaned her name as he spilled his seed into his palm, imagining himself buried to the hilt in her soft walls.

Violet nibbled her lower lip in her teeth, curling her fingers into her gown while she searched his eyes. Christopher had to set his glass down on the floor, certain he would break it if he didn't get it out of his hand. Good Lord, she was so unsure of herself – so unaware of her own desirability – and the inexplicable thought drove him to madness.

Without any measure of rationality, he stood from his chair. Violet stared in bewilderment as he cleared the space between them in a single stride. When he came to stand in front of her, he stared down at her flimsy nightgown. He studied the way her shallow breaths pulled the ivory lace across her chest. A tiny whimper escaped her parted lips with his uninhibited perusal, making him groan along with her needy little noise.

Christopher sank to his knees before her. He sank to his knees, even though he'd sworn in this very house that he would never allow himself to love a woman enough to let those emotions rule him. He knew what it felt like to be forced to his knees, and he'd vowed he would never feel that way again. Yet here he was, kneeling before her openly and willingly, no matter how much pain it caused now or would cause in the future.

He reached for Violet as he collapsed to the ground, laying his head in her lap while his hands sought her waist. He curled his fingers into her hips and closed his eyes, pushing the top of his head into her thinly clothed belly and breathing in deep. Her familiar scent of sweet cream and honeysuckle filled his senses while he secured her in place beneath him.

Violet's fingers moved instantly to his hair, ruffling through the short strands, making him moan with the intoxicating sensation. Sweet hell, how could this woman not understand the level of his emotions? How could she not know how much he wanted her heart and soul, as well as her body? How could she ever doubt his demanding, incessant need to be inside her in every possible way?

Christopher pressed his cheek against her gown before turning his face fully into the juncture of her thighs. He'd laid his head on her lap many times before tonight, taking his rest while they sat together on the gazebo bench. Yet it had never been quite like this, with so little clothing to separate him from her. The nightgown she wore now was little more than gauze and the warmth of her skin seeped immediately into his.

He nudged the fine fabric with his nose, pushing the top of his head even harder into her stomach so he could center his face over her sex. He breathed in, fully and deeply, wanting to smell her desire for him. Her hand trembled against his scalp as he absorbed the faint but heady scent of her arousal. He was not subtle in his actions and figured she must comprehend them. He expected her to start talking. He expected nervous words to pour from her lips at any second. For once, Violet remained silent.

She didn't speak at all, which worried him enough to consider stopping what he'd started. But she didn't resist him, either. If anything, she held him to her with her fingers twisted greedily into his hair. Christopher accepted her desire wholeheartedly, seeing as it entirely matched his own.

He allowed one of his hands to uncurl from her hip and ease slowly down her leg, his fingers dragging over her nightgown as they roamed. The ivory fabric felt smooth the entire way down her thigh and calf, but it didn't compare in the least to the silk of her flesh once his hand slipped below her hem. Violet gasped when his fingers curled around her bare ankle, but she didn't speak up in protest, nor did she attempt to move away.

He ceased his actions for a moment, allowing her to become accustomed to the feel of his skin on hers. He'd touched this part of her body once before, when they'd sat together on a blanket in the Wilmington field, after she'd asked him to remove her shoes and stockings so her toes could wiggle freely. He'd put his hand up her skirt that day, too, just as he was about to do now. Yet this experience was going to be completely different from that one, and he felt fairly certain she understood that fact as well as he did.

Christopher allowed Violet all the time she needed to settle herself. Only when her breathing returned to a normal – albeit slightly elevated – pace, did he begin moving his hand. He circled his fingers around her ankle several times, with his head still planted firmly in her lap and his other hand still gripping onto her hip. He breathed slowly and steadily over her sex as he touched her in this rather innocent manner, knowing that if he stopped right now, nothing truly unsuitable would have happened between them.

But he didn't stop. He pushed his fingers beneath her nightgown instead, sliding them with deliberate purpose up her bare leg, until he reached her knee. He explored that soft circle, listening intently as she succumbed to shaky laughter. The delightful sound made him smile into her lap, since he already knew she was ticklish here.

Christopher raised his head, lifting his eyes to look into hers, wanting to watch her while he tickled her knee. He expected to see her face lit with joy. He expected her to be smiling, at the very least. She was not. Violet was not amused at all.

She looked drunk with desire, her sky eyes mired by unruly emotion and yet wholly focused. Her mouth parted on panted gasps. Her lower lip lay swollen from the voracious bite of her teeth. Her entire body hummed with energy, honed in on him alone.

Holy hell, she looked like a siren of the sea. A savior and a sinner, all wrapped into one. The kind of temptress sailors told tales of, as warnings to other seafaring men: *Steer clear of a woman such as this one, lad. You'll never recover your heart after you've looked into her eyes. You'll never be right again without her.*

Christopher heard the warnings in the back of his mind, but he didn't want to listen. He shifted his hand over her knee to watch Violet's eyelashes flutter and hear her breath hitch in her chest. He understood now that he was taking inappropriate liberties with her. Not that he wasn't aware of that a few minutes ago; he was most certainly aware. But now, seeing the stark arousal written across her face with the barest of touches, he definitely knew he was taking advantage of her virginal status. For even if Violet could be his wife – even if he could stay right here, say his vows to wed her, and keep her by his side forever – she was not his wife at this moment.

Still, Christopher couldn't bring himself to care. He needed to touch her. He needed her to know, without any doubt, how feverishly he longed for her. And he needed to soothe her desires before he left, even if it could only be in this one small way.

He shifted away from her, just slightly, just enough to give his fingers more freedom to move. He watched Violet intently, seeing her arms fall to her sides and her fingers dig into the couch cushions as he continued his exploration of her leg. Christopher held her hip steady in one hand while skimming his other hand up her thigh, caressing her smooth flesh as he worked his way gently and methodically toward her sex. The ivory fabric of her gown gathered over his bare forearm and bunched just above her knee. Her constant refusal to wear knickers felt rather dizzying to him once his fingers slid closer to the apex of her thighs, and especially when she parted her legs to grant him further access.

"Violet," he said, her name barely edging past his constricted throat.

She held his bold stare even when her voice trembled. "Y-yes?"

Christopher slipped his hand down between her thighs, skimming lightly across the curls covering her sex. "Have you ever touched yourself here?"

She whimpered and shook her head.

"You've never touched between your legs? Never touched your sex?"

"No," she admitted, her fists denting the leather of the couch. "Although it feels like you're already touching me there. I mean, deeper there."

"It does?" he asked, his fingers twitching on the outside edge of that warm, beckoning place. "Tell me how your body feels down here right now."

Violet sucked in a breath. "My skin is throbbing. And it's...it's..."

"Wet?"

"Yes."

"Mmm. Have you ever felt wet between your legs before?"

She nodded slowly. "A few times, when we're together and you're touching me. Like that night you held onto me in the carriage, and that day you pulled me into the gazebo. And also, um, sometimes when..."

"When what?"

Violet licked her lips. "When I wake from my dreams."

"Really? What kind of dreams?"

"Dreams about you and me. About us together."

Christopher's jaw clenched. He remembered all too well the day he'd dragged her into the gazebo after realizing she'd had an erotic dream about him. He remembered how goddamn ravenous she looked at that moment, how her body vibrated for him just as it did now.

His fingers shifted closer to her sex, quite of their own volition, which caused Violet to inhale sharply. "Tell me more," he commanded. "I need to know what I'm doing to you in your dreams. God, I beg you to tell me."

"Oh. You're just...you're kissing me. And touching me. I mean, not like this. Not this kind of touching, but rather touching overtop of my clothes."

"Hmm. Is that all I'm doing in your dreams?"

"Well, I assure you, it always feels like quite a lot."

"I see," Christopher considered, offering a gentle smile while squeezing his hand into the gown over her hip. "I do like touching you overtop of your clothes. But as lovely as that is, it's not enough for me anymore. I want to touch you underneath your clothes, as well." His smile faded as quickly as it came. "I want to touch so much more of you, Violet. I want to touch your sex, to feel the soft, slick skin between your thighs. I want to slide my fingers all the way into your body, so I can know how just wet you are for me."

She moaned with his words as he pressed his chest against her knees, struggling to keep his hand from moving. "Can I touch more of you?" he questioned, the words a deep growl in his throat. "I shall need your explicit permission to do so, because we both know I am not your husband. We have not made those vows to each other in the proper way, and yet I still want to feel you. I want to feel you so desperately. You have no idea."

If he expected her to shy away from his immoral advances, or admonish or reject his demanding requests, he would have been sorely disappointed. Violet didn't refuse him. Not even in the slightest.

"We may not have said our vows properly yet," she sighed, releasing one of her fists in order to slide her hand up his jaw. "But you are my husband, Christopher. No one can tell me otherwise."

He heard the conviction of her words, and felt the pure, undiluted tenderness of her touch. The sensation currently swamping his chest was one he'd never experienced in his life: squeezing and harsh, barely leaving him room to breathe, and yet as freeing and faultless as any feeling in the world. He wasn't quite sure what to do about it, so he held entirely still, waiting for her to instruct him.

"I want you to touch me," she said, her hand dropping from his face back onto the couch. "Please."

Christopher exhaled. "Thank God."

～

VIOLET WASN'T sure where her courage came from. She'd only stolen away to her husband's chamber tonight for a hug, and perhaps a kiss. Well, most definitely a kiss. Or two.

She hadn't expected much else, though. She hadn't truly expected anything. She'd only longed for his attention and affection, hoping to gain some assurance that he still wanted her – both her heart and her body.

What Christopher had already given her tonight was more than anything she'd ever imagined. Honestly, she would have been content to wander back to her room a while ago, after he'd told her he was here for her and not her father's money. His assurance granted her such ease that she was finally able to confess her fears over the distance she'd felt between them recently. She'd hoped he would tell her that the detachment was all in her mind and did not actually exist. But never in her wildest dreams did she think he would come to her like this: sunk down onto the floor, fallen to his knees, looking up to her face as if she was the only light in a world of darkness.

Violet also never expected him to touch her. Not like he did now. She never expected him to slide his hand beneath her nightgown, or to ease it slowly up the flesh of her leg, or to press his fingers so close to the entrance of her sex. But she would not refuse him. She would never refuse her husband's desire to touch her, especially not when she ached for his touch in the most agonizing way.

She knew her thoughts were wicked and wrong, and that she should feel guilty for her wantonness. However, she meant what she'd said. Christopher was her husband, and no one could tell her otherwise. She accepted his touch unreservedly – not just because the gentle glide of his fingers over her sex made her flesh hum and spark – but because he stared directly into her eyes, as if there were no shame at all in what they were doing. His steadfast certainty enabled her to meet his intent gaze as she basked in the feelings he coaxed so masterfully from her flesh.

He eased his hand even further between her legs as the wetness from inside her sex seeped out onto his skin. Her body's juices coated the roughness of his fingertips, making everything slick and smooth. He'd barely touched her at all, yet she could feel him everywhere. The powerful sensations he wielded made her thighs tense and her back arch, which tilted her hips down and pinned his hand beneath her on the couch.

"Oh, goodness. I'm so sorry," she panted. "I did not mean to stop you."

"Don't be sorry," Christopher soothed. "But if you can, I'd like you to lift your hips and move down on the cushion, so you are a bit closer to me."

Violet bobbed her head, raising her bottom to free his hand from its confines as she shifted toward him. "How is this?"

"It's perfect, my sweet. Now, I want you to part your legs even further. Can you do that for me?"

"I can," she answered, digging her fists into the cool leather while spreading her thighs. She bit hard into her lower lip, keenly aware that she'd opened herself entirely to him, even if her nightgown still concealed most of her skin. His pupils darkened wildly while he stared at her mouth.

Christopher straightened his upper body and pushed forward, settling his hips fully between her knees, making it impossible for her to be anything but open. "God, you're beautiful," he breathed, his gaze dragging from her mouth up to her eyes. His hand shifted beneath her gown, smoothing over her wet skin. "I have wanted to touch you like this forever."

Her nipples hardened to the point of pain, making the soft fabric pulling across her chest feel rough as wool. "I have wanted you to touch me forever," Violet admitted, not feeling the least bit ashamed.

He gave her a tempting smile. "I'm going to touch you deeper now."

"Yes, I...I understand."

"You can tell me to stop at any time."

"I don't want you to stop. Not ever."

He chuckled, the gravelly sound seducing her even further. "Well, in case you change your mind, just know that you have the option to tell me."

She nodded, unable to voice her agreement before his fingers slipped into the outer folds of her sex. Violet groaned from deep in her chest when he ran the pad of one finger down her soaked skin. All her sounds garbled as that finger drew back upward, making contact with a little circular nub of flesh at the very top of her folds. He pressed down, firm and exact on that specific area, catching every surface of her flesh on fire at once.

"Oh, great heavens," she moaned, digging her nails into her palms. "What is that place you are touching on me?"

"It is a sort of pleasure center for your body."

"Good Lord, has that always been there? I mean, I know it has. I realize you didn't just create a new part of my body. Although it does feel that way."

He slid his fingertip over the tiny bud again, causing her spine to arch and her shoulders to push back into the cushion behind her. "I didn't create this place, Violet. But I can certainly use it to bring you pleasure."

"Yes, please. Please do that," she urged, even as her thighs attempted to clench around his hand.

Christopher shifted closer, keeping the lower half of his body wedged firmly between her knees, with her legs spread around his hips. He fixed his gaze on her face as he circled her pulsing nub of flesh with his finger, watching the air puff from her lips in broken pants. Violet tried her best to manage the intense sensations he created while every muscle in her body coiled.

Her sex grew wetter, which she didn't know was possible. She'd most likely drenched the fabric of her nightgown and made the couch cushions damp with her eager juices. She thought to apologize, but then his finger left her tiny yet powerful pleasure center and drifted down through her folds, pressing deeper as he explored her skin. Before she realized his intentions, Christopher slipped his finger directly inside her body.

He performed the action quickly, driving that one finger very decidedly up into the walls of her sex without any forewarning. Violet sucked in a steep breath, although not due to discomfort, since the slickness of her flesh allowed him smooth, easy entrance. It was more the fear of discomfort – and the shock of the deed itself – that caused her surprise.

With her swift inhalation, Christopher halted his actions and steadied himself before her. At least, he attempted to steady himself. For the first time since he'd eased his hand beneath her gown tonight, she saw the pain of restraint written on his face and felt the subtle tremble of his tensed muscles.

"How does this feel to you?" he asked as he searched her eyes.

Violet worked very hard to focus on his question, since she wanted to please him with a proper response. She felt the callouses on his finger within the walls of her sex, and after all the nights she'd watched him practice his sword in the gardens, she knew those callouses came from the hilt of his blade. That coarseness felt absolutely wonderful right now, planted deep inside her. And while his hand was indeed warm, his skin still felt cool within her snug sheath, given the wild inferno raging through her body.

She attempted to place all her scattered thoughts in some sort of sensible order, and even though it was difficult to get words out, she tried. "Having your finger inside me feels...it feels full. And definitely tight."

The muscle in Christopher's jaw twitched furiously with her answer. "I know you are *tight*," he growled. "Bloody hell, you do not have to inform me of how *tight* you are. What I want to know is if this feels *good* to you."

Her cheeks flushed hotter beneath his piercing stare. "Oh. I see. Yes, it does feel good. Everything you've done to me tonight feels good. Honestly, everything you ever do to me feels incredible."

His shoulders eased from the level of his ears. "Wonderful. That is truly wonderful. I'm so sorry I growled at you. I'm finding it arduously difficult to control myself right now. Please forgive me."

Violet held his piercing stare. "You're forgiven."

He smiled softly. "Thank you, my dearest. I'm going to keep this finger steady inside you for a while, so you can get used to the feeling." His eyes finally left her face, to drift down to the delicate laced ties that pulled across her chest. "However, I am going to move my other hand. If you'll allow it."

She felt his other hand – the one still clinging to her hip – shift over her nightgown. "I'll certainly allow it. I'll even beg for it, if I must."

Christopher huffed out a laugh with her zealous words, the warmth of his breath brushing across her face. He ran his other hand over the lace of her gown, from her hip to her belly, to draw circles across the curve of her stomach. She hummed with his attention to this new part of her, even if it remained clothed. Yet her contented hums mutated into crude groans when he smoothed his palm upward, over her ribcage and onto her chest.

The moment he took her breast in his hand, easing his fingers around that mound of flesh, Violet shut her eyes tight. Not because she didn't want to watch him, but because she needed to give herself a moment to absorb every sensation. She'd not yet grown fully accustomed to having his finger up inside her, and with his palm now supporting the weight of her breast, her mind began to unhinge.

She tried to tell herself she possessed the ability to remain calm, seeing as he'd already touched her chest on the night of the ball. Unfortunately, when they were in that carriage, she'd had a corset and bodice tying her in place.

Those impediments no longer existed between them, and she could practically feel his flesh on hers as the heat of his skin penetrated her airy gown.

Christopher shifted his thumb, brushing it across the tip of her nipple. The touch was feather-light, but the bud of her breast was so tight that it felt as if he'd raked it with sandpaper. "Oh, God," she groaned, trying to keep her hips steady while digging her fists into the cushions beside them.

He brushed her nipple again, harder this time, stroking over it with the roughened pad of his thumb. Then he did it again, and again. Flashes of lightning sparked from that touch, shooting straight to where his finger lay deep inside her, now warmed entirely to match the torrid heat of her body. Violet mewled and panted in a vain attempt to keep still.

"How does this feel to you?" he questioned her again.

With the sound of his rasping voice, she looked to his face. His eyes were as dark as the surrounding night, and she knew just how to answer him this time. "It feels so good. It's magnificent, honestly. As if the two are connected."

"Which two?"

"My breast and my...my sex."

He stared into her, long and hard, before nodding. "Well, then. I think we should definitely connect the two."

"Connect the two? How exactly are you going to...*ooh.*"

Her words faltered the instant he coordinated his touches. His finger slid out of her sex before pressing back in, just as the thumb of his other hand stroked over the taut peak of her nipple. Violet moaned, her eyes rolling back in her head as the rushing waves swept over her body. Her hand flew to his bare forearm, her fingers digging into his skin to hold on for dear life.

Christopher didn't retreat from her shameless, lustful grasp. If anything, he moved closer, shifting on his knees to push his body as near to hers as the couch frame allowed. His hips kept her thighs pried apart while he continued his assault on her senses, drawing his fingers over the most sensitive parts of her body, taunting and tantalizing her skin.

"Damn it," she cursed beneath her breath, fighting hard to remain stationary beneath the onslaught of sensation. "Damn it, damn it, damn it."

He groaned with her curses, pushing his thumb harder against her nipple while driving his finger further inside her sex. With the inciting sound of his matching desire, she couldn't resist her body's needs any longer. Violet began to move, arching her hips off of the couch cushions, using her grip on his forearm as leverage. She didn't know exactly what to do, but the feel of his slick finger inside her pulsing walls felt even better when she controlled her actions like this, running herself up and down on his hand.

Christopher growled a stream of fiercely foul words as she ground her body down on his finger again and again. He sucked in a deep breath before moaning her name. "*Violet.*"

"Mmm?"

"You are thrusting your hips. Do you realize that?"

She forced herself to stop the seemingly natural movement. "I...I do realize it," she admitted, opening her eyes to search his. "Is that not the right thing to do?"

He pierced her with a brutal stare. "You do not ever have to worry about right or wrong. Not with me. I assure you that thrusting your hips is quite excellent. You are doing precisely what I need you to do, but I want you to do even more. I want you to drive yourself onto my hand – hard or soft, fast or slow – any way you want. Any way that feels pleasurable to you."

"Then I shall," she agreed, dropping her head back on the couch and letting her eyes fall shut again. She gripped his forearm as she started to move her hips. This time, she tried going soft and slow, since he'd given her that option. She liked it very much. The leisurely slip of his finger in and out of her body allowed her to concentrate on the feel of his rough skin, and how slick her body's wetness made them both. Yet that smooth, gliding sensation also caused her pulse to sputter wildly, making it impossible to maintain the gentle pace for long.

Violet sped up, thrusting herself onto his finger. Everything inside her grew tense and stiff, and yet warm and perfect, all at once. She thought nothing in the world could feel better until he surprised her with more. Christopher kept his finger wedged inside her sex while he pushed the thumb of that hand up through her folds to press against the tender nub at the top. A blinding spark of sensation shot straight into the walls of her sheath, making her hips stutter and slow.

"Keep moving," he directed when she faltered. She nodded, instantly restarting her rhythm with barely a beat missed. Yet now, when she ground herself down onto his hand, she felt the very direct stimulation of her pleasure center, as he'd called it. Although that seemed like a dreadful misnomer, given the pleasure she felt across every part of her body.

"Christopher," she cried, her voice louder than intended while she struggled to withstand the throbbing pressure deep within her sex. "Christopher, Christopher, Christopher. More, please. More."

Violet wasn't sure what she begged for, but she felt something building inside her, a sensation she couldn't quite define no matter how hard she tried. It coiled in her belly, making her slick walls contract around his finger. She heard her own voice from a distance, calling his name louder and louder as she rocked her hips onto his absurdly skilled hand.

He slid his other hand off of her breast to move it upward, grazing her cheek with his fingers. "Violet. I need you to look at me."

She stopped just long enough to gaze into his gorgeous blue. "Y-yes?"

"In a few moments, I'm going to make you scream."

"My goodness. Are you really?"

"I am. In an entirely good way, I assure you."

"I see. Very well, then. I shall scream for you."

He laughed, the mirthless sound quite dark and delicious. "No, that's... that's the problem. These walls will not conceal every sound we make. We must be quiet, so no one hears us."

"Oh. Right. I understand."

"And do you think you can do that? Can you stay quiet for me?"

Violet honestly didn't know, but she wanted to do as he'd asked. "I'll try, Christopher. I'll try my very best to stay quiet."

"Good. I'd also like you to do something else for me."

"What is that?"

He moved his finger inside her, drawing another whimper from her throat, as his other hand returned to cup her breast in his palm. "I want you to keep your eyes fastened to mine. I want to watch you the entire time."

"You want to watch me?"

"Yes, I do. Very much."

She nodded, not exactly sure what he thought was going to happen, but trusting him wholeheartedly. "Then I shall look at you the entire time."

Christopher gifted her with a sinful smile before resuming his intent focus on her body. He thrust his finger into her sex and pressed his thumb on her little bundle of nerves while dragging his other thumb over her stiffly pebbled nipple. He coordinated every sensation with meticulous precision, playing her flesh like an instrument, as Violet whimpered in tune.

She still wasn't sure why he thought she would want to scream. But as she watched her husband's profound longing spark deep within his eyes, she knew desire at a level she'd never before imagined. When his tongue darted out to moisten his lips, a strangled noise erupted from her throat that she did not consciously create. When he pressed his finger up inside her slick walls again, and pushed his thumb into the tiny circle at the top, her hips rocked entirely of their own accord.

The rhythm he set for her was utterly decadent, sending shocks of light-ning pulsing from her tight nipples to the tight walls of her sheath to her tight little bud of pleasure. Christopher never left her body at peace, staring his intentions into her eyes while he stirred her blood, inflamed her flesh, and drove her to the brink of maddening euphoria. Violet mewled as her muscles wound to the point of breaking, not understanding everything he made her feel and yet needing to feel it. When she knew for certain that her entire body would snap in two without some form of release, she found herself on the edge of a precipice, struggling to keep air inside her heaving chest.

She remained on that unknown, teetering brink for seconds only. In the next instant, Christopher showed her exactly how he would make her scream. He played her flesh in precisely the right way, so every nerve in her body fired at once, flooding her with pleasure a thousand times more intense than anything she'd ever known. She dug her fingernails into his forearm, clamped her legs around his waist, and stared hard into his eyes, struggling to harness these waves of wicked, torturous bliss. Yet despite her best efforts, she could not escape such an overpowering force of ecstasy. Violet allowed herself to feel everything all at once.

She screamed.

Christopher reacted the instant she cried out wildly into the night air. He yanked his hand from her breast to press it against her lips, clamping her mouth shut beneath his thick fingers. Violet's hips bucked frantically as he muffled her animalistic shrieks. Somewhere in the back of her mind, she understood that he was merely trying to protect her from herself. But in the delirium of her pleasure, all she knew for certain was that his skin lay against her lips. Yearning to feel even more of him inside her, she opened her mouth and bit down on his finger.

Every muscle in his body jerked when her teeth closed around his flesh. "Fuck, fuck, fuck," he growled, the curses ripped from his throat as he focused wholly on her mouth. Violet would have apologized for her scandalous actions, except he didn't look at all angry. If anything, his eyes flared even deeper with desire, his breaths forced harsher from his lungs.

With his obvious arousal – combined with the earthshaking tremors still quaking her body – she found the boldness to bite down harder. He groaned with her actions, pushing his finger past her teeth to place it fully into her mouth. She didn't bother to question what he'd done. She just clamped her lips around his skin and sucked him inside her, wetting his roughened flesh with her swirling tongue. Honestly, she wasn't sure if he would even enjoy such a thing. But when his eyelids fell to half-mast, and he rewarded her with several more deliberate flicks of his other thumb against her throbbing nerve bud, she believed she'd done well.

Violet dwelled in each sensation he gave her for as long as she possibly could. Eventually, her hips stopped their frenzied thrusts and settled back into the couch cushions. She no longer produced any more ravenous, unseemly noises, yet Christopher still touched her. Even after he withdrew his finger from her mouth and traced that hand down her chest back to her hip, he kept his other hand settled firmly between her thighs. He eased his finger in and out of her pulsing sex as his thumb pressed against her tiny nub of pleasure, creating aftershocks that zipped through her limbs and kept her skin constantly humming.

She could do nothing but respond to his every move, a puppet on his strings, marveling at him as he studied how each touch affected her. Violet loved him so deeply in this moment, for showing her what her body could do, and for caring enough to make her feel such incredible things. She loved Christopher more than she'd ever loved anyone or anything in her whole life, and she couldn't wait for the day when he would love her back.

Finally – when all the shocks in her body had settled completely – he slipped his finger out of her sex. She moaned with his withdrawal, partly because the slick movement still felt glorious, and partly because she became instantly hollow and missed having him inside her. Her shoulders fell as he pulled his hand away.

Christopher sat back on his heels to remove his arm from beneath her gown. When he brought his hand to his chest, Violet's gaze fastened on the finger he'd just had inside her. His skin shone in the firelight, still coated with her body's juices. She began to apologize for making such a mess, but then he did something she would never, ever have suspected. He drew his hand to his face and sucked his wet finger into his mouth.

Her jaw unhinged. "*Christopher.* What on earth are you doing?"

He didn't reply. He merely continued to savor his finger.

Violet leaned toward him. "Are you...are you tasting me?"

"I am," he admitted, his voice low and raw as he took a moment to run his tongue over the tip of his thumb.

"But, why?"

"Because you taste perfect. So incredibly perfect."

She lost her voice with that statement. Violet could hardly comprehend such an act, and yet she adored that he wanted her inside his body just as she wanted him in hers. She kept staring at him, with her eyes wide and her heart wider, wondering what she'd ever done to deserve such a man.

Once he'd cleansed his skin of her taste, Christopher stood from the floor, straightening to his full height while reaching his hand out for hers. She placed her fingers inside his palm and allowed him to help her up, but not before she noted the very full state of his manhood. His daunting shaft stood firmly at attention beneath the straining resistance of his breeches. She whimpered with that view while he pulled her onto his chest.

Violet enveloped him as soon as she could, throwing her arms around his neck and arching up on her tiptoes to press the side of her cheek against his. He banded her onto his body, clutching her so fiercely that he nearly squeezed the air from her lungs. She struggled to catch her breath, both from the ferocity of his grip and the stiff jutting of his manhood into her stomach.

She'd felt her husband's rigid length on several occasions before this one, so she was no longer uncertain or shy about his virile state. In truth, she felt quite empowered by his ardent, blatant yearning for her body. "You're so hard," she whispered against the line of his jaw, rejoicing in the magnificence of his desire as she pressed lingering kisses to his coarse scruff. "You're so incredibly, wonderfully hard for me."

With her breathy words, Christopher leaned back to pin her drunken gaze. "God, yes. I'm so fucking hard for you," he admitted with an aching moan. Then he grabbed her face in both hands and lowered his mouth, claiming her lips with a level of desperation she'd not felt in weeks, if ever.

Violet opened herself to him, readily accepting his tongue the second he slid it past her teeth and twisted it against her own. He tasted like brandy with just a hint of salt, which she knew was the taste of her body's wetness licked from his finger. That understanding sent another devilish pulse of energy shooting down through the tender walls of her sex.

She pushed closer to him, rubbing her thinly clad stomach against his strained breeches. She relished the imposing stiffness of his shaft, certain he would fill her with it now – Christopher would fill her tight sheath with his thick, unyielding length – wholly and completely. In truth, that reality was still a bit unnerving. Yet it was also exhilarating, since she knew her husband would make her feel so many amazing things.

When he finally released her from his grasping, greedy kiss, he rested his forehead onto hers. He struggled to breathe, the air puffing from his lips in warm pants across her face. For a long while, he merely held her against him. Then he ran his hands up into the loose curls of her hair. "Violet?"

"Mmm?" she murmured, drawing her fingers from his shoulders to curl them around his tensed forearms.

"There is one more thing I need you to do for me tonight."

"What do you need, Christopher? I'll do anything. Anything at all."

He took another labored breath. "I need you to leave. I need you to go back to your room. Alone. Can you do that for me?"

Her forehead crinkled as she looked to his eyes. "What? You can't actually desire me to leave you. Not when I shall be most happy to..."

"Please, Violet. I'm asking as kindly as I can." His hands tightened in her hair. "I beg you to leave me of your own will, for I do not currently possess the strength to resist this ungodly need I have for you. I cannot be trusted to act as a gentleman right now, not after witnessing the utter beauty of your pleasure. And definitely not with the taste of your sex still on my tongue."

She stared at him in both bewilderment and confusion. After all, she knew exactly what she wanted to do right now. She wanted to tell him to stop being a gentleman. She wanted to command him to sweep her into his arms, carry her to the next room, and lay her down on his bed. She wanted to insist that he take all of her, entirely for himself.

Violet opened her mouth to make her heady demands. But then she felt the tremble of his strained muscles, and remembered how she'd promised to help slow things down between them, at least until their wedding day. Her actions tonight had been entirely contrary to that vow – and any further actions would make her a liar as well as a sinner – so she grudgingly settled back on her heels and released her formidable grip on his arms.

"I shall go," she whispered, feeling the weight of his body sag against hers with her submission. "I shall go because you wish it, even though I do not."

He exhaled heavily. "I appreciate your struggles, my dearest. I hope you'll forgive me for mine."

"There is nothing to forgive. You are a gentleman of the highest order and I thank you for it most sincerely. But I also want you to know that I meant what I said. You are my husband, Christopher. No one can tell me otherwise."

A pained smile pulled at his lips before he leaned down to press one last kiss to her mouth. "Goodnight, my sweet Violet."

"Goodnight," she said, disentangling from his clinging grasp before forcing herself to walk away.

THE NEXT AFTERNOON, Violet glanced around the guest bedchamber of the Kastle manor, reassuring herself that she'd collected all of her things. She patted the pocket of the crimson riding cape she wore, making certain she'd remembered to put her spectacles back inside. Although she knew she had, because she'd already checked three times.

She'd actually packed her trunk quite early this morning, and Aunt Tildy's coachman had come many minutes ago to take the luggage to the carriage, yet Violet still stood in this room. Stepping to the window, she looked out at the twisty tree standing proudly within the tangled gardens. She drank in the splendor of its gnarled branches stretching broadly from its sturdy trunk. She wanted to stay right here, in the place that would soon be her home, looking out on the Kastle family tree while knowing she belonged among its bright, colorful leaves.

Sadly, she hadn't known if she truly belonged here when she'd been climbing with the twins yesterday. Given the way Christopher had acted toward her in the past two weeks, Violet wasn't sure if she would ever belong. But after last night, she didn't doubt her husband's wishes. After all the things he'd said to her, and all the ways he'd touched her, she no longer questioned anything. Lord Kastle definitely wanted her as his wife, and she wanted him in every way possible.

Violet grinned as she gazed out at their family tree. She looked forward to the day she would return to this manor as Lady Kastle. And she especially looked forward to never having to sleep in the guest bedchamber again.

"Do you need any assistance, Violet?"

Turning at the sound of her name, she watched Daniela enter the room.

"The coachman has settled your trunk onto the carriage," Daniela told her. "But I can help you further, if you require anything else."

Violet's gaze roamed over the woman's plain gray dress, lacking in any decoration that would highlight her stunning brown hair or matching eyes. She felt grateful her father's money would bring many opportunities, as well as fine clothes, to all the wondrous women who lived in this home. "Thank you for the offer, Lady Daniela. You have been very kind and gracious to me throughout my visit."

Daniela stepped further into the room. "You do not need to thank me. I am happy to do it."

"Are you truly?" Violet wondered aloud, since this woman had been the most reticent of the sisters in accepting her.

"Most truly," Daniela assured, "for you have made such a difference in Christopher. My brother is not the same grumbling, growly creature he was when he returned from sea, and I know that has everything to do with you. It is a difference all his sisters notice, and we are grateful for it...and for you."

Tears misted Violet's eyes. "Oh, my. Thank you so much for that. All I ever wish is to be a beacon of light in the dark world he's been forced to witness. Therefore, your assurances mean more to me than I can say."

"Good heavens," Daniela remarked, her head tilting as she surveyed Violet. "You really do love him. Don't you?"

"I do," she answered without a second thought, seeing no need to guard herself here. "I love Christopher with all that I am."

Daniela gave her a tender smile before glancing to the floor. "I'm happy for you, then. For you and my brother both."

Violet stepped toward the woman whose heart now lay open before her. "And I am happy for you, Lady Daniela."

Her eyes rose when Violet stood in front of her. "For what?"

"For the happiness you found with Mr. Marlow. Please forgive me for mentioning it in such a forward manner, but I could see it so clearly when we were all together at the Chaney's ball. You love him and he loves you."

A whimper escaped Daniela's throat. "I do love him. I have loved Nicholas Marlow for as long as I can remember. Perhaps longer."

"You loved him even as a child?"

"I did, in a childish way. But that love grew and changed, day by day. I loved him when we were little, when I would jump from the branches of the twisty tree and he would catch me in his arms. I loved him when he was a young man, despite the fact that he acted like a spoiled, foolish sop alongside my brother. I loved him after that, when he struggled to act as a proper gentleman, trying to earn my guarded affections. I loved him even when he left me to join the Royal Navy. I loved him when I thought he was lost to the sea. And I love him still."

Violet reached out to gather her hand. "And he loves you. I barely know him at all, but I could tell that much in an instant."

"You are right. Nick does love me."

"Well, then. That is perfect, for you can be together now."

Daniela clutched Violet's fingers. "On the contrary, it is not perfect at all. My brother will not condone our union. He never approved of Nick as a suitor before they left for the sea, and approves even less since their return."

Violet's brow furrowed. She couldn't comprehend Christopher's rejection of such a wealthy suitor, especially since Nick was his oldest and dearest friend. "I want to help you," she declared. "I think I could, if I spoke to Christopher. If I just explained to him how much you and Nick love each other, then perhaps I could convince him to change his mind."

Daniela sighed. "You are very kind, and I appreciate your desire to help. But I do not wish to cause any discord between the two of you, especially since Christopher almost never changes his mind once he is set upon a course of action. Besides, if anyone should talk him out of his decision to keep Nick and

I separated, it should be Mr. Marlow himself. If he wants to be with me as much as I want to be with him, then I must believe he will find a way to make it happen."

"I suppose I understand," Violet acknowledged. "If you're certain you do not wish me to say anything to your brother about this, then I shall not."

"I am certain. But thank you again for the offer."

"No need to thank me, Lady Daniela. I would be happy to help you."

"And I would be happy if you did not call me Lady Daniela anymore," she offered with a gentle squeeze of her hand. "Just call me Daniela, please."

"Thank you so much, Daniela."

"Of course. Now let us get you to your carriage, shall we? I'm sure my brother will be along shortly."

CHRISTOPHER STOOD IN THE HALL, staring at the door to his father's antechamber, trying to convince himself to go inside. He had to leave their home in mere moments, and must leave England this very night, so he needed to see his father one more time. After all, it would most likely be the last.

With a deep breath, he knocked on the door.

"Come in."

The croaked words sent a shiver down his spine as he stepped into the room. The Earl of Nightingale sat in front of the window, as always. Christopher walked toward him with weakened legs, stopping beside his chair to behold his wasted features. "Hello, Father."

"Hello."

"I must take Violet back to the Wilmington estate today. I do not know when I shall be able to return, so I wanted to say goodbye to you."

Quinton glanced down to his hands. "It's odd how life works, isn't it? How it all boils down to a few moments – just a few brief instants – where you must make the decisions that shall affect you forever."

Christopher assessed his father's sickly form as the old man reminisced. He wanted to agree with those words, and confess to the appalling decisions he'd made, and admit how those shameful choices now tore his life apart. Yet as he watched Quinton's yellowed eyes draw back to his, and saw his chafed lips suck in another labored breath, Christopher remained silent.

"I do not have much longer on this earth, my son, so I hope you will indulge me with a few moments of your time. I wish to say something to you, and I desire you to listen, before my words are gone."

Christopher fought back his tears. "Of course. I will always listen."

Quinton stared straight into his son's eyes. "I want to tell you that I believe in you. I believe you deserve the title of Earl of Nightingale, more than I ever did. I believe you can be the man, and the leader, the people here deserve. Not just to your sisters, and not just to your betrothed, but to all the people of Nightingale. You can do so much for them and for us. You can return respect and glory to our family name. I know you can."

A tear slid down Christopher's cheek. He scrubbed it away with the back of his hand. "Thank you, Father. I appreciate your faith in me, although I do not know that I deserve it."

"You deserve it," Quinton insisted. "Trust me."

"Thank you again," Christopher said, taking one last long look at the man who'd raised him with every privilege. "Well, I suppose I must leave you now."

"Yes. I understand."

He pivoted on his heels that instant, striding toward the door.

"Christopher?"

He stopped short, turning back to meet his father's eyes. "Yes?"

"I want to offer you another piece of advice."

"What is that?"

Quinton smiled softly, like he used to do when Mother still lived. "Love your wife. Love her every moment of every day, and never take her for granted. For she will take care of you in ways you cannot possibly imagine, and she will give you strength you never knew you could possess."

Christopher absorbed his father's words with nothing but regret. He could not bear to tell him that his son would never be the man he wished him to be. He could not admit that he would leave Violet in just a few hours, to set out to sea and resume the life of a pirate. And he refused to ruin this last moment with a dying man, so he merely plastered a smile onto his lips.

"I appreciate the advice, Father. I shall heed it as best I'm able. Also, I want you to know that I...I love you."

Quinton held his remorseful gaze. "I love you, my son."

With those words, Christopher nodded and left the room.

As soon as he stepped into the empty hallway and pulled the door shut, he leaned back on the heavy wood and closed his eyes. He needed a moment to himself. A moment to be still. A moment to rest. A moment to breathe.

"You don't have the time you need," Cora said, her disembodied voice answering his thoughts as if he'd spoken them aloud.

"Good God, where did you even come from?" Christopher grumbled when he opened his eyes to find her standing directly before him.

"I was waiting around the corner, until you finished with Father."

He stared at his sister with utter incredulity.

"You don't have the time you need," she repeated. "But you can change that, you know. You can simply tell Nick you are not ready to set sail. If you do, it will give you more time with the family, and Father, and Violet. After all, the ship cannot depart without its captain."

"You're wrong, Cora. I have no more time. Max is being tortured as we speak. Villages are being burned. Innocent people are suffering." Christopher raked a hand across his face. "Besides, this is hard enough already. I have no desire to prolong the agony."

Cora sighed. "Well, then. I shall say goodbye to Father as well."

Christopher lowered his voice. "Did you leave the money for the family?"

"I did. Nick's gift is in the chest at the foot of my bed. I'll leave a note under my pillow before I sneak out tonight, explaining to everyone that we had to leave Nightingale urgently to assist a distant cousin who is unwell."

"Hmm. I don't think anyone will believe that."

"Perhaps, but I cannot exactly tell them the truth. This way, they'll have some explanation for our absence. I shall also explain that Nick offered us passage on one of his family's merchant ships, on which he will accompany us, and that he left them all funds for their use until our return. They may not believe every word, but they shall at least be prosperous without us."

Christopher stared his little sister down. "Is there truly nothing I can say to change your mind about accompanying me on this journey?"

Cora tilted her head, looking at him as if he had three heads of his own.

He huffed out a laugh while grasping her shoulder. "I'll see you on the ship at midnight. Be safe, Cora."

"Aye, Captain. I shall."

At this moment, the look in her eyes was one of understanding, acceptance, and even admiration. Christopher bore a small sense of peace when he left her standing by their father's door. He hadn't embraced the idea of Cora at sea, but he now believed she would be dutiful and compliant, which meant there was the tiniest possibility he could bring her home safely.

After walking away from Cora and his father, Christopher proceeded down the staircase to bid farewell to the rest of his family. The front door stood ajar, and he spied the coach from the Wilmington estate at the entryway. All of his other sisters awaited him outside, along with his Violet.

Violet. He'd already seen her once today, at breakfast. That was the first time he'd laid eyes on her since the moments they'd shared in his room last night. She'd walked to the table with a full blush on her cheeks, nibbling her lip even before she saw him. She'd sat down in the chair to his right, and gave him a gorgeous, crushing smile, so he'd reached for her. He took her hand inside his own without thought of consequence, leaving their entwined fingers on the tabletop the entire time they'd eaten their meal.

His sisters did not seem to mind the open display of affection, although each of them did glance to their tangled hands at some point. Christopher knew he shouldn't still be touching her, and definitely not so transparently. Especially when Cora looked to him with her brow cocked, making him question his actions more than he already did.

Despite Cora's silent condemnation, nothing could prevent his desire to feel Violet's skin against his at the breakfast table. Even now, as he saw her standing by the carriage, his entire being begged to touch her. Christopher stepped through the door to approach the waiting women, his heart pounding in his chest the instant Violet's gaze drew to his. She wore a sky-blue dress today – one that matched her eyes perfectly – with her crimson cape overtop. Yet he still saw her in that little ivory nightgown she'd worn to his room last night, sitting on his leather couch with her eyes wide and her legs wider, as she came apart beneath his touch.

He strode directly to her with no one else in sight. Violet kept her gaze fastened to his for every second of his approach, until he reached her side and wrapped his arm around her back. He gathered her body onto his, tucking her into his shoulder and pressing a lingering kiss to her hair. She hummed serenely beneath her breath, placing her hand over his where it rested on her waist, as he breathed her scent into his lungs.

"Oh, bother," Octavia whispered to Stanzi, her voice carrying rather loudly. "Is it always going to be this way between the two of them?"

Stanzi giggled and spun in a circle.

"It is time for us to say goodbye," Juliette refocused the younger girls.

"And now you must release Violet for a moment, Christopher," Ruby insisted. "For we all demand proper hugs from the both of you."

"Yes, do let go of her, won't you?" Pearl added, stepping up to Violet's side. "You cannot be so greedy with her, dear brother. After all, the two of you have your whole lives for such displays of affection."

His fingers twitched under Violet's, since his sister's words were devastatingly untrue, and he did not wish to release her even for an instant. Christopher forced a nod as he stepped aside. He bent down and spread his arms, allowing Stanzi and Octavia to launch themselves onto his chest.

He hugged every one of his sisters in turn and watched while they each hugged Violet. Even Daniela hugged her, which was quite odd to him, since the eldest Kastle sister did not easily warm to people. When the unexpected embrace ended, Daniela turned to him and offered a genuine, heartfelt smile. Christopher smiled in return, no matter how much it hurt, because he knew his Violet had truly won over his entire family.

When their goodbyes ended, he followed his betrothed up the single step into the carriage chamber. After pulling the door shut behind them, he knocked on the hood to alert the coachman. As the horses moved down the gravel entryway, Christopher waved to his sisters from the window while they shouted well-wishes and begged for promises to return home soon. He didn't reply. Eventually, he pushed himself back against the bench, averting his eyes from the gut-wrenching sight of his beloved family disappearing from view.

Violet continued to wave, leaning over his body to reach her hand out of the window, while the carriage shimmied away from the manor. The heat of her skin permeated his clothes with treacherous ease. Christopher struggled to sit still as the side of her chest bounced against his whenever the wooden wheels hit a rough patch in the ground. When his frayed nerves could take that vexing contact no longer, he reached for her still-waving fingers and brought them to his mouth.

She focused wholly on him the instant his lips touched the back of her hand, her eyes brightening while she watched him kiss her flesh. "That feels wonderful," Violet whispered, staring at his lips as if he'd never pressed them against her before.

"You feel wonderful," he responded. And he didn't even feel guilty.

She curled herself onto him, resting her head against his shoulder and shifting her hips as close as she could without actually sitting in his lap. Christopher wanted her in his lap. He nearly pulled her straight onto his thighs before he reminded himself that it was the middle of the day and the trip from the Kastle estate to Wilmington took very little time. He found a small measure of satisfaction by wrapping his arm around her back and banding her tighter to his chest.

"Mmm. It amazes me how good you always feel," Violet hummed, her warm breath ghosting over his neck. "Every single time I am with you, your body is just so perfect in mine."

Christopher groaned.

"Oh, goodness! I meant to say *on* mine," she corrected. "I mean, your body has never been *in* mine. Well, I suppose certain parts of your body have been in mine. Your tongue has been in my mouth many times. And last night, there was your finger. It was definitely in my body – quite far into my body.

More than one finger, actually. For one of them was in my mouth, and the other was in my…"

"Violet, please," he begged, needing her to stop these rambles so he could control his urges in this very well-lit coach. Hell, he'd barely managed to get her out of his chamber last night before the point of no return. In truth, the second she'd tiptoed into the hall and closed his door behind her, he'd untied his breeches and taken his rock-hard cock into his hand. It took just three strokes for him to come undone, spilling his seed into his palm. He'd chanted her name, over and over, lingering on the memory of her inner walls contracting around his finger as she'd come apart so willfully and gorgeously beneath his touch.

"I'm sorry. I'll stop talking about it now," Violet acquiesced, pressing her palm to his shirt directly over his heart.

Christopher remained silent after her apology, although he did place another kiss in her hair. She snuggled onto him and sighed in contentment, the soft sound slicing his skin as sharply as any blade. He'd fully intended to separate himself from her these past days, yet he'd failed quite utterly.

After last night, when he'd allowed himself to touch her in such intimate ways, he knew he'd destroyed any sense of separation that may have existed between them. He knew Violet felt as one with him, and honest to God, he felt exactly the same way. As far as he was concerned, it made no sense to pull away from her now. Not until he absolutely must.

Urging her even closer, Christopher secured her fully to his chest. He pressed his lips to her loose curls over and over before resting his cheek on them. He closed his eyes, absorbing her warmth into his skin and his heart, acknowledging that he was incapable of slowing anything down between them. There was nothing slow at all about this overwhelming love he bore for her, and since they only had hours left with each other, he would keep her as near to him as he could.

Several stretched, easy moments passed before he heard her voice again.

"Christopher?"

"Hmm?"

Her fingertips fluttered against his chest. "I know I just said I wouldn't talk about it anymore, but I do want to thank you."

"Thank me? For what?"

"For what you did to me, or rather *for* me, last night."

He grinned despite himself. "You're welcome."

"Also, I would really like to talk about it further. If you'll allow it."

He braced himself, knowing such a conversation would be hell on his already ragged nerves. Yet he still nodded, fully aware that he owed her this much, at the very least. "You know you can always talk to me, Violet."

"I do, but I don't exactly know what to say in this circumstance. The things you made me feel as you touched my body last night went far beyond my scope of knowledge. They were astonishing, and I don't even know what they were. Do those sensations you gave me have a name?"

He eased his hand over her arm. "There is a name for the peak of your pleasure – the moment when you screamed. It is called an orgasm."

"An orgasm," she contemplated, as if tasting the word on her tongue. "That is a funny name, although it was not a funny feeling. It was a truly exceptional feeling."

"Good. I'm glad to hear it."

Violet's fingers twisted around the buttons of his shirt. "Do, um, do men feel orgasms, too?"

"They do. Most definitely."

"And do you think they are as pleasurable as a woman's?"

Christopher blew out a breath, fanning a gold curl across her cheek. "I do not know precisely what a woman feels, but I can assure you that a man feels a great deal of pleasure in the act of lovemaking. A man's orgasm coincides with the spilling of his seed and that release is beyond compare."

"I see. However, that does make me curious about something else."

"What is that, my sweet?"

"Well, it sounds as if a man's orgasm is necessary during lovemaking for the creation of a child. But a woman's orgasm doesn't seem to be necessary at all – even though I think it should be, since she is the one to carry the child afterward. I suppose I don't understand why a woman's pleasure is not inextricably linked to the act of lovemaking, the same as a man's. I mean, except when she is with a man who cares enough to make her feel wanted and cherished, like you did for me last night."

Christopher covered Violet's fingers with his own, pressing them to his heart, as he lowered his voice and spoke very clearly. "What you felt last night is how you should feel, each and every time you are with a man. He should always make you feel wanted and cherished, no matter what."

She lifted her head to look into his eyes. "Then I thank the heavens that you are the one and only man I shall ever be with. For I cannot fathom feeling those things with anyone but you."

If Christopher had thought his heart was already breaking, it was nothing compared to the sensation currently swamping his chest. All he could do was lean down to press his lips to hers. He contentedly drowned himself in the beauty of her innocence, since he could not imagine that even a scrap of his heart would remain after he left her tonight.

Their kiss was warm, soft, and comforting. Violet didn't say anything after it ended. She just curled herself into his chest again, returning her head to his shoulder and her hand to his heart. Christopher merely clung to her for the rest of the trip, since that was all he was capable of doing.

The carriage arrived at Wilmington far too quickly. He gripped onto Violet's fingers as they stepped down to the ground. Mr. Rodchester awaited them to ask about their travels and to have her trunk brought up to her room. Christopher just stood beside her and nodded.

After they left Mr. Rodchester to his duties, Christopher led Violet up the entryway and into the grand foyer. He guided her to the staircase, trying very hard to not squeeze her hand too tightly. She turned toward him at the bottom step. "Unfortunately, I think it is too late to go on our walk in the gardens today."

"Yes," Christopher sighed. "I suppose that's true."

"Well, I guess I should go up to my room and start to unpack my trunk. Then I shall meet you here for dinner."

"I will meet you right here. For dinner."

With his confirmation, Violet arched up on her toes, pressed a quick kiss to his lips, and floated up the staircase.

THE TIME CHRISTOPHER spent alone before dinner was excruciating in every way, shape, and form. Yet it was nothing compared to actually sitting across the dinner table from his betrothed, seeing the joy in her eyes as she gazed at him over their meal. He was barely aware of the presence of Lady Wilmington, or of the servants, or of the food on his plate.

He could only see Violet. He could only hear her. He only wanted her.

Christopher hardly spoke a word, even when he guided her down the hall after dinner, back into the grand foyer. When they arrived at the bottom of the staircase as they had so many times before, he forced himself to smile while Violet grinned up at him. He forced himself to grasp her fingers and kiss the back of her hand with gentle assurance. He forced himself to hold entirely still as she ascended the stairs with a luminous glow in her eyes.

Cursing every decision he'd ever made in his entire life, Christopher escaped to his bedchamber to pace the floor while he waited for the end. His ship did not depart until midnight, which meant several hours remained before he had to be at the Wharf Street docks. It meant that several hours remained before he had to tell Violet that he was abandoning her.

Yet as he moved restlessly over the floor, with his heart in his throat and his gut in his feet, he realized he could not wait that long. He needed to get this over with, because he'd had all the time he could have with her. He'd had two months of being in her presence every day – of talking with her, learning about her, touching her, kissing her, and falling madly, desperately in love with her – and now he needed to walk away.

Christopher stopped pacing and stood entirely still, fighting to focus. He straightened his black coat and fiddled with the tall white collar of his shirt. Then he moved forward, opening the door and stepping into the hall.

No servants roamed the corridors, so he was accompanied only by the dim glow of the wall lanterns as he proceeded. He knew exactly where to go, since Violet had told him the location of her room just two weeks ago. She'd invited him to her bedchamber to spend the night asleep in her arms, and he despised the fact that he must now tarnish that pure and glorious offer.

Christopher passed the top of the staircase, striding silently over the lush hall carpet, to the fifth door on the left. He stood in front of her bedchamber for a long minute, struggling to regulate his breathing. When he could unclench his fingers, he reached for the latch to ease the door open.

He stepped inside her room as quickly and quietly as possible, his eyes zeroing in on her the moment he closed the door behind him. Violet stood in front of her bed with her back to him, folding up the dress she'd worn today. The only thing covering her body was a thin, laced ivory nightgown, identical to the one she'd worn to his antechamber last night.

Christopher swallowed hard. "Violet?"

She startled with the sound of her name, spinning around to pin his eyes. "Christopher!" she gasped, cringing as she worked to lessen the volume of her voice. "Goodness, you surprised me. I did not expect you here, but I'm so glad you finally decided to come to my room."

She took a step toward him, but he was the one who cleared the distance between them. He strode forward until he stood directly before her.

"I'm thrilled that you are here to spend the night with me," Violet said, leaning in closer. "I think you should be able to sleep quite well in this bed. At least, I hope you will."

He grasped each of her hands in his. "Violet, I…"

"I'm sorry I've already put on my nightgown. I can put my dress back on, with your assistance, if me being further clothed would make you feel more comfortable with our sleeping arrangement. Had I known you were coming to my bedchamber tonight, I would have simply remained dressed. But since we stayed up so late together last night, I found myself rather tired after dinner. I decided to change out of my dress a bit early and…"

Christopher kissed her. Mostly to stop her words, because he needed her to focus. But also because he just wanted to kiss her, one last time.

His lips lingered against hers. Violet's mouth was so warm, her sighs so sweet. He held tight to her hands, soaking in her soft, tender acceptance. It was all he could do to pull away from her.

"Mmm. That was lovely," she murmured as she reopened her eyes. "I guess that means you do not need me to dress before we get into bed?"

He fastened her gaze while he shook his head. "Unfortunately, I am not here to sleep."

"You're not? Then why are you here?"

"I'm here with…with bad news, actually."

"Bad news?" she echoed, her finger gripping onto his. "What is it?"

He pried his clenched jaw open. "I – I have to go away. I have to leave England again. To go back out to sea."

"*What*? You're being called back out to sea? But I thought you were no longer a sailor with the Royal Navy."

"You're right. I'm not."

"Then I don't understand. Are you being called out for other reasons?"

"I am."

"What other reasons?"

Christopher witnessed the concern building in her eyes. He sucked in a sharp breath. "Violet, do you remember the orphaned lad I told you about? The boy who was with me nine years ago when my ship was attacked?"

"Yes, I remember. You said his name was Max."

"His name *is* Max."

"You mean he is still alive?"

"He is."

"Well, that is wonderful to hear. I had thought, since you and Nick did not bring Max back home to England, that he had perished at sea."

"He did not perish then, but he may now. Max is in very grave danger."

Violet gasped. "My heavens, that is awful. Are you certain he is in danger?"

"Yes, unfortunately. Nick discovered the truth of it. He is worried sick, as am I. Max is like a brother to us, and I cannot stay here when he is in such terrible need. I must go to help."

She studied him. Christopher could practically see the wheels turning in her mind – her brilliant, gorgeous, perfect mind. Eventually, she sighed. "I understand. If your friend is in danger, you must go."

His fingers shook against hers. "You truly understand?"

"I do," she assured. "So, when must you leave?"

"Very soon."

"How soon?"

Christopher shifted on his feet. "Tonight."

"Tonight? You mean *tonight* tonight?"

"Yes. My ship sets sail in just a few hours."

She whimpered. "Just a few hours?"

He held tighter to her hands. "Yes."

"Oh," she said, staring into his eyes for the longest seconds of his life. After forever, she nodded. "Well, then. I shall have to come with you."

"Come *with* me?"

"Of course. It is short notice, but I can pack quickly." Violet released his hands, pivoting toward her bed to gather her dress. "It won't take me but a moment to collect my things. I shall call Mr. Rodchester to fetch my trunk again, and I'll be ready to leave in no time at all."

Christopher's heart thudded against his ribcage as he watched her collect her gown in frenzied haste. He reached for her shoulders and turned her back toward him. "Violet, I need you to stop this, please. I – I cannot take you with me. I wish I could, but it is not possible."

She stilled herself as she gazed on his face. "Why not?"

"Because I don't know what's waiting for me out there. The journey is too long and dangerous, and I will not risk your safety."

"But if it is so dangerous, then must you truly go? I need you to be safe, too, Christopher. Just as you need me to be safe."

"I am aware of that, but I have no choice in the matter. I have things to accomplish and obligations to fulfill. I wish I didn't, but I do."

Her eyes dropped to where her hands lay clenched against her stomach. "Very well," she whispered, nibbling against her lip before stiffening her spine. "We shall simply have to get married tonight, then."

"We...what?"

"It will be a bit difficult, certainly, but not impossible. Thankfully, my father has many connections. Swift arrangements can be made, especially if we offer enough reward. If we leave now, I'm certain we can find a magistrate who will perform the ceremony within the hour. Sadly, we shall have to wait until your return before we can have a proper wedding night. I mean, unless you think we'll have time to be together before your ship departs? Although I'm perfectly happy to wait for you to come back home to me. I shall go to the Kastle manor tomorrow, to remain there with your sisters, and I'll await your return while you..."

"*Violet,*" he breathed, his voice breaking on her name.

She stopped formulating her plans in order to focus on him. "Yes?"

Christopher absorbed the hope in her eyes, horribly aware that he would never see such promise again. He dropped his arms to his sides and said the words he couldn't bear to say. "We are not getting married."

Her face fell that instant. "Wh-what do you mean?"

"I mean exactly what I said. We are not getting married."

Tears sprang to her eyes. "But I don't...I don't understand. Do you not desire me anymore?"

He dug his nails into his palms. "Dear God, you know that's not true."

"But then why would we not get married?"

"Because I cannot."

Her shoulders shook as the tears slid down her face. "Is it because I talk too much? Have you finally grown sick of my voice?"

His chest constricted while he slipped his fingers up her cheek, brushing over her wet skin. "Violet, I've told you a hundred times: I love your voice. When you speak to me, I know that everything is right with the world. I shall miss hearing you talk. More than you can imagine."

"But then why will you not marry me? Am I not refined enough? Not accomplished enough? Not pretty enough? What is it that I lack?"

"Nothing," he vowed, tracing the outline of her face. "You lack nothing, my dearest. It is I who am lacking. I cannot marry you for a million reasons, all of which are my fault. Please be certain that this has nothing to do with you and everything to do with me. Me, and the many, many sins of my past."

Her lips trembled. "How many sins are there?"

He dropped his hand from her cheek. "More than I can count."

Violet's eyes remained fastened to his. She studied him forever before finally offering a watery smile. "What if I forgive you for your sins?"

Christopher thought his heart might actually explode. He thought his whole body might burst open entirely, and he could remain in her presence no longer. "Thank you for the generous offer, my sweet. Regrettably, even if I could accept your forgiveness, I cannot escape my atonement."

"But what if..."

Reaching out, he grasped her shoulders in his hands and pulled her to him. He rested his forehead onto hers and breathed in deep, filling his lungs with her scent one last time. "Go and live your life, Violet. Please live your life and be happy, because knowing that you are happy is the only way I will survive what I must now do."

Christopher didn't give her a chance to respond. He pressed a tender kiss to her forehead, released her body, and turned away. He walked out of her bedchamber without looking back at all – no matter how much he wanted to see her just once more.

～

VIOLET HELD VERY STILL, staring at the door Christopher had just disappeared through. She stood beside her bed, with her arms sagging and her legs barely supporting her, as tears streamed down her face. She knew her heart still beat in her chest, but it was thick and heavy and wretchedly painful.

She shuddered from head to toe as Christopher's words echoed in her ears: *Go and live your life, Violet. Please live your life and be happy.*

"Live my life?" she whispered. "Live my life and be happy?"

Her legs started to collapse, forcing her to take a shaky step back to the bed so she could sink down on the edge of the mattress. Violet twisted her fingers together on her lap, hanging her head to watch her tears fall from her cheeks onto her hands. "How am I supposed to be happy without you?" she questioned her husband, still feeling the warmth of his lips on her skin.

Good Lord, he'd gone. The only man she'd ever loved had gone and left her here alone. Utterly alone.

She shook her head, over and over, just now realizing that she wouldn't be alone for long – not when everyone heard that Christopher had returned to sea without marrying her. Once Tildy learned the news, she would send Violet directly back to Pennyshire. And once she arrived on her parents' doorstep, they would barely greet her before packing her up again. They would gather all her belongings, wrap her up in a tightly corseted dress, and send her straight to the Duke of Dunworthy.

She could practically hear her father's voice now: *I told you, Violet. I told you that you must marry, and I even gave you an option. If the heir to the Earl of Nightingale is no longer that option, then the Duke of Dunworthy will be. He is your only other option, whether you desire him or not.*

Violet heard Papa's words so clearly, knowing he would not tolerate her failure in acquiring a husband. She would instantly be sent off to marry the ancient duke. At which point, she could only pray for the lesser of two evils – to watch him fall asleep in his soup bowl each night until she died of sheer boredom, or to sit hopelessly by the man's side until he expired of extreme old age – and she didn't know which was worse.

"And if I do survive him, what can I hope for then?" she asked her tear-soaked hands. "To still be young enough to go out into society, only to be mocked as the pickiest princess, rejected by an earl and widowed by a duke? Or will I merely cower in isolation until I'm an old hag? Will I be surrounded by servants paid to listen to me drone on about the days I once spent at Aunt Tildy's, the only days I ever truly lived with the only man I ever truly loved? Oh, God. Dear, sweet, merciful God. This cannot be happening."

Violet groaned, wishing she could think more rationally, since she truly did understand what Christopher told her. His friend was in trouble and he felt obligated by honor to offer assistance. That part of his speech was logical and matched his flawless character. Yet everything he told her afterward made no sense at all.

She'd seen him practice his sword many times, his movements as lethal as they were graceful. She knew he could protect her, so why would he not allow her to accompany him on this supposedly dangerous journey? And even if she must remain behind, why on earth could they not get married? Why couldn't she become his wife this very night, and then live at the Kastle manor with his sisters to await his return?

Violet couldn't comprehend any of it, because it simply didn't make sense. Nothing about this made sense. "And I never once told him that I love him," she realized, the breathy words barely making it past her lips.

She stood from her bed to feverishly pace the floor, with every nerve in her body stripped raw. "Great heavens, I never told him I love him. There are so many things I never had the chance to say. There is so much more to discuss. If Christopher will just listen to me, I'm certain we can work this out." Her hands balled to fists as she stared at her incessantly moving feet. "I must speak with him. Right now. I must find him and beg him to listen."

Violet made herself smile, clinging to the hope of a future in which all of this nonsense lay firmly in their past. Yet her smile fell just as quickly, because it sounded like an impossible dream. Her husband had already left Wilmington, and he would sail away from England in just a few hours.

Her feet stopped, frozen to the spot. "Just a few hours," she said, repeating the words he'd spoken to her mere minutes ago. "Christopher is going to sail away in just a few hours, which means he is still here somewhere. It means I still have time to change his mind, if only I can figure out where he's gone."

Her mind labored in haste, searching frantically for answers. Would he have gone back to the Kastle manor, to see his family once more? Would he have gone early to the docks, to ensure his ship was ready to set sail? Or would he have gone somewhere else entirely?

She bit her lip as she considered her options, wondering what destination her husband would choose at a time when his emotions must be in such great upheaval. That consideration was all she needed, for it drew forth the memory of what she'd overheard Nick Marlow say to Christopher on the night of the ball: *I know these feelings you have for Violet are overwhelming you entirely. So, if you ever realize you're in too deep, and you need a little time and space to clear your head, feel free to use my spare room in Nightingale Port.*

"Nick's room on top of the tavern!" she shrieked. "The one closest to the Wharf Street docks! That has to be it!" The words no sooner left her mouth than she began running toward the door, yanking on the latch and stumbling into the hallway. Violet glanced down the empty corridor for seconds only before realizing she wore nothing but her nightgown.

She huffed at her unfortunate state of undress, having neither the time nor the assistance to change into a formal outfit. She scurried back to her room and grabbed the crimson riding cape she'd worn home from the Kastle manor earlier today, pulling it over her shoulders and fastening the single toggle at her neck. Unable to bother with lacing up her boots, she tucked her bare feet into the pink silk house slippers resting beside her bed.

The next instant, she took off running again. As stealthily as possible, Violet escaped her bedchamber, hurried across the hall, dashed down the staircase, and flew through the foyer. She fled from the grand entrance of the Wilmington manor without looking back even once, sprinting full force to the stables to acquire whatever horse she could find. Christopher's steed was already gone from its stall and there were fresh hoofprints in the soft earth – prints she hoped to follow in the steady stream of pale moonlight.

As she coaxed a black stallion from one of the stalls, she said a word of thanks to her mother, who'd made her take riding lessons back in Pennyshire. Violet could not have been more grateful for her ability to ride, since she definitely had somewhere she needed to be right now. And someone she most definitely needed to be with.

CHAPTER 12

Truths

Christopher rode his horse from the Wilmington manor to the tavern on Wharf Street with singular purpose. He tried like hell to not think about Violet as he guided his steed through the cool night air. He tried to not think about how she looked while standing in her bedchamber, wearing nothing but her soft little nightgown, staring up at him with tears streaming down her face. He tried to ignore the devastating pain in his heart, knowing he'd done such damage to hers.

When he arrived at his destination, he pulled his horse to a halt at the side of the building. He dismounted and tied up his steed before walking around to the entrance and through the tavern door. The fire in the hearth raged just as it had the last time he'd come here, only two weeks ago, to meet with Nick. Christopher turned away from the vile flames, ignored the countless other people in the crowded room, and stepped over to the bar.

The same furry barkeep stood in front of the liquor shelves. Christopher captured the man's attention, declared himself a friend of Mr. Marlow's, and insisted that Nick had granted him use of his private chamber upstairs. The barkeep side-eyed him, but still offered a key along with a pointing finger. Christopher mumbled his gratitude before turning in the indicated direction, which led to a narrow staircase at the back of the main room.

Weaving through the throngs of bar patrons, who were all quite drunk and garrulous at this dark hour, he made his way up the winding, creaking staircase. The steps opened out at the top to a short hallway on the second floor.

Only one door stood at the end of the constricted corridor, so he strode to it and used the key for access.

Nick's home-away-from-home proved to be a rather simple place. The room was moderate in size, currently lit only by moonlight seeping through the window on the far wall. Christopher glanced around in the dimness, spying a desk with a single chair and a slim bed with a table beside it, which bore a candle and matches. He pushed the door closed behind him, somewhat muting the raucous noises of the tavern patrons downstairs.

Stepping to the bedside table, he snapped a match to light the candle in its brass holder. The ensuing flame cast the room in a soft yellow glow. Christopher appreciated the light, if not the fire itself. He sat down on the bed, which was little more than a cot with a tan blanket covering the mattress. It was still comfortable enough to sit on, though. It was also probably comfortable enough for Nick to sleep on when he was too drunk to find his way home.

Nick.

Christopher should rightly be with his brother now. He should be down at the docks this very minute, helping with the final preparations for the voyage they would embark on in mere hours. He should have ridden his horse directly there from Wilmington and boarded the ship as its captain.

But he couldn't do it. He needed a little more time. He needed these last moments to just be Christopher. He needed to be Lord Christopher Kastle for as long as humanly possible, before he had to become someone else entirely.

With a labored exhale, he reached down to tug off his boots. He set them next to the bed and planted his bare soles on the wood floor. He stretched out his toes, appreciating the simple feeling, since he would not have such unwavering ground beneath him again for a very long time.

Drawing his eyes up from the ground, he looked to the desk and chair sitting against the wall. Several items lay on the desktop: paper, quill, ink, and wax. He wondered if the letters Nick had sent him were written right here – the letters that changed the course of Christopher's life – the letters that took away his one and only chance at happiness with his Violet.

He moaned with the sound of her name in his head, the punishing ache in his heart resurfacing with a vengeance. He stood and marched to the desk, glaring down at the paper and ink, wanting nothing more than to swipe his arm across the surface and knock it all to the floor in a fit of rage. With great effort, he restrained his temper and shed his coat instead, tossing the stiff black fabric over the back of the chair.

Christopher unfastened the top few buttons of his shirt as he stepped to the window. He looked out into the distance, spying the docks so close by. He could see the hulls of the many clipper ships and the inky waters beneath them, shining black in the pale moonlight.

Goddamnit. He didn't want to go there. He didn't want to leave his wife. Not ever. And yet, he already had. He'd stood in her bedchamber and told her he was leaving. Even after she'd offered to come with him on his journey – even after she'd offered to marry him this very night – he'd stood there and told Violet he was leaving her. Despite every torturous scar that marred his body, Christopher had never felt pain like that before.

Now, all he could do was stand alone in this pitiful room. All he could do was stare out to the waters he would soon call home, thinking of the woman he never wanted to leave. The woman he loved with all his heart. The woman he would most likely never see again.

He placed his hand against the wall, trying to hold himself steady on his feet and not collapse beneath his anguish. He wasn't sure how long he stood and stared out of the window. He only knew that at some point, the door opened behind him. He heard the hinges creak and his breath caught.

He didn't have to turn around to discover who now stood here with him. He didn't have to see her reflection in the window to know she'd come. He could smell her sweet scent from across the room. He could hear the tiny puffs of air moving in and out of her chest, even over the riotous tavern noises filtering up the stairs. He would know her anywhere.

Christopher's gaze slid down to watch the candle flame cast shadows on the floorboards. He inhaled deeply and exhaled slowly, but he could not turn around. He could not look on her. Not even when he spoke to her.

"How did you find me, Violet?"

"I overheard you and Nick speaking on the night of the ball. He told you he had a spare room over a tavern on Wharf Street where you could go if you needed to get away. He said you should come here if your emotions ever overwhelmed you, and I figured tonight was more than a little overwhelming."

Christopher smiled despite himself. "You are quite the spy, aren't you?"

"Are you judging me?"

"No. I'm proud of you," he corrected before clamping his mouth shut. He let the room fall silent, strengthening his will before he turned to see her.

Violet stood in the doorway wearing nothing but her ivory nightgown and crimson riding cape. His first inclination was to yell at her. Good Lord, how dare she come to a goddamn tavern in the middle of the fucking night wearing so little clothing! He nearly screamed at the top of his lungs. But then he glanced down to the pink silk slippers on her feet, and at the dirt scuffing their edges, and realized she'd come here barely dressed because she'd felt desperate to reach him. Which was entirely his fault.

Christopher held his anger close to his chest as he glanced to her face. He drank in the sight of her gold hair hanging about her shoulders, the rosy flush of her cheeks, and the determination in her sky-blue eyes. Violet was color and light and life. She was an angel and a siren, and his heart pounded against his ribcage while he looked on her.

Bloody hell, she wasn't supposed to be here. Not just here in this room, but here in his heart. She wasn't supposed to be here, and yet she'd found him. Violet found him because she was too intelligent for her own good. And too kind. Too gentle. Too innocent. She was so fucking innocent, and he was anything but.

She took another step inside the room, closing the door softly behind her. She left them utterly alone together, just like she'd done last night in his antechamber. She also wore the same gauzy slip of a nightgown, making Christopher despise that scrap of fabric that barely concealed her from his eyes. He needed it to conceal much more of her. He wanted it to conceal much less.

"I had to see you," she spoke in the dense silence, taking a step closer.

"Why?" he demanded, his voice coming harsher than he meant. But it stopped her from advancing further, which was precisely what he needed.

"Because I don't think we finished our conversation," Violet answered.

"Yes, we did. I told you I had no choice but to leave England tonight. There is nothing more to say."

"I don't believe that's true. I believe there is much more to say."

"No. There is nothing left."

"But I'm sure there is! If you want to be with me, and I want to be with you, then I'm certain there is a way we can work all of this out!"

Christopher bore witness to the fortitude in her body as she yelled at him above the noisy clamor emanating from downstairs. He raked a hand through his hair, fully aware that there was so much about himself he needed to tell her – so much he *should* tell her. If Violet knew the truth of his past, she probably wouldn't be standing here right now, trying to resolve their issues. If she knew the truth, she would most likely spin on her heels and run like hell in the opposite direction.

Or maybe she wouldn't. Maybe she would remain by his side despite all his sins. Because she was his, just as he was hers.

He shook his head. "Violet, I understand why you've come to speak with me. I appreciate your need for resolution, but this is not what you think it is.

We cannot stand here, have a productive conversation, and make everything right between us. I'm sorry, but we cannot possibly do that."

"Why not?"

"Because."

"Because why?"

Christopher huffed. "Because this journey I must now take is not only about rescuing my friend, Max. There are things happening here that you know nothing about. There are forces acting against your will, as well as my own. Forces that reach far beyond your knowledge."

She took another step forward, her eyes pleading along with her voice. "Then tell me about them. If you have sins for which you must atone, tell me what they are and let me help. I believe a productive conversation could allow us the opportunity to work through so many things. Just talk to me. Please."

He absorbed the conviction in her eyes while his gut clenched. He absolutely could not tell her the truth. If he did, she would either scream and run, or dig her heels in and remain. Right now, he honestly didn't know which would be worse.

"Are you really not going to tell me?" she asked after arduous moments, with the candlelight reflecting her gathering tears. "After all the time we've spent together, after all these weeks devoted to learning about each other, after all the laughter and confidences and touches we've shared, are you truly going to stop everything and just walk away from me?"

This was the second time in the last few hours that he'd brought her to tears. The droplets that hadn't yet fallen from her eyes raised his heart from its grave just to murder it again. It took every ounce of resolve in his body to produce one single word. "Yes."

Violet's lips quivered. "And is there nothing I can say to change your mind? Nothing about my hopes for us? Nothing about my dreams for our future?" Her voice dropped to a mere whisper. "Is there nothing I can say about how I feel for you? About how very deeply I feel for you?"

Christopher's heart leapt. He already knew what she meant to tell him, yet he couldn't let her speak her feelings aloud. He couldn't stand here and look on her sweet face as she confessed her love for him, because hearing her say those words would be both the best and worst things ever.

"No," he insisted. "There is nothing you can say, Violet. Nothing will change my mind. Nothing at all."

She stared at him. She stood tall and resolute, even as she swiped at her tears. She stared at him until he actually wanted to cower and hide. But he did not. He fully met and matched her intent gaze.

After several minutes filled with only the distant tavern racket, Violet seemed to resolve herself to their unwinnable situation. When she raised her chin and brushed her hair from her damp cheeks, Christopher assumed her tenacious pursuit of the impossible was now over. He figured she would turn and leave this place without another thought of him. He actually hoped she would leave, as much as he dreaded it. He stood still as stone, waiting in petrifying anticipation, until she spoke again.

"Well, then," Violet said, her tone firm despite the tremors plaguing her body. "I suppose there is only one thing left for me to ask of you."

He straightened himself, keeping his chest puffed out and his shoulders squared. But inside, he recoiled. Because he could already hear her next words.

I want you to go to hell.

That is what she should say to him. That is what she should ask for.

I want you to go to hell, Christopher.

He knew those words were coming. He also knew they were justified. In truth, he was already engulfed in flames of his own making, so he simply braced himself for the added impact of her damnation.

I want you to go to hell.

Violet pinned his eyes. "I want you to make love to me," she said.

Christopher stopped breathing. Everything in his entire body froze. He stood, utterly dumbfounded, for an eternity.

Eventually, he managed to ask one question. "What the hell, Violet?"

"I want you to make love to me," she repeated, as if it was the simplest and most obvious suggestion ever. "Right here. Right now."

"My God! You cannot possibly expect me to…"

"Why on earth not?" she demanded, cutting off his words as she took another step toward him. "Give me one good reason why I shouldn't ask this of you. After all, you said earlier that you want me to live my life and be happy. You said the only way you can survive what you must now do is to know that I am happy. But I'm never going to be happy without you, because we both know what shall happen to me when I must remain here, unmarried in the eyes of the rest of the world."

In the eyes of the rest of the world. He didn't miss her implication. He knew she considered him her husband. And he definitely considered her his wife. But their beliefs wouldn't matter to anyone else, not if their vows hadn't been spoken in front of church and family.

Violet's entire body shuddered. "Shall I recount to you what will become of me when you leave?" she asked. "I need to be sure you know. I need to be sure you understand that when I arrive back home, alone and unwed, I shall immediately be sent off to the Duke of Dunworthy, in all his glory. The Duke of Dunworthy, who is old enough to be my grandfather. I'll be sent to live out my days in a gilded cage, with no chance for freedom and no hope for happiness. And all I will have to sustain me, in my unrelenting life of familial servitude, are my memories. All I will have are my recollections of you and I, and of the blissful moments we've shared."

She paused to breathe and struggled to continue. "After you leave me, I will have nothing to look forward to except for growing old. I will grow to be a sad, withered old woman, who smells of soup and regret. And the only things I shall possess, of any real value, will be my memories. My priceless memories of your voice, and your smile, and your touch."

Violet took a step toward him. "Those precious remembrances of you are all I will truly own, Christopher. And I want them. Dear God, I *need* them. Therefore, I must ask you to forgive the impropriety of my request. For just once in my life – for just *once* – I want the man I love to make love to me."

The man I love.

The man I love.

He heard the words, and he knew the truth of them. Yet he still couldn't fathom them coming from her unspoiled lips. He shook his head, again and again, unable to comprehend anything at all.

She took another step forward. "I want you to make love to me."

"No," he said, barely getting the word out. "No, that's...no."

"Why not?"

"Because I cannot. I simply cannot."

"Why? Because it wouldn't be *honorable*?"

"Exactly," he insisted, matching her indomitable gaze. "I may not have a choice in leaving you, but I have the ability to do it in a gentlemanly fashion."

"Well, just so you know, even if you leave my honor here, you'll still be taking my heart with you. And that is something I can never get back."

Christopher clenched his jaw until he thought his teeth would shatter. Violet searched his eyes, looking for answers he could not give. When she found nothing, her face crumbled.

"Please do not do this to me," she entreated. "Do not leave me to marry that man. I honestly don't think I can live through it. I will wither away. I will wither away to nothing."

"No, you will not! You are strong. So strong. You will survive."

"I will *survive*? Is that all I have to look forward to, then? Will I be forced to sit at the duke's dinner table every evening, filling a chair like a place card? Must I go to his bed at night and allow him to climb on top of me? Must I endure him touching my body in any manner he desires, as I pinch my eyes shut and pray it will all be over soon?"

Christopher's hands fisted like bricks. "Don't talk about that, I beg you. I cannot listen to it."

"But you need to listen. You need to acknowledge what is going to happen to me. I will be sent to the duke and he will have me in his bed. He will have me naked, and he will run his hands all over me, and..."

"Good Lord! Do you think I *want* that? Do you truly think I want to leave you to another man? My God, I cannot fathom any other man ever touching you. For that is my privilege, and mine alone. You are everything to me, Violet. You are all I have ever wished for in my entire life. You are bright, bold, beautiful, and perfect, and if this were a perfect world, I would marry you right now. Hell, I would have married you the first moment I met you, when you introduced yourself as my wife."

Christopher's voice caught with that memory. All he wanted in the world was to go back to that day and live it over again, just to have more time with her. But the only thing he could do now was watch his wife quiver before him, while still standing so far away.

Violet gasped for air. He knew his confessions hurt her more than they helped, yet he still needed her to hear them. He softened his words, focusing his entire being on hers.

"I want you to know something without doubt, my dearest. I want you to know that if I were another man, leading another life, I would fight to call you mine. I would fight like hell against anyone who dared to say I couldn't be with you. But the fact remains that this is the life I lead. I have no choice but to tell you goodbye, even if it rips me apart to do so."

Fresh tears sprang to her eyes, brimming so quickly that they slid down her cheeks before she had the chance to blink. She made a choked little sound in the back of her throat, sniffling while her fingers twitched. He took a step toward her, thinking his closeness might be a comfort, but she wouldn't let him come any further. She held her hand out forcibly in front of her, stopping him in his tracks.

"Violet," he whispered, needing to reach her in some way.

She shook her head as she scrubbed the tears from her face. "No. You don't get to do that. You don't get to say beautiful things to me at the same moment you say you're leaving me here alone."

"Violet..."

"God, please do not say my name like that."

"Like what?"

"Like you love saying it. Like it is your favorite name in the world."

"But it is my favorite name."

"Damn it, Christopher! I don't want to hear how much you adore me! I don't want to hear how you wish we could be together! You said you were mine! You said you would remain beside me for as long as I desired! You said I would be your wife! You said you would make love to me thoroughly, completely, and exhaustively, as soon as we were married! What do you have to say about those vows now? What about *all those vows* you made to me?"

Christopher stood witness to the extraordinary courage radiating from inside her. He wished Violet could see herself the way he did. He wished she could see the fearless strength on full display before him.

He offered a tender smile as he answered. "I kept my vows to you."

Her eyes flew wide. "What? Are you being serious?"

"I'm perfectly serious. I kept them all, in different ways."

"Great heavens! How on earth do you figure that?"

"Because I am yours. In my heart, I have been yours since the moment we met. And I can promise you that my heart will remain beside you for as long as you desire, because it most certainly is not leaving this room with me tonight. It will stay right here with you."

Christopher paused to take a breath, watching as she struggled to claim one of her own. "And you are my wife, in every way that matters to me. You have been my wife since the night we spoke our vows in that carriage," he professed, keeping his voice low and gentle. "As for making love to you, if we had ever been given the chance to say our vows properly, then you may have never left our bedchamber again. Because I would have kept your naked body pinned beneath my own for every second of every day you allowed."

Violet's eyes sparked, yet that flash of hope fled as quickly as it came. She stared into him with unhinged emotions darkening her sky-blue. In the next instant, her gaze fell to the floor. "That is truly unfair, Christopher."

"What is unfair?"

She studied her scuffed silk slippers. "It is unfair of you to say those things to me. It is unfair to taunt me with such sublime words, and I must now insist that you stop saying them. I cannot listen to your sweet nothings anymore, because that is all they are – sweet and nothing."

Her admonition broke something inside him. Christopher threw his arms in the air. "Bloody hell, woman! I've spoken as openly and plainly as I possibly can! I don't know what else you expect from me!"

Violet's gaze flew to his face. "I just...I just want you to..."

"To what? Tell me! Goddamnit, just tell me what you want!"

"I want you to be cruel to me! If there's nothing I can do to stop you from leaving, then I want you to break my heart! I want you to crush it into a million pieces! Because I never wish to feel it again!"

His entire body revolted. Christopher had to lock his knees while his stomach twisted in knots, making him feel sicker than he ever had in his life. "Violet," he breathed, reaching out in the only way he could. He barely realized he'd said her name again – like it was his favorite in the world – until her shoulders sagged and a tiny sob escaped her throat.

"Please," she begged. "Please break my heart." Her eyes settled on his, full of tears and determination. "Tell me you never wanted this marriage. Tell me all the moments we've shared meant nothing to you. Tell me you don't love me. Tell me..."

Christopher cleared the distance between them in two strides. He had her face in his hands before he even knew what he was doing. He had her lips beneath his own before he could think to stop himself.

Violet molded to him in an instant, her fingers clutching at his forearms as their mouths and bodies fused, each sinking seamlessly into the other. He'd kissed her a thousand times before and yet this felt like their first. It also felt like their last. He poured all the emotion he could into this single touch of their lips. When he eventually eased back, to look into her eyes as they slowly lifted to his, the injustice of her request became more than he could endure.

"I will not tell you any of those things," he said, keeping her face steady in his hands so he could stare the words inside her. "I could never say them, for they would be the foulest and gravest of lies."

Christopher held her gaze for long, warped, slurred seconds. He listened to the tiny, panted breaths escaping her parted lips until he could no longer suffer the anguish. He released her then, so she could walk away from him. He expected Violet to turn away directly, to escape this place and never look back, because he knew this should truly be the end of them.

He'd felt her soft, sweet kiss one last time, and he'd heard her say she loved him. That should be all he needed in this life: to know he was redeemed and whole within the heart of this one woman. To know she could look on him with her sunlit eyes, filled with such purity, and see only the good inside him. All of that should be enough for him.

But when she arched up on her tiptoes, with her gaze focused solely on his lips, Christopher didn't stop her. He didn't say a word in protest before she touched her mouth to his. He didn't prevent her timid kiss in the slightest.

He simply allowed himself to taste her again, to revel in the warmth of her body pressed onto his. He stood very still, with his arms at his sides, as Violet eased her lips slowly and gently over his own, lingering for several seconds before tracing the seam of his mouth with her tongue. Then he watched as she settled back on her heels and gave him an encouraging smile.

Christopher searched her eyes, witnessing an entire world inside them. He could see her sheer, undiluted yearning for him. He could see her hunger, her passion, and her love. He could see her willingness to give him anything he wanted – to give him everything he wanted.

He watched her with his heart in his throat and his entire body taut with desire. At this moment, he finally accepted the atrocious truth. He wasn't strong enough to leave Violet's innocence here. He needed it too much. He needed to take it with him, and hold onto it in the darkness, if he was ever going to have a chance to make it back home alive.

Christopher reached for her. He grabbed hold of his wife, accepting that she would be his tonight. Even if it was just for this one night.

Violet didn't resist him. She rushed into his arms, matching the demands of his mouth without falter. She pushed herself into his ferocious grip, threading her fingers into his hair to clutch him to her, opening to the exploration of his tongue while he tasted her with feral need. She thrust herself so ardently and feverishly onto his body that Christopher had to pry his lips away, just to be absolutely sure.

"Violet," he moaned, his rapid, heated breaths mixing with hers. "Are you certain about this? I need you to be unquestionably certain, for if this is what you truly desire from me, I shall give it to you. God, I want you so much. I want you more than you can possibly fathom. But you must understand, even if I make love to you now, it cannot change the fact that I'm leaving tonight."

Her arms tightened around his neck. "I'm certain, Christopher. I want you to make love to me. Please. *Please.*"

He didn't need any further assurances. He sank back into her, melding their mouths together, slipping his tongue past her parted lips so easily. Violet sighed into him, her body sagging as her fingertips slid across his scalp. He felt the release in her muscles, felt her complete acceptance of his touch. She gave in to him entirely, making him want to both claim and protect her, all at the same time.

Christopher wanted to give her the experience she deserved. He wanted to devote hours and hours to loving her. He wanted to spend lengthy, deliberate moments kissing every inch of her skin, exploring every part of her body, and giving her orgasm after orgasm, before ever seeking his own release. But as much as he wished to do all of that, he simply did not have the time. He forced himself to wrench his mouth from hers, needing to focus on the rest of her body, intent on giving her as much pleasure as possible in the scarce minutes they had remaining.

He looked down to her riding cape, which was the only thing she wore over her thin nightgown. The sight of the crimson fabric conjured the memory of the first time he and Violet walked in the Wilmington gardens together, when she assured him that he had free rein with her body after just one kiss to her hand. He remembered feeling like the Big Bad Wolf that day, come to steal her virtue under the guise of a trusted companion. Now, it seemed quite fitting that she should offer herself to him while wearing a red riding hood, and that he should divest her of it before claiming her innocence for himself.

Reaching to the single clasp at her throat, Christopher undid the simple toggle with a flick of his fingers. He watched the coat slip off her shoulders and slide to the floor. Then he stared down at the flimsy slip of ivory fabric she still wore, seeing it pull across the lush, round curves of her chest.

Only a few simple ties held her nightgown together at the top. He reached for them next, tugging on the tiny, delicate strings that started at her neck and moved down to the valley between her breasts. Violet's breathing turned shallower as he worked, her hands falling to her sides and twisting against her hips. Once he pulled the last laces free, and her gown gaped and caught on the upper swells of her breasts, he refocused on her face.

Her eyes were wide, filled with uncertainty tempered by determination. Christopher knew she was trying to be brave for him. He also knew she wasn't questioning her decision to allow him inside her; she only feared the unknown. But he didn't want her to be afraid, since he was determined to give her all he could in the brief moments they had.

Leaning forward, he ghosted his lips over hers. "Kiss me," he pleaded, needing to feel how starkly she longed for him, fully aware that his longing for her could destroy him entirely.

Violet nodded, but she didn't come to him right away. She swallowed hard, the movement shifting the long, smooth column of her bare throat. She pushed up slowly on her tiptoes and slid her hands up his arms, all the way to his shoulders. Resting her barely covered chest against his shirt, she sighed into his mouth and touched their lips together.

Christopher let her control the kiss as long as he could. He allowed her to taste him in her own way, tangling their tongues in a tender exploration while her body softened against his. He gave her time to accustom her mind to the reality of what she'd asked him to do to her.

When Violet eventually eased away, smiling up at him beneath heavy-lidded eyes, he grasped her arms and urged her gently backwards. He stepped with her until they reached the wall, her lips parting on a huffed breath when her spine flattened against the wood surface. He released her then, holding her in place with only his gaze as he reached for her gown.

Christopher watched her intently while bringing his hands to the laced edge of her neckline, slipping his fingers beneath the gauzy fabric to pull it across her shoulders. Violet whimpered when he eased the material down her upper arms. She gasped when the edge of the gown caught against the peaks of her nipples, just before he freed her breasts from the confines of her scant clothing. She bit into her lip when he let the nightgown fall, allowing it to pool entirely at her feet. He didn't have to remove her knickers, because she didn't wear any. They both knew that.

The doubt in her eyes as she searched his made Christopher's gut clench. "You're beautiful," he assured, still fixated solely on her face.

"But you...you have not even looked on me yet."

"You're absolutely beautiful, Violet. Trust me."

She gave him a bashful smile. He returned her smile as he took a half step back. Then he lowered his gaze to look on her bare body.

In this moment, Christopher wished he could have the full force of the sun at his back. He wished to have every speck of light on earth at his command, to illuminate every little bit of her. Yet he still treasured the view he now possessed – in the dim glow of a single candle flame – even if the shadowy light could not possibly do her justice.

She stood entirely naked before him, with the curves of her form as bare to him as the love in her eyes. Sweet hell, his wife was truly stunning. He wanted to worship her. With his hands and his heart. With his mind and his body. He wanted to make love to the woman he loved. Just once.

Christopher wished to start right away, but he also didn't want this to ever end. He barely knew what to do with himself, so he simply gazed on her. He could have stood here and stared at her until the end of time, yet Violet chose otherwise. She stepped into him and pressed her mouth to his.

Her movements were both hesitant and assured, and he met her lips with forced restraint. He worked to remain calm, not wishing to frighten her with the ferocity of his desires while he touched her for the first time. He slipped his hands onto her shoulders and she gasped into his mouth, even though his movements were gentle and his skin warm. He took a great deal of time smoothing his fingers up her neck and back down her arms, accustoming them both to the seamless glide of his flesh on hers. Eventually, when she'd settled fully into his touch, he eased his fingers onto her chest.

Christopher cupped one of her breasts in each of his palms. Violet stopped kissing him, her gaze falling to her chest. She marveled at his hands as they glided over her skin, caressing her soft curves with his roughened fingers. She watched intently as he edged his thumbs over her taut nipples, pulling them even tighter. A bare second later, she closed her eyes and dropped her head back against the wall.

He examined her expressions while he touched, seeing her lips part and cheeks flush with his continued stimulation of her peaked buds. The sounds she made were needy and frenzied, but he could hardly focus on them. He'd wanted to touch her flesh like this for so long that it felt like a dream, and this was only the beginning of all the things he wanted to do with her.

Tearing his eyes from the pleasure written across her face, he leaned down to taste. He bent over and sucked onto one pebbled nipple, pulling it fully inside his mouth. Violet cried out and grabbed his hair, fisting the short strands to secure him against her chest. He rewarded her feverish desires by sweeping his tongue over that perfectly hardened peak, causing all her muscles to tremble. Christopher felt grateful now that he'd pushed her up against the wall, since she required the support. They both did.

Dragging his mouth from her breast, he ran several kisses across her chest before sucking her other nipple deeply inside. He tasted her thoroughly, trying very hard to not use his teeth. His wicked urge to mark her as his nearly overcame his sensibilities, until he heard Violet whimper to the point of crying. The tender sounds of his virginal wife's newly flourishing desires reminded him to be gentle.

Christopher pulled his lips from her breast, giving her a few seconds of vital reprieve before he kissed a path further down her body. He sank to his knees – an otherwise vile action he now fully embraced in her presence – keeping his mouth and hands in contact with her skin the entire time. He drew his fingers from her breasts onto her ribcage and then to her waist, grasping for the curves of her hipbones. He gripped her hips as he smoothed his mouth over her stomach and onto her bellybutton, pressing his lips to that tiny circle the moment he settled onto the ground.

Violet opened her eyes again, staring down at him while flattening her hands to the wall at her back. He met her unflinching gaze from his place below her, witnessing the curiosity, lust, fear, excitement, and need warring within her eyes. He continued watching her while he slipped his mouth downward, sliding his lips across her stomach until he could press a kiss into the soft curls covering her sex. When she gasped in surprise, he worked like hell to keep his attention on her face. He kissed her there again, breathing in the scent of sweet cream and honeysuckle, mixed now with the intoxicating fragrance of carnal desire.

Christopher eased back to see his wife better in the candlelight. Her body appeared so stunning from this angle, with her tight, wet nipples peaked up in the night air, her loose, gilded hair falling across her shoulders, and her wide, darkened eyes focused entirely on his. He honed in on that gorgeous blue as he urged one hand away from her hip to draw it down between her thighs.

He didn't have to ask her to part her legs. Violet spread herself open freely, although not too far, since she didn't possess her full balance right now. But she did ensure that he could touch her as he had last night.

Christopher didn't hesitate. He slid his hand between her legs and slipped one finger into the delicate folds of her sex. Good Lord, she was already wet. Violet was so fucking wet for him.

His ridiculously stiff cock – which he'd been fighting to ignore this entire time – pulsed in his breeches, straining the material near to bursting. He clenched his jaw, struggling to keep that monster at bay, disregarding the cries of his rigid shaft as it begged to be inside her. Instead, Christopher pressed only one finger up inside, relishing her tight walls when they surrounded his flesh. He began to move that finger with leisurely insistence, slipping in and out of her slick sheath.

Violet mewled with his invasion, spreading her fingers against the wall to maintain her balance. She adjusted her legs to accommodate the size of his hand, sighing indelicately as he edged gently out and back inside. Christopher stifled the imploring screams of his own body, fully aware that she wasn't prepared to take all of him yet.

He knew he must put more than one finger inside her now. Last night, one had been enough to bring her to orgasm. He hadn't needed to concern himself with stretching out her tight walls, since he'd had no intention of making love to her. But that was last night. Tonight, he needed her snug walls stretched as much as possible beforehand. He didn't want Violet to feel pain when their bodies joined, even though he knew she would. He only hoped he could make it easier for her.

Christopher pressed his finger inside her again and again, gliding across her slippery flesh. He gauged her reaction, seeing her eyes fall shut and hearing her stuttered breaths. When she began to move, driving herself onto his hand, he gripped onto her hipbone even harder.

Violet bucked against his hold, her erratic thrusts lodging his finger high into her wet walls. Christopher stared in wonder as she sought her pleasure in the same way he'd taught her last night. He cursed beneath his breath while he absorbed the splendor of her flushed cheeks, the determined furrow of her brow, and the rhythmic motions of her body. When her harsh moans turned harsher, he shifted his hand to introduce another finger alongside the first. Unfortunately, the second one didn't fit in quite as easily.

Violet stopped moving and looked to him. "My heavens, Christopher. Do you have two fingers inside me now?"

"I do. How does it feel?"

She gave him a teasing smile. "I'm not supposed to say it feels tight, am I?"

He chuckled, remembering how he'd growled at her for telling him that the night before. "You can say anything you wish to me, Violet. Although, I'm quite aware that you are tight. As you well know."

"Hmm. Then I suppose I will tell you it feels very lovely to have you inside me. One finger or two, they both feel wonderful."

"Good," he said, drawing both fingers out and thrusting them back in.

She groaned deep in her chest and fisted her hands against the wall. Christopher stared up at her in sheer longing while working his fingers in and out of her sex. He tried to spread them apart as he thrust into her body, but the barrier of her taut skin prevented him from stretching her out so far.

Violet gazed down at him the entire time he manipulated her flesh, focused wholly on his actions. She looked open and willing and quite simply glorious, and Christopher fully intended to bring her to orgasm right now. He had every intention of watching her come apart as she had last night, just from the touch of his fingers. But when he shifted his hand to press his thumb against the tiny nub at the top of her sex, she shook her head.

"No," she breathed.

"No?" he echoed, ceasing his actions immediately. "Am I hurting you?"

"Oh, God, not at all. I am fully aware, based on your actions last night, that you are only trying to bring me pleasure right now. But I don't want to have my orgasm this way. Tonight, I want you with me."

"I am with you."

"No, Christopher. Not this way. If I am to experience such pleasure again, then I want you *with* me."

He smiled with her needless concern. "I appreciate your consideration, my sweet, but you do not need to worry yourself over my pleasure. I will find my own release within your body soon enough. Besides, I can give you more than one orgasm. Fairly easily, I imagine."

"More than one? Can you really do that? Can I really do that?"

"Absolutely. Just give me the chance to show you."

Violet considered his words for lengthy seconds, until he stroked his thumb purposefully over her tight little nub. She sucked in a breath, yet still shook her head. "No. Not like this," she insisted. "I want you with me."

She reached for him then, with her palms facing up, offering to help pull him from the ground. Christopher drew his fingers from her body to place his hands inside her own. When he stood and aligned his clothed body to her naked one, she stared up at him with equal measures of love and lust.

His blood rushed through his ears while he brought his fingers to his mouth, needing to taste her lingering wetness like he had last night. Violet didn't appear shocked by his actions this time, and merely observed him as he cleansed his skin of her juices. He figured she would wait patiently until he'd finished, yet he barely had the chance to taste her sweet sex before she grabbed hold of his wrist and tugged his hand to her lips. She gazed up at him while she sucked his fingers into her mouth and swirled her tongue over his flesh. Christopher nearly spent himself inside his breeches.

"Holy hell," he growled, wrenching his fingers from her mouth to dig them into her hair. He pinned her against the wall as he plastered his lips to hers, sinking his tongue inside her so they could taste her sex together. He kissed her deep and hard, trying to soak her body fully into his. But he couldn't, not with all of his goddamn clothes still on.

Violet must have felt his frustration, or perhaps her own, because she reached to unbutton his shirt. Her fingers trembled as she worked, barely getting two buttons undone while she struggled to match his frenzied kisses. She made heady little noises, sounds of both necessity and desire, and he understood her emotions all too well.

Christopher needed the barriers between them gone just as much as she did. He released his tenacious grip on her in order to grab hold of his shirt, clutching the hem in both fists to yank the material up over his head. It took a mere second before he tossed the fabric to the floor, leaving him clothed in only his breeches. He looked to Violet's eyes the instant his shirt fell, wanting to see that glorious blue while he took her back into his arms.

But just as he reached for her, he stopped. Every muscle in his body stilled when her gaze shifted to his chest. Christopher realized, right at this moment, that he'd forgotten about his scars. For once in his life, he'd actually forgotten how mutilated he was. He'd forgotten how each one of the gashes and gouges he possessed could ache in reminder of all he'd done wrong. He'd forgotten all of it, because he'd only wanted to feel her against him, skin on skin.

Now, as Violet scrutinized his tattered body, he remembered everything. Every lash. Every stab. Every burn. No one had seen his disfigurements in so damn long. Not one single person had seen him unclothed in the whole past year, and the few who'd seen him before that had looked on him with either absolute horror or utter disgust.

Christopher stared at his wife with his heart in a vice. She didn't move at all. She simply examined his chest, her eyes absorbing each and every scar within her view. She seemed to catalog them all in her mind, in brief instants that felt like lifetimes. Then her gaze dragged back up to his face.

He braced himself for what he would witness when she looked at him now. He prepared himself for her disgust. Her pity. Her fear. But he could never have prepared himself for what he actually saw in her eyes.

Violet looked at him in awe. In respect. In reverence. She looked at him as if he'd conquered the entire world, and brought the crowns of every kingdom back to lay at her feet. She looked at him with more love than he could imagine, and certainly more than he ever thought he deserved. Then she reached for him, wrapping her arms around his neck and pressing her lips to his.

Christopher seized hold of her, trying his damnedest to absorb her into his skin. He pulled her bare chest flush with his, crushing her perfectly rounded breasts against his marred flesh. Violet writhed against him, in an ineffective yet determined attempt to climb him like a tree, so he assisted her. He reached down and grabbed two handfuls of her sumptuous bottom, pulling her body straight up off the floor. She banded her legs around his waist, the seamless motion bringing his aching cock to rest between her spread thighs, which made them each groan into the other's mouth.

He'd grasped onto her ass so greedily that he now felt its soft center seam parting with the pull of his hands. Her wet entrance teased the tips of his fingers from behind, coating his skin further with her juices. He barely took note of her feet shifting over his low back to kick off her little pink slippers, but he did have the presence of mind to step over the dirt-covered silk when he turned her toward the bed.

Christopher started walking as best he could beneath the intoxicating sensation of her mouth, hands, chest, and legs plastered onto him. He managed to carry her the few paces to the cot, with the strained material of his breeches the only barrier remaining between them. God, he didn't know how many times he'd imagined this moment, when he could finally lay her naked body out before him.

He'd always wanted to lay her on a plush mattress, bathed in silk sheets. He'd wanted to place her on a massive bed, swathed in decadent pillows. He hadn't wanted to take her innocence on a shifting bench, like that night in the carriage. He most certainly hadn't wanted her first time to be on a dingy cot in a room above a tavern, with the boisterous sounds of drunken men seeping through the floorboards. But at least no one would hear them, or care, if they both screamed out together. And at least his wife would be in some sort of a bed, instead of on a bench.

Christopher laid her down with great caution, easing her head onto the pillow and resting her spine against the blanket. She released him when he pulled back, dropping her hands to her sides as he straightened to stand beside the bed. His eyes drifted over her body, absorbing her untarnished beauty while the candlelight licked her skin. He drank in every curve and hollow until he could endure their separation no longer. Reaching to the waist of his breeches, he untied them and dropped them to the floor.

He observed his wife intently once he'd stepped out of the last of his clothes. He knew his erect flesh appeared rather formidable at the moment, and hoped she wasn't too nervous seeing him fully for the first time. After all, she'd definitely felt his stiff cock before, pressed eagerly against her body on several previous occasions.

Christopher studied her face as he stood completely naked before her, but Violet wasn't looking at his face. She stared directly at his rigid length with her mouth gaping. He didn't move at all. He simply let her look for as long as she needed. Although he couldn't prevent his cock from jerking with the fierceness of her stare, and that movement made her brow arch to her hairline.

Eventually, her features softened. Her gaze drew up over his abdomen, across his chest, and onto his face. She met his eyes and smiled, looking up at him with complete and utter trust. She parted her legs then, settling her bare feet to either edge of the bed and reaching out to him.

He didn't hesitate. Christopher took her hand, kissing the backs of her fingers before lowering his body onto the cot and settling himself between her legs. He rested onto his forearms, placing them at the sides of her chest to keep his full weight off of her. He also made sure to shift his hips over a bit so he could nestle his shaft into the crook of her thigh, not wanting her to feel that pressure against her sex just yet.

"Am I hurting you?" he questioned.

She shook her head, her gold curls feathering over the pillow. "Not at all. I had a dream once where you were hovering overtop of me, sort of like this. But in my dream, I never got to feel your skin on mine."

"Do you want to feel my skin on yours?"

"Definitely," she insisted, wrapping her arms over his shoulders and pulling against his back. "I want all of you."

Christopher allowed himself to slip off of one arm, pressing their chests together. Her peaked nipples flattened against the wall of his muscles, making his throbbing shaft twitch into her leg. He sucked in a steadying breath as he traced the outline of her face with his fingertips.

"Better?" he asked.

"Better," she agreed. "Even better if you kiss me now."

A laugh escaped his throat with the beauty of her words, causing his heart to ache in the best way. He kissed her, soft and slow, trying to keep his actions simple so she would feel comfortable and safe. She'd told him once that she trusted him to take care of her the first time they made love, and he very much wanted to prove himself worthy of that trust.

Violet accepted his gentleness for a long while. But ultimately, she sought more. She sought the winding of his tongue with her own. She sought the pressure of his body, with her hands tugging against his scar-coated spine. She sought the movement of his hips by arching hers upward, making his already unyielding cock tighten to the point of pain.

With a deep groan, Christopher eased his lips from hers and traced his fingers down her cheek and onto her neck. He watched his hand smooth from her neck to her arm before he shifted his hips so he could settle that hand between their stomachs. He reached further down until he felt the familiar softness between her thighs, slipping his finger over her wet folds.

"Oh," Violet moaned, biting into her lip.

He lowered his mouth to her neck, kissing up to her jaw as he thrust his finger in and out of her warm inner walls. She responded instantly, lifting her bottom to meet his hand even as the weight of his body pressed her into the mattress. She cried out when he eased a second finger inside her, yet she still arched up to seek his intimate touches. He had to stop kissing her to grit his teeth together, fighting his overwhelming urge to possess her this instant.

Christopher drove his fingers into her body over and over, ensuring she was as stretched and ready for him as possible. Once her moans began to escalate along with the rhythm of her hips, he drew his hand away. "Are you sure you don't want me to give you an orgasm with my fingers?" he asked when she looked to him with hazed eyes. "I could do that right now."

Violet shook her head. "I want you with me."

He sighed with her persistence but still nodded. He pressed a tender kiss to her lips before reaching for his cock. Taking the thick length in his hand, he shifted his hips to line them up precisely with hers, running the tip of his fully hardened shaft up against her soft folds. He worked to maintain his focus on her face as he coated himself in her wetness, ignoring the sinful sensation of her slick skin sliding against his demanding flesh.

Violet's fingers squeezed into his back while he rubbed himself against her.

He leaned down, running the tip of his nose over hers before meeting her gaze. "All is well," he assured. "I'm not going to enter you yet. Very soon, but not yet. Not until you're truly ready."

She eased her fearsome grip on his spine. "I trust you entirely."

Those words settled deep in his chest as Christopher kissed her lips, feeling her smile against him while he continued running the tip of his shaft up and down her folds. Her juices were more than plentiful and lubricated his skin perfectly. He used his fingers to spread the wetness across more of his length, making certain he would glide into her as easily as possible. Then he shifted his hips upward, to press against the tiny nub at the top of her sex with the head of his cock.

Violet inhaled sharply. "God, that...that feels good."

"Just remember this will all feel good, eventually. I promise it will."

When she nodded, he drew his rigid length back down through her folds to press his tip into the entrance of her body. His flesh was nearly as wet as hers now, and with the effort he'd made to stretch her with his fingers, he hoped he would slip inside a bit easier. But she was still quite tight, and he instantly met the resistance of her flesh.

She moaned with the pressure of his inflexible shaft at her opening. He used all his strength to keep his hips in place as he slid his hand up the side of her body. He suspended himself very precisely over her, not moving at all.

"Violet," he breathed.

"Mmm?"

"I want you to hold my hands. Both of them, please."

She instantly dropped her arms to the cot, spreading her fingers out to either side of her head. Christopher balanced on his forearms as he reached for her, placing their palms together.

"When I enter you, you can squeeze onto my hands as hard as you like," he offered, fighting to steady his hips with the head of his cock pressing against her sex. "I don't want you to worry in the least about hurting me."

"Are you worried about hurting me?"

"Yes. I hate that this part will hurt you, even briefly."

"Don't be worried. I promise I'm ready," she said, looking up to him with utter trust, tempered by the slightest hint of fear.

He pressed several kisses to her nose and her cheeks before pausing over her lips. "I want you to kiss me now, my sweet. Will you do that for me?"

She arched her head off the bed to meld her mouth with his, slipping her tongue past his teeth. Christopher allowed her tentative explorations for a moment only before he took over, pushing his tongue deeply and fiercely inside her. Violet rested her head back against the pillow as she welcomed his determined actions. He moved his mouth resolutely across hers while she made mewling little noises that vibrated in his ears and on his lips.

Christopher made sure to keep his tongue inside her mouth, because he wanted it there when he claimed her. He squeezed his eyes shut and took a swift breath in through his nose. The next instant, he thrust his hips forward as quickly and decisively as he could. He drove the full length of his taut shaft into Violet's body in one single motion, tearing past the barrier of skin at the opening of her sex. He seated himself wholly inside her, completing the action in the blink of an eye, before she even had the chance to clamp her thighs around his hips. And he did it all with his tongue pushed far inside her.

She bit down. Hard. Violet clenched onto his fingers, dug her nails into his hands, screamed into his mouth, and bit into his tongue, all at once.

He'd expected her to do all of those things. Honestly, he'd craved it. He already knew her biting his tongue would be painful, since she'd accidentally bitten him on their carriage ride. Yet he desired to feel that pain again now, knowing she was in true pain and not wanting to take any pleasure in it.

Christopher did not want to relish the inconceivably flawless sensation of her tight, wet sheath cradling the full length of his manhood. Not yet. Therefore, he kept his tongue inside her even when she bit him, and tried to relax his fingers while she dug her nails into his hands, and worked to keep his hips entirely still as her thighs now squeezed fiercely onto his waist.

Violet regained her control almost instantly. After her initial undoing, she eased her grip on his hands and opened her teeth to release his tongue, although she did still keep her legs fastened around his body. Christopher didn't withdraw his tongue from her mouth right away. He kissed her a bit longer, until she returned his affections. When he felt satisfied that she'd calmed, he drew back just enough to look on her face.

Violet slowly opened her eyes to gaze up to his.

"Are you with me?" he asked when he could see her sky-blue again.

"Yes, Christopher. I'm with you."

"I'm sorry I hurt you."

She gave him a shy smile. "I'm sorry I bit your tongue."

"That's all right. I wanted you to bite my tongue."

"And I wanted you inside me, so we both got what we wanted."

He huffed at the practicality of her words, especially since he wasn't ever going to get what he wanted. He couldn't have her. Not after tonight. Not after these few blissful moments.

But he did have her now. He had Violet utterly and completely, as she lay here beneath him with his body buried inside hers. He would always have her in this one way. He would always be the first man inside her. No other man would ever know her exactly like this, and that knowledge was a tiny triumph in a world of pain and defeat.

Christopher knew he should feel guilty for the satisfaction he took in claiming her. Yet he couldn't bring himself to feel any guilt whatsoever. For he would remember this moment every day – and most certainly every night – for the rest of his life.

"Please tell me, Violet. Is the pain still bad?"

She crinkled her nose. "It's definitely still there."

"Do you want to keep holding my hands?"

"Honestly, I think I prefer to use my hands."

The instant he released her fingers, she threw her arms around his shoulders and reached for his hair. He brought both his hands to her face, to cradle her cheeks and ground her to him. "Just let me know when you're ready for me to start moving."

She kept her eyes locked with his. "I think I'm ready now."

"You don't have to rush yourself."

"No, I...I really do think I'm ready."

Christopher smoothed his fingers up her cheek. "Very well, then. When I move, it may still feel a bit uncomfortable. Not for long, hopefully."

Violet nodded and held onto him tighter.

He shifted his hips, pulling slightly out of her body. When she cringed, he halted. "Are you still with me?"

"I am. I'm right here. Just go slowly, please."

"I'll go very slowly. I promise."

He shifted again, clenching his jaw to combat the urge to move any faster than a snail's pace. He eased his cock nearly all the way out of her, taking as much time as possible. When he'd withdrawn almost to the tip, he pushed back in, slowly and surely, until he seated himself entirely inside her again. She released a harsh moan, raising her knees to adjust her thighs around his hips.

Christopher watched her closely. "How are you doing, my sweet?"

"I'm well. I think."

"Well enough for me to keep going?" he asked, all of his muscles tensed as he restrained his visceral desire to thrust and claim and conquer.

"Yes. Keep going. The pain is getting better."

"Good," he breathed, pulling out again before easing tenderly back in.

She gasped the moment his body lodged up against hers. "My heavens. That is...that is..."

"Pleasurable?"

"Almost. Do it again. Please."

"You don't have to say please. I'll do anything you ask of me."

Violet stared up at him as he withdrew and reseated himself once again. She ran her fingers over the coarse scruff on his jaw. "I know you will. But I still like to say please."

Christopher held her with his eyes as he pushed his hands into her gold curls, tightening his fingers against her scalp. He pulled his cock almost entirely from her sex, keeping his actions simple yet deliberate. He studied her as he sank back into her wet heat, seeing her eyelids fall to half-mast and her lips part on a sigh.

"Oh," she breathed when his hips settled down onto hers.

"Is that a pleasurable sound?"

"Yes. Very."

"Thank God," he hissed.

Violet stared raptly up at him during his next withdrawal and unhurried thrust. She released another tiny gasp when he settled fully back inside. Her fingers shifted nervously in his hair. "How, um, how do I feel to you, Christopher? I mean, do you like being inside my body?"

He blew out a kempt breath. "Bloody hell, you don't have to question that. I love being inside you. You're perfect. So incredibly perfect."

"Do I feel warm?"

"Very warm."

"And soft?"

"Most definitely."

"And wet?"

"Gorgeously wet."

"And tight?"

"Fuck, yes," he groaned, his cock twitching inside her sheath.

Violet whimpered with that sensation, her tongue darting out to moisten her lips. "So, may I assume that my tightness is a good thing in this instance?"

"For me it is. Although it makes things uncomfortable for you."

Her brow creased. "I don't think I'm too uncomfortable anymore. I think you can move faster now."

"Are you sure about that?"

"I am."

"And you know you can tell me to stop at any time?"

"I do. I promise I do."

Christopher kept his fingers curled into her hair when he began. He moved very slowly at first, making sure Violet felt pleasure and not pain. But he saw no signs of distress in her eyes, not even when he increased the speed and strength of his thrusts. She only held tighter to him, with both her arms and her legs, as her quick little bursts of breaths ghosted over his face. When a smile of unmistakable pleasure drew up the corners of her mouth, he decided it was finally safe to rejoice in the feel of her.

Violet was indeed warm, soft, wet, and tight, as she thought. But she was so much more than that. She was comfort, elation, desire, need, and bliss. She cradled him so fucking remarkably inside her, even as her arms and legs embraced him quite zealously on the outside. He let his eyes close when he sank his mouth onto hers, kissing her with all intents of possession, while driving his stiff length into her body again and again.

She clung to his neck, returning his kisses as feverishly as he gave them. She even started to move her hips a little, to mirror the actions of his. He had to wrench his lips away from hers, struggling to maintain his control, while the fueling sounds of her delicate whimpers inflamed him entirely.

"Oh, yes, that feels incredible," she panted, tugging on his neck to urge him closer. "Faster, Christopher. Go faster."

He groaned with her demands. Partly because he felt relief that Violet found joy in their lovemaking. Partly because he didn't want this to ever end, even though it must. And partly because he knew he would have to pull out of her soon, to spill his seed on the blanket and not inside her body.

"Faster. Please," she begged, grasping his earlobe between her teeth.

"Damn, I love it when you bite me," he growled, grabbing tighter to her hair while plunging his cock deep inside her sex, over and over.

Violet bit into his ear again. She nibbled a path down the side of his face, biting fully into his jaw before running her tongue over his scruff. She spread her thighs all the way apart, wrapping her legs securely around his waist and linking her feet behind his back.

Once she'd opened herself to him without any further uncertainty, his desires took over completely. Christopher bucked into her, slamming his eyes shut as he drowned in the feel of her slick juices coating the thick flesh of his cock. She was perfect. So goddamn fucking perfect, panting in his ear while clinging to his neck and nipping at his jaw.

He didn't want to leave her body. Not ever. Definitely not tonight. He wanted to stay inside his wife, and spill his seed deep within her walls, as he'd never allowed himself to do with any woman in his life.

But he shouldn't. Christopher knew with absolute certainty that he shouldn't. Even as he lunged into her, letting her softness surround him and pull him further inside, he knew he had no right to empty himself within her walls. Yet her legs wrapped around him so tightly. Her whole body wrapped around him, clinging in desperation and desire, binding him to her. She moaned and writhed beneath him, seeking her own release so faultlessly.

When he opened his eyes to look on her face, Violet met his gaze that instant. God, she was a beautiful woman. He already knew that; he'd known it since the moment he'd first seen her picture in his locket. But right now, as she accepted every one of his thrusts with complete and utter pleasure, she'd never enchanted him more.

Christopher wanted her more than he'd ever wanted anything in the world. He needed her more than he could even comprehend. He loved her more than he ever thought he could love anyone. She was his home, as he was hers. Violet was his whole, entire life and he wanted to live in her.

In this perfect moment, he made the very conscious decision to remain inside. He would not leave her body. Not until they were both completely sated in each other. This would be their only time together, so he intended to be with his wife in every way he could.

He sank himself into her soft, sweet heat, again and again. He watched her face with every movement he made, making sure she felt worshipped and loved. He believed she did, especially when she began chanting his name.

"Christopher, Christopher...oh, God, *Christopher.*"

He focused even harder when she moaned, needing her to reach her peak, to feel the satiation he would experience without question. He drove into her with as much precision as he could manage, tilting his hips up at the end of each thrust to stimulate the tiny nub at the top of her sex. Violet encouraged his efforts in the best way, meeting the downward pressure of his hips with the upward lunge of her own, while she groaned and gasped beneath him.

The sounds she made grew louder as his muscles shook with the effort of control. Then she clamped her legs around his waist, drawing him fully into her body, at the same moment she pressed her cheek against his. Violet stilled herself beneath him, just for an instant, to whisper into his ear.

"I love you, Christopher. I love you. I love you."

He nearly burst into tears. That desolate display was only prevented by the forcefulness of his other emotions – the ones driving him fiercely to completion. All he could do was chant her name as he wrapped his arms around her body and clung to her with everything in his power.

"Violet. Violet. Violet. *Violet.*"

She came undone then. She came apart entirely, wrapped in the shelter of his embrace, with her body utterly open to his. She screamed into the warm night air and Christopher thrust into her just once more before joining her in pure oblivion. They shouted out together, in untamed, carnal cries that echoed through the room.

Her inner walls contracted around his full length while he emptied himself deep inside her, with all the muscles in his body tensed at once. Her cries turned to moans as he gripped her to his chest, his own moans now joining hers in a fitful chorus of release and pleasure and love. *Love.* Good God, how he loved her. Not that he questioned his feelings before this moment – he didn't question them at all – but now he knew he would never love anyone else. Not like this. Not ever again.

"Violet," he breathed, soaking her scent into his lungs while he pressed his lips to her forehead, her cheek, and her nose. He pushed his pulsing length further into her softness, needing to feel himself as deep inside her as possible.

"Oh, Christopher. My Christopher," she whispered, lifting her head to fuse their mouths while her body continued to quake beneath its release.

"I am yours," he promised against her soft lips. "Forever, my dearest."

When she sighed with his declaration, he slid his tongue inside her. He kissed her for long, tender, flawless minutes as he lay buried deep within her walls, feeling her arms wrap tighter over his shoulders and her fingers ease across the scar on the back of his neck. Right now, Christopher didn't care about the scar. He didn't care about the sins of his past, or about atonement, or even about forgiveness. He only cared about her.

For these few perfect moments, the entire world narrowed to just the two of them. It was the only world he wanted to live in, ever again.

Violet eventually pulled her lips from his to catch her breath. He rested his forehead on hers and ran his hands into her gold curls, pinching his eyes shut tight to keep everything else out of his mind. He had to hold his demons at bay for just a little while longer. His wife needed him right now, and this was exactly where he wanted to be.

"Mmm," she hummed after several silent minutes, her fingers tracing over his scar again before pushing up into his hair. "Mm-hmm."

He smiled against her lips. "I hope those are good noises."

"They are better than good."

"I'm glad," he said, trying not to take too much pride in the joy she'd given them both. She shifted beneath him, making him realize how much of his weight he'd placed on her body and how tight her inner walls still felt around him. "I should pull out of you now, so you do not feel any further soreness."

Violet nodded. "Go ahead."

Christopher eased out of her, groaning as she gasped. He angled his hips to rest his wet shaft against her inner thigh. Honestly, he was still half-hard and could probably make love to her again with even the slightest provocation. But he definitely didn't have time for that, especially since he still wanted to hold her, even if only for a short while.

"Why don't you turn on your side, Violet? That way, I won't be crushing you beneath me anymore."

Her eyes flew open. "You're not leaving already, are you?"

He stared into her in the dim light of the room. "No, I'm not leaving yet. Not before I get the chance to hold you."

She searched his face before she acquiesced. Christopher lifted himself so she could roll onto her side. Then he settled back down in front of her, lining their bodies up from head to toe, even though his feet hung off the bottom of the cot and hers did not.

He reached out, grabbing onto her hipbone to pull her closer to him. Resting his head on the pillow beside hers, he stared into her eyes. He wanted to say a thousand different things to his wife in this moment. But he knew none of those words could change anything, so he remained silent while tracing his fingers across the curve of her hip.

Violet matched his fixed gaze. She watched him while she ran her fingers up his jaw and over the curve of his ear. She didn't say anything at all, which both relieved his mind and crushed his heart.

After some time passed, she tucked herself fully into him, curling her chin down and burrowing into his chest. He enveloped her with both arms, pulling her further into the warmth of his body. He realized just now that they'd never gotten under the blanket. Fearing her being cold, he spread his fingers out over her spine and pressed his heated palms to her skin.

He wanted to make sure Violet felt entirely protected and secure and safe at this moment. Sadly, it was the worst thing he could do. After all, she couldn't be protected or secure or safe – not with him.

Christopher waited with her for a long while. Probably too long. He waited with her, and held her to him, and reveled in the warm puffs of air that escaped her lungs and ghosted over his chest. He hated himself more and more as he lay wrapped around her body, knowing what he must now do to her. He definitely deserved to feel pain and suffering after all the sins he'd committed in his life, but his wife did not.

He allowed himself to hold her a little longer. Just a little while longer. Then he drew back to press a kiss to her forehead. "Violet," he whispered into her hair. "I have to go now."

She didn't respond, but she also didn't cry. She looked into his eyes with tears welling in her own, but didn't cry at all. He loved her even more for that.

Christopher forced himself to sit up on the edge of the cot, to ease his feet to the floor and reach for his breeches. He pulled them up, tugged on his boots, and marched over to the wall to collect his shirt and shove it over his head. Once he'd fastened the buttons, he picked up Violet's nightgown and riding cape from the ground. He walked back to the bed to set her clothes on the end of the mattress.

She still lay on her side, watching him, although her body had curled up nearly to a ball. He noted a spot of dried blood on the blanket behind her thigh. He wanted to fetch a pan of warm water from the barkeep downstairs and bring it back up here to cleanse her skin. He wanted to take care of her, to give her the attention she deserved. But that was no longer his place.

Christopher reached out instead, running his fingers over the side of her face and slipping a curl of gold hair behind her ear. He gave her a soft smile before making his final request. "Be safe, my love. Please."

She still didn't say anything to him, and that was fine. She certainly had the right to stay silent, even though he already missed her voice and wished he could hear it once more. He took one last long, hard look at his Violet. Then he spun on his heels, grabbed his coat from the chair, and exited the room as rapidly as he could. He closed the door and stood in the narrow hall for another minute, giving himself time to breathe.

As Christopher stared at the confining walls, he tried like hell to ignore the excruciatingly hollow ache in his chest. He tried to accept the fact that he'd just abandoned his heart in the room behind him, leaving a giant, gaping hole beneath his ribcage. He assured himself that leaving his heart here with Violet was for the best. He did not wish to possess such a vulnerable thing anymore, for it would do him no good at all. Where he was going, a heart would only be a burden, and a hindrance, and an adversary.

He shoved his arms into his coat sleeves and drew up to his full height, squaring his shoulders beneath the stiff fabric. Christopher stared ahead with virulent intent as he strode toward the staircase. He told himself he no longer possessed a heart. He told himself his future was set in stone and he must make himself as hard as stone to survive it.

He told himself he could no longer be Lord Christopher Kastle. Not anymore. Now, he must be something else.

～

VIOLET LAY VERY STILL on the tiny tavern cot, curled up into a ball, watching Christopher leave the room. She watched him walk right out and shut the door behind him, with only these few words: *Be safe, my love. Please.*

She shook her head the instant he'd gone. "I don't want to be safe," she spoke into the cool night air. "I want only to be with you."

Violet sat up on the mattress, wincing with the action since she was still quite sore. A very distinct yet unfamiliar ache pulsed between her legs – the ache of where Christopher's body had been buried deep within her own – and it hurt. Not just physically. It hurt to know he would never be inside her again. It hurt to know how sweetly and gently he'd loved her, trying his damnedest to keep her pain to a minimum while ensuring her pleasure. He'd taken such beautiful care of her, and now that it was all said and done, Violet knew without doubt that she could never accept any other man inside her. Not ever.

She hadn't really understood what she would feel when she'd asked her husband to make love to her tonight. At the time she'd made her illicit request, she honestly believed she could live her life without him as long as she possessed one memory of them being fully together. What she had not realized was how the bond they already shared would deepen exponentially in that act.

Violet hadn't known that her love for him would grow, in supremely rich and wondrous ways, in those precious moments when their bodies merged. She hadn't known of the endless binding of her heart to his heart and her soul to his soul. But now that she did know, she could not imagine performing the act again with any man other than him.

In truth, she simply refused to imagine it. She would not offer herself to anyone but Christopher ever again. She would certainly not offer herself to the Duke of Dunworthy, allowing him to climb on her and invade her body by any means he chose. Violet would never let that man touch her at all.

She'd already come to that conclusion when Christopher was still here. Just minutes ago, when they'd laid side by side after making love – when he'd pulled her into his chest to keep her warm and safe for as long as possible – she realized she could never be with anyone else. Lord Christopher Kastle was her husband, and no one could tell her otherwise. She just had to find him again, so they could be together from this day forward, to truly honor the vows they'd made on the night of the ball.

Christopher swore many oaths to her on that fateful night, and he somehow believed he'd kept them all. However, she wasn't presently concerned about the vows he had made to her. Violet was only concerned about the ones *she* had made to *him*. She'd promised to be his. She'd promised to put her faith in him, always and completely. She'd promised he would never again have to endure agony alone, not so long as she had breath in her body.

Her husband believed the journey he embarked on tonight would cause him great agony, and since she was still very much alive and breathing, she had no choice but to be with him. Violet had no intention of allowing him to endure his agony alone, which meant she could not stay here a moment longer. She needed to move. She needed to leave this tavern right now, figure out which ship Christopher had boarded, and sneak onto the exact same one. She needed to be by his side where she belonged.

Violet lunged for her nightgown. She snatched it from the bottom of the bed, yanked it over her head, and crammed her arms through the sleeves. She cinched up the delicate ties against her chest while she stood to pull on her cape, determined to find her husband as quickly as possible. But as she shoved her feet into her pink silk slippers, a devilish voice niggled her mind.

What if Christopher truly doesn't want you with him? What if you find your way onto his ship and he refuses you? What then?

Violet cringed with her unbidden doubts, yet she refused to let them deter her. "Christopher will want me with him," she assured herself. "Perhaps not at first, but he will always keep me close and safe, because he loves me."

She smiled with her words, hoping they were true. She hoped his love for her would overcome his disdain for her actions. Yet even if it didn't, she had no choice but to leave England tonight. Her body ached from where her husband had been inside her, and her heart ached from where he remained inside her, and she refused to go backwards.

Violet wouldn't go back to Wilmington. Or to Pennyshire. And she would definitely not go to Dunworthy. Even if the worst possible thing happened when she found Christopher's ship – and he rejected her yet again – then she would simply have to find her way in the world on her own. She would move forward no matter what, because she refused to allow anyone but herself to decide her fate. Not even Christopher. And especially not her father.

"I'm sorry, Papa," she whispered, feeling the guilt of her defiance even as she decreed it. "I'm sorry I cannot fulfill my duty to my family."

Her breath caught when she thought of the family she'd always loved: of Papa in his silly white wig with a forced look of sternness on his lips; of Mama in her lush dresses with her arms open for hugs; of Gwen with a smile on her face as she lay her head in Violet's lap. She could see them all in her mind's eye and didn't want her actions tonight to hurt any of them. Yet she must still leave, for deep in her heart, she was no longer a Bell. She was a Kastle.

"I must write them a letter," Violet realized. "To fix whatever I can."

Rushing to the desk on the other side of the room, she surveyed the writing materials spread across the tabletop. She reached into the pocket of her cape and pulled out her spectacles, grateful she hadn't removed them after her return from the Kastle manor. Placing the wire rims on her nose, she reached for the quill and ink and began putting her thoughts on paper.

She addressed her letter to Papa, Mama, Gwen, and Aunt Tildy. Violet wrote that Christopher had been called to sea on urgent business, which was terribly important and quite unavoidable. She wrote that he had asked for her hand this very night, and that she'd happily accepted, and that they'd been married in a quick, private ceremony by a magistrate in Nightingale Port. She wrote that they were now to debark on Christopher's voyage with her accompanying him as his wife. She wrote that she would come home as soon as she was able.

Violet paused her furious scribbles to examine the page with tears in her eyes. This was a letter of fairytales and falsehoods, and she hated writing such lies to her family. She also hated how much she wished it were all true.

Gwen's face sprang to her mind, making Violet wince with the thought of how unhappy her sister would be without her. Nevertheless, Gwen had Welly beside her now – and the Chaneys had accepted her in a very public manner – so she would be a Lady of Centreville regardless of the reckless actions of her elder sister. Violet simply couldn't worry about how her choices might affect anyone else. For once, she must do what was right for her.

She fortified her courage as she put quill to paper once again. *Please proceed with Gwen's wedding as planned. I do not know when Christopher and I shall make it back home, and I do not wish for Gwen and Welly to have to wait for our return. Please know I will be with you in spirit during every festivity, and please be certain that I love each of you. Always.*

Violet stared at the words for a quick second before adding a few more: *And Papa, please send the funds from my dowry to the Kastle manor, in care of Lady Daniela, to ensure the well-being of my new sisters until Christopher and I come home. Thank you so very much. Yours, Violet.*

She blinked away her tears as she pulled her spectacles from her nose and slipped them back into the pocket of her cape. After tucking the letter into an envelope, she grabbed the candle from its brass holder to drip wax over the seam. She pressed the wax with the stamp that lay on the desk, imprinting the same "M" insignia she recognized from the envelope Christopher had received from Nick Marlow two weeks ago. Once her letter was sealed, she riffled through the drawers of the desk until she found what she hoped the very wealthy Mr. Marlow had left behind: a few random coins.

Clutching one thick piece of gold in her hand, Violet blew out the candle before escaping through the door. She flew across the narrow hall, down the crooked staircase, and back into the main room of the tavern. Pulling the front seams of her cape together to cover the nightgown beneath it, she hid her state of undress just as she had when she'd arrived here tonight. She glanced at the drunken patrons still scattered about the room, but they paid no attention to her while she stepped over to the bar.

"Excuse me, Sir," Violet addressed the portly barkeep when she caught his eye, hoping he would be as considerate to her now as he was earlier, when he'd directed her upstairs to Nick's spare room.

"Hello again, Miss. What can I do for you?"

"Do you know of the Wilmington manor here in Nightingale?"

"Aye, that I do."

"Wonderful. I have a letter I need delivered there tomorrow. Could you do that for me, in exchange for this?" She presented him the gold coin, watching his eyes widen at the severe overpayment for such a simple task.

"I can certainly do that for you," he replied, snatching the coin with one hand as he took the letter with his other. "Rest assured."

"Thank you. And would you also return the black stallion that is outside your tavern to the estate? The Wilmington caretaker is Mr. Rodchester and I'm certain he will be most grateful to see the horse. Please tell him Miss Violet said to offer you a return trip to Nightingale Port in the Wilmington coach, in exchange for your good deeds."

The barkeep nodded, giving her a toothless grin. "I can do that. However, the man who came down the stairs before you told me to keep his horse."

"I see," she sighed, abhorring the thought of Christopher abandoning such a beloved possession. "I'm sorry I cannot offer you this horse as well, but it is not mine to give."

"Eh, I prefer the gold anyway. I'll get your letter to Wilmington."

"But no sooner than tomorrow."

"Yes. Tomorrow."

"Thank you. Goodnight."

"'Night, Miss."

She offered the man a warm smile before turning and fleeing the room. Violet rushed through the tavern door but stopped short on the stoop. The roads before her were barely lit by the sparsely situated oil streetlamps, yet she still took a moment to pull her hood over her head to conceal the brightness of her hair. She gathered the front seam of her cape even tighter as she moved forward, winding down the still bustling streets of Nightingale Port. She did not have to question her current path, since the peaks of the clipper ships' masts loomed in the distance and she could track them easily over the dark gables topping the buildings nearest the docks.

Dread filled her gut as she stole forth so late at night, even though the sights, sounds, and smells of Nightingale Port were not unlike those she remembered from the London of her youth. Soused old sailors, who reeked of gin and urine, still snored in the alleyways. Painted women, eyeing any man who staggered past them in well-tailored clothes, still lingered on the corners. Tiny street urchins, much like the one she'd been, still scoured the ground in search of forgotten coins. Emaciated rats, in desperate search of food, still scurried past her feet to disappear into the shadows.

The world Violet now saw around her, in this dark underbelly, was nothing like the life she'd led in the bright countryside of Pennyshire these past ten years. But that didn't mean she couldn't exist in conditions such as this. If Christopher rejected her, setting her back on shore the instant after she boarded his ship, then she believed she could survive on her own. After all, she'd grown up in the dregs of London. She knew how to subsist on little food and the barest shelter. She also knew how to play cards and could make money gambling, if necessary. She would do whatever she must in order to live free from the expectations of English society.

Of course, she did not desire to survive solely on her own. She did not want to become a vagrant gambler with no home, no family, and no husband. She wanted her husband to accept her presence aboard his ship. She wanted him to realize she belonged beside him, no matter how dangerous his journey.

Violet lamented her wishful thoughts as she scurried down the gloomy streets. She knew Christopher would not simply welcome her aboard his ship with open arms. She was fully aware of how upset he would be with her over her decisions tonight. He would be shocked, horrified, irate, and perhaps even furious. But regardless of all that, he still needed her with him. He could not leave his heart behind in England with her, as he'd assured her he would. He required it in order to live, and she'd be damned if she allowed the man she loved to face any sort of danger without his heart present.

The sound of lapping water filled her ears the instant she turned the last corner, pulling her thoughts to the scene that lay before her. Excitement raced through her veins at the promise of seeing Christopher again, yet her heart sank to her feet the moment she drank in her surroundings. Violet stood stiffly at the entrance to the Nightingale docks, looking at all the ships stretched out before her eyes – all the many, many ships.

God, she'd not even considered the possibility that there might be more than one vessel to choose from. In her haste and naivety, she assumed Christopher would simply appear before her like a figurehead ornament on a clipper's bow. She hadn't stopped to consider the amount of activity on the docks, even at this late hour. But she should have expected it, because she knew Nightingale Port had grown to nearly the size of London itself.

For the first time since she'd made her decision to escape from England, Violet truly questioned the prudence of her choice. She had no idea which of these ships her husband was actually on. She could not even comprehend how she would make a proper decision on which one to board.

Think, Violet! she commanded herself silently but firmly while tucking her body into an alley between two salt-weathered buildings. Concealing her form as best she could, she searched for clues on the many clippers lined beside one another. She worked to recall all the times she'd sat on the docks in London, watching the vessels in childish wonder as they prepared to sail into the sea.

Whatever ship Christopher is on should be occupied by many men, and bustling with activity, and have its small sails prepped for departure.

Violet nodded her head as she drew on her long-lost memories. She looked for the vessels which bore the most movement of sailors, sighting three in the near distance. Each of those three ships had gangways attached to them, with men carrying large wooden crates and barrels up the plank entrances, and a spread of small canvas sails hanging from the masts. They also had glowing lanterns attached to posts on their main decks, highlighting the flurry of activity onboard.

That narrows your choice to three, she assured, now examining the sides of the ships for markings. *You must pick one with a Marlow Merchant Company insignia, since Christopher will most certainly be with Nick.*

Her eyes scoured the vessel markings, and for once, Violet was grateful to be far-sighted instead of near. She searched until she saw the distinct "M" on the side of one ship. It was the same "M" from Nick's wax stamp on his desk, which she'd used to seal her letter to her family. Unfortunately, that "M" was on the side of another of the three vessels, as well.

"Well, that narrows my choice to two," she muttered, looking back and forth between those two Marlow Merchant ships, trying to discern the faces of the men shuffling about on the decks. Alas, she was too far away, and the night was entirely too dark, even despite the lighting of the lanterns. She could not see Christopher, nor Nick, no matter how hard she tried.

You will have to choose the ship most prepared for departure, she determined, certain Christopher's journey would begin in no time at all. She examined the two vessels for one more minute before deciding that the clipper to her right was fully loaded with rations and looked well prepared for a lengthy voyage. She noted that several of the extensive, stretched ropes which attached the ship to the docks had already been loosened. She also saw oars poking out from openings in the lower deck, set to row the ship to open waters where the full sails would be raised.

That must be the one. That must be the ship Christopher is on.

Violet forced a smile of assurance to her lips, just to feel a bit better about her decision. She glanced to her left and right, ensuring that she was alone and would have no difficulty going forward. Tightening the edges of her cape with clawed fingers, she ducked her head under her hood.

She tiptoed onto the docks, her silk-covered feet silent on the wood slats, as she hurried toward the ship she'd chosen. Her heart raced in her chest, causing her blood to rush in her ears while she slipped noiselessly over the planking. Gratefully, most of the men on this part of the docks were already aboard vessels, or quite busy moving supplies, and she could scurry through the shadows unnoticed.

As she neared her chosen ship, Violet crouched low to the ground beside many crates of various shapes and sizes. She spied two gruff-looking sailors hoisting a large wooden barrel up the gangway. Once they reached the main deck, she saw no other souls in her immediate surroundings. She took her opportunity and dashed forward.

Violet rushed up the gangway, from the ground all the way to the top, keeping her body low and her movements quick. She made it onto the clipper without discovery before scrambling off the side of the plank. She ducked her body behind several giant barrels on the main deck, close to the ship's railing.

Plastering her spine against the back of one rounded wood container, she worked to settle her panted breaths. She also fought back a cough, since this barrel she hid behind obviously held a very potent rum and the sharp stench burned her nose. *Stay still and quiet*, she reminded herself. Not that she needed reminding, since she had no idea what would become of her if Christopher was not actually aboard this ship.

Breathing through parted lips, she turned her body to peer into the small space between two of the rum barrels, trying to discern the faces of the men moving about the main deck. The only person she wanted to see was her husband, but the only people she could see were the two brawny, crusty sailors who'd hauled the last barrel up the gangplank. She now felt appreciation for the intense odor of rum in her nostrils, since she felt certain the stench of these men would have knocked her to her knees otherwise.

Within seconds, Violet heard the scurrying of many footsteps, the shouting of deep voices, and the scrape of twine on metal and wood on wood, as the last of the ship's ropes were loosened from the dock and the oars below deck were thrust into the water. Next, she heard the gangway being pulled in from the ship's hull. The floor of the vessel shifted beneath her feet, which meant they'd left the safety of land and she had no secure means of escape. Right or wrong, Christopher or no Christopher, Violet was now an inhabitant of this vessel.

Her fingers fisted into her cape, pulling the fabric further around her body – her very scantily clad body. As she watched the two men before her mop their dirty brows of sweat, she now understood how truly reckless her actions had been tonight. Even if they were entirely justified.

"My name's Gibson. Horace Gibson," the first meaty sailor said, addressing the man beside him. "S'pose I should introduce myself, since we're going to be sailing together for some time."

The second sailor, who appeared a bit more refined, nodded to his new travel companion. "Good to meet you, Gibson. I'm Barnaby Atwell."

"So, then. Do you think it's true, Atwell?" Gibson asked, his voice as gritty as it was skeptical.

"About what?"

"About what? About who the captain of this ship is, of course."

Violet's ears perked up even as the vessel rocked beneath her body, floating across the waters that lay beneath them all.

"Well, the First Mate says it's true," Atwell responded with a shrug. "And since he's the one handing out the gold, I'm not going to question him."

Gibson huffed, sliding his thick fingers through his dense, grimy beard. "But how can it be true? How can the captain be here in England? The newspapers say he's in India."

Violet felt the ground shift under her feet again, but she couldn't be sure if it was from the motion of the water or simply the unease in her body. Talk of India sounded familiar to her, in an eerie sort of way. She pressed her lips shut tight to learn all she could within the sailors' words.

"You don't actually believe what you read in the papers, do you?" Atwell chided. "Newspapers are just gossip told on a grander scale."

"Are you saying I'm stupid?" Gibson grumbled, his stocky chest puffed out at the taller man beside him.

Atwell held his hands up. "No, no. I'm not saying that at all. But if you really want to know why the captain is in England instead of India, you should just ask him yourself."

Both men turned, directing their eyes toward the other side of the immense deck. Violet followed their line of sight straight to another person: a large, thickly muscled man who stood near the opposite railing. He stood stiff as a rod with his back to them, looking out to the dark distance. She could not see all of this other sailor in the light of the lanterns, but she saw enough to know that he wore a black coat trimmed in gold, with a matching tricorn hat that most likely belonged to the captain of this ship. He also had long, straight black hair that hung halfway down his back and was tied between his shoulder blades with a strip of leather.

"So, that's him," Gibson said, his voice far more reverent as he looked on the black-haired captain. "That is the legendary pirate Blackheart."

"Aye, that's him," Atwell confirmed.

"Oh, God, no," Violet breathed, clamping her hand over her mouth the moment she spoke aloud. *That is the pirate Blackheart! Good Lord! The pirate Blackheart is the captain of this vessel!*

She screamed inside her mind, the ground shifting fully beneath her quavering legs. *I've boarded the wrong ship! Dear merciful heavens! I'm on the wrong ship!*

Violet needed to vomit. Now. But she could not, because the wretched noise would surely reveal her presence to everyone here. She pinched her lips shut with her fingers as the ground rocked again. The swaying motion made her wonder if her legs were actually collapsing – although she knew this rocking came from the ship, since the sailors shifted on their feet, too. At least, Gibson and Atwell shifted. Blackheart stood tall, without moving in the slightest, as if he was one with this vessel and with the sea itself.

"M-maybe I will go introduce myself," Gibson announced, squaring his shoulders when his unsteady voice betrayed his bravado. "After all, the pirate Blackheart is only a man."

Atwell shook his head. "Not from what I've heard, he isn't."

Violet's whole body shook with those words, her mind scrambling to recall the things she'd heard her maids say of the notorious Blackheart. According to Harriet and Beatrix, the pirate was a vicious creature with long, stringy black hair, who ate the limbs off of children for breakfast. On the other hand, they'd also described him as a stunning Adonis with long, flowing black locks, who bedded a dozen wenches a night. Violet felt certain her maids did not relay either of those tales with complete accuracy, but they did get the part about the pirate's lengthy black hair correct.

She couldn't stop staring at Blackheart's hair now, as Gibson took his first few hesitant steps toward the captain. Violet remained focused on that dark ponytail because it looked rather inhuman – so thick and coarse – much like the mane of the black stallion she'd ridden to the tavern earlier tonight. She wondered what sort of foods Blackheart ate to make his hair grow like that, and she prayed his diet did not include tiny arms and legs.

Great heavens! Stop thinking such ridiculous things! she chastised herself, blinking her eyes in an effort to sharpen her muddled brain. She needed to stop this nervous rambling in her mind and focus on her new reality. She needed to deal with the fact that she was onboard a ship with a dreaded criminal, who was the deadliest pirate presently known to the world. She needed to embrace the reality that she'd stolen onto the wrong vessel, a vessel whose hull sliced through the dark waters just beyond Nightingale Port.

Violet had to get out. Now. She must escape from the pirate Blackheart by any means necessary, even if that meant flinging her body over the railing and plunging herself into the cold, inky sea. She must swim back to the docks to free herself from Captain Deadly Madman. She must take yet another chance on finding her way aboard Christopher's ship.

"Christopher," she breathed, his name sneaking past her sealed lips.

Good Lord, what if I didn't choose the wrong ship? What if Christopher is here? Could he be a sailor in the crew of the pirate Blackheart? Is that why he never wished to speak of his time at sea? Was he too ashamed to be associated with the infamous pirate himself?

Violet shook her head, not wanting to believe such harsh conjectures. Although, if they were true, then much of what she'd seen and heard in the past two months would make perfect sense. Like the fact that Christopher nearly choked to death at the dinner table when Aunt Tildy mentioned Blackheart's name. And the fact that his Royal Navy ship had been attacked by pirates. And the fact that his body bore horrible scars. And the fact that he'd said there were forces working against them – forces she knew nothing about.

God, can it be true? Did Blackheart capture Christopher six years ago? Was he tortured by the bastard until he finally gave in and succumbed to his captor? Does Blackheart actually control my husband?

Violet held onto her stomach as the acid within churned violently. She couldn't possibly hoist her body over the railing right now. She could not attempt her escape until she knew for certain that Christopher was not here. For if he was here, he needed her more than ever.

"Pardon me, Captain," Gibson announced, finishing his approach by coming to a standstill to the pirate's left. "My name's Horace Gibson. I'll be sailing under you for this voyage."

The captain didn't reply. He only stood stiff as a board while staring out over the shadowy waters.

"I *said* I'll be sailing with you," Gibson reiterated, his words turning coarser as he attempted to match the captain's imposing height. "I'm introducing myself because I hear you're the pirate Blackheart. I'd like to know if that's true."

The captain remained rigid as a plank, making no effort to respond.

Gibson crept closer, his eyes narrowing in the glow of the lanterns. "So? Is it true? Are you Blackheart himself?"

"Aye," the captain growled in reply, finally turning his head to look the other man in the face. "I am the pirate Blackheart. And you'd do well to remember it, Mr. Gibson, for I do not expect you to speak to me again without being spoken to first. Is that understood?"

Gibson faltered instantly, cowering from the pirate's fierce words and fiercer glare. However, Violet didn't truly see the sailor's response to the captain's commands. All she could see was the captain's face.

She could only see the lips she'd just been kissing. And the jaw she'd just been running her fingers across. And the eyes she'd just been gazing into, as his body filled hers completely.

The man she saw before her could not be the man she saw before her. But it was. It was him. It was Christopher.

The captain of this ship was the man she loved. And the captain of this ship was the pirate Blackheart. Which could only mean one thing.

Christopher Kastle is the pirate Blackheart.

The whole world closed in around her, squeezing the air from her lungs. Her ears buzzed, her vision blurred, and her skin burned. Blackness overcame her entirely. Violet collapsed to the floor behind the rum barrels, fainting straightaway.

Looking for more romantic adventures by Tina?
Visit Day and Knight Romance Publications
DayAndKnightRomance. com

For lovers of Young Adult Romance:

Are you yearning for the softness of first love,
this time with a supernatural twist?
Set yourself on the path of ***The Watching Trilogy***.

For lovers of Adult Romance:

Are you searching for a fun, frolicking adventure?
Enjoy a sexy escapade with ***Sweet Revenge***.

Are you interested in trekking off the beaten path?
Take the road less traveled with ***On Vacation***.

Whatever your desire for romance,
Tina promises a voyage like no other!

Tina is the author of multiple books and the owner of the publishing company Day and Knight Romance Publications. Writing as Day for her young adult novels and Knight for her adult novels, she offers a wide variety of journeys to satisfy your appetite for romance, love, and passion. Tina enjoys couch surfing, movie theaters, steamy reads, and bonding with fellow obsessive romantics who 'ship all the 'ships there are. Fortunate enough to have stumbled onto her soulmate back in the 1990s, she has been married for over a quarter century to a man who still tells her she's beautiful, no matter how many wrinkles she grows or cupcakes she eats. They live in Virginia with their two children, multiple fish, a fuzzy kitten, and a silly puppy, who are all frankly just too darn cute.

Visit Tina Online:
Facebook.com/TinaKnightBooks
Instagram.com/TinaKnightBooks
Twitter @TinaKnightBooks